BARBARA WINSLOW, REBEL

LECTOR HOUSE PUBLIC DOMAIN WORKS

BARBARA WINSLOW, REBEL

ELIZABETH ELLIS

ISBN: 978-93-90198-64-1

Published: 1906

LECTOR HOUSE LLP
E-MAIL: lectorpublishing@gmail.com

MISTRESS BARBARA WINSLOW

BARBARA WINSLOW
REBEL

BY

ELIZABETH ELLIS

ILLUSTRATED BY
JOHN RAE

1906

PREFACE

Whether James, Duke of Monmouth, would have succeeded in his enterprise had a different fortune attended his army at Sedgemoor, is a favourite subject for speculation among historians and others who interest themselves in the consideration of such strange chances as have not infrequently led to the downfall of great hopes. Certainly, had victory attended the invader's troops in their first battle, many waverers would have thereby been drawn to his standard, and the ranks of his supporters might have been swelled by that large class of politicians who measure the righteousness of a cause by its success.

But it was not ordained that Monmouth should free England from the abuses and injustice under which she struggled during the latter days of the Stuart dynasty; not into the hands of such men as this are entrusted the destinies of nations. This slight man, torn by weak hopes, weak fears, weak ambitions, small throughout his life, exceeding small and pitiful in his death, was not the instrument to overthrow the power of even so insecurely throned a monarch as James II. The history of the world is the history of individuals, and proclaims in all its pages the inexorable justice of God. A cause may be righteous, its vitality may be fanned by the devotion of thousands and watered by the heart's blood of heroes, but if the man in whom are centred the hopes of its supporters be unworthy, if his life be undisciplined, his aims selfish, his own faith weak, the glory of the struggle is clouded by the shadow of his personality, and failure is preordained to wait upon the enterprise.

James Monmouth, like his grandfather before him, like his cousin after him, inspired in the hearts of his followers an enthusiastic devotion that recked not of consequences, that gave all and asked nothing with unquestioning loyalty. In him his followers saw the man sent by Heaven to protect their religion and to purify the government of their country, the defender of their faith and freedom, and they were ready to lay down their lives at his bidding. But God, who reads the hearts of men, saw in the pretender a man of petty vices, of pitiful ambitions, weak, and selfish as the King he strove to dethrone, and though Monmouth offered at the altar of destiny many hundreds of devoted hearts, God refused the sacrifice and scattered his armies like the ashes of the offering of Cain.

So Duke Monmouth failed. The history of the world's triumphs is the history of individuals, but the world's failures are written in blood upon the hearts and lives of thousands; for though the reward of success may be the glory of one man, the suffering of many is the penalty demanded for failure. Duke Monmouth failed and the story of this abortive rebellion of the west is the story of the suffering of the innocent for the sins of the guilty. Many of those who prompted and led the invasion escaped in safety, to win pardon later from William of Orange and to live out their lives in peace and prosperity. Monmouth indeed died on the scaffold; but his worthless life was not to pay the price of rebellion. It was for the poor misguided peasants who had left their homes to fight for a religion dearer to them than life and happiness; it was for them, by cruel torture and death, or by weary years of suffering in the Plantations, to expiate their misplaced trust in a leader unworthy of the cause they cherished.

And where are we to look in this to find the infallible Justice that regulates the chances of this life?

Not indeed in the fair west country given over to pillage and the sword, her towns shambles, her countryside a waste of ruined crops and deserted farms; not in the attendant heartbreak and despair are the workings of justice transparent to our eyes. But looking across the years that followed is seen the reassuring ray of promise. The sacrifice offered at the hands of Monmouth was indeed rejected, but the sacrifice was not therefore vain. The wretched peasants had offered their lives for the establishment of religion and truth, and the offering was accepted. Their lives were indeed demanded of them on the battlefield, on the scaffold, in the slave cabins of the Plantations—who shall say that they did not receive their reward; and who, having regard to the wonderful growth of religious tolerance, of justice and national honour in England during the eighteenth and nineteenth centuries, will deny that the seeds sown with blood and tears in that short-lived rebellion of the west have blossomed in fadeless flowers? Here is a tale of two who threw in their lot with those who followed Monmouth; not for love of the Duke, but impelled thereto by an unexpected chain of circumstances. Two whose lives drifted together on the fierce tide of war and in whose hearts love was awakened by hatred of tyranny. It is a tale of dangers, of sorrow and of suffering, yet of some merriment, of courage and of great happiness withal, for she who inspired it was not one to let fear of the future darken the present, or present suffering weaken the spirit to endure. Rather she accepted whatsoever the Fates might send with a quiet courage, laughing in the face of frowning fortune, and found among the ashes of suffering and seeming desolation an exceeding great treasure. If the memory of Barbara Winslow inspire any to face the monotony of life with the same blithe courage with which she faced the horrors of death, her story will not have been told in vain, but will prove a seed bearing fruit in the life of a brave woman.

CONTENTS

Page

LIST OF ILLUSTRATIONS

BARBARA WINSLOW
REBEL

CHAPTER I

"Truly, Sir Peter; 'tis a great honour you do me. Yet bethink you; if every fugitive felt it a duty to offer his hand to each maid who had favoured his escape, there would be busy doings in these troublous times."

"Duty, Mistress Barbara, i' faith! 'Tis no thought of duty your presence inspires."

There was an ominous glint in the speaker's eyes which caused his companion to interrupt him quickly with a nervous laugh.

"In that case, sir, 'twere best I should leave you; 'twere small good urging upon you the duty of saving your life by instant departure, if my presence play traitor to my words by bidding you stay. So fare thee well; I wish you a safe journey."

"Alas, madame, and will you indeed send me away without one word of hope? I will die an you do. What is life to me without your favour? I entreat you, have pity."

Sir Peter's protestations were eager, nay ardent, but they tripped too glibly from his tongue, they smacked too much of experience in the art of wooing and moved Mistress Barbara to naught save amusement.

"Nay, but listen to me, sir," she answered with mock solemnity. "As you well know, there are many who since the rising have been in hiding like yourself. For Rupert's sake, I will give help and shelter to all who need it, but it were too much to expect me to give to all such unfortunates what now you seek. Bethink you what complications might arise hereafter."

"But, madame, 'tis possible all will not adore you as devotedly as do I."

"'Twere scarcely worth my while to consider such a remote possibility, sir," she answered demurely. "Nor do I see reason why you should prove an exception."

A man and a maid seated together on a bank of moss in the moonlight have been seen oft in England; nor, if the maid were fair and not unwilling to listen (and what maid ever refused?), was it ever matter for surprise if the man has made wise use of the opportunities the Fates had given to him to perfect a romantic harmony of time and place by pouring forth protestations of undying devotion and of admiration for the incomparable charms of his companion; for moonlight is in truth a marvellous loosener of tongues; the greatest matchmaker of the universe is the pale witch queen of the night.

But natural though the affair may at first sight appear, in the present case it was attended by certain untoward circumstances which would have rendered the conventional occupation of Sir Peter and the lady productive of astonishment to an onlooker.

For it was but a week since the disastrous engagement at Sedgemoor where Sir Peter had commanded one of the foot regiments in Monmouth's ill-fated army. And though the ardour of his wooing for a time almost led him to forget the fact, he was nevertheless a condemned rebel with a price upon his head and little hope of life unless by some means he could reach the coast and so compass his escape from the country. Within a mile of where he sat there were those who were seeking high and low to take his person, dead or alive; yet despite his danger he seemed oblivious to everything beyond his immediate surroundings. He devoted himself to the wooing of his companion's favour with the same passionate assiduity which he had ever displayed in more peaceful days in the calm precincts of Whitehall, or even in the perhaps less reputable regions of Old Drury.

Three days after the rout at Sedgemoor, after experiencing the miseries of starvation and despair which fall to the lot of a hunted man, Sir Peter Dare had reached the village of Durford, hoping thence to escape to the coast. Driven by hunger and distress to desperate ventures, he had presented himself at the Manor House, trusting to his ready tongue, his handsome face and his large experience in the management of the sex to gain the sympathy and assistance at least of the women of the household. He met with a welcome even more kindly than he had dared to hope for. Mistress Barbara Winslow had a tender heart for all rebels, her own brother, Rupert, having also ridden with Monmouth, and being himself even then in hiding, she knew not where. Therefore, she and her cousin Lady Cicely gave shelter to Sir Peter gladly, and for some days he remained at the Manor House, lauding the Fates for directing him to such a pleasant haven, and employing his time, having nought else to do, in losing his heart to his fair hostess, who, being a woman, thought no worse of him for his obvious admiration, which, to do her justice, she considered but her due.

But not many days could the wanderer remain in safety at Durford. The country was closely patrolled by those searching every hole and corner for fugitives from Monmouth's army, and a small search party had their headquarters in the village itself. The Manor House was suspected, and the Winslows could not hope longer to conceal the presence of their guest, especially as their household consisted exclusively of women—creatures of unquestioned loyalty but irresponsible tongues.

In the meantime, however, news had been received of a fishing vessel lying off the coast, some three miles from Listoke, and with the help of one Peter Drew, a smith by trade, and a devoted admirer of Mistress Barbara, arrangements had been made with the skipper to take the fugitive on board.

Four days, therefore, after his arrival, Sir Peter reluctantly bade farewell to his hostess, and prepared to ride away once more upon his wanderings.

But ere he started finally on his journey, Mistress Barbara, moved either by the beauty of the evening, or by pity for his somewhat forlorn condition, proposed to accompany him to the end of the narrow lane, leading from the Manor House to the high road, and so set him on his way.

Now at the side of this lane ran a mossy bank, and the night being warm, and the moonlight inspiring, it befell that an hour after his departure from the house, Sir Peter was still seated on the bank at the feet of Mistress Barbara, oblivious alike to her repeated assertions that if he would not depart she at least could remain no longer, and to her warning that each moment's delay meant additional danger.

Still they sat there, until Sir Peter, moved by the sweet tones of his companion's voice, by the gleam of her eyes in the moonlight, and by gloomy reflections on their approaching separation, threw prudence to the winds, and burst forth into desperate, and for the time being heartfelt, protestations of devotion, mingled with entreaties that she would at least give him hope of one day winning her favour.

But Mistress Barbara, though she had found satisfaction in Sir Peter's open admiration, was in no wise pleased at so serious a turn to the conversation. She shrewdly suspected that it was by no means the first time such vows had passed his lips, and was consequently quite unmoved by his despair; but this unexpected change from moonlight dreams in the present to practical discussions of the future brought back her mind to realities with a sudden shock. She had no inclination to enter into a serious discussion of the matter, so she put a sudden end to the affair by springing to her feet and insisting upon her companion taking his departure forthwith, lest he miss the tide.

Sir Peter, recognising that further pleading would be useless, heaved a forlorn sigh, at which Mistress Barbara smiled under cover of the darkness and they walked to the end of the lane in silence. Here they paused and Barbara gave her final directions.

"I can go with you no further. I would we could have kept you with us longer, but indeed it is not safe; they have traced you here and are hunting high and low for you. Your only hope is to cross the water. I have told you the road; two hours' riding should bring you to the place. Pray Heaven you fall not in with Captain Protheroe and his men. But if you do you should soon outstrip them, for their horses will be weary; they have been out seeking you since daylight, though thanks to their belief in their own intelligence they have sought diligently in the wrong direction. But they will come back to quarters presently and you must be gone. Farewell, my friend, and a pleasant ride."

Sir Peter stooped to kiss her hand and mounted his horse reluctantly.

"Farewell, madame. It were useless to try to thank you. But at least I shall hope for some future occasion of repaying my debt."

"I shall deem it well repaid if you can contrive to send me word of Rupert's safety," answered the girl with a sigh. "That he will escape I am assured; Rupert could never come to harm; but the waiting for news is weary, and on some days hope is only a duty, not a consolation."

"See what it is to be a brother," exclaimed Sir Peter mournfully. "You care more for his little finger than you do for the offer of my heart."

"Well, sir, and is not the rarer commodity ever the more precious?" she answered saucily. "Rupert hath but two little fingers, whereas——"

"I have but one heart, madame."

"True, sir; but what limit to the times it may be offered?"

"Ah! Mistress Barbara, you know naught of the matter, for you yourself have no heart at all."

"And I marvel that you should still have one, considering how frequently you have lost it."

"I vow——"

"Hush!"

The jingle of accoutrements sounded round the corner of the road, and at the same moment they became aware of horses slowly approaching, a sound which hitherto they had been too much engrossed in their conversation to heed.

"Alack! 'Tis the troopers," whispered Barbara. "Back, ere it be too late."

But the time for escape had passed; for even as she spoke, and before Sir Peter had fully grasped the situation, the troopers had rounded the corner of the road, and were face to face with the fugitive.

They could scarcely be described as an imposing-looking force. Since daybreak they had been out scouring the country for rebels, beating the woods, ransacking the barns, following a wild-goose chase after false information extracted from the sullen country-folk, and were now returning to the village, worn out, dejected, and mud-stained. It would have been difficult to find a more forlorn-looking crew, even among the unfortunate men whom they hunted.

But at sight of the couple before them their dejection instantly vanished. The man's rich dress, handsome still, despite its draggled appearance, his presence on the road at this hour, and the horrified exclamation of the girl, all tended to prove that this was the man whom they sought. With a quick exclamation, the leader sprang from his horse and striding up to Sir Peter seized his horse's bridle, crying sharply, "I arrest you in the King's name. Surrender like a wise man, or take the consequences."

Sir Peter reined his horse back abruptly, and glanced round at his enemies with a muttered curse. But in Mistress Barbara the danger only roused a spirit of excitement and mischief. She flung up her head and laughed.

"Cock-a-doodle-do! Who is afraid of you?" she sang saucily.

Captain Protheroe was somewhat discomfited by this unexpected answer. He threw an angry glance in the direction of the girl, and otherwise ignoring her presence, turned again to his prisoner.

"Come, sir, I ask you again, do you surrender, or must I order my men to seize you?"

"And I repeat," remarked the girl again, "that you crow too loudly, noble sir."

One of the troopers in the background laughed, and the captain turned furiously on Barbara.

"Peace, wench," he began sharply. But at that moment, when all eyes were turned on the girl, Sir Peter dealt a furious blow in the captain's chest, driving him back against the bank, and at the same time wrenched the reins from his grasp and dug his spurs into the horse's flanks. The animal leaped forward suddenly, and before the men could recover from the confusion and make a further move to stop him, the prisoner was clear of the surrounding circle and galloping rapidly down the road, while Mistress Barbara clapped her hands and laughed delightedly at their discomfiture.

Captain Protheroe sprang to his feet in an instant, furious with rage, but quickly realising that it would be vain with their wearied horses to attempt to overtake the fugitive, he opened his lips to give the order to fire, that the man might be stopped, dead or alive. But ere he could speak the word, two arms were flung round his neck, and two soft hands were pressed tightly over his lips, while again the girl's mischievous laugh rang in his ears.

For a moment the captain was too much astonished to move, then astonishment gave place to anger.

Roughly seizing the girl's wrists, he pulled away her hands and shouted to the men to fire at once. But it was already too late, the fugitive was out of sight, and though several troopers presently set out in pursuit, it was obvious that the hope of recapture was very slight, seeing he rode a fresh horse, and the moon, already low in the sky, promised soon to give the pursued the protection of darkness.

Then, balked of his prisoner, Captain Protheroe turned furiously upon the cause of his failure.

"You hussy," he exclaimed harshly, "I will teach you——"

He stopped abruptly, for the girl's hood had fallen back, and he found himself gazing into the most wonderful eyes he had ever beheld.

Then a soft voice drawled in sympathetic tones, "'Deed, captain, hath he really escaped thee? How vastly annoying. For, an I mistake not, the orders were to take him at all costs, dead or alive, and now, being but few miles from the coast, and being well mounted, 'tis very like he may be altogether quit of the country by to-morrow morn. I vow 'tis too bad. But sure, you are eager to pursue him, so I will no longer delay you. I wish you a very good even."

She dropped him a sedate curtsey and turned to walk back to the house.

But by this time Captain Protheroe had recovered from the effect of her eyes. He seized her roughly by the wrist and dragged her back.

"Not so fast, my girl. I must have some information from you first concerning this same rebel."

Barbara eyed him in grave astonishment.

"You are hurting my wrist," she complained reproachfully.

The captain dropped her wrist instantly, and she held it out to him gravely, that he might see the red marks of his fingers on the white flesh.

"Come," he began, somewhat abashed, "tell me but this: Was that Sir Peter Dare who hath escaped us, and if so, where and how did you fall in with him?"

"Indeed, sir," answered the girl demurely, "you are surely forgetful of the place and hour. Bethink you, 'tis scarce meet that I remain here alone, parleying thus with strangers."

"Tut! girl," answered the captain, laughing, "that excuse will not avail. You thought it no shame ten minutes since to remain here parleying with one man. There is safety in numbers."

"Ah! That is a different matter, sir," she answered with a most innocent glance. "He was a gentleman."

"A gentleman! Well! What then?"

"Such do not mishandle women, sir," she said and pointed again reproachfully to her injured wrist.

"Peste!" muttered the captain angrily. In truth he was somewhat puzzled as to whom the girl might be. She wore a rough scarlet cloak and hood common to all the country maids, and he could not see her dress beneath. Furthermore she spoke with a slight Somersetshire accent, and this, together with her saucy manner, had at first led him to suppose her to be merely a simple country wench. But now the suspicion grew that she was but masquerading in the part.

The only thing of which he felt certain was that she had the sweetest voice and the most bewitching dimple in the corner of her mouth of any woman he had ever met.

"Come now," he continued more gently, "I am sorry I hurt thee, girl, but an answer I must have. Who was the fellow?"

She looked at him gravely.

"Well, sir, an you will have it, he was—he was a certain Captain Miles Protheroe."

Captain Protheroe laughed unwillingly at her coolness.

"Come, you must give a better account of him than that, mistress."

"Nay, is that no good account?" she exclaimed with elaborate astonishment.

"Marry! How one may be deceived. I have ever heard Captain Protheroe spoken of as passably honest, though perchance not overwise, and decidedly hard-featured."

But this was too much, and Captain Protheroe lost all patience. Yet if the girl persisted in her saucy masquerade, he resolved at least to play up to her, and let her see how she enjoyed the part.

"A truce of this fooling, girl," he began harshly.

"Faith, sir, an my conversation please you not, I will e'en take my leave," she interposed quickly, and again turned to leave him.

But Captain Protheroe seized her cloak and held her fast.

"Listen to me, my girl," he said sharply, "and bridle your saucy tongue. Give me the information I require or, by Heaven, I'll march you back to the village and keep you prisoner till you learn to obey. Make up your mind. Which shall it be?"

Barbara turned and regarded him gravely from head to foot.

"I like you not," she remarked coolly, as the result of her critical survey.

"That may well be," he answered, smiling scornfully. "But an you answer not my questions, and that speedily, I must find means to make you do so. Now speak; which shall it be?"

Barbara glanced round eagerly for a way of escape, her mouth drooped, her eyes opened wide with fear, her hands were clasped convulsively at her throat, the fingers fidgeting with the ribbons of her cloak. She shook her head once or twice helplessly, casting at the captain glances of indignation, pleading, and reproach.

But he remained resolute. Then she began in a trembling voice:

"Well, sir, if there be no other way of escape, I must—I must e'en——I must run!" And as she spoke the word, with a quick movement she twisted herself free from the cloak which she had previously unfastened, leaving it in the captain's hands, and darting up the bank by the roadside, disappeared into the plantation beyond.

One or two of the troopers made a motion to pursue her, but the captain called them back.

"Let her go. You would never find her in the dark." And added, laughing, "The wench deserves her freedom. Fall in, men, and back to quarters; we can do no more to-night."

Nothing loth, the troopers resumed their way back to the village; but ere he departed, Captain Protheroe stooped and tore a ribbon from the discarded cloak, and with a short, half-shamed laugh twisted it round his wrist.

CHAPTER II

A man might journey far afield and find no sweeter spot than the village of Durford as it appeared on a certain sunny September afternoon in the year of grace 1685. The low white houses with their heavy overhanging thatched roofs were bowered in roses; while in each miniature garden the riot of colour and perfume intoxicated the senses. The low sun spread the long, cool shadows of the trees across the brilliant emerald and gold of the meadows, and lighted up each leaf and flower distinct from its fellows. The square tower of the old grey church and the grey-green clump of the yew trees behind it were silhouetted against a golden haze like the head of a haloed saint. The summits of the distant hills faded in golden mist like the mystic scopes of Paradise. In the neighbouring orchards the trees bent beneath the weight of their russet burdens, the fields spread golden with the harvest, and the wooded hills burned with the bright, burnished tints of early autumn. It was as though in this, the evening of the year, mother earth were moved in emulation of the sky to deck herself in all the varied colours of the autumn sunset.

In the woods the birds were practising for their autumn chorus, voicing the ecstatic joy of life in little unexpected trills and bursts of song, while the heavy drone of the bees and the occasional cry of the grasshoppers denoted a more sober contentment. The soft, warm air was heavy with a myriad delicate scents; breathing over the imagination faint, suggestive memories of a happy past and formless dreams of a golden future.

But as the heart of man is still untamed by the sweet influences of nature, so, on the afternoon in question, a scene was being enacted on the green before the Inn, as foul as the surrounding picture was fair, as though heaven and hell, God's love and tenderness to man, and man's brutality and cruelty to his fellows, were here met side by side.

In the centre of the green stood a tall whipping-post, and tied to this was a small boy of some nine years of age. His back was bare, his eyes were wide with fear, and his teeth were resolutely clenched to repress the sobs which ever and anon forced their way through his lips.

Over the boy, whip in hand, stood a man dressed in the uniform of a corporal of the 2d Tangiers Regiment, a stout, purple-faced fellow, with scrubby black hair and beard, near-set cunning eyes, a cruel mouth, and over all an air of supreme importance and self-satisfaction. This was Corporal Crutch, a man whose life was alternately glorified by his own assurance of his remarkable ability and embittered by the world's blindness towards the same.

Some half dozen troopers stood around watching the scene, and on the edge of the group were three or four sobbing women and a crowd of wide-eyed, terrified children.

"Now, my lad," cried the corporal, with a gleeful chuckle, "let us have no more of this obstinacy. Nay, an thou wilt not speak, I warrant me a taste of this whip will help me to the finding of thy tongue, and doubtless of thy father into the bargain. An thou beest a wise lad thou'lt speak now, once my arm gets to work on thee 'twill not be so ready to stop, maybe."

Some of the troopers laughed, and the women's sobs increased, but the boy remained resolutely silent.

"So thou wilt have it then," cried the corporal; and the whip descended with a sickening swish on to the boy's bare back.

Once! Twice! Thrice! The boy shuddered and sobbed, but no word came from his lips, and the corporal, angered by this unexpected determination on the part of his victim, doubled the weight of his blows.

Suddenly a shout interrupted the proceedings and a loud, clear voice rang out imperiously:

"Hold, fellow! What art thou doing to the child? Loose him instantly."

The crowd round the corporal fell back hurriedly, and he himself paused and slowly turned his head in the direction whence the voice came.

The speaker was a tall, slender girl, with a face of such exquisite beauty as men may hope to see but once or twice in a lifetime, and having seen, may never hope to forget. The beautiful oval face, clear-skinned and glowing with colour, was outlined by soft dark hair, shading to black in the shadows, waving back from the low white brow in soft rippling curls. The clear-cut perfection of her features was relieved from coldness by the unmanageable dimple at one corner of her mouth, and by the frank directness of the deep blue eyes, which looked out upon the world from beneath their dark lashes with habitual fearlessness. The expression of her face was habitually happy and friendly, only the firm lines of her mouth and chin belying the general expression of good-tempered recklessness.

She was mounted on a rough pony, and had drawn rein at the top of the hill leading down to the village, moved by an idle curiosity to learn the cause of the crowd before the Inn.

The faces of the sobbing women brightened when they saw the girl, and the men glanced at each other sheepishly.

"'Tis Mistress Barbara Winslow from the Manor House," muttered one. "Thou hadst best send the lad about his business, corporal."

But Corporal Crutch was an obstinate man, and one moreover who was imbued with a strong sense of his own importance; he had no mind to allow any woman, whether of high or low degree, to interfere with his chosen occupation. Moreover the Manor House was suspected of harbouring rebels, and its occupants were judged little better than rebels themselves. So paying no heed either to the command or the advice, he turned his back upon the advancing figure and raised his whip for another blow on the back of his trembling victim.

"Hold! I tell thee, fellow," cried the girl again angrily. "Dost thou not hear me? Nay, an thou wilt not, by Heaven I'll make thee obey."

Without further ado she galloped straight at the group on the green which scattered to right and left as she passed, then with a sudden quick movement cracked out the long lash of her riding whip, curling it lasso-like around the corporal's neck, and not checking her pace dragged him stumbling and stuttering backwards till he fell to the ground. Then releasing the whip handle and reining back her pony to admire her handiwork she burst into a peal of laughter. And indeed 'twas a fit subject for merriment, for the corporal was stout and angry and the lash was exceedingly long and heavy. The corporal alternately swore and struggled, and the lash became every minute more tightly entangled round his neck.

Presently Mistress Barbara checked her laughter, slipped from her pony and crossed to the whipping-post where the sobbing boy stood watching the scene with eager eyes in which hope and fear still strove for the mastery.

"Loose him," she cried imperiously, and the troopers hastened to obey her.

"My poor brave laddie," she murmured, bending over him tenderly. "Ah! but they have hurt thee cruelly. Get away to thy mother and fear not. They shall not touch thee again."

Then drawing herself up to her full height, and she was more than common tall, she faced round upon the group of men.

"Brutes," she cried. "Brutes ye are, and no men to treat a poor helpless laddie thus. What! Have ye no manhood? Think shame of yourselves to stand by and let such work go on. An I were but a man I'd teach you a lesson you would not soon forget."

"'Tis well enough to talk," grumbled one of the troopers angrily; "but the lad's father is in hiding and we must know where he is, The boy could tell us well enough an he would speak. We caught him slipping thro' the wood an hour back. Yon basket of food he carried was for him, I warrant."

"'Tis very like," answered Barbara coldly. "What then?"

"What then? Why the fellow is a rebel."

"And what of that, pray? An his father be a rebel to King James, is that reason why the lad should be traitor to his own father? Shame on you! You who are fathers yourselves; would you have your sons cast such a teaching in your teeth?"

By this time the corporal had freed his neck from the lash and recovered his equanimity. Now he bustled to the front with an air of importance.

"Best beware, mistress," he cried roughly. "Best beware. 'Tis ill work to interfere wi' the just punishment of traitors."

Barbara turned to him and laughed softly.

"Ha! Sir Gallows-Bird. So thou hast escaped the hemp; welcome on thy return to this wicked world."

"I tell thee, madame," stuttered the corporal angrily, "'tis ill work jesting — —"

"Peace, fool!" she cried imperiously. "I marvel thou art not ashamed to show thy face after this day's work. I knew already you and your masters think it no shame to fight against women, but at least methought children might go unharmed. They can do but little harm to King James."

"Pshaw! Ye know nought of the matter," blustered the corporal. "I brook no interference in the exercise of my duty. Bring back the boy, Sam Perry, and proceed with the interrogation."

"Do not attempt it," answered the girl quietly, "for I will not permit it."

Sam Perry hesitated.

"What!" roared the corporal, "are ye afraid of a chit of a girl? Why do you not obey?"

"At your peril," cried Barbara sharply, moving before the men.

How the matter would eventually have terminated is doubtful had not a second interruption occurred.

The door of the Inn opened, and a figure emerged at sight of which the troopers shrank back sheepishly, and the corporal's air of importance vanished pitifully.

"What is the meaning of this disturbance?" sharply demanded the new arrival.

Barbara turned eagerly towards him.

"Are you the leader of these butchers, sir?" she enquired haughtily.

Though somewhat astonished at this unexpected mode of address, Captain Protheroe, for he it was, smiled slightly and answered politely enough:

"I am the captain of these men, if that is what you would ask, madame. Are all soldiers butchers in your estimation?"

"Soldiers!" she cried scornfully. "Call ye them soldiers? But perhaps you are even as they, and 'tis by your orders they torture women and children and make a veritable hell of God's earth. I wish you joy of such work."

"Pardon my dulness, madame," answered the captain calmly, "but I have not the least idea to what you are alluding or how I have incurred your displeasure."

"No? Then hearken, sir." And in burning words she described the cause of her indignation.

The captain listened with a gathering frown to her story, and at the conclusion turned on the corporal with a look that boded ill for that self-satisfied mortal.

"So, sirrah! Is this the way you carry out my orders? Have I not said I will have no violence to the village folk? And by Heaven I will be obeyed. I have long known thee for a knave. Art fool and coward, too, that you must needs force children to help thee with thy work? Is this thy notion of a soldier's work? I'll teach thee better knowledge of thy duty ere I've done with thee. 'Tis not the first time I've heard such complaints; see to it it be the last, or by the saints 'twill be the end of thy service. I'll have no bullies in my troop. Go, sirrah!"

The discomfited corporal slunk off down the street casting an ugly glance over his shoulder at the girl who had brought such a rating upon him. But for her part Barbara laughed and waved her hand after the retreating figure.

"Fare thee well, Sir Knight of the whipcord," she cried gaily.

When the corporal had vanished, followed by other troopers, the captain turned towards Barbara with a bow and said coldly:

"I trust you are satisfied with these orders, madame."

"I shall be satisfied, sir, when I know that the orders are executed," she answered coolly.

"Madame, I command here. Where I command I am obeyed."

"'Twere easy to believe it, sir," she answered with a half-smile and a glance at his resolute face. "But I have heard there be many orders delivered thus readily in public which privately are never intended to be performed."

The captain flushed hotly, but gave no further sign of anger at this insinuation.

"Indeed, I know not wherein I have deserved your distrust, madame."

"In such troublous times as these my distrust is given before my confidence, sir; and pray what have you done to prove that distrust is misplaced? You claim to be a gentleman, but by Heaven 'tis no gentle's work to hunt down poor wretches led astray by others who should have known a wiser path; 'tis no gentle's work to harry helpless women and children; 'tis no gentle's work to listen behind doors and spy through keyholes. By my faith, sir," she continued, her temper increasing at the remembrance of her many grievances; "By my faith, sir, this poor wretch of a corporal whom you have so rated is virtue itself compared with you. He but executes the orders which you conceive, hiding yourself behind the name of gentleman."

The last words were delivered with biting scorn, and having concluded her tirade, Barbara turned her back upon him and stepped towards her pony.

Captain Protheroe had remained politely silent during this harangue. When her back was turned he smiled slightly and followed the indignant lady.

"Permit me to assist you to mount, madame," he said with grave politeness.

Barbara drew her skirts around her and answered with as much haughty dignity as her rising anger would permit:

"No, sir. When you have shown yourself capable of a gentleman's work you may be worthy of a gentleman's privileges. Until that time I prefer to mount alone and keep myself from the pollution of your touch."

But instead of being crushed as she had intended he should be, Captain Protheroe merely smiled again and stood politely aside to watch her mount. The pony was restless, two or three attempts were necessary before the feat was accomplished, and during the struggle both Barbara's dignity and temper suffered considerably. Captain Protheroe wisely made no further offer of assistance, but watched her efforts with an amused twinkle in his eyes.

Suddenly an idea struck him. He laughed softly, and placing a detaining hand upon the pony's bridle he turned once more to the lady, an ironical smile playing about his lips.

"Madame, since I am unworthy to touch your foot, I fear I am equally unworthy to retain this small token of remembrance which you so obligingly bestowed upon me that evening some weeks ago when you did me the honour to embrace me." So speaking he placed his hand in the pocket of his coat and drew forth the scarlet ribbon of the cloak which she had left in his hands when she fled from him at their first meeting.

Had there been magic in the small piece of ribbon it could not well have wrought a greater change in Barbara. Her attempt at dignity vanished. A wave of crimson passed over her face, her eyes blazed, and when she spoke it was in a voice choked with passion.

"How dare you, sir! 'Tis a most cowardly lie. 'Twas no embrace, as you might know well. 'Twas—'Twas—an assault."

Her persecutor was as unmoved by her passion as he had been by her rating.

"No embrace?" he drawled in polite astonishment. "Nay, then I pray you pardon my mistake, which you will grant me was a natural one. Truly an that be your manner of assaulting your enemies, I forgive the Fates for having ranked me among their number, and shall desire of them nothing better than continuous battery at your hands."

"Have your desire then," cried Barbara furiously, and doubling up her first she dealt him a fierce blow on the side of his face.

With a quiet smile he turned his head.

"The other cheek, madame?"

Barbara gasped and for a moment stared down into the cool face raised to hers. Then suddenly her eyes twinkled, her mouth dimpled, and she broke into a soft, half-angry laugh which, however, she as quickly repressed.

"By Heaven, sir, an you be not the most aggravating man in the kingdom, Heaven grant I may never meet him. How dare you detain me thus? Loose my pony instantly."

He drew back with a low bow.

"Your pardon, madame, your way is free. In the meantime I will keep this token till ye redeem it by another embrace—I should say, assault."

"Then you will keep it forever, sir."

"It is nought but the alternative that I should desire more," answered the captain still with the same quiet smile. But Barbara was too furious to answer, and whipping up her pony she galloped away.

The captain stood silently watching her till she disappeared from the narrow village street, then he turned and walked into the Inn.

In the taproom sat the corporal, his wounded pride somewhat soothed by generous potations, holding forth upon the subject of his grievances to the half-dozen troopers collected there.

"'Tis a fine state of things when any blue-eyed wench is to be allowed to interfere in the administration of justice and say this ye shall and this ye shall not do, for all the world like the general himself. 'Tis no sort of work. 'Twas very different in the old days wi' Captain Carrington. Then an a lad would not speak we had ways to teach him. But now — —" He paused cautiously and confided his criticism of his superior officer to the depths of his tankard.

"This Mistress Barbara is a bold wench," ventured Sam Perry cautiously.

The corporal's face darkened.

"Mistress Winslow had best be careful," he muttered. "Her brother is attainted as a rebel, and lieth somewhere in hiding, and I warrant yon haughty wench knows where. Zounds! I'll keep a careful watch of her—and I doubt not soon to surprise her secret. 'Twere a sweet revenge," he muttered, rubbing his fingers gleefully; "and 'twould teach her 'tis scant wisdom to bandy words wi' them in authority and fling whips i' an honest man's face."

Meanwhile Barbara rode home slowly, talking to herself as was her wont.

"Odd's bodikin! as Rupert would say, but how the fat corporal did puff and splutter. Poor Cicely would say 'twere wicked folly thus to anger our enemies against us, but sure such a prank can do no harm. The corporal is patently a fool, I fear him not; and as for the other— —" Here she paused and laughed half-angrily. "He surely would not venge his quarrel with me on Rupert. But what an immovable fellow it is. How I would love to see him angry. 'Twere perchance a dangerous experiment, but I were no true woman did I not long to try. Ah! well, an he remain here much longer I fear he may have many chances to taste of my temper. 'Tis a brutal world." And so alternately laughing and frowning, she rode home to the Manor House.

CHAPTER III

The Durford Manor House, which for many generations had been the home of the Winslows, was a low, rambling structure of grey stone, full of strange nooks and corners and curious hiding places. Part of the house dated back to the fifteenth century, and had sheltered fugitives from Bosworth field. It had witnessed many strange scenes during the years of the Civil War; many a Royalist had found refuge there, and it had been twice besieged. Here, in the great oak-panelled hall, Lady Elizabeth Winslow, grandmother of the present Sir Rupert, had entertained the Parliamentarian officers to supper while her husband was held prisoner in the neighbouring room, and after disarming their suspicions by her wit and gaiety, had eluded their vigilance and slipped out of her window when her guests had retired for the night, and ridden through the darkness to Taunton. Here she roused the townsfolk, and herself riding at their head had surprised the small force conducting her husband to Gloucester and rescued him just when all hope of escape seemed dead. Here Mistress Penelope Winslow, the proud beauty of the House, whose portrait, a stiff, lifeless shadow of the beauty which had set fire to all the hearts in the countryside, still hung above the stairs, had refused her twenty suitors and finally given her hand to a nameless Scotch soldier and ridden away with him to the wilds of his Highland home. Here Richard Winslow, that renowned soldier, had been brought after the battle of Worcester, the very remnant of a man, spared by the clemency of Parliament to drag out a weary existence in the house of his fathers, and dream what his life might have been had not a fatal shot left him at once blind, deaf and paralysed. Here Stephen Winslow, after impoverishing his house and risking his life for his sovereign, had eaten his heart out through long years of baffled ambition and bitter disappointment, learning the gratitude of kings.

The Winslows had ever been loyal to the Stuarts, giving all and asking little in return, and, though she would not for the world confess it, it had been a sore trouble to Mistress Barbara that her twin brother Rupert, the last representative of his line, should have chosen to cast in his lot with the usurper Monmouth and rebel against his lawful sovereign.

She had acquiesced, as she acquiesced in all he proposed, but her heart boded no good of the matter, and when the fatal battle of Sedgemoor had sent Monmouth to captivity and the block, and had made of her own brother a fugitive from home, in hiding she knew not where, she experienced anxiety and misery indeed, so far as her sunny hopeful nature would allow, but no surprise.

More than two weary months had passed since that fatal morning, but no news of the wanderer had reached the Manor House. From time to time her more humble neighbours crept back in secret to the village they had left so hopefully that bright morning in June when they went out to join one whom they believed to be the Heaven-sent defender of their faith and freedom. But they came back, alas! only to creep away again to some dreary hiding-place in moor or wood, for the village was watched by the soldiers and home could no longer offer safe refuge to the weary, despairing men. From time to time came rumours of the escape or capture of this or that follower of the Duke and terrible stories of punishment meted out by brutal judges; still no news of young Sir Rupert Winslow came to allay the anxiety of his sister or soften the hopeless misery of his young cousin Cicely, to whom he had been betrothed but three short weeks before his departure. But no suspense, however terrible, can last forever, and at length, early in September, the longed-for news arrived.

Mistress Barbara and her cousin were at breakfast in the sunny parlour of the Manor House, and the former had just sought to win a smile from the sad face of her companion by relating her adventure with Corporal Crutch in the village on the previous afternoon. When she ended her story Cicely looked up fearfully and shook her head.

"Indeed, Barbara, thou art too rash. Thou hast but made an enemy of the man, and God wot we have enemies enough already."

"Nay, prithee do not chide me," answered her cousin coaxingly; "the fellow can do us no harm. And indeed, Cicely, I must be merry sometimes, or I verily believe I should die."

"Merry!" exclaimed Cicely somewhat bitterly. "Ay, perchance thou canst be merry, Rupert is but thy brother; yet to me——"

"He is thy betrothed. Then truly by all showing I should be more distressed than thou. New lovers may be gotten by the score, but by no power could I win me another brother. Nay, dear, I did but jest, I meant not to vex thee," she added contritely, seeing her cousin's lip quiver unsteadily; "thou knowest my tongue runs ever faster than my brain, plague on it."

"Thou hast not vexed me, Barbara, only—— I would I had the secret of thy courage."

"Nay, thou hast courage enough, only somewhat too much thought. Were I to sit and dream all day of what evils might befall Rupert I should be as sad-eyed as thou art. But indeed no news is good news. The world is a good place, and I see not why one may not hope for happy days until sad ones befall us, eh!"

They were interrupted by the entrance of the waiting-maid. "I were loath to trouble ye, Mistress Barbara," she began, "but 'tis a zertain tiresome vellow, Simon the pedlar, who asks to show you his wares. To my thinking he hath nought worth a glance, and I had zent un about his bizness speedily; but a be a mozt stubborn fellow and will not depart until a zee ye. A zays a hath zomething of great value but a be a vellow will say aught to gain a hearing, I know un well."

Barbara's face brightened suddenly and she sprang eagerly from her seat.

"'Tis well, Phoebe, take the fellow in; I will come on the instant."

"Why, Barbara!" exclaimed Cicely in astonishment; "what would you with the man? Would'st plenish thy store of linsey or tapes that thou art so ready to see him?"

"An I dream not, Cis, he will have wares more precious than those."

"What!" cried Cicely with awakened interest. "Is it possible the fellow hath stuffs from London with him? I would willingly buy, an it be so."

Barbara laughed and pinched her cousin's chin. "Thou little vanity! Thou worshipper of gauds and ribbons!" she cried with much solemnity; "I verily believe thou would'st sell thy soul for two dozen yards of Genoa velvet. But come; we will see what he has to show us."

On entering the large wainscotted hall the girls found the pedlar standing in the embrasure of one of the windows, his pack tying unopened at his feet. He was an aged, wizened-looking creature upon whose face greed and cunning had laid their stamp.

Cicely eagerly eyeing the pack addressed herself to him with a slight air of hauteur.

"Well, fellow, where are your wares? Have you aught of rarity or value to show us?"

"Ay, that have I, mistress," he answered in a high-pitched grating voice, with an air of impertinent familiarity. "I have that here which will bring light to the dullest eye, a blush to the palest cheek, and joy to the saddest heart. 'Tis not over rare neither, yet 'tis ever held to be of the greatest value."

"Why what mean you? What should this be?"

"A letter, mistress! a love-letter I doubt not."

"A letter! From whom?"

"From one of whom your ladyship hath long wished to hear, and hath wellnigh heard from no more," he answered with a brutal laugh.

Cicely's eyes flashed, her whole body trembled with eagerness.

"Ah! give it me, give it me, my good man; why hast thou delayed so foolishly?"

"Softly, softly mistress," answered the fellow coolly. "Here is the letter sure enow," drawing a small white packet from his valise—"And 'tis from Sir Rupert." Here he showed the direction. "But first give me my price."

"Oh yes, thou shalt be paid, never fear," cried Cicely with increasing impatience. "Now give me the packet."

"Not so fast, mistress," he answered curtly; "I yield not up this packet before I see my reward."

"Oh! you foolish fellow! name your price then."

"Five hundred crowns," he answered coolly.

"Five hundred crowns," cried Cicely in horror; "why, man, thou art mad, I have not such a sum."

"Mad or no, that is my price."

"But I could not pay thee such a sum; you are a very extortioner, you wicked fellow."

"Listen to me, mistress," interrupted the pedlar roughly; "and be not so glib with thy tongue; hard words win no favours. I know nought of politics, and Sir Rupert may hang twenty times for all I care. All I know is that this letter is worth my price, and if ye will not pay it there be others not a mile away who will be right willing to buy the information it contains."

"Ah, sure you could not be so cruel," began Cicely piteously, but Barbara intervened.

"Peace, Cicely, let me deal with the fellow. Now, my man," she continued, turning on him sharply, "we will give thee twenty crowns for that letter and not a penny more, dost hear me?"

"Oh, ay, mistress, I hear thee," drawled the pedlar jeeringly. "Well, 'tis but a small matter after all, 'tis but one more job for Tom Boilman. I doubt not your ladyship hath heard the sentence of these rebels," he continued turning to Cicely; "'Tis hanging, drawing and quartering for them all. Oh, I warrant me they'll spare no toil to give Sir Rupert a worthy death. He'll have music in plenty for his last dance, and in case he find the hanging wearisome they'll cut him down and cut him up before he chokes." He laughed brutally at his joke and added coolly, "Maybe he'll live long enough to feel the boiling pitch, they say some of them have done so, and Sir Rupert is hardy enow."

Cicely covered her face with her hands and sank shuddering to the ground.

"Oh! Barbara, Barbara, what can we do?" she sobbed, while the pedlar laughed once more.

"Plague take the man," muttered Barbara in desperation; "what could Rupert be doing to trust in such a rogue! Well, something must be done, but what?"

She looked round for inspiration and her glance rested on a long rapier which lay on the central table. She turned again to the pedlar and her eyes gleamed with excitement and triumph.

"He is but a poor creature," she muttered, "and by his face he should be but a coward. I can but try it."

"Well, mistress," continued the fellow harshly, "am I to offer the letter for sale down at the Winslow Arms yonder?"

"No, my man," answered Barbara calmly, "for an ye will not deliver it fairly I purpose to take it myself." So saying she stepped aside, picked up the rapier and raised the point full at the breast of the pedlar.

The cunning smile died from the man's face and he looked doubtfully from the shining blade to the resolute face of the girl.

Barbara watched him with a cheerful smile. "I fear me, fellow, you have made a sad mistake," she remarked coolly, "an you deemed you could act the bully undisturbed. We be two women, 'tis true, but not defenceless, as you will soon learn an you try to resist, for I can wield a rapier as well as any man; Cicely, reach me hither yonder pistol; 'tis loaded? Yes. Now my man, the letter, if you please."

This turn of events was totally unexpected by the pedlar. He half-doubted the girl's threat, but few such men as he would care to risk a rush against a loaded pistol and a rapier wielded by a resolute hand. He made an attempt to snatch the rapier but the girl easily fenced his attempt, and the rapidity of her disengagement showed him that her boast of skill had been no idle threat. Barbara stood betwixt him and the door, the window was closed, he could see no way of escape.

After a moment or two of hesitation during which Barbara watched him breathlessly, he decided on a prudent course; placed the letter on the window-seat and answered sulkily:

"There is the packet then, give me the twenty crowns and let me go."

"Not so, friend," answered Barbara sweetly. "The Winslow Arms is still conveniently near, and I have not so low an estimate of your cunning as to doubt your knowledge of the contents of yonder letter. We must keep you here a little space. Oblige me by mounting those stairs."

The hawker made a step forward, only to find the point of the rapier against his breast, and seeing resistance to be useless he turned with a muttered curse and commenced to climb the wide staircase. Barbara followed him, the sword in her right hand, the pistol in her left, for being thoroughly skilled in the use of the rapier she felt more confidence in that weapon than in the pistol, which latter aroused in her as in many of her sex feelings rather of doubt and suspicion than of confidence, in fact she carried it but to give an air of greater resolution to her action.

"What a grace it is to be firm of countenance," she chuckled to herself as she slowly followed her victim. "The poor fool! and he did but know how my heart trembles, for in truth, if he resists, I could not hurt him. If I did pink him with my rapier 'tis very like I should but faint at sight of his blood, but he is too great a coward to attempt it. What a tale this will be for Rupert."

Now when either man or woman is embarked upon any hazardous undertaking 'tis but scant wisdom to indulge in triumphant rejoicing before the success of the enterprise be thoroughly assured. Had Barbara borne this in mind and given less rein to her hopeful imagination she had doubtless been better prepared for what followed. For as they approached the top of the stairway and she was hugging herself over the success of her bravado, the pedlar suddenly stumbled forward upon his face, slipped down two steps, striking his boots against the girl's ankles, and before she rightly realised what was happening had twisted himself backwards under the guard of her rapier, knocked up her arm and flinging her roughly aside he started down the stairs.

Barbara clutched at the balustrade to save herself from falling headlong, and in so doing dropped the pistol. The suddenness of the attack had completely shattered her nerve, she could do nothing save cling to the oak railing and gaze help-lessly after the retreating figure of the pedlar.

As for Simon, he paused neither for his pack nor his letter, but made all speed to reach the open door of the hall, and he would assuredly have escaped unop-posed but for the sudden intervention of an unexpected enemy.

He had already reached the threshold, and in another minute would have been free, when Cicely, with a sudden thought born of the very nearness of the danger, sprang to her feet and gave a shrill whistle. There was a low, fierce growl, a quick rush of feet.

"Down with him, Butcher, at him! at him!" cried Cicely, and the next moment the pedlar was pulled to the ground and struggling wildly with the enormous wolfhound which had answered his mistress's eager summons and now stood over Simon shaking and worrying him as if he had been a rat.

If the man's life were to be saved there was clearly no time to be lost, and the two girls hurried to the spot to interpose between the dog and his victim.

It was no easy task, for the dog was savage with fury, but at length Cicely succeeded in dragging him away, while Barbara fell on her knees beside the man anxiously inquiring of his injuries.

"Oh! I can trust thou art not greatly hurt," she gasped; "tho' in truth 'twere but thy deserts. Canst not speak, fellow? Nay, prithee what ails thee? Alack! I fear me Butcher has hurt thee sorely, and yet truly I would it were more. Indeed the dog should be chained, tho' I am right thankful he was free."

So she continued, torn between a woman's compassion for his overthrow and a deep sense of relief at their escape.

Meanwhile Cicely having somewhat pacified the indignant Butcher returned to the pedlar's side. She could not repress a smile as she listened to her cousin's contradictory outburst. She had no pity to spare for the man who had so threat-ened the life of her lover.

"Tut, Barbara! 'tis my belief the fellow is but little injured save in the loss of his garments," for the pedlar's coat was in rags. "Come," she continued, turning sharply to the man, "be thankful the dog has dealt so gently with you, 'twould not be so the next time an ye attempt to escape again. Up with you, fellow."

With many groans and heartfelt curses Simon struggled to his feet. As Cicely had suspected he was rather terrified than hurt, but the dog had shaken out of him what little courage he possessed. He turned without further attempt at resis-tance, and slowly mounted the stairs, followed once more by Barbara, who, having well-nigh paid dearly for her experience, did not relax her wariness until she had safely secured him in one of the upper chambers whence there was no possibility of escape.

This done she hurried down into the hall, where Cicely sat engrossed already in her letter, and burst into a merry laugh.

"Well done, Cis, well done," she cried, flinging herself down beside her cousin. "I vow thou art a very virago, but for thee he would have escaped. Alack! 'tis small use to have the wrist, eye, and skill of a man when one has but a woman's nerve. But what news, coz; what says the letter?"

"He is safe, he has reached the coast, and to-morrow will take sail in a vessel bound for Holland. He— — But I will tell thee the rest anon," answered Cicely somewhat hurriedly, and then passed into the garden still reading her letter.

"Plague take these lovers!" exclaimed Barbara, looking after her whimsically, "they are not too generous with their news. But now, how to rid me of yon same discontented gentle upstairs." She paused and bit her lip thoughtfully. "Ah! well, there is time for that; he is safe enough now, and belike a plan will suggest itself later."

Then she stretched her arms as though a great load were lifted from her shoulders, and laughed again softly.

"'Tis selfish to be happy when there be so many still in sorrow," she murmured. "But with Rupert safe again I cannot feel a care. All! 'tis a good world, a good world, and therefore," she cried, springing to her feet with a laugh, "I will go out and rejoice in it."

CHAPTER IV

The old-fashioned garden was the glory of the Manor House. Generations of flower-lovers had tended it year by year, and every nook and corner bore testimony to the loving care of its owners. As Barbara tripped along the trim box-edged paths between banks of hollyhocks and proud-faced dahlias and sweet clusters of late roses, she looked, in her soft blue gown, with her happy face and shining eyes like the very spirit of Hope just escaped from the box of Pandora, and meet to face and vanquish all the evils of the world. But when she emerged upon the lawn and came in sight of the grey stone sun-dial she stopped short, for on the steps of the dial sat Sorrow herself in the person of Cicely, her head leaning forlornly against the stone pillar, her eyes streaming with tears, her hands clasped and her breast convulsed with bitter sobs.

The laughter died out of Barbara's face, and was replaced by a look of the utmost astonishment and desperation.

"Now may I be forgiven, Cicely, an thou beest not the most ungrateful girl in Christendom," she exclaimed reproachfully. "Shame on you to sit there weeping like a very fountain, when thou shouldest be glad and thankful at Rupert's escape."

"Ah, indeed, Barbara! I am thankful, but——"

"Nay, then Heaven preserve me from such a melancholy display of thankfulness," responded Barbara drily. Then seating herself beside her sobbing cousin she continued coaxingly, "Come, tell me what ails thee, Cicely. Thou sayest Rupert has reached the coast in safety and to-morrow will take ship for Holland where he will wait until we can make his peace with the King. Is it not so? I confess I see no great cause for tears in news such as this."

"Ah, Barbara, 'tis different with thee, Rupert is only thy brother."

"Well, and were he ten thousand times thy sweetheart, I still cannot see why thou shouldest weep at his escape."

"Thou dost not listen, Barbara," answered Cicely somewhat petulantly. "I thank Heaven for his safety, but, oh, Barbara! I cannot let him go without seeing him once more, just once; and he says likewise he will not go without seeing me. Bethink you, we may not meet for years, and so he being but ten miles distant, he purposes to ride over to-night and bid farewell; and so I must weep, Barbara, for if he comes he will assuredly be taken, and if he comes not I shall assuredly die."

Barbara sprang to her feet with a gesture of despair.

"Now a plague on you both for a pair of mad lovers. He cannot come here, 'tis madness. Thou knowest, Cicely, the house and roads are watched night and day by these scarlet-coated, scarlet-faced troopers, and they say yonder dark-visaged captain of theirs is a very dragon of vigilance. 'Tis clear they deem such a visit likely, seeing how closely they watch our movements; 'twere fair courting capture if Rupert came."

"I know the risk well enow. But, oh, Barbara, I cannot live another day without seeing him. Ah, to feel he is so near, so near, and I may not see him, feel his hand, hear his voice. Oh! I cannot endure it," and leaning her head once more against the cold stone pillar of the dial, she burst into a passion of sobs.

Barbara regarded her with an expression of helpless bewilderment.

"'Tis passing strange," she murmured. "Come, Cis, I am Rupert's self in face and figure. I will kiss and cozen thee and call thee pretty names to thy heart's content; why may not that suffice thee?"

In spite of her tears Cicely could not repress a smile at this strange offer of a substitute.

"'Tis very clear, Barbara, thou hast never loved."

"Truly no," was the frank rejoinder. "I know nought of the matter; it passeth my understanding altogether and indeed methinks it is but nonsense. Rupert is very well where he is and you shall see him in a year or two at most. What more can you wish tho' you were a thousand times in love. Come, Cis, dry thine eyes, and we will send to forbid him to come."

But Cicely only wept the more persistently.

"Ah! Barbara, thou hast no heart, I must see him once again, indeed I must. I must let him hold me in his arms, and feel him near me. Barbara, you do not understand, but I shall die if I may not see him. Sure thou couldst help me an thou wouldst. My heart will break else. Oh, Barbara! try to understand."

Barbara gave a sigh of sheer desperation, then yielded to her cousin's plea.

"'Tis stark madness, Cis," she cried; "but thou shalt have thy way. Only look cheerily and Rupert shall come. But now how to devise it." She clasped her chin in her hands and bent her brows in thought. "What said he in the letter?"

"Thou mayest read it, an thou wilt not laugh."

Barbara took the note and turned away to pace up and down the lawn lest her cousin should see the involuntary twitching of her lips as she read the tender epistle; it was so strange to her to think of Rupert writing thus—Rupert, who to her seemed the personification of boyish gaiety.

As she raised her head from perusing the note her attention was momentarily arrested by a rustling sound from within one of the large laurel bushes bordering the lawn and a strange shimmer behind the leaves. She stared at the bush a moment in surprise and then passed on towards the foot of the garden still deep in thought. Here she paused long, gazing into the stream which there flowed by the garden, her face wrinkled with anxiety and bewilderment as she puzzled her brain over the situation, her eyes darkened with a shadow, of fear.

Suddenly with a flash the inspiration came. Her bent brows relaxed, her eyes glanced mischievously, she gave a gasp at the very magnificence of the idea, and breaking into the gayest laughter she fairly danced back to her cousin, clapping her hands with delight.

"Cicely, Cicely," she cried, "never let it be said again that Barbara is a brainless madcap. I have conceived the properest plot, a very prince of plots. Thou shalt see thy Romeo to-night, my poor lovelorn Juliet, and I——faith! I will have the maddest prank that ever woman played." And flinging herself on to the grass, she laughed till the tears ran down her cheeks.

Cicely stared at her in undisguised astonishment.

"Barbara," she remarked solemnly, "I verily believe thou art mad."

"Thou wouldest say so indeed an thou knewest my plan."

"Come then, tell me."

"Not I," laughed Barbara. "Be thou content with thy beloved Romeo, and leave me my jest to myself."

"But, Barbara, I am afraid. What if the plan should fail!"

"Talk not to me of failure, Cis. There is a risk, I do not deny it; but," she continued, laughing, "if danger befall can we not fight our way out? Butcher is a mighty ally; I am well nigh as handy as Rupert with the rapier, and thou mightest perchance discharge a pistol or so, if it were possible to do so and cover thine ears at the same moment."

"In Heaven's name, Barbara, what have you in your mind?" cried Cicely in dismay.

"Fear nothing, coz; leave all to me. Listen, Peter the smith can always be trusted; he or little Jacky Marlow would carry our message to Rupert. If he start at twilight he should be here before ten. We can hide him——"

"Whist, Barbara!" interrupted Cicely softly, "didst not hear a rustle in yonder bush? Can anyone be in hiding there?"

"Tut, tut! thou trembler! Thou wouldest see a spy in every pansy face. 'Twas but a rat or a rabbit. Get thee in and send for Peter; I will write my note to Rupert."

"I know not why I trust you, Barbara," said Cicely doubtfully, "for thou art ever a madcap. But I must see him."

"Well so thou shalt, so thou shalt; now leave me alone to think."

Left alone by the sun-dial Barbara resumed her favourite attitude for thought, one foot tucked beneath her, her head bent, her chin resting upon her clasped hands.

She thought deeply. Twice or thrice she raised her head and laughed aloud suddenly, as though catching some new and entertaining idea. Once indeed her face grew grave and her eyes fearful, and she shuddered as she weighed the dangers before her, but presently with a laugh she banished the thought. Was she not a Winslow? and whenever was Winslow yet who let fear turn him from the path he chose to tread?

At length she drew paper and pencil from her reticule, and wrote a short note. Then gathering up her flowers she rose and walked towards the house.

As she passed the clump of laurel she paused and plucked a few sprigs, glancing sharply through the leaves the while; then with a laugh and a shake of the head she passed on.

But having passed, there lay behind her in the centre of the path two roses and the little white note which had slipped from her fingers to the ground.

No sooner had Barbara vanished from sight than the branches of the laurel were parted and a purple face peered cautiously out. The face was followed by the stout figure of Corporal Crutch, who crawled from behind the bush, pounced upon the paper, and with a low chuckle of delight disappeared with his prize, leaving the garden once again deserted.

CHAPTER V

Corporal Crutch, having obtained possession of the coveted note, and seeing nothing more to be gained by remaining at his uncomfortable post, withdrew softly from the garden. Stealing into the adjoining coppice, he seated himself beneath the shady trees, mopped his brow and proceeded to decipher the letter, pausing occasionally to chuckle slyly and congratulate himself upon the unexpected success of his espionage.

The letter was written in a bold round hand, and ran as follows:

> DEAR RUPERT.—Thou art indeed the very apostle of rashness, but seeing thou art resolved to venture here to bid Cicely farewell, 'twere waste of words to attempt to dissuade thee. Yet prithee think no shame to be cautious, for the risk is great; we are much suspected and the house and lanes are closely watched. But to-day I will convey a message to this worthy captain, as from a trusted informant, that it is thine intention to meet me at the Lady Farm. These troopers swallow any bait; 'twill go hard an they ride not thither on a wild goose chase. As for you, an you come with caution over the hill and down the stream (the boat is moored among the willows at the old place) you will surely escape them. Once in the garden thou art safe enough; they dare not show their faces there and they love not the copse at night, deeming it damp,—as assuredly it is,—and haunted,—as doubtless it may be. We will be on the watch for thee, and the old hiding place is ready, an it should be needed. Farewell, thou rash and lovelorn fool. Thy sister,
>
> BARBARA.

"Ods zooks! here's a prize!" chuckled the corporal, tossing the paper in the air and catching it again in the very ecstacy of delight. "Ha, Ha! my pretty mistress, thou'lt sing a different tune ere I've done with thee to-night. Now what to do? What were best? The captain (curse him) is away to Spaxton wi' three o' the men, to search the Squire's papers; he'll not be back till nightfall. The better fortune that; I'll see to this business myself, and 'twill go hard an I have not this same 'rash and lovelorn fool' in my safe keeping ere day dawns. Now how to work it?" he mused. "It were easier had they but said where the fellow lies. Should I set one to follow her messenger, and so discover his hiding-place? Yet that were difficult, perchance dangerous; 'tis very like we would but be led astray; these peasants are cursedly untrustworthy, and monstrous shrewd. Or post men up the stream, and take him on the road? That, too, were risky. Perchance 'twere wiser to watch him into the house, and there trap him. Yes, by Jupiter!" he muttered excitedly, "trap him and trap them all. Two traitors are better than one, and if she be not judged traitor for thus harbouring rebels, may I dance to Kirke's music myself. Why, 'tis no less than Mistress Lisle lost her head for last week. Yes, it must be so. Ah! the pretty fool, wi' her prince of plots. She may plot, ay, and counter-plot, but she'll not out-plot Jonathan Crutch, I warrant me. But soft, who comes here?"

It was Peter Drew, the smith, from the village, who strode through the coppice on his way to the Manor House. He greeted the Corporal with a scowl.

"Good-day, fellow," began that worthy. "What do you up here?"

"My lawful business, which is more than you can say," growled the smith, and passed on towards the house.

"Hum! So yonder is her messenger," mused the corporal. "Well, let him pass, he'll lime our bird for us."

Then he arose, and cautiously resuming his post of observation within the laurel bush he tossed the note back into the garden. Scarcely had he done so when Barbara came down the garden, searching eagerly for the missing paper. Presently she espied it where it lay on the lawn, and picking it up she placed it carefully in her pocket and returned to the house, while the corporal chuckled again over his success.

Ten minutes later Peter Drew came into sight round a corner of the building. He led a sturdy pony by the bridle, and his right arm was firmly linked in the arm of the unfortunate hawker, who was helpless in the grip of the powerful smith, and with rage in his heart was forced to walk along apparently on terms of the greatest friendship with his companion. For behind them marched the wolfhound, and the hawker knew that at the least attempt to escape he would be given over at once to the mercy of this relentless foe. They turned in the direction of the smithy and soon disappeared from sight. Then all was quiet once more and the corporal, again extricating himself from the sheltering laurel, set off for the village to collect his men and make his dispositions for the evening.

He proceeded with the utmost caution. Two of his men he posted on the main road to Cannington, where a path turned off over the hill to the river, and two more some distance up the stream, that they might watch and follow Sir Rupert should he by chance elect not to visit the Manor House itself. These he instructed not to interfere with Sir Rupert, unless he showed signs of scenting a trap, but to allow him to reach his house unmolested. The remainder he ordered to conceal themselves in the plantation near the house, and after dusk at a signal from him quietly to surround the building. He enjoined on all the greatest caution in concealing themselves, and bade them take good note of all who entered or left the mansion, but not to prevent any or show themselves until he gave the signal.

This done he returned to the Winslow Arms and proceeded to fortify his spirits and strengthen his wits by a hearty meal, thanking his stars the while that Captain Protheroe's absence gave him the opportunity to direct the operations in his own way.

"If the matter were but left to the captain, there would be but little fear for Sir Rupert; he hath neither wit nor stomach for such a job. Like as not he would have left the women alone, to harbour what rebels they choose. I marvel how he hath already risen so high in favour, save that the general is always easy tempered. If the business had been in my hands alone, the fellow had been laid by the heels long since."

So mused the worthy corporal, as he devoured his dinner and complacently reviewed his crafty proceedings of the morning.

His meal and his meditations were alike presently cut short by the entrance of the host, who announced that a man stood without clamouring for instant permission to speak with the captain, or if that might not be, with the corporal of the troop.

"'Tis a most persistent fellow. He saith he hath information of great moment for your honour, but I'll not vouch for the truth of it; he is a pedlar by trade, and such have ever glib tongues," continued the host with some scorn.

The corporal started on hearing the man's message; but remembering that a part of Mistress Barbara's plan was to send a messenger to the captain he smiled cunningly and ordered that the pedlar be instantly admitted.

"'Tis some traitorous rogue she hath employed, I doubt not," he muttered, "and a daring fellow withal to venture thus into the net. 'Twere well that such an one be speedily laid by the heels."

Then the door opened and in hurried Simon, the Pedlar.

Breathless and eager, and glancing nervously over his shoulder the while, he ignored the curt greeting of the corporal and broke at once roughly into his story.

"'Tis concerning Sir Rupert Winslow," he began. "I have certain information to sell. I know where he lies hid and likewise whither he purposes to ride this very night. An it be not so, you may hang me for a lying rogue. Give me my price and I will deliver him over to you within three hours. But first I must see my reward."

Had the hawker's mind been in a less agitated condition, had he been less nervous of pursuit and interruption he had assuredly gone about his business in a more cautious manner; but so fearful was he lest even at the eleventh hour he might be prevented from driving his bargain that he failed entirely to note the effect of his words upon the corporal.

As for that self-complacent mortal, ever since the unceremonious entrance of the pedlar whom he instantly recognized as the smith's companion of that morning, his indignation had increased, until at the final rough demand for money, it overflowed in a furious burst of anger. Even had he believed the man honest, it is doubtful whether he would have listened long to one so utterly wanting in all the obsequious attentions which he considered due to his dignity, but convinced as he was that the fellow was no more than an impudent impostor, his rage knew no bounds.

Springing from his chair, and banging furiously with his fist upon the table he roared at the astonished pedlar, pouring forth upon him such a torrent of abuse and threats that Simon was terrified. In vain did the unfortunate pedlar attempt to remonstrate, in vain did he plead that his tale might be put to the proof, the corporal would hear no more, and before he could grasp the reason of this unexpected anger he found himself marched away between two troopers and securely locked into an upper chamber of the inn, where he was left to meditate in solitude upon his second unsuccessful attempt at bargain driving, and to curse the ill fate that had led him so to over-reach himself.

Then, with a pleasing sense of duty done and villainy outwitted, the corporal soothed his ruffled feelings with a cooling draught of cider, finished his dinner in peace, and departed once more to take up a position behind his well-tried laurel bush, whence he could survey at once the stream, the lawn, and the entrance to the house itself.

Ten minutes after his departure an anonymous note was left at the Inn for Captain Protheroe. The note lay unheeded on the table, but Barbara's mission had already been unwittingly fulfilled by the very man who sought to betray her.

CHAPTER VI

Time passed slowly for the corporal as he crouched wearily at his post.

The garden remained deserted. Late in the afternoon three maid-servants chattering gaily, he supposed at the prospect of an evening holiday, came out and set off for the village, calling back saucy messages to Phoebe Marlow, who, from the doorway disconsolately watched them depart. Then again all was silent.

The bright promise of the early morning hours was not fulfilled. The evening sky was heavy with clouds and dusk fell early. The corporal had changed his position a hundred times, had yawned and sighed, and even nodded once or twice before the longed-for hour arrived.

But at length, about ten o'clock, a light twinkled in one of the windows of the dark and silent house, and presently the soft swish of a paddle up the stream was audible.

The corporal held his breath and craned forward, looking and listening eagerly. He heard the dull thud of the boat against the bank, a paddle drop, soft footfalls on the lawn, and presently the dark figure of a man loomed into sight, and passed quickly toward the house.

But ere he reached the building, the door was flung wide and a woman appeared on the lintel with outstretched arms, crying loud, "Rupert! At last! At last!"

For an instant the figures stood revealed in the glare of light from the doorway, and the corporal noted a tall, slender youth with bright complexion and dark, curling hair, falling in love-locks to his shoulders, as Barbara had described him, herself in form and feature. Taking the woman into his arms, they passed into the house together, and the door was closed.

For a few moments the corporal waited cautiously, then as all remained quiet, he crept from his hiding-place and, cracking his fingers with delight at the success of his enterprise, gave the signal for his men to surround the house.

In five minutes they were posted to his satisfaction, so carefully that not a cat could escape unobserved, and having ordered them to let any enter who would (for he had as lief catch a dozen rebels as one), but to allow none to leave the building without his express command, he approached the entrance and delivered a thundering blow upon the door.

There was no answer. The echoes died away in the distance and the house remained silent as night.

He raised his arm for a second blow, when a light touch on the shoulder caused him to spring round in astonishment and fear, for his heart was already in his mouth with excitement and self-importance.

Behind him stood Captain Protheroe, regarding him grimly.

"How now, corporal?" demanded the captain sharply, "What is the meaning of this? I came riding down the lane when I find three troopers crouching by the gate yonder, for all the world like conies in their burrow, and I learn, forsooth, that you have surrounded this house and were even about to force an entrance. What warrant have you for this, and why was I not informed sooner of the matter? Must I again teach you, sirrah, that you take too much upon yourself?"

The corporal regarded him sulkily.

"There is a traitor within, captain," he muttered.

"Bah! another of your mare's nests, I make no doubt. What proof have you?"

"Proof enough and to spare," answered the corporal stoutly. "Witness my own eyes and ears," and he rapidly reported all that had passed. The captain's face hardened as he listened and he glanced sharply up at the house.

"Ah! it seems you are on the right track for once. But zounds, fool," he continued angrily, "why, in Heaven's name, didn't you trap him before he entered the house and leave the women-folk in peace? I warrant we'll have a bad business now. Dolt! Well, there is no other way now. Knock again and on with the work. 'Twill be a wretched business," he muttered with a shrug and a wry smile.

The corporal again knocked loudly, and after a considerable interval, footsteps were heard inside, and a voice demanded timidly who was there.

"Open at once, i' the King's name," roared the corporal.

"Marry, then, which king?" answered the voice, "there be so many kings nowadays."

"Open in the name of King James," was the angry answer.

"Now wherefore King James? King Monmouth was far better favoured," answered the voice.

"Zounds, fellow!" interrupted the captain angrily, "wouldest parley all day?" Then dealing a furious blow on the door, he shouted angrily:

"An ye open not instantly, I must break in the door."

"Beshrew me! Here's a gentle visitor!" was the answer, and then the door yielded to their pressure and the captain, followed by the corporal and three troopers, entered the house.

They paused, however, on the threshold, and Captain Protheroe muttered a despairing exclamation, for the hall was empty save for Mistress Barbara, who, dropping them a mocking curtsey, demanded gravely to what cause she owed the honour of such a visit.

Captain Protheroe quickly recovered his composure and bowed politely, mentally observing that never before had he done full justice to the girl's beauty, or fully realised the fascination that may lurk in soft dark curls trailing over a snowy forehead and nestling into the nape of a beautifully formed neck.

"It grieves me to be thus forced to intrude upon your privacy, Mistress Winslow," he began gently, "but I must obey orders. Methinks you need scarcely pretend ignorance as to the reason of my presence."

"Bless the man!" exclaimed Barbara cheerfully, "does he think his business is writ large on his brow? I assure you, sir, I know nothing whatever of the cause of such a visit."

Captain Protheroe raised his eyebrows.

"In that case, madame, I must inform you. I have certain knowledge that a fugitive has taken refuge in this house, and it is my intention not to leave the place until I have found him."

"A most laudable intention, sir, though I fear me it means that you will remain here for the rest of your natural life. But pray tell me, how long has it been the custom for an honourable gentleman to turn man-hunter?"

The captain reddened angrily.

"It is not a task I would gladly choose, madame, as you might know. But I am not here to discuss the virtue of my orders, I am here to search for this rebel."

"Then in Heaven's name go and search for him elsewhere. I assure you he is not here," exclaimed Barbara petulantly.

Captain Protheroe looked at her for a moment questioningly.

"Will you swear to me that such is the truth, madame?" he asked.

Barbara hesitated for a moment. Then she turned away impatiently and walked back into the room.

"Nay, an my word be not enough, I will swear nothing. Yet I assure you the man you seek is not here."

But even as she spoke the words, she stopped with a stifled cry, for in the centre of the floor lay a man's hat, stained and draggled, but serving, with its long plume and jewelled clasp, as an outspoken traitor to its master.

The captain's glance fell on the hat at the same moment, and he turned to Barbara with a questioning smile. But she had recovered herself in an instant. Walking coolly forward, she concealed the treacherous hat beneath her skirt, until with a dexterous movement she swept it out of sight under the table, while at the same time she unconcernedly (though a trifle breathlessly) repeated her former statement that the man they sought was not in the house.

Captain Protheroe, marvelling greatly at a woman's strangely discriminating sense of honour, which will permit her to assert a fact but not to swear to it, smiled at her statement and bowed politely.

"So be it, madame. Then nought remains save for me to order my men to commence the search at once, since you so resolutely refuse to give up the traitor. I am distressed to disturb you, but search I must."

"Marry! sir, then search," cried Barbara, with a sudden suspiciously hysterical laugh. "Perchance he lurks behind this curtain, or cowers beneath the table. Think you he is concealed in yonder snuff-box, or is hid beneath my petticoats? Prithee, search well, for there is no telling where the rogue may lie," and assuming a mock air of importance closely resembling that of the corporal, she commenced a solemn burlesque of the search, hurrying about the room, and carefully examining the most impossible hiding-places, while the captain bit his lip to prevent a smile, and the troopers watched her mimicry of their efforts with embarrassed indignation.

When she had concluded her tour of the room, Barbara turned to the astonished soldiers and remarked with mock solemnity:

"You see, I am correct, he cannot be here."

"We are deeply indebted to you for this entertainment, madame," interrupted the captain with grave politeness. "Now we will commence the search in earnest."

The laughter died from Barbara's face, and a strange hunted look crept into her eyes. She glanced round helplessly, as though seeking means of escape, then casting a pleading glance at the captain, she said in a trembling voice:

"If you still persist in your error, you must e'en do as you list," and with a low sigh she turned away and sank wearily into a chair.

Captain Protheroe gave the necessary orders and the corporal and troopers departed on their errand. Then he turned doubtfully towards the girl.

"I am very sorry for this intrusion, Mistress Barbara," he said gently. "My corporal, who is but a blundering fellow, made these dispositions while I was away, otherwise, be assured, I should have taken the fellow before he entered your house."

"Yes, that would have been far easier for you," she answered calmly.

"For you, madame," he corrected her, smiling. "May I hope I am forgiven for thus doing my duty?"

Barbara directed upon him a beaming smile.

"Why, as to that, sir, 'tis I who must crave forgiveness for my inhospitality. I' faith, seeing he is not here, I know not why I should be so angry at your visit, I should rather pity such a wild-goose chase. Is it not so?"

"*If* he were not here, Mistress Barbara, we should deserve no pity, our intrusion would be quite unpardonable."

"But I have told you that he is not here," she answered eagerly.

"True. And I have told you that he is."

Her lips trembled at his resolute tone, and she turned away her head. But in a moment she answered brightly:

"'Tis clear, sir, this is a most unprofitable subject for discussion, seeing we shall never agree. Time must show who is in the right. In the meantime we will conclude the matter thus: If he be here, the worse for him; if he be not here—why, the worse for you. What say you now?"

"Madame, your argument is unanswerable."

"Then hence with argument, hither with supper. Come, captain, we'll sign a truce for the nonce. If I mistake not, you have had a long ride and spare rations this evening. You are well come. I was about to sup when you interrupted me, so while your men search the house, you shall bear me company. You refuse? Why, what fear you? The house is surrounded, not a creature can escape," she continued bitterly, "and you need not fear lest the wine be drugged or the meat poisoned, for I, too, intend to partake of them."

"Ah, madame, those are not the dangers I fear." He shook his head, with a smile.

"What, then?"

"Look in your mirror, Mistress Barbara, perchance you will understand."

Barbara gave a sudden, laugh of pleased amusement.

"Nay, sir, I protest I have no desire to bewitch you," she answered with a bright blush.

"Then, madame, why do you look at me?" asked the captain, and his eyes said more.

Again the dimple deepened and again the lips curved into a smile. Captain Protheroe detected himself watching for that dimple with a quite inexplicable and, considering his errand, inexcusable eagerness.

"Methinks the conversation is astray upon a bye-path," she answered demurely; "let us return to the high-road. I am dying of hunger, and 'tis but dreary to sup alone. Will you not join me?"

As Captain Protheroe had tasted no food since early morning, the offer was too tempting to be refused.

"Madame, you overwhelm me with kindness," he answered.

She led him to the upper end of the hall, where a table was already laid with three covers.

"Do you always sup in company with two empty chairs, madame?" he asked quizzically.

Barbara flushed crimson and hesitated.

"I—I expected friends, sir," she stammered. Then recovering, she darted a bright glance at him and continued. "And you see my expectations have been fulfilled, for are you not come?"

"Does not another lady dwell here with you?" he queried indifferently.

"Yes—my cousin, Lady Cicely Winslow. But she—she is out," stammered Barbara again nervously.

"Ah! so she is sharing the fellow's hiding-place," muttered the captain to himself. "A piece of folly only possible in a couple of lovers."

Throughout the meal Barbara laughed and chatted gaily, evidently exerting all her efforts to entertain her guest. She led him on to tell strange stories of his adventures and his travels, to which she listened with that eager interest and open admiration of his doings, so dear to the heart of man; she made him laugh heartily at her quick jests and saucy answers, and ever and anon as she talked she raised her dark lashes, and turned upon him the full depths of her wonderful eyes.

But Captain Protheroe was not altogether unversed in the ways of women, and though he enjoyed to the full the pleasant companionship of her manner, and drank deep of her beauty, he was in no wise mindful to allow her charms to turn his thoughts from the matter in hand.

And as he watched her carefully, he noted how from time to time she would break off abruptly in the middle of a sentence and listen anxiously to some distant sound in the house, while the smile died from her face, and her eyes widened with fear. She twisted her fingers nervously together as she talked, and her laugh was high and shrill.

"She plays her part admirably," he muttered to himself, "but she should not show her eyes."

"'Tis strange how falsely that base churl Rumour reports," he began, when Barbara paused once to listen anxiously to the movements of the searchers overhead. "Now concerning you, madame, methinks he hath totally misspoken."

"Why, what saith Rumour concerning me?" questioned Barbara with interest.

"In the first place," he continued, eyeing her steadily, "he reports that you are fearless both of men, mice, and devils."

"And what then?" she asked, her eyes flashing proudly.

"Why, I say he is a lying fellow, for I see you are as timid as—as a woman."

"I, sir, timid!" she cried indignantly.

"Aye, madame, you start and tremble at every sound."

"Nay—I assure you—I—I do not so," she stammered, trembling with eagerness. "Why, wherefore should I tremble."

"Nay, I know not, madame. Save as the poet saith—'A guilty conscience——'"

"I thank you for the suggestion, sir," she answered with a faint smile. "I will consult my conscience."

There was a pause, the silence broken only by the distant movements of the searchers.

"Is there a ghost in the room, madame," asked Captain Protheroe suddenly.

Barbara started violently.

"A ghost, sir?" she exclaimed.

"Aye, a ghost. I saw you staring at the wall behind me with so horrified an expression, methought you beheld an apparition at least, peeping over my shoulder."

Barbara dropped her head and bit her lip.

"'Twas but my own thoughts. There is nothing else."

Captain Protheroe wheeled round in his chair, and stared thoughtfully at the full-length portrait of an old Winslow knight in armour which confronted him.

"Now what is there in this same old gentleman (for I trust 'twas not my appearance that had such a horrifying effect upon you), what is there here to terrify you?"

"Nothing, sir, I assure you," repeated Barbara faintly.

"Yet there is certainly a strange look about this portrait," he mused. "There is a glint in his eye that mislikes me. One might almost believe," he continued, turning towards her, "that he hid some secret behind that fixed countenance."

Barbara stared at him a moment with terrified face, then she rose abruptly from the table.

"I—I wish you would leave me, sir," she answered curtly.

"That is a hard saying, madame," he exclaimed in mock astonishment. "Did not yourself bid me to supper?"

"Yes. But I am weary of you and now I bid you go."

He laughed quietly.

"That is easily said, madame, but not so easily answered. I may not——"

He was interrupted by a hurried knock at the outer door.

Barbara gave a slight scream and ran across the hall, but Captain Protheroe was at the door before her.

"Pardon me, madame, I must see to this," he said sternly.

He flung the door wide, standing himself in its shadow, and Peter Drew, the smith, rushed quickly into the hall.

"Ah, Mistress Barbara," he exclaimed breathlessly, not noticing her sign to him to be cautious, "the villain hath escaäped me, and I can't faind no traäce of un anywhere."

"Very much my case, my friend," interrupted the captain, shutting the door quickly, and confronting the astonished smith with a quiet smile. "But what may be the name of this same escaped villain?"

Peter gasped at him stupidly.

"Come, fellow, out with it," cried the captain sharply.

The smith glanced at Barbara and shook his head.

"I don't know," he muttered sulkily.

Captain Protheroe turned to Barbara.

"May I—er—advise you, madame, to order this reluctant henchman of yours to be more speedy in his replies."

"You may tell the captain all you know, Peter," she said after a moment's hesitation. "Methinks 'twill not greatly enlighten him."

"'Tweren't nobbut a certain hawker, your honour. Her ladyship bid me keep un zaäfe till marnin' zo I fastened un oop zafe i' my farge. But when I were awai—er—awai on my biznez thicey marnin' my waife, plague on a meddlezome fingers, zay I, muzt needs oppen door, to zee, forzooth, whai it were zhut, and zo the fellow hath vled."

"Good! Why was this hawker to be thus secured?"

"He had angered me, sir," interrupted Barbara haughtily.

"Ah! summary justice, madame," answered the captain, laughing. "But hardly, methinks, within the measure of the law."

"I care nought for the law."

"So I can well believe. But come, I must know a little more concerning this hawker."

"That you cannot, sir," answered Barbara calmly. "For the simple reason that Peter knows no more, and I, who do know, do not purpose to tell you."

Captain Protheroe hesitated a moment. Then he continued lightly, but eyeing Barbara steadily the while:

"Ah, well! 'Tis of small import. Doubtless it will not be difficult to find the fellow himself and learn all I wish from his own lips."

Barbara's face grew suddenly white.

"Yet another man to search for," she exclaimed lightly, but with a strange hoarseness in her voice. "I' faith, captain, yours is no easy post. It must indeed be a wearisome life to seek and seek for that which like the philosopher's stone, is never to be found."

They were startled by a sudden clamour which arose in a distant part of the building, the clatter of pans and dishes, the angry shouts of the men, and above all the shrill voice of a woman pouring forth a torrent of furious abuse.

"What in the devil's name——" began the captain, striding across the room.

"Oh! 'tis nothing," interrupted Barbara coolly. "Your men have doubtless encountered my waiting-woman, Phoebe. She is somewhat hot and hasty in her humour and—I am sorry for them."

As she spoke the door was flung open and the corporal rushed angrily into the room. He was a miserable sight to behold. His head was saturated with greasy broth which dripped from the ends of his scrubby hair and beard and trickled down his rubicund countenance; he was covered from head to foot with flour and dust, and he held his hand pitiably to his temple where a large bump, the size of an egg, was rapidly rising, to embellish his appearance.

Behind him marched Phoebe, weaponed with a besom, her face blazing with anger, her hair dishevelled, and her sleeves rolled up to her shoulders, showing the brawny arms of this amazon.

At sight of this couple, Barbara fell back into a chair, and laughed till her eyes filled with tears.

"My poor Sir Knight of the Whipcord," she gasped. "What hath befallen thee? Ah me, Phoebe, but thou art a very dragon!"

"A very devil," spluttered the corporal.

"Devil in thy teeth, fellow!" cried the enraged waiting-woman. "Mistress Barbara, what think ye? this fellow hath tramped through every hole and corner of the house; he hath rent the hangings, broken the chiny, forced open the closets, and made the place a very desolation. And then—then he was for trapesing into my kitchen, my kitchen that I had but just redd up, with his great muddy boots, to poke his nose into all my places, because, forsooth, he swears I have a man hid among the pots and pans! A man, indeed! The meddlesome fool! I warrant me 'tis no man, but the victuals that he is in search of."

"Patience, good Phoebe, patience," laughed Barbara. "As thou sayest ever, men are but fools and know no better."

"Humph! Mayhap they knew no better, but they know better now, I warrant. Though it repents me that I wasted the whole of a good basin of broth and a bag of flour i' the teaching of it."

Meanwhile Corporal Crutch, having mopped his brow, and beaten off much of his outer covering of flour, made shift to resume his customary air of pompous dignity.

"This woman, sir," he explained with a wave of the hand in the direction of Phoebe, "withstood us in the doorway of her kitchen, powerfully ammunitioned with pannikins. 'Twas, indeed, a post of some vantage, therefore I deemed it wisdom to lead her off, as you behold, by a feigned retreat, while the men make a flank attack, and secure the position by entering through the window."

On hearing this Phoebe set up a howl of rage, and disappeared speedily in the direction of the kitchen, to oust the intruders from the spot. The sounds of battle which presently arose proved the success of the corporal's manoeuvre.

Captain Protheroe drew the corporal aside.

"Well! You have searched?"

"Aye, sir, every nook and cranny in the place. Not a rat's hole has escaped us. He must be hid somewhere in this room, for there's no other place unsearched."

"'Tis very like, and I think I can put my finger on the place," answered the captain softly.

Barbara looked up.

"Well, captain, if you are satisfied that I have spoken the truth, perhaps you will take your leave, for I protest I am weary of you."

"One moment, madame," he answered, "I will but examine into the secret of this same cross-eyed ancestor of thine, and then you shall be no further troubled."

He turned, as he spoke, towards the picture, but Barbara sprang to her feet with a sharp cry, and darting past him, placed her back against the frame and turned to him full of defiance.

"Nay, sir, that you shall not," she cried resolutely.

Corporal Crutch paused in his search, and gazed at her in open-mouthed astonishment, but Captain Protheroe strode quickly to her side with a sharp frown.

"Come, madame," he began impatiently, "this is sheer folly. We must proceed with our work. I do, indeed, regret the painful business, but by your leave we will not prolong it. Be so good as to show me the secret of the spring."

"I will not."

"Then, madame, we must open it by force."

"You shall not pass me," she cried defiantly. "I will not move aside."

Captain Protheroe swore in desperation.

"Come, Mistress Barbara, be reasonable," he urged. "You know well that resistance is quite useless. I were loth to use violence, but an it must be so, methinks it were possible to move you without much injury to either of us."

Suddenly Barbara began to cry, leaning her head back against the frame and sobbing bitterly. But she did not cover her face with her hands as is the manner of most women.

"Oh, go away, I beseech you," she pleaded, clasping her hands in entreaty, and raising tearful eyes to his face. "Rupert hath done you no injury, suffer him to escape this once, and I will be your debtor forever."

Captain Protheroe stared down at her, wondering vaguely whether her eyes looked more lovely when bright with merriment, or when wide and soft with welling tears, and why he had never before noticed how inviting was a full quivering lip. Then suddenly recollecting the unprofitableness of such considerations, he glanced indignantly at the corporal and swore at him beneath his breath.

"You are making my duty very hard for me, madame," he pleaded gently.

"I—I want to," she sobbed. "Please go away."

"No, Mistress Barbara, I cannot," he answered firmly.

Barbara stopped her sobs and stared at him for a moment in astonishment. Then she suddenly turned on him furiously.

"You will not? You will not?" she cried. "Then have your way. See what lies concealed."

She pressed a small button cunningly hidden amid the carving of the frame, and the portrait slipped back, revealing a large recess in the wall, deep enough to hold three men.

The recess was empty.

The two men stared at each other in utter astonishment, but Barbara flung herself into a chair, clapped her hands, and burst into a paroxysm of laughter.

"Fooled! Fooled!" she cried, pointing at them mockingly. "Was ever man, since the days of Adam, so bravely fooled. Oh! I shall die of laughter," and again the room rang with her merriment.

Captain Protheroe turned to her grimly.

"Pardon my dulness, madame," he said harshly, "and be so kind as to explain what this means."

"Means! Why, marry, it means that I have spoken truly. Rupert is not here, moreover, he never has been. Have I not said so throughout."

"Not here? Impossible! Then these tremblings, entreaties, tears were all——"

"All a comedy, sir, which I trust you enjoyed as greatly as did I. Oh! tell me, sir, should I not make a brave player?" She danced a few steps towards him and dropped a mocking curtsey. "I await your applause, signors," she cried with a saucy laugh.

Captain Protheroe strode the length of the room and swore to himself heartily, but Corporal Crutch was not so easily convinced.

"'Tis false, sir," he cried. "She is fooling us again. Why I saw the fellow enter, myself."

"That you did not, corporal, an I may make so bold as to contradict you," laughed Barbara. "Though I wouldn't deny," she added solemnly, "the possibility of your having seen someone enter."

"Aye, someone hailed by the name of 'Rupert,'" sneered the corporal.

"What's in a name?" quoted Barbara, laughing.

"Whom did he see, then?" demanded Captain Protheroe sharply.

"How should I know?" she retorted cheerfully. "'Twas not I who saw him. Ask the corporal."

"An 'twere not Sir Rupert, 'twas the devil himself in his likeness. I saw him as plain as I see you. He is the very counterpart of yon wench, his sister."

"That is true enough," answered Barbara calmly. "We be so alike that times have been known when we were mistaken for each other. And yet I will swear 'twas not Rupert whom you saw."

"Will you have the goodness to explain the matter, madame?" interrupted the Captain impatiently.

"With all my heart, sir, though 'tis a somewhat lengthy tale. Know then, it commences with a stout corporal but half concealed behind a large laurel bush.

Ah, ha! Sir Whipcord, you look guilty! Now this same corporal was a spy and an eavesdropper, and eavesdroppers must not be surprised if at times they overhear that which *is* intended for their ears. 'Twas so in this case. The corporal, who bore a strange resemblance to this gentleman, overheard a pretty little plot, discussed especially for his edification, he stole and read a cunning little note, written for his eyes alone. Being a gentleman of extraordinary blindness, he walked into the trap as prettily as a bird. The rest was simple. It remained but to send a messenger, whom your soldiers kindly permitted to pass, to inform Rupert of our arrangements. Cicely and I, disguised but in linsey petticoats and woollen hoods ('tis passing strange how dress can make or mar a man) went down to the village this afternoon, and later I—I returned, alone. Perchance—I say perchance, 'twas I whom your corporal saw enter; and yet, sure, how could it be?"

"And your cousin?"

"Cicely? Oh, she is away passing the evening with Rupert, who, thanks to the corporal's kind thoughtfulness, in withdrawing all his men from the roads and the village, was enabled to visit her with perfect safety at a certain house we wot of. But, indeed, the time has passed so quickly while you have been here, that he will by now have returned whence he came, and I fear—I greatly fear you have missed him."

Then at last Corporal Crutch, convinced of the truth of her statement, opened his mouth and commenced to swear; to swear so roundly that Barbara covered her ears, and Captain Protheroe curtly bade him be silent.

"'Tis thine own doing, thou blundering fool," he said angrily. "Wherefore didst not follow the messenger and trap the fellow in his hiding-place?"

"Nay, captain, give me some credit for the business," interposed Barbara cheerily. "'Twas a most excellently conceived plan. And yet," she mused, "I doubt if ever men were more easily fooled."

"And may I ask, madame, what part in the plot this evening's entertainment served?"

"Oh that! Well, I cannot say that was altogether necessary, though I desired to keep you here till Rupert was safe away. But," she added roguishly, "'twas vastly amusing. And besides, methinks you deserved no better treatment after forcing your way thus churlishly into a lone woman's house."

Captain Protheroe turned brusquely on his heel.

"There is nothing further to be gained by remaining here, corporal," he said. "Call up the men and march them back to quarters. And as for this fellow," he added, pointing to the smith, who had watched the scene with deep enjoyment, "keep him safe till morning; we may have need of him."

"And what of the wench, captain? Can't we lay hands on her for aiding and abetting?"

Captain Protheroe scowled.

"Leave me to deal with her, sirrah. I will follow you anon. And harkee. There is a certain hawker wandering in or near the village. Yon fellow can describe him. If we can lay hands on him, I doubt not he can tell us what may prove useful."

Corporal Crutch started guiltily.

"A hawker, captain? Why, I know the fellow. I have him safe under—that is—er—I doubt not I can speedily lay hands on him."

"Do so. See to it to-night, and we may yet catch our hare. Now begone."

The corporal saluted and went out.

Captain Protheroe glanced at Barbara, and he saw that no trace of her triumphant merriment remained.

He turned and walked to the window and stood for some time in silence gazing out into the darkness while the last echoes of the retreating footsteps died away. Then all was still.

CHAPTER VII

Captain Protheroe stood gazing out into the dark night, asking himself savagely why he still waited there, why he did not leave the girl at once and return with his men to the village, preparatory to setting out in pursuit of this man who still escaped them.

It was clearly his duty to go—and yet—— There was still time, nothing could be done until the hawker was discovered, and his secret, whatever it might be, was learned. And in the meantime he could not resist the temptation to remain a little longer, to learn more of this girl who, while she mocked and flouted, yet fascinated him in spite of his anger against her. To punish her a little for the way she had outwitted him, aye, and to watch how she bore the punishment. So while he cursed himself for a fool in so doing, yet he remained.

Barbara sat bolt upright, watching him furtively with eager eyes. Her hands were tightly clenched, and her lips pressed together in anxious thought. "Oh! what shall I do now?" she murmured again and again desperately. "What shall I do? The pedlar hath escaped. I have tried tears, they are useless. Oh, God! help me to play out the game."

At last he turned, and crossing the room seated himself beside her. Leaning forward, his hands clasped between his knees, he eyed her steadily and spoke in a low even voice. "Mistress Barbara, have you ever heard tell of a certain Mistress Alice Lisle?"

Barbara shuddered quickly, and her face grew very pale, but she answered him bravely:

"Aye, sir, she who was beheaded last week at Winchester for harbouring rebels."

"Good. And hast also heard of Mistress Judith Barge, condemned to be flogged for a like act of treason?"

"Indeed, sir, her story likewise is well known to me."

"Ah! so you were forewarned. You did not act in ignorance of the fate awaiting you?"

His face and voice were hard and her heart beat wildly, but she fought the rising fear and answered proudly:

"Captain Protheroe, none but a fool goeth to war without counting the cost. I am no fool, sir."

Suddenly his whole bearing changed, his face softened, and, raising her hand to his lips he said gently:

"Madame, I salute the bravest lady I have ever known."

Barbara flushed crimson.

"Nay, not so, sir," she answered, smiling bravely, "for there is yet a third story I have heard. For I have heard that in these last days it has been everywhere the custom for king's officers stationed in our villages to take up their quarters in the houses of the rebels, driving forth the occupants and taking unto themselves all their goods. Yet Cicely and I have remained here undisturbed. So I knew well, sir, that in playing my part I had to deal with no Kirke or Jeffries but with a gentleman of heart and honour, in whom a woman could place her trust."

"Can so small a matter win a woman's trust?" he asked doubtfully.

For an instant Barbara sat silent, twining her fingers together nervously, and breathing hard. She was preparing for her last great stake.

Then she turned to him. Her eyes betrayed her fear, but her voice was firm:

"Captain Protheroe, my brother lieth hid in the fisherman's hut, three miles eastward along the coast from Watchet. From thence he will escape to-morrow morn in a vessel bound for Holland."

He sprang to his feet and turned on her in sudden anger.

"In Heaven's name, madame, why have you told me this?"

"Ah! sir, because an I had not you would have learned it elsewhere. This mad pedlar who hath escaped me, knows my secret; to-night he will betray it to you. So I prefer to tell you myself and throw myself on your mercy."

"You play high, madame."

"Aye, sir, to lose or to win all."

He turned from her and paced the room angrily. So this was the result of his effort to punish the girl (fool that he was to try it), she flung herself on his mercy and challenged him to betray her confidence. Well, why should he not, seeing the confidence was given unasked. But his pride loathed the thought. He had never yet betrayed a woman's trust; the chivalry of his nature had remained unsoiled by the cynicism and callousness of those among whom he lived, and that chivalry now forbade him to profit by her moment of confidence.

That he, Miles Protheroe, should fall a prey to the fascinations of a woman! He laughed savagely at the thought. And yet that this girl fascinated him he could not deny. Not only by her beauty (he was too much a connoisseur of woman's looks to be deeply moved by them), nor by her gaiety, infectious though it was; no, to him the charm lay chiefly in her manifest courage, for courage was his God, and she seemed the very personification of fearlessness.

So he mused, warring betwixt pride, anger, and tenderness, while Barbara sat still, watching him with a desperate eagerness.

"Are you a soldier only, or a man?" she pleaded. "An ye be the first, go do your work. But oh, an ye be a man, ye cannot sure betray a woman's confidence."

"You have taken an unfair advantage of me, madame, and you know it."

"Aye, sir, 'tis true enough. Think not I feel no shame. But—Rupert is my brother."

Her voice broke piteously over the last words. She was worn out with the terror and excitement of the day, and could scarce keep down her tears. She bit her lips, and her breast heaved with a strangled sob. He drew near and stared down at her gloomily.

"So because you are a woman and this rebel chances to be your brother, my honour must go bail for his life! Do you understand, Mistress Barbara, what you ask of me?"

For an instant she hesitated. Then she raised her head and turned to him proudly:

"Yes, sir, I understand, and—I ask it."

He bowed.

"So be it, madame, your brother is safe from me."

He turned coldly, and taking up his hat, walked to the door.

Barbara followed him timidly.

"Captain Protheroe," she pleaded softly. "Honour may be one of the first virtues, but there is a greater even than Honour,—Charity."

But now his anger mastered him, he would not relent.

"It may be so, madame," he answered curtly. "But in your presence I find the defence of my Honour more than I can well attend to. I bid you good-night."

And turning abruptly he left the house.

Barbara remained gazing after him, her cheek slowly flushing with rage and shame.

"And has not a woman honour too?" she cried at last fiercely. "Am I not dishonoured enough already by this night's work that he must needs fling his taunts in my face? There be women, perchance, who will play with men's honour as lightly as they throw the dice, and he may think it a little thing for me to ask this of him, but oh, were it not for Rupert I had sooner have died than thus have shamed myself."

Flinging herself back into a chair she gnawed her clasped hands, and beat her foot upon the ground in silent fury.

Half an hour later the door opened softly and Cicely stole cautiously into the room, Cicely with dishevelled hair, red eyelids, and her face alight with eagerness and terror.

"Barbara! Barbara!" she cried, coming eagerly forward, on seeing the room unoccupied save by her cousin. "The village is all astir, the troopers are busy looking to their horses, and David Marlow hath heard that on his return to the Inn, the Captain gave orders that they be ready to start on some expedition at three o'clock in the morning. Think you, Barbara, he can have heard even now of Rupert's hiding-place? Or think you they will intercept his return. He left me but half an hour since. Speak, cannot you?"

Barbara looked up slowly, her face very pale. "Aye, he hath heard, I told him myself."

"Barbara! Art thou mad, child?"

"Indeed I verily believe I am," she answered in a dazed voice. Then collecting her thoughts she told her cousin all that had passed in her interview with the captain. "Think you, Cicely," she continued nervously, "after that it were possible that he has betrayed me?"

"Possible!" cried Cicely in a voice of scorn and fury. "Why, thou little fool, 'tis the man's profession to spy and snare and betray us. Oh! Barbara, how could you be so rash, so wicked? Now 'tis too late to save him."

Barbara roused herself.

"Nay, Cicely, I will not believe that of him. I have his promise. He is a hard man, but he will assuredly keep his word; he would never betray my trust."

"Oh, thou art bewitched by his fair words. Nay, speak not to me. I will go pray, 'tis all that is left for me now."

Sobbing bitterly she left the room.

Barbara sat upright in her chair, clenching the arms with her hands and gazing straight before her.

"An he dare to do it?" she murmured under her breath. Then she sprang suddenly to her feet. "He *shall* not do it," she cried. "I must to the village—there is no other way. And yet,—sure,—nay, I cannot. Bah! I have shamed myself once before him, what matter an I do it once again!"

CHAPTER VIII

Captain Protheroe strode thoughtfully up and down his room at the Inn, puffing furiously at his pipe and staring at the floor.

On his return from his interview with Barbara he had found awaiting him an order to proceed at once to Taunton, and in the yard without he could hear his men still busy with preparations for their early start on the morrow. But though wearied in body with his long day's work the captain felt no inclination for sleep, and, his thoughts still busily occupied with the events of the past few hours, he passed the time pacing his room. His promise once given, he was not the man to waste many regrets upon what was passed, yet as he thought over the affair his brows puckered into a frown, and he ground the stem of his pipe savagely between his teeth. To wink at the escape of a rebel was indeed no great matter in those days. He knew well to what extent corruption and bribery were rife among his fellow officers and how few would hesitate to allow a rebel to slip through their hands could they thereby help to line their pockets. From the Lord Chief Justice downwards the custom was openly practised. Even the Queen's maids of honour, delicate women whose sensibilities were wrung by the death of a beetle, and who would have swooned at the idea of crushing a moth, even they openly trafficked in pardons, and complained bitterly when the life ransoms extracted from the impoverished friends of the prisoners failed to satisfy their demands. But hitherto Captain Protheroe had prided himself upon keeping his fingers clean amid such general corruption, and it enraged him to feel that at last he too had succumbed. Not indeed for a bribe's sake, but because a woman believed him worthy of her trust and his pride would not allow him to betray it.

But was it in truth for that reason alone? Might not it also be because the woman was possessed of a pair of wonderful eyes and knew how to use them?

"Bah!" he muttered angrily, pausing to knock the ashes from his pipe. "How a woman may play the deuce with a man's work!" Then drawing from his pocket a small bow of scarlet ribbon, he gazed at it for a few moments with a strange expression on his face, and with a short laugh flung it from him into a corner of the room and resumed his promenade.

He was interrupted at length by a loud knock at the door, and at his summons Corporal Crutch entered to say that after diligent search he had discovered the missing pedlar, and that the fellow confessed to having certain matters of import to make known to the captain alone. The corporal had no desire that Captain Protheroe should hear of his first interview with Simon, feeling that his customary acuteness had slightly failed him on that occasion, and after a vain attempt to extract some information on his own account from the sulky pedlar, he was at length forced to hand the man over to his superior officer, threatening him first, however, with dire penalties should he breathe a word concerning their previous encounter.

"Bring the fellow in, I will see him," answered the captain, on learning that the pedlar was without.

The order was obeyed and the hawker, glancing furtively from side to side, was pushed rather than ushered into the room.

"Well, my man," Began Captain Protheroe, eyeing him sharply, "what is your business with me?"

"An it please your honour, I have information to sell to your honour concerning the hiding-place of a certain rebel."

"To sell to me!" answered the captain sternly. "It is not for a loyal subject of his Majesty to drive bargains with his officers. We do not buy information, we exact it."

The manner in which these words were uttered caused the hawker to modify his tone.

"May it please your honour," he whimpered, "is there no reward for the arrest of a rebel?"

"If your information be correct, and above all of value (which I greatly doubt), you shall have such money for your services as they deserve. Now for your story, and waste no more of my time."

Thus driven to a corner and moved as much by desire of vengeance as by greed of gold, the hawker related how he had received the letter from Sir Rupert Winslow, and the information it contained.

"Then the ladies know nought of the matter as yet?" enquired the captain.

"Nothing whatever, your honour."

"But this letter—where is it?"

"I—I have mislaid it, sir—but——"

"You are lying to me, knave," interrupted the captain coldly. "By Heaven! an I find you trying to deceive me you shall taste o' the rope's end before an hour is passed."

The hawker cowered before such a prospect, and discovering after much protestation and evasion that the captain evidently knew more of the matter than he had expected, he decided to tell the truth. Thereupon he gave a full account of the transaction, up to the time of his escape from the smithy, omitting only (out of respect for the Corporal's threats) to refer to his interview with that worthy.

Captain Protheroe listened attentively to the narrative, smiling slightly at the complaint of Barbara's treatment. When it was ended he turned coldly on Simon.

"That will do. You can go."

"But the reward, your honour," began the hawker nervously.

The captain eyed him sternly.

"An I had my will with you, fellow, you should to the pillory as a thief and extortioner. But as, in this world, a rogue must be paid for his roguery, take your liberty and deem it meet reward for information which I received an hour since. Be off with you."

The hawker, with a deep, heartfelt curse, shuffled out of the room.

"I would that I had seen her braving the fellow," muttered the captain as he recharged his pipe.

So engrossed was he in his meditations that he paid no heed to a sudden clamour in the yard without, and he sprang to his feet with an oath of astonishment when the door was flung wide open, and the corporal burst violently into the room.

"We have him, captain!" he cried, almost dancing with eagerness, "we have him at last, the very fellow himself. Caught as clean as a bird in a net."

"What means this, sirrah?" interrupted the captain sharply. "Art mad, or drunk; or both together?"

The corporal's face fell. He pulled himself together and saluted in a somewhat crestfallen fashion.

"Your pardon, captain," he continued more calmly. "But an it please you, we have taken Sir Rupert Winslow himself."

It was now Captain Protheroe's turn to betray excitement.

"Taken Sir Rupert Winslow! Why, fellow, 'tis impossible. You are dreaming."

"Dreaming or no," answered the corporal sulkily, "he is without. We spied him skulking round the stables to the back o' the Inn. I doubt not wi' intent to steal a fresh horse. There we ambushed him. He made a fierce resistance, but," with an air of supreme complaisance, "I soon overpowered him."

"The devil take the rash fool!" muttered the captain. "Well, bring him in, corporal. And do you see that the men get to rest, we must be off at daybreak to-morrow. I will see to the security of the prisoner."

The corporal saluted, and a moment later ushered his prisoner into the room.

Captain Protheroe looked up curiously at his entrance, and for some minutes silently surveyed him, until the prisoner, weary of such intent scrutiny, tossed his hat on to the table, and flung himself back into a chair with a half-embarrassed, half-reckless air.

The captain broke the silence.

"This is a strange ending, sir, to so lengthy a chase," he said gravely.

"Ah, well! 'twas bound to end sooner or later, and as well this way as another," he answered with a short laugh. "In truth, 'twas a hole and corner business, and I am weary of it."

"You have been to visit your sister at the Manor House?" queried the captain.

The prisoner looked up haughtily.

"My past movements are my own affairs, sir; you and I are concerned with the present alone."

"I take you, sir," answered the captain quietly. "Moreover, I understand the reason of your presence here, and I honour you for it. It is irregular, of course, but under the circumstances, I cannot refuse to give you every satisfaction."

"Satisfaction!" exclaimed the prisoner in astonishment.

"Aye, sir. You doubtless understand me."

"Not I. I have no personal quarrel with you, that I know of."

"No quarrel! Then am I wrong in supposing you to be the brother of Mistress Barbara Winslow?"

"And what then, sir," demanded the prisoner sharply. "What of her?"

Captain Protheroe shrugged his shoulders.

"Ah! I see I am mistaken," he replied. "I deemed, sir, you had ventured hither in order to seek me and to demand satisfaction for my behaviour towards your sister. But since— —"

"Will you have the goodness to explain, sir," interrupted the prisoner fiercely.

The captain smiled calmly.

"Egad! I confess 'twas a somewhat low piece of work. But the wench was so exasperating and withal so pretty. And I give you my word," he added with a cynical laugh, "she showed no over-great reluctance to my kisses."

The prisoner sprang to his feet, his fists clenched, his eyes blazing with passion.

"May Heaven have mercy on you, sir, but 'tis a most dastardly lie."

"Heaven will need have mercy on you my friend, if you give the lie so freely," answered the captain coldly. "But perchance you are willing to fight now, sir, unless" —with a laugh—"you have smaller regard for your sister's reputation than I surmised."

"Now, by Heaven! you shall swallow your words," cried the youth, white with fury.

Captain Protheroe rose.

"I am at your service," he answered coolly. "I have two rapiers handy, there is no time like the present, and as for place, why this chamber will serve as well as anywhere."

The prisoner bowed assent, and after a moment's hesitation flung off his cloak and turned to take his rapier.

"One moment, sir," continued the captain. "Seeing that I am in no manner bound to grant you, my prisoner, this satisfaction, before I indulge you there is one stipulation I would make."

"Name it."

"That the encounter be *à entrance*." Then seeing his opponent hesitate, he continued:

"Mark me, sir. An the advantage be mine, you shall have your choice of meeting death by my hand presently, or on the gallows some few weeks hence. If, on the other hand, the victory fall to you, you will doubtless use the opportunity to regain your freedom, and since my life must go bail for your safe-keeping, I claim the right to a similar choice. If you refuse these conditions I must withdraw the privilege I would confer."

"Have it as you will." cried the prisoner impatiently.

"Draw then, and defend yourself."

They took their positions and the blades crossed.

After the first few passes a look of surprise crept into Captain Protheroe's eyes as he realised his adversary's skill. He, himself, had studied the art in many countries, and knew that few swordsmen in England were his equal, yet he found this youth no mean opponent. From the outset he felt no doubt of the result—a skilled swordsman soon gauges the extent of his adversary's powers.

As for the prisoner, after the first fierce attack his fury subsided, and he steadied himself to parry with eager watchfulness the captain's point. His eye was quick, his wrist supple, and he was well practised in the art. But he lacked strength. Slowly he was driven backward, backward, across the room, till at length he was fighting with his foot pressed against the wall. Even then he showed no fear, nor relaxed for an instant his resolute defence. Suddenly the captain's wrist seemed to relax its merciless strain and with a quick movement the prisoner had twisted the blade from his grasp and it flew with a clatter among the furniture of the room.

Captain Protheroe clasped his hands behind his back, and fixing his eyes full on his opponent's face waited what should follow.

The prisoner stood for a space staring at him in silence, the expression of his face changing from astonishment to triumph, from triumph to deep dismay. Then he dropped the point of his rapier and turned away.

"HE DROPPED THE POINT OF HIS RAPIER AND TURNED AWAY"

"'Tis enough, I am satisfied."

"But pardon me, sir, I am not," answered Captain Protheroe drily. "Methinks you have forgotten my stipulation."

The prisoner bit his lip and answered coldly: "I do not choose to comply with it; nor do I hold with such folly."

"'Tis a pity you did not express that opinion before, sir. Yet there remains no choice for you. I prefer death by the sword to death by the scaffold. I am ready. You will therefore carry out our contract at once, or forfeit all claim to be counted a man of honour."

The prisoner flushed angrily and once more raised his rapier. But meeting the quiet smile and steady gaze of his opponent he dropped the weapon upon the table and turned away.

"You must wait. I cannot kill you now."

"Your reason, sir?"

"I—I am not in a killing humour."

Captain Protheroe's lips twitched, but he answered gravely:

"Then may I beg you, sir, to overcome your humour without delay."

The prisoner breathed quickly and was silent.

Then Captain Protheroe laughed quietly. "Ah, well! from time immemorial women have loved to delay their *coup-de-grâce*. You but carry out the traditions of your sex, madame."

The prisoner turned to the captain a pair of wide blue eyes filled with horrified amazement.

"Ah! I thought I could not be mistaken, Mistress Barbara," continued the captain, smiling. "Pray be seated, you must be worn out with fatigue."

Barbara sank unresisting into the chair he pushed forward, and drooped her head in silence.

"May I ask, madame, to what cause I owe the honour of this visit?" queried the captain politely.

"Cicely said—we thought——" she began. Then recovering herself she continued firmly. "I had a suspicion that you might play me false, and might even now be about to set out to arrest Rupert."

"Indeed! So you affected this—er—disguise to prevent our departure. Is it so, madame?"

"I knew no other way," muttered Barbara.

"I gave you my word."

"Aye, but I liked not the manner in which you gave it. You—you angered me."

"That is a pity," he answered quietly. Then seating himself on the edge of the table beside her, he eyed her coolly, and continued with a slight drawl. "Ah, well! the resemblance is certainly a strong one. Sir Rupert, methinks, is a trifle broader in the chest, and—there be one or two more details," he added, slowly surveying her figure.

Barbara drooped her head still lower, and flushed angrily at the veiled insolence of his tone.

"You will wonder how I noted the difference," continued the captain. "The fact is, as I was riding home alone, after my visit to the Manor House, I chanced to encounter the real Sir Rupert, and we had some conversation together."

"You met Rupert!" cried Barbara, forgetting all in her astonishment. "Oh! where is he?"

"He should by this well-nigh have reached the coast."

"Alone?"

"Alone, madame."

"So you have kept your promise?" she cried in amazement.

"Yes, Mistress Barbara, strange though it may seem to you, I have. It is a pity you did not trust me, you would have spared yourself the inconvenience of this—masquerade."

The covert sneer in his tone stung her to a sudden anger.

"And why should I trust you?" she cried haughtily. "You are my enemy."

"I was your enemy, madame, but I had believed myself now to have some claim upon your trust and friendship."

"I see not upon what you base such a belief," she answered still in anger.

"Why else, madame, think you, did I set your brother free?"

"I have but your word concerning that transaction," she answered scornfully. "You were alone when you encountered Rupert."

"Certainly. What follows?"

"My brother, Captain Protheroe, hath his sword."

"A sword!" he laughed. "Why so have I, madame."

"Verily, sir," she answered with a mocking laugh, "yonder it lies."

Captain Protheroe, in astonishment, glanced from her face of triumph to the distant corner where lay his discarded rapier.

"Damnation!" he muttered with a short angry laugh. "I had forgot."

"Aye, so I thought, sir," she answered, smiling scornfully. "And my brother is a better swordsman than I. Yet 'twas a prettily conceived story."

"Mistress Barbara, in good truth, I swear——"

"I have already heard more oaths this evening than I am accustomed to," she interrupted. "I will not trouble you to further tax your powers. I wish you good-evening, sir."

She rose to depart, but he stepped quickly before her, and leaned his back against the door.

"A moment, madame, I beg," he said, his voice harsh with anger. "Since it has pleased you to withdraw your trust in me, I see not that I am any longer bound to respect your confidence. 'Tis but an hour since I parted from Sir Rupert. He can yet be overtaken."

Barbara raised a terrified face to his.

"Oh, no! You could not do that," she said.

"And wherefore not?"

"Oh, because—because——" she faltered.

"Well, madame, your reason?" he demanded again harshly.

Barbara flung up her head defiantly, and snatching her rapier from the table raised the point to his breast.

"Because, sir, by your own showing," she replied, facing him boldly, "your life is now mine, to do with as I will. Make one motion towards my brother's undoing, and I swear by Heaven I will run you through as blithely as ever I ran needle into cloth."

For a space they stood thus, she with face alight with excitement, he staring down with astonished admiration into her blazing eyes.

Then he laughed quietly.

"Pardon me, Mistress Barbara," he said, eyeing her coolly. "Your doublet is awry."

Instantly she dropped her rapier, her hands flew to her waist, she looked down in deep consternation. All her newborn resolution had vanished, she was but a woman once more.

"My doublet is not your concern, sir," she muttered.

"Your pardon, madame," he answered pleasantly. "I should in truth have thought a doublet rather my concern than yours; but as you will. If you prefer to wear it thus, of course——"

"I—I knew not exactly how it should be worn," she faltered, glancing doubtfully at her figure. Then recollecting herself she continued angrily. "My dress is my own affair, sir. Why should I not play the Rosalind, an it so please me?"

"No reason whatever, Mistress Barbara," he continued lightly. "I can only rejoice at my good fortune in being present at the performance. By my faith, the dress becomes you wondrous well." And again he submitted her to a critical survey from head to foot.

Her head drooped, her breast heaved, and turning suddenly from him she sank into a chair and burying her face in her outstretched arms upon the table, she burst into bitter sobs.

Captain Protheroe regarded her doubtfully.

"Woman's last weapon?" he queried with a cynical laugh.

The sobs redoubled in force; they shook her whole body.

"Come, come!" he protested roughly, "this is useless, madame. I have already once this evening had the pleasure of seeing your tears; I know their value. Besides, you should bear in mind your character; tears are ill-suited to doublet and hose."

Still she sobbed on, unheeding.

He moved impatiently and hummed a tune which quickly wandered away into incoherence. "I would I knew if it were counterfeit," he muttered.

Still she wept, with quick-drawn breath, and short, gasping, helpless sobs, very terrible to a man's ears.

He took two steps towards her, and then paused. "No," he muttered. "I will not. She hath already duped me twice, I will be hanged if I let her do so again. 'Tis but counterfeit."

He turned from her resolutely and seating himself with his back to her waited stolidly until she should see fit to relinquish this last design.

Minute after minute passed. Soon the sobs died away.

"Ah, good!" he thought with a smile. "So my lady has decided to try another plan."

He waited impatiently for her next move. There was no sound in the room save an occasional sobbing gasp.

At last he could wait no longer, but rising quickly hurried to her side. Her eyes were closed and she lay very still. Then he listened for the regular breathing. There was no doubt of the matter, she was asleep, asleep as peacefully as an infant.

"So it was no counterfeit," he muttered slowly; "she hath sobbed herself to sleep. What a brute she must think me! What a brute I am!"

He stood close beside her gazing down at the graceful yielding figure, at the dark lashes curling on to the flushed, tear-stained cheeks, at the rosy half-opened mouth, at the loose mass of hair framing her perfect face. His breath came fast, his heart beat quickly.

Suddenly he turned from her and hurried from the room, locking the door behind him. Away from the room, away from the Inn, away to the river-bordered meadow behind. And there he paced the night through, puffing unconsciously at an unlighted pipe, until the first rays of dawn softened the sky.

Before he set out he crept once more into the room where Barbara still lay asleep. He paused first to throw a cloak gently over the form of the sleeping girl, then he turned to pick up his sword and collect his papers.

But ere he left the room he hesitated once more, and turning strode into the far corner. Here he knelt down and searched eagerly for a certain knot of scarlet ribbon, which being found, he folded carefully and with a short half-shamed laugh, placed in the pocket of his doublet.

So Captain Protheroe and his men rode from the village. But Barbara slept on peacefully, while the sunbeams stole into the room and played with her dark curls. And there an hour later Phoebe found her, when, in answer to a message sent by the captain ere he left, she came down from the Manor House to search for her missing lady.

CHAPTER IX

It was with many a sigh and much inward misgiving that the Reverend Marmaduke Peters ascended his pulpit steps in the little church of Durford and prepared to deliver his discourse to his flock on the morning of Sunday, September 15, in the year of grace, 1685.

The Reverend Marmaduke was stout and placid in person, kind-hearted and nervously sensitive to a degree; and having as his aim in life the threefold longing to satisfy his superiors, to breed the best poultry in the country-side, and to live at peace with all men, he wondered what cruel humour of fate had placed him in such a hot-bed of rebellion as was the little village of Durford.

A while ago, with sorrow and amazement, he beheld his flock straying wilfully towards the abhorred wilderness of rebellion, but his doubts then lest possibly the rebellion might prove successful, forbade the cautious soul to use what influence he might have had in holding their allegiance firm to the king.

Now, however, when the rebellion had failed, and the rebels had been scattered, the same caution forbade him to display openly the deep sympathy which his kind heart could not but feel for the sufferers, many of whom were personally dear to him.

Truly his was a delicate position, and the ingenuity with which hitherto he had maintained a neutral position, and in both his Sabbath discourses and his week-day intercourse with his flock had succeeded in ignoring the very existence of the rebellion, displayed an amount of thoughtfulness and steady perseverance which would have done justice to a nobler effort.

But the most far-sighted prophet may be o'erthrown by circumstances.

During the few weeks in which Captain Protheroe and his men had occupied the village a severe and inexplicable malady had kept the worthy minister prisoner in his house, and had prevented any untoward collision between himself and these representatives of the Royal cause.

With the withdrawal of the soldiery on the previous Wednesday, however, he had once again recovered full health and strength, and had resumed his duties.

But the week was not out when, to his dismay, six troopers under the command of Corporal Crutch returned, and he received a polite but firm intimation from the corporal that as he himself proposed to attend the service on the morrow, a discourse upon the sinfulness of rebellion would be regarded by the authorities as a satisfactory proof of the preacher's loyalty and submission. The intimation was accompanied by a clear hint that the Reverend Marmaduke's loyalty was regarded in certain quarters as of a questionable quality.

The Reverend Marmaduke was dumbfounded.

In vain did he represent to the corporal that sermons could not be prepared on the instant, that a discourse worthy of such a theme would require days of careful thought and study; in vain did he endeavour by every device in his power to escape the ordeal thus set unexpectedly before him, but escape was impossible; for the worthy corporal, finding himself in a position of unquestioned authority, was once more minded to enjoy it to the full. He could not enter the pulpit himself, but he was resolved to cause such a discourse to be delivered as should bitterly condemn all rebels, and surround with a halo of glory his loyal, law-preserving self. A few judiciously suggested threats concerning the suspected disloyalty of the minister were sufficient; the worthy doctor recognised his helplessness and he submitted.

Not, however, until he ascended his pulpit on the morning of the Sabbath had he fully realised the enormity of the task he had undertaken.

Beneath him stretched row after row of benches, well filled with the parishioners who loved and trusted him, and the majority of whom had sent their best-beloved to aid the rebellion which he was to condemn. To his left sat Corporal Crutch, attended by two troopers, sitting as judges upon the loyalty and fervour of his discourse. While immediately below the pulpit sat "the quality," as represented by Lady Cicely and Mistress Barbara Winslow, and when his glance fell upon the face of the latter, he knew that the ordeal before him was desperate indeed.

He had chosen for his text the words of the psalmist, "Kings with their armies shall flee before Him," hoping that the allegorical allusion to Monmouth as a king might soothe the feelings of those who believed in their hero's title. The delivery of these words, applicable as they were to recent events, instantly aroused the attention of his hearers. The worthy preacher groaned inwardly; would they but sleep or allow their attention to wander, as was ordinarily the custom, all might yet be well; this unwonted interest was but another cruel jest of Fate. Barbara, after a sharp glance in the direction of the corporal, whose presence she had noted with surprise and anxiety, settled herself to follow the discourse with a defiant light in her dark eyes, and even Lady Cicely looked up with unusual interest.

The Reverend Marmaduke mopped his brow, sipped his glass of water, and sighed deeply. Then summoning all his resolution to the task, he plunged into his subject and wandered for some time among the ramifications of the history of the Israelites, until an impatient movement from Corporal Crutch warned him that it was inadvisable longer to delay the application of his text to current topics.

Thereupon he fixed his glance resolutely upon the countenance of the corporal and burst forth into an eloquent reference to the triumph of the supporters of the Lord's Anointed, as represented by the king's troops in the late battle, and the downfall of his enemies.

Presently he became uncomfortably aware that Lady Cicely Winslow was weeping silently into her kerchief, while many of his parishioners at the back of the building were giving vent more noisily to their grief. The faces of the men were dark with anger, and below him the figure of Mistress Barbara grew more and more erect, her head thrown back, her lips pressed tightly together, and her eyes flashing upon him glances of indignation and scorn.

The preacher hastily diverted the flow of his discourse into a cautious condemnation of rebellion in general, but was again driven forward by the threatening glances of the corporal to particularise and condemn more thoroughly.

Now, however, he was interrupted by a sharp fit of coughing from Barbara, loud and aggressive, which ceased when he paused, and when he continued broke out with new vehemence. For full three minutes the struggle continued, till Cicely's whispered entreaties induced Barbara to allow the unfortunate preacher to proceed in peace.

Alas! his nerves were now unstrung, his thoughts hopelessly astray. Desperately he grasped at a last straw and sought to compromise.

Truly, he protested, rebellion is as the sin of witchcraft, and rebels are ever to be abhorred. (This to soothe the corporal.) But had not many rebelled in ignorance, led astray by misrepresentations, by wolves in sheep's clothing, and for such there was not condemnation, but pity.

This appeared to the worthy doctor an excellent position to adopt, and for the remainder of his discourse this position he maintained, endeavouring by appreciative references to the noble supporters of justice on the one hand, and by an attitude of tender consolation towards the rebels on the other, to satisfy both sections of his congregation.

But to Mistress Barbara Winslow such a compromise appeared nothing short of direct insult. Condemnation as a rebel she could endure, but pity as an ignorant fool incapable of judging her own path, she felt was more than any maid should be called upon to accept in silence, and but for Cicely's restraining hand and entreating whispers she would have left the church. In deference to her cousin's feelings she remained, but her indignation was so apparent that the unfortunate pastor could not continue, and bringing his discourse to an abrupt and bewildered conclusion he withdrew from the pulpit.

When Barbara rose to leave the church she was a confirmed rebel. Hitherto she had taken but small interest in the great rising, except in so far as it concerned her brother, and had certainly been no ardent supporter of Monmouth, but the worthy doctor's discourse had aroused in her a keen feeling of anger and opposition.

Now 'tis with a woman as with a stream; endeavour to resist or to direct her course with argument or reason, and the current of her actions will but flow the stronger in the ever-narrowing channel.

Barbara's first impulse was to waylay the Reverend Marmaduke in the churchyard, and there, outside the sacred edifice, pour forth upon his offending head the vials of her wrath. But discretion and a lengthened indulgence in the seclusion afforded by the vestry secured the peace-loving occupant from an encounter not wholly unanticipated. In ignorance of the exact nature of the events which had passed in the churchyard during the interval, but satisfied at last that his congregation had dispersed, he made his way to the safe haven of the rectory.

Disappointed of her intention, Barbara looked round in search of some other victim, but there appeared only the corporal, and she would not demean herself to bandy words with him. Throwing a disdainful glance in his direction, she swept haughtily down the grass-grown path to the lych-gate. Here she was perforce delayed. Her cousin had paused to speak a few words of hope and sympathy to an old woman whose only son lay in Taunton gaol, awaiting his fate, and as she waited Barbara glanced carelessly around her.

On the green near the church she noted a couple of mounted dragoons in charge of four spare troop-horses saddled and bridled, and a third in charge of a rough-looking cart. She noted these preparations for departure with satisfaction, and wondered what had been the reason for such a short and sudden visit.

As the crowd in the churchyard parted, and the corporal, followed by his two attendant troopers, came down the path to the gate, she was soon to be enlightened, however.

The corporal advanced and laying his hand on her shoulder, cried in a voice wherein pompous dignity and elation strove for the mastery:

"Mistress Barbara Winslow, I attaint you as a rebel, and arrest you in the name of his Majesty."

Too much astonished to speak, Barbara was conscious, however, of a murmur of anger and surprise from the crowd of villagers and of Cicely's voice enquiring sharply:

"What is the matter? What means this?"

"There is no call to answer questions," replied the corporal pompously. "But an ye must know, it means that this woman is attainted as a rebel, and I hold a warrant for her arrest, with orders to conduct her instantly to Taunton gaol to await trial."

"But it is impossible! she is no rebel."

"She is known to have sheltered rebels, many have been hanged for less," answered the corporal, with a sinister glance of triumph at his prisoner.

"Yet surely it cannot be as ye say?" cried Cicely helplessly. "Taunton gaol! Why she is a woman, ye cannot. Nay, she is but a child. Oh! 'tis monstrous, monstrous."

"No words, no words," cried the corporal fussily. "You will learn, madame, that in such affairs of state, least said is soonest mended. Now, mistress," he continued roughly, turning to Barbara, "we'd best be moving."

But a growl of anger broke from the still lingering crowd, and Peter Drew, the blacksmith, sprang upon the low wall of the churchyard.

"Hey, lads!" he cried; "they red-cöats be vor taäkin oor young Miztrez to Taunton gaol. Zhall her be taäken, lads? Zhall her go? Hey lads, we be vaive to one. Zhall her go, lads?"

Peter was no orator, but eloquence was not needed. Love for Barbara, that old feudal love for their lord; resentment for the many acts of ill-treatment sustained at the hands of the troopers during their occupation of the village; and lastly, the spirit of revolt against injustice and opposition which lurks secretly in every heart, all combined to rouse his hearers to fury, and it needed no words of the smith to fan the flame.

They greeted Peter's harangue with a wild shout of triumph, and closed in round the corporal and his men with gestures which threatened every moment to develop into a fierce attack.

Barbara's face flushed and her eyes glittered with triumph. Wild projects flashed through her brain. To overpower the half-dozen troopers, then to fortify the Manor House, and hold it against all comers; to rally round her the many secret supporters of the late rebellion, to recall the exiles from Holland, and to succeed in establishing justice and the Protestant Religion, or die fighting for the Cause. Had not other women done as much! These men, she knew, would cheerfully fight to the death for her; the country was still full of malcontents; one failure could not be regarded as the death of the Cause. Hope was high, all things seemed possible. Who shall say what mad dreams passed through her thoughts during those few moments while she stood there, the centre of that enthusiastic mob?

But it was not to be. From out the crowd there pressed forward an old woman, who flung herself trembling at Barbara's feet.

"Eh; Miztress Barbara, dearie," she cried, seizing her hand, "don't-ee, don't-ee, then. A'll swing for it, for zure a wull if a faight. And zee there," pointing with her trembling hand at a tall stalwart fellow, prominent amongst the throng, "thiccy's arl I've left now. Three others have been taäken. If they taäk un I maun die, for zure I maun. Don't-ee, now."

"Vor shaäme, mother," cried the lad referred to. "Would ee have un taäk the young Miztress to Taunton? Vor shaäme."

But the dreams had passed. Barbara's eyes were opened and she recognised the hopelessness of any resistance. She could not, she must not sacrifice these lives.

Gently disengaging herself from the clinging hands of the old crone, she sprang on to the wall at Peter's side and caught his uplifted arm.

"No, no, friends!" she urged; "it won't do. We could not hope for more than a short-lived victory. She is right, there would be vengeance and ye would all swing for it. This fellow saith he hath the Royal Warrant for my arrest, an that be so I must e'en go with him. Be assured they cannot harm me; I have done no wrong. Besides," she added proudly, "I would not have them think me afeared to go. Peter, be silent. Nay, I thank you indeed, but there must be no resistance. Go home quietly. You women, look to your men folk. No harm shall come to you for my sake, and none must think I fear to go."

Thus she stood upon the wall, a bright figure in her dainty muslin gown, smiling down upon them, until with reluctance, and many incoherent mutterings, the crowd, somewhat reassured by her words, slowly dispersed. Then turning she addressed the corporal:

"So that is ended. Now, an you will permit me first to return to the Manor House to collect some necessaries, I am ready to go with you to Taunton."

"I am rejoiced, mistress," he assured her pompously, "that you have decided to submit peaceably to my orders."

"Aye, corporal," answered Barbara, with a smile at his perturbed countenance. "I do not doubt but you are indeed rejoiced. But come, I must to the Manor House, to prepare for the journey. I presume you will allow me so much grace?"

"The escort will accompany you thither."

"I had thought my submission had been proof enough of my good faith, but as you will," answered Barbara carelessly, passing through the gate.

"Barbara, I must with you to Taunton, indeed I must," pleaded Cicely, as she hastened after her cousin. "'Tis monstrous that you should go alone with these men."

"Thou, Cicely? Impossible! What could'st thou do there? Where could'st thou lodge? Not i' the gaol indeed."

"There be many kindly folk in the town who would house me, and they will perchance advise too what 'twere best to do for thee. There is good Mistress Lane, the wool-merchant's wife, I will seek her out. But go with you I must indeed."

"In truth, Cicely," answered Barbara with a quick sigh, "I would fain have thee near, if 'twere only to teach myself the folly of my fears by laughing at thine."

With a tyranny born of his newly acquired importance, Corporal Crutch refused to allow his prisoner more than a few minutes' preparation before her journey to Taunton, but having resigned herself to fate Barbara had no mind to delay, and in less than half an hour after their return to the house the two enforced travellers were ready for departure.

Barbara's resolution was by no means strengthened at sight of the ramshackle cart provided to convey her to Taunton.

"To what low estate our fortunes have fallen!" she muttered with a wry face.

"Rebels cannot expect to be treated like honest folk," remarked the Corporal complacently.

"Set a watch on thy tongue, Master Corporal," retorted she angrily. "I am no rebel till I be proved such, therefore I warn thee 'twere best be more careful of thy words," and turning abruptly from the startled man she took her seat in the cart.

For the first few miles of their journey each of the girls devoted all her efforts to the difficult task of cheering the other. Upon leaving the village and their friends behind them, some sense of the utter helplessness of her position filled Barbara's mind, and she was but a sorry comforter.

But hers was not a nature to sigh long, and soon the fresh air, the bright sunshine, and the interest and amusement she found in watching her escort, had their effect. The result of this reaction from her former depression was a mood of high spirits and brighter hopes.

"In truth, Cicely," she broke out suddenly with a laugh, "we are both fools. At worst 'tis but a matter of a night or two in gaol, where I doubt not I shall meet much good company; an interview with Lord Jeffreys (I would fain see him, they say he is a right handsome man, for all he has such a tongue); then perchance a fine, and so home. Why 'tis not worth a sigh. 'Tis but an adventure, and thou knowest I love such."

"Aye, Barbara, you speak truly," answered her companion, with a desperate attempt at cheerfulness. "They would not dare to harm a woman. I make no doubt these tales of my Lord Jeffreys' punishment and—and of Lady Alice Lisle, are gross exaggerations." This last she added with a tentative air—Cicely longed for corroboration of that statement.

At mention of Lady Lisle Barbara's face fell slightly, but she resolutely dismissed her fears.

"There is not a doubt of it, sweet. Yet even an it were not so, they could prove nought against me. They have no testimony to show that we housed or aided either Rupert or Sir Peter."

"That is so," assented Cicely joyously. "And in justice none could punish us for what is unproven."

"Oh! Cicely, look at yon red-headed trooper, didst ever behold so scarlet a poll?"

"Aye. And mark how he sits his horse. I wager he will be over its head ere he sees Taunton. Note his face when the creature pricks his ears; 'tis a very picture of terror."

"Didst note the corporal as we passed trough the village?" laughed Barbara. "The poor fool feared an ambuscade at every corner, and well-nigh fell from his horse with fright when old Mother Gilkin's pot fell down as we reached her cottage. I hate the fellow, yet I cannot but laugh at his antics."

Thus for a while the two chattered bravely as they clattered and bumped along the rough country roads to Taunton. But as night drew on the sky became overcast with clouds, and a cold wind and drizzling rain added to the discomfort of the journey. Their conversation became more and more desultory, and finally ceased altogether.

Only once again did Barbara break the silence.

"Cis," she asked with some slight hesitation, "thinkest thou that Captain Protheroe knows aught of my arrest?"

"Knows aught!" cried Cicely in astonishment. "Why, Barbara, child, who else hath accused thee?"

"Nay, nay; I will not believe that of him," answered Barbara stoutly.

"Believe what thou wilt, I tell thee it is the truth. Thinkest thou he would tamely endure to be duped as thou hast duped him, without some revenge? Oh! I tell thee as I have ever done, the fellow is to be mistrusted, and to take such revenge on thee were but his nature."

"In truth, Cicely, you do not know him," pleaded Barbara. "He is not—I would trust him."

"Why, Barbara! Hath the man bewitched thee that thou art so ready in his defence?" cried Cicely, looking at her curiously. "What hath he done to win such trust? Or dost thou deem, perchance, that thou hast bewitched him, and so bound him to thy cause? I' faith, coz, I warn thee, trust not too much to the power of thine eyes; all men be not so easily ensnared."

But Barbara answered not, only sighed lightly and stared thoughtfully into the gathering darkness, her eyes wide with wonder and with doubt.

The distance from Durford to Taunton is scarce twelve miles, and 'twas little past noon when they set out on their journey, but the progress of the cart was slow, owing to the bad roads.

A horse, too, cast a shoe, and they must needs stop at the next village to seek a smith. The escort halted more than once for refreshment, and in fine it was night before they reached their destination.

Perhaps the darkness was not without its compensation. At the cross roads were scenes ill-suited to a woman's eyes, traces of that wholesale butchery which for many weeks had devastated the fairest county of the West. Gaunt figures swinging in their chains from the sign-posts, tokens of the merciless punishment meted out to those even suspected of rebellion, had been no cheering welcome to such travellers as they.

When they entered Taunton the streets were almost deserted, and the dwelling houses closed and in darkness, but the windows of the White Hart Inn, the headquarters of the royal troops, blazed with light, and the shouts of laughter and snatches of song from within indicated that the soldiery were holding revelry, heedless alike of the hallowedness of the Sabbath, of the misery of the townsfolk, and of the despair of hundreds of prisoners who lay awaiting their doom in the crowded gaols of the town.

As the cavalcade passed before the Inn an officer lounged into the light of the doorway, and stared carelessly at the passing company. Barbara with a gasp of astonishment half rose to her feet, but Cicely's hand restrained her, and reluctantly she sank down beside her cousin.

The cart passed, leaving Captain Protheroe to continue his inspection of the night all unconscious of whom the vehicle conveyed.

CHAPTER X

"So! Now am I in prison. Well, I had as lief be elsewhere," muttered Barbara when she awoke after her first night in gaol, and proceeded philosophically to take stock of her surroundings, which she had been too weary to notice on the previous night.

She was not confined in the regular gaol of the town; for nigh two months past that had been filled to overflowing. Those arrested within the last few weeks, together with the unfortunates sent on from Exeter in the van of the dread-inspiring Jeffreys, were lodged in convenient sheds and storehouses, situated in various parts of the town; bare, dreary places with little or no suitable accommodation for the wretches herded within their walls, but affording enough shelter in the opinion of the authorities for rebels during the short interval which must elapse before their trial.

The building wherein Barbara awoke was a large wooden shed, originally a storehouse for wool, some few bales of which still remained piled in the corners. A large door closely guarded and windows high in the roof were the only means of egress, and no provision for the accommodation of the inmates had been made beyond a few straw pallet-beds for the women prisoners, roughly screened from the rest of the shed by a dilapidated piece of sacking. Even in the most hopeless moments since her arrest Barbara had calculated on nothing so dismal as this.

She had slept late after the fatigues of the previous day, and when at length she awoke, the other occupants of her corner had already risen, and passed beyond the partition into the shed.

Barbara seated herself on the edge of her bed and stared forlornly at the bare wall opposite.

"Well! Many better women have been in worse plights, there is not a doubt. I must e'en comfort myself with that," was her verdict after musing some minutes upon her situation. "Now let me see. Rupert would say that the duty of every woman under every circumstance is to look her fairest, but there seemeth little scope for that maxim here, and I see not wherein lies the vantage of tending one's looks when here is no mirror to show the result. However, for lack of other advice I'll e'en follow Rupert's."

Having come to this laudable conclusion, Barbara opened her bundle and proceeded to arrange her curls, and make such improvements in her toilet as the scanty means at her disposal allowed. This done she drew aside the partition and stepped into the room beyond.

It was a curious sight that met her eyes. The shed was totally destitute of furniture, unless as such might be designated the few bales of wool and some bundles of straw, used by the prisoners indiscriminately as couch, chair, or table.

The place served as lodging for about fifty prisoners, many of whom had been from two to three weeks in captivity. The majority of them were rough, ignorant peasants, who, having faithfully followed their leaders into a quarrel which they themselves but half comprehended, now awaited their doom with that same half-puzzled, stolid patience and dogged courage which had helped them already to face death on the fatal field of Sedgemoor.

There were some, too, of the yeoman class, some of the richer townsfolk, and here and there a noncomformist divine, but save perhaps in a certain intelligence and eagerness of expression, there was nothing to distinguish the man of learning or station from the poorest peasant. All alike were dirty, ragged, and dishevelled; unshaven, unwashed, with ill-kempt beards and hair. Existence in such a prison, following in many cases upon days of homeless wanderings, had wrought this levelling effect upon them all. Their money, what little they once possessed, was long ago exhausted. They could pay their gaolers for neither books, amusements, nor drink. They talked little; what was there to talk of? For the most part they were plunged in the deepest apathy. They had fought, they had failed; now they awaited what was to come in silence. They showed no fear, no despair, no hope, only a great patience.

Barbara gazed on the scene with the utmost astonishment and indignation. Were these men, indeed, the same wild enthusiasts who a while ago had so eagerly cheered Monmouth through the streets of Taunton? Aye, and not only cheered him, but aided him loyally, leaving work, home, wife, children, and all, that they might follow him and strike a blow for the Cause. Were these indeed those who, armed but with stake or scythe, had made such a gallant stand against the best disciplined troops of the country; those who (men were forced to confess) would but for an accident, undoubtedly have won an unprecedented victory? Could these indeed be the same? She stared with anger and scorn at their silence, their apathy, their unkempt looks. Her ardent young nature had no understanding of this submission to the Inevitable; she had not yet learned that an Inevitable might exist.

Her birth and breeding afforded her no comprehension of the stolid bravery of the peasantry. The farther man is removed from the natural state, the greater the advance he has made in civilisation, so much the more does he deem it necessary to hide his emotions beneath an artificial mask, to seem to be that which he is not. A century later in the massacres in Paris the victims were for the most part nobles and gentlemen; they went to their doom bravely, with a smile in their eyes, a jest upon their lips. In this great Rebellion of the West the victims were the poorest of the peasantry; they faced their doom no less bravely, but they faced it gravely, in silence.

Barbara's family traditions had taught her nothing of this. She had expected her fellow prisoners to be a company of merry dare-devils such as her brother Rupert, or Sir Peter Dare, men who laughed at danger, mocked their gaolers, and turned misfortune, nay, death itself, into a subject for jest. Men, too, who could fight fiercely and endure bravely on occasion, yet would scorn to appear serious in any circumstances (save perchance when discussing the set of a doublet or the colour of a bow), and who looked upon gravity as a sign of cowardice. Such were the rebels she knew, the rebels she had dreamed of, gay, careless, defiant to the end; not such as these, silent, sunk in a helpless submission to their fate. She could not understand. She looked round upon them in indignation, her lips curled in scorn.

But while she stood there surveying the scene she had herself been the subject of observation; presently one of the prisoners approached her and interrupted her meditations.

"What are you doing in this place, my child?" he asked gently.

The speaker was a small, spare man, with bushy white hair and beard, a face seamed and lined with age, yet full of kindliness and humour, with a pair of bright, piercing eyes; a face calculated to win friends or to daunt foes.

Barbara turned to him at once as to an old friend; his voice invited confidence.

"I was arrested but yesterday, sir, on a charge of sheltering rebels, and I am here, as the rest of the company, to await my trial."

"You are very young, but you have a stout heart," he said, smiling kindly.

"Why, sir, I hope so," answered Barbara cheerfully. "I am Barbara Winslow of Durford Manor, and no Winslow yet was ever written coward," she added proudly, with a scornful glance round the shed.

"Noblesse oblige," he quoted, smiling at her sadly. "Ah, child, your strength may seem great, but trust not in it too wholly, lest in the hour of darkness it prove but a broken reed."

Barbara was puzzled. "What mean you, sir? Sure, 'tis not sinful to be brave for a name's sake."

"Nay, I say not that," he answered gently. "There be three qualities that have power to beget a courage unto death—Faith, Love, and Pride. But of these three only the courage born of Faith has never been known to fail. Yet whencesoever it springs, courage is the gift of God and a blessing to man, and as such must be honoured."

Barbara looked at him curiously.

"You are a divine, sir, are you not?"

"Yes, I am indeed a servant of the Lord, though for many years I have been withheld from openly preaching His word. For fifty years I have lived and worked secretly among the miners of the Mendip Hills, and when they marched to support the defender of our religion, I followed to give them the comfort of my words. I thank God that I shall follow them to the end. Ah, child," he continued earnestly, "you cannot understand what it is to be silenced, to be dumb, as 'twere, for twenty-three years; to be torn to pieces 'twixt the burning in my heart to speak the Word, the fear in my breast of meeting the punishment. It is worth a thousand deaths to have had at last this chance of testifying once again to the truth."

Barbara looked at him gravely.

"No," she said, "I do not understand."

His earnestness vanished. He gave a soft resigned sigh and smiled at her, as at a child.

"No, you do not understand; you are young and fearless."

"It should be easy to me to be courageous," she answered lightly. "I have nought to fear. 'Tis for me but some few days in prison, and then perchance a fine. In justice they can do no more."

He smiled at her a trifle sadly.

"Aye, child, as you say, *in justice* they could do no more."

She looked up at him doubtfully, but forbore to question further the meaning of his words.

"But these folk," she continued, looking round, "have doubtless more to fear."

"There is indeed little hope for them this side the grave," he answered calmly, "save for a speedy and merciful death."

Barbara was startled.

"Surely not so—and yet—I had not thought on't," she muttered. "Verily, sir, if this be true, my scorn was ill-timed, they have courage. They are but rude peasants, with neither pride of birth nor name to strengthen their hearts, yet they await death as calmly as any noble. How comes this?"

"So thou deemest courage a monopoly of gentle folk, eh?" he asked, laughing softly. "Ah, child, thou art young. But indeed," he continued more seriously, "these men have fought in the Lord's cause, there is no fear but He will send them strength to fight their battle bravely to the end."

"How can it be God's cause when it hath failed?" asked Barbara bluntly.

"Failed, child? What mean you?"

"Why, call you not this failure?" she asked, glancing round.

"This! In good sooth, no; this is but the beginning of success, only the times were unripe for rebellion, the leaders were unworthy of the cause. Think you these men will die in vain? In God's name I tell you, no. A cause strengthened by such devotion cannot but succeed; for every drop of blood shed to-day there will spring up seeds of justice and resolution in the hearts of the survivors which shall blossom forth into a mighty power. I shall not see it, but thou mayest, for the day is not far off when justice, toleration and true religion shall once more flourish in this kingdom. Failure! Never! We are but the necessary martyrs, the runners of success. The cause of justice was never yet won save by a path of blood and tears."

His enthusiasm communicated itself to Barbara. Her face glowed with eagerness; at that moment she had resolution to face block or scaffold that she also might die for the Cause.

"Ah!" she cried, "this is the courage of which you spoke, the courage born of Faith."

He bowed his head in assent, and there was silence between them while Barbara pondered on his words. Presently she continued:

"And the third, the courage of Love? What mean you by that?" she asked.

Instantly his face was transfigured by a smile of great tenderness.

"I will show you," he answered gently. "Look."

Barbara followed the direction of his eyes. In a far corner of the shed, apart from the rest of the prisoners, sat a man and a woman. She lay in the circle of his arm, her head dropped back upon his shoulder, and oblivious to all around them they sat gazing in one another's eyes. Pale, ragged and unkempt, as were all the prisoners, yet beautiful in each other's eyes, and transfigured by the light of perfect happiness, by the glory of their love.

"It is their wedding-day," he continued softly. "I married them at seven o'clock this morning."

"But who are they?" asked Barbara in bewilderment.

"He is the son of the squire of Hardon, and an officer in Monmouth's army; she, the daughter of a rich cloth-maker of Taunton, who joined the army and met his death at Sedgemoor. He lodged in her father's house when the army was first quartered here. Later, she was attainted a rebel, and they met again, in prison. See now how mighty is love, that it will even force its way into such a desert as this. They have lived here together for three weeks as in a Paradise, and yesterday, feeling the time of separation draw near, they besought me to join them forever in God's sight, as man and wife. I know not whether I rightly consented, yet who could refuse?"

"And the future?" whispered Barbara eagerly.

He shook his head.

"She has money, the charge against her is but slight, her friends will buy her freedom. But for him, an officer in the rebel army, there can be little doubt— — Is it not wonderful?" he continued softly, as though to himself. "Thus they sit hour by hour. Hopes and fears alike have faded in the great light of their love, and for to-day at least they live as in the Garden of Eden, where there is neither past nor future; nought but the present and themselves."

Barbara gazed silently at the couple, until suddenly a great sense of loneliness overcame her, and her eyes darkened with a mist of tears. She turned to her companion with a pathetic gesture of helplessness.

"Alas! ere I came here I had believed myself so strong, so fearless. And here I find all others are brave, and I but a helpless fool."

There was something bewitching in this sudden confession of weakness, and her companion's face softened for an instant as he looked at her. Then he laughed, and his laughter was wise, for it stung her pride, and recalled her former resolution.

"In truth, this discovery is to be deeply regretted, Mistress Winslow," he answered lightly, "seeing I had hoped to enlist the services of one so stout-hearted in the work of cheering the weary hours of some of our unfortunate comrades."

"My services! Why, what think you I can do?" asked Barbara eagerly. "Wouldest have me clamber on a bale of wool and harangue these men upon the duty and virtue of courage?" she added merrily.

"Nay, that were hardly woman's work. And 'tis not for men your help is needed."

"For whom, then?"

"There is a poor girl, she is scarce more than a child, who was brought hither yesterday with her younger sister. They were among those maids of Taunton who presented to the Duke his banners, and for this innocent action they have been arrested. I think, indeed, there is little fear for them; they have rich friends, people of influence, who can save them at a price. But the poor child is fragile. Terror hath gripped her by the heart, and if she be not roused and cheered 'tis to be feared her brain may give way."

"Take me to her, I will try."

"Come, then. Her sister is beside her, but the poor child is very young and can do but little. It may be that you will be able to cheer her."

Barbara gathered up her dainty skirts and followed her companion. As she passed along she was greeted by many a look of surprise and admiration, but so intent was she upon her errand she scarce noted the interest she aroused.

They found the two ill-fated children—they were both little more—crouched against the wall in the darkest corner of the shed. Near them sat a poor peasant woman weeping bitterly, while a second woman offered rough attempts at comfort. Close beside the latter was a thin, elderly woman, with the severe mouth and narrow forehead of a fanatic, who stared straight before her, muttering rapidly to herself, oblivious to her surroundings. These few, with Barbara and the young bride, were the only female prisoners in the shed.

Barbara paused a moment, surveying the group curiously, then she advanced slowly towards the two sisters. The elder of the two was scarce sixteen, fragile and pale. She crouched beside the wall, her chin sunk on her breast, silent, immovable, but when Barbara, touched her on the shoulder she raised her head suddenly, and displayed a face so frozen with despair and eyes so wild with terror that the girl was horrified. In an instant all other considerations vanished before the great pity and tenderness that filled her heart.

"My poor, poor child," she exclaimed gently, "what have they done to thee? Nay, look not thus, none shall hurt thee, I promise it. See, I will sit thus beside thee. Come, now thou art safe and hast nought to fear."

She sank down beside her, drew the child close and encircled her tenderly with her strong young arms.

The bright face, cheery smile, and gentle voice, all tended to excite confidence, as did also the firm pressure of human touch. The child gazed at her for a few moments in doubt and bewilderment, then suddenly clung to her fiercely and burst into wild tears.

"Oh! they will kill me," she sobbed. "Do not let them. Do not let them take me away."

"No, no, they shall not, I swear they shall not harm thee," answered Barbara soothingly, though with more rashness than conviction. "Only look cheerily, sweetheart, and be brave and all will be well."

"Will you take me home? Prithee, take me home," she begged, sobbing.

"Nay, we must bide here for a day or two, but what of that? It will not harm you, and 'tis for a great cause. Bethink you of the saints, of the martyrs; they suffered even death without fear. Bethink you, childie, how many women have striven and suffered manfully for their cause, and be you courageous and proud to suffer thus little for yours."

"Tell me of those women," whispered the younger child, creeping near to their new-found protector. She was stronger; she did not suffer as did her sister, but her poor puzzled brain could not understand why this imprisonment had befallen them; she grasped eagerly at the reference to martyrs. 'Tis easier to be brave in paths which others have trod before us.

So Barbara settled herself between the two children and bent all her efforts to recollecting and relating to the best effect every tale of heroism she had ever read, heard, or imagined, incidents culled from the histories of many nations, from romances, ballads, and legends. From her earliest childhood she had loved to listen to all such tales of prowess and brave endurance; her store seemed unlimited, she had a clear memory, and above all, she possessed that rarest of all gifts, the art of story-telling.

The two children were soon listening with deep interest. She raised her voice, that beautiful voice, not the least of her many charms, and presently the woman sitting near them ceased her sobbing to listen; some of the men even raised themselves from their lethargic musings and drew near, so that she became in time the centre of a large group of prisoners. Cheered with this success, Barbara braced herself to an increased effort. She related story after story of the heroes of many countries and times, stories of love and tenderness, of fierce passions, of high devotion to a worthy cause, till her audience were infected with the enthusiasm and followed her words with startling eagerness. For a time prison walls faded away, trial, punishment, death were forgotten, they lived again in the past.

It is a wonderful power, the art of story-telling, and is given to few, especially among Western peoples, but it is a power which, when combined with the magnetism of a beautiful presence, is irresistible.

Thus intermittently for several hours Barbara continued, and to her hearers the long day passed quickly, until late in the afternoon the pealing of bells and a roll of drums were heard from without. These sounds betokened, as some guessed, the expected arrival of the king's judges. On the morrow, therefore, would commence the Assize trial, which was to decide for each whether he, too, was destined to follow in the footsteps of the long line of martyrs and heroes who had suffered and died in the cause of freedom.

The charm cast around them by Barbara was broken, and she finished her narrative lamely, as her audience grew inattentive and relapsed into moody restlessness. As the darkening shadows gathered in the wool-shed a silence fell, the silence of an overhanging doom.

Suddenly and with startling effect the silence was broken by a clear voice which rang through the room. "Be strong and He shall 'stablish your hearts, all ye that put your trust in the Lord."

The words seemed to echo like a battle-clarion, an incentive to lead all men to victory.

It was Barbara's friend of the morning, Mr. Hardcastle, the noncomformist divine.

When other comfort had failed he was at hand to show these untutored peasants the true source of strength in danger, of consolation in affliction, the promise of their God. Few and simple were his words, yet charged with the fervour of belief, they served their purpose well. Again the courage of Faith strengthened them, the peace of God filled their hearts, and when at the close of his address he besought all to sing with him the eighty-sixth psalm, they joined him with a cheerful heartiness which made the rafters of the barn ring again.

So night drew down upon them, but there was light in their hearts, and they settled to rest in peace.

Barbara carried off her children to their pallet bed in the corner. With the darkness the poor child Katherine's terror had revived somewhat, and for a time she could not be induced to lie down. But gradually Barbara soothed her, talking hopefully of her probable return home on the morrow, and crooning tender child ballads such as her mother sang. Nature was merciful; clinging to the hand of her protectress she sank at last to sleep.

Barbara herself lay long awake listening to the heavy breathing of the sleepers around her and to the dull tramp of the sentries in the street without.

Sleep! the very thought of it seemed ill-timed with the lives of all these men at stake, and some way, surely some way was to be found, could she but think of it, to save them. To her active spirit it seemed past belief that escape should be impossible; intolerable to think that these forty or more around her, strong and healthy men, should go quietly to their deaths without one bid for freedom.

She tossed from side to side upon her mattress, racking her brains to devise a plan. Had she not wit and cleverness more than common? Sure she could find some way! But in vain; her thoughts wandered round and round in a circle, a circle she could not break. At length she sprang to her feet in desperation.

"'Tis no use," she exclaimed, "I can think of nothing. But he hath brains and he cares for their safety, I will go to him. Together surely we may devise some means of escape."

Softly she stepped out into the shed, and picked her way carefully among the sleepers, looking right and left for the face she sought. The moonlight poured in through the windows high in the room so that her passage was not difficult. She came at length upon the man she sought, the Reverend Mr. Hardcastle. Half the night he had spent at the side of one or another of his weaker comrades, cheering and strengthening each by his sympathy. Now at last he had found time for repose, and lay sleeping quietly, his Bible still open at his side. His slumbers were light, for he awoke at her slightest touch, and raised himself to his feet, instantly alert.

"What is the matter, child, do you need me?" he cried.

Barbara's face was pale in the moonlight, her eyes gleamed strangely and she clutched his arm with desperate eagerness.

"Surely something can be done to save them all," she cried confusedly. "It cannot be impossible."

"What mean you, child?"

"Why, here are fifty brave men, at most but half a dozen guards. Can we not break prison, rush the door, devise some mode of escape? 'Tis intolerable to sit here in idleness while the lives of all these are at stake. 'Tis monstrous. Sure, something can be done!"

"Peace, child," he answered sternly; "you know nought of the matter. We be fifty to six, 'tis true, but those six are armed and behind them are many more. If the door were passed we could not escape the town, or if perchance we won from the town where could we hide? The royal troops are everywhere. 'Twere but a hopeless venture which must cost the lives of all."

"Yet, sure, 'twere better to venture some effort than to sit thus helplessly awaiting their fate," she pleaded impatiently.

"Ah! Mistress Barbara, you have yet to learn that the highest courage may lie in such waiting. And I charge you, child, say nought of this to the men. They are nerved now to meet their fate, I will not have them distressed by false hopes. You have played your part well to-day, your place is with yon poor children. Go to them now, and leave these men to me."

Unaccustomed though she was to contradiction, Barbara was yet too strongly awed by his air of command to disobey. Reluctantly she turned away and with a glance of hopeless pity at the sleepers around her, passed beyond the partition and again took her place beside the weary children.

So the long night hours passed slowly away and the first morning of the Bloody Assize of Taunton grew rosy in the east.

CHAPTER XI

When Cicely Winslow was parted from her cousin she went at once to seek a lodging in the house of Master Thomas Lane, one of the most flourishing wool-merchants of Taunton. For many years the Winslows had purchased their stuffs from the house of Lane, in fact ever since the time when the founder after a long and devoted service at the Manor House had established himself in business at Taunton. Therefore, when Cicely presented herself at the house of the worthy merchant she met with a hearty though respectful welcome, and felt confident of all possible assistance.

But though comforted by the warmth of her welcome, Cicely was not slow to perceive that while the long business connection betwixt the two families assured to her every consideration and respect, yet the political opinions of her family met with anything but approval from her host.

For, indeed, the Lanes, unlike the majority of the townsfolk of Taunton, were the staunchest of Tories. They had ever stood firm for the King, and having suffered considerably for their opinions during Monmouth's brief reign of power in the West, it was perhaps but natural that now they should feel harshly disposed towards those who had favoured the Duke in his rebellion against their lawful sovereign.

The household was about to sit down to supper when Cicely arrived, but they waited respectfully until she was ready to join them in the large lofty room, where, according to the fashion of the day, it was the custom for master and family to sup in company with the apprentices and others forming the household.

Knowing well the differences of opinion which existed between themselves and their guest, Master Lane and his good wife endeavoured to avoid all reference to current events, but the all-pervading topic would not be stayed from creeping into the conversation, and so at length Master Lane deemed it best boldly to set their relations on a more definite and clear footing.

"You are heartily welcome, Lady Cicely," he began gravely, "and I will gladly render you what help I can; at the same time I cannot disguise from you, indeed it were not right to do so, how heartily I disapprove of the step young Sir Rupert has taken. So much opposed to what I am sure his father would have wished. Sir Rupert in thus wilfully aiding rebellion against his lawful sovereign has proved himself unworthy of his noble name, and of the high and honourable position he should hold in the country."

Cicely's eyes filled with tears at this unexpected attack. She had not Barbara's spirit, and could not enter into eager discussion with her sedate and solemn host, as her cousin would doubtless have done under similar circumstances. She had no full knowledge of the questions which stirred men's hearts at the time, only to her, what Rupert did was right, and now in her loneliness it tried her sadly to hear his actions thus ruthlessly condemned, and that, moreover, by one whose opinions she could not but respect.

But the good merchant was quite oblivious to her distress. He knew nothing of the close relations between her and Sir Rupert, and was intent only upon removing any misapprehension on her part as to what were his real feelings, while at the same time he deeply pitied the misfortunes which had overtaken the family with which he had been long honourably associated.

"The late Duke of Monmouth," he continued solemnly, "set foot in this realm in open rebellion; not only so, but he and those under him deliberately invented and spread abroad scandal concerning the religion, the honourable intentions, and the virtue of our noble sovereign. Moreover, he had the effrontery actually to declare himself, here at Taunton, lawful King of Britain, thereby seeking to depose his own uncle. Furthermore, he hath since proved himself coward, not alone by his conduct upon the field of Sedgemoor, but also by the manner of his meeting death. That men should be so ready to turn from allegiance to their king, to support the claims of such an one, so worthless and so base, betrays a condition of mind unstable and untrustworthy. For howsoever they may choose to prate of religion and justice, they show but shallow reasoning. For religion and justice are protected by our lord, the King, and need no other defender, and the alleged dangers threatening the Protestant Church are but the inventions of fools. 'Tis no regard for religion and justice which directs such men, but a love of excitement or a hope to escape from patient, honest toil by a chance turn of events in the fortune of war." Here he cast a severe glance down the table in the direction of his apprentices. "For Mistress Barbara," he continued, "I will, if only for her honoured father's sake, do what I can, and I have small fear but that all severe punishment may be averted. But a woman hath no reason to interfere in such affairs, and she must not be surprised if she meet her reward. I rejoice, for his sake, that Sir Rupert hath escaped, and pray that his misfortunes and hardships may tame his hot blood. 'Tis indeed a sad business."

So the old man droned on solemnly, his wife from time to time nodding approval, till Cicely choked over her meat, and felt she could endure no more, but must scream aloud to stop this dreary tirade, every word of which was a sword-thrust in her over-wrought heart.

But diversion came from an unexpected quarter.

Among the apprentices at the lower end of the table sat a broad-shouldered, long-legged youth, whose sharp, eager face was surmounted by a shock of fiery red hair. Throughout this discourse he had evinced the utmost restlessness, shaking his head, clenching his fists, half-rising from his seat, and showing all the signs of entire dissension from the speaker. At length he could restrain himself no longer, but bidding defiance to all custom and etiquette at his master's table, he leaned forward eagerly and broke into the conversation.

"An it please you, sir, 'tis not so, and I must speak," he exclaimed desperately. "'Tis unjust to talk thus of those who fought for Monmouth, unjust and untrue. We—they—'twas not a search merely for excitement; 'twas not for evasion of lawful duties, but was to uphold the sacred cause of justice; 'tis—'tis a slander to say else. Indeed, sir, would men risk their lives, their homes, for a jest? Would they fight, as the Duke's men fought, for a mere whimsey? 'Tis false to say they had no reason, nor grievance. When religion is endangered and when justice is o'erthrown men have grievance enow! You urge the King's justice," he continued with scorn. "We hear enow of the King's justice in these times from Exeter or from Dorchester. We shall watch it this week in Taunton an I mistake not. But for the Duke's men, 'tis unfair to speak of them as though they had been a band of rowdies. They were true men, gallant men, and I would I had been among them."

He stopped as suddenly as he had begun, crimsoned to the roots of his flaming hair, and glanced around him with a look of dogged recklessness, as of one who had said his say and cared nothing for what should befall him.

There had been a sudden astonished silence, all eyes fixed upon the lad who had dared thus to beard Master Lane at his own table.

The elders regarded him with horror, the younger apprentices with awe not untouched with a certain admiration. For Master Robert Wilcox's opinions were well known. It was also well known that he had intended to join the rebel army had he not been forcibly detained by his godfather, Master Lane, who at the first sign of rebellion had packed the fiery lad off to Portsmouth, where he had remained safe under the sharp eye of his uncle, a retired shipmaster, till the danger had passed. But despite the fact that Master Robert was a somewhat privileged person and, notwithstanding his turbulent spirit, a favourite with his godfather, that he should have dared to enter into public discussion with his master, and upon such a subject, passed the bounds of previous belief. All held their breath in expectation of the sharp reprimand which they knew must follow, and which was, indeed, hovering on Master Lane's lips, when he was once again interrupted, this time by a member of his own family, a traitor, so it seemed to him, on his very hearth.

The Lanes had two daughters. The elder, Deborah, was the image of her mother, a solemn, staid, and eminently practical maiden, not, indeed, without a certain love of excitement, but yet in most points a typical burgher maid. Of the younger girl, Prudence, 'twas a matter of constant wonder how such a madcap could spring from a family so grave, so unemotional, as were the Lanes. Pretty, spoiled, saucy, mischievous, she was the delight of her father; adventurous and romantic to a degree, she was the plague of her mother; and in every respect she was a constant alarm and puzzle to her duller-witted sister Deborah.

Now she chose to electrify her family by taking up the theme where Master Wilcox had left it. First casting a bright, approving glance in his direction, which caused that ardent youth to blush more crimson than before, she proceeded to expound her views upon the subject with a directness that amused the apprentices mightily and horrified her mother and sister.

"Rob is right, dad. 'Tis mighty unfair to speak thus of the Duke's men because they fell into the Bussex Rhine instead of winning the victory. For all the world knows they had won if—if they had not been defeated. For my part, I am for the Duke and for all who rode with him. And I think 'twas splendid of Sir Rupert," she added, with a bright glance at Lady Cicely, who could not resist a grateful smile in return, at her saucy defender.

Mistress Lane frowned sharply, but the merchant only shook his head indulgently at his spoiled daughter.

"What! here is a traitor indeed. Has my little Prue turned political?"

"Nay, dad, I care naught for politics, I only say 'tis finer to risk life and fortune and all for—for principles, whatever they be, than to sit year in and year out among ledgers and wool bales and to care nothing for country and church, but think only how to keep a whole skin and get money enow to live at ease and grow fat. 'Tis contemptible. Nay, daddie, I meant not you," she added penitently. "You have fought, I know well. I spake but of younger men who had as lief see their country go to rack and ruin as risk a crown of their wealth or a scratch to their finger to set it to rights."

She paused out of breath with her torrent of indignation. Her father laid his hand on hers tenderly and shook his head gravely at her words.

"Nay, Prudence, Robert, children both, you know nought of the matter. Perchance I spake unkindly of the rebels. I would not be unjust. But I am growing an old man, I have passed through one civil war, and I pray Heaven night and day that England may never see another. Had you been living as was I through those terrible years, had you seen the country devastated, families divided, brother against brother, aye, father even drawing sword upon his own son; homes ruined, wives widowed, children left fatherless through the whole length and breadth of the land—had you seen these things, my children, you would understand better why I speak thus harshly of those who raise the standard of rebellion within our fair realm. Men may use all just, all peaceful means of redressing their grievances, but should they fail, then, I say, 'twere better to endure those grievances, aye, even injustice, in silence, than bring the curse of civil war upon their country."

There was silence for a space. Then Prudence, whom no solemnity could long depress, again broke out merrily:

"For all that, daddie, the Duke's a main handsome man, and one worthy to be followed."

"Why, Prue?" exclaimed her sister teasingly, "methought you cared for none save brave men. How canst speak thus of such a proved coward?"

"The Duke is no coward," exclaimed Prue hotly. "They be but lying knaves who say otherwise. He is worthy to be followed and," with a saucy glance at her father, "when he comes again I'll follow him myself."

"When he comes again!" cried Deborah in blank astonishment. "La! child, where be thy wits? Dost not know he was beheaded on Tower Hill, two months since?"

"Aye, so they say in London," answered the little rebel scornfully. "But what should they know on't there? Here in the West 'tis known that the Duke escaped, and that 'twas his servant, dressed in his coat, and as like him as pea to pea, whom the soldiers took. He died in his master's place as would many another, and the Duke will return again to venge himself upon this bloody King."

Deborah stared in blank astonishment at the exposition of this astounding theory which, notwithstanding its extravagance, did not lack many believers other than the pretty Prudence. But Mistress Lane would endure no more, and interrupted her daughter sharply.

"Prudence, you give your tongue too much license, as I have told you oft. Go to your room and rest there till you be of a better mind. Nay, Thomas, 'tis for the child's own good; who can say what trouble may befall her if she will not curb that saucy spirit? To your room instantly, Prudence; three days with bread and water will tame you, let us hope, and let us hear no more of this nonsense."

Prudence rose slowly with pouting lips, and cast glances of entreaty in the direction of her father, who resolutely refused, however, to meet the eyes of the daughter whom as he knew too well he spoiled.

Robert Wilcox's countenance assumed terrible contortions in its endeavour to express at the same time admiration of Prue's bravery and indignation at Mistress Lane's severity, but he dared make no more outspoken remonstrance.

Prue saw no escape and was leaving the room to go to her imprisonment when Cicely intervened.

"Prithee, Mistress Lane," she pleaded gently, "forgive her. I make no doubt 'twas but consideration for me made her speak so rashly, she will be more careful hereafter. Nay, an you will forgive her, I will be her surety for the next three days that no word of folly pass her lips. You will grant me this, else shall I feel that I have brought dissension into your household, and that would grieve me indeed."

She pleaded gently, but urgently, and Mistress Lane could not refuse so honoured a guest. So Prudence was forgiven, after receiving a lecture upon the virtue of silence in the presence of her elders.

But so ardent were the looks of gratitude for her interference which Cicely received from the red-headed apprentice, that she learned at least one secret that evening, and intercepting a glance or two 'twixt him and the pretty Prudence, she suspected that she had learned yet another.

The Lanes were an early household, and when Cicely rose in the morning, having slept late after her journey of the previous day, she found they had long been about their duties of the day. Nor had her affairs been forgotten. Master Lane had been early to the prison to ascertain of Mistress Barbara's comfort, but discovered, to his chagrin, that admission was strictly forbidden.

He had next sought out the governor, hoping an exception might be made in favour of so staunch a Tory as himself, but the governor informed him, courteous-ly enough, that such a favour was impossible. Hitherto a visit to the prisoners had been an easy matter to compass, but in consequence of the escape of some of the prisoners who accompanied the train of the chief justice on the road to Exeter, an order had been issued that no access should be allowed to the prisoners on any pretext whatever. The governor expressed his regret at being obliged to refuse the request, but he could make no exceptions. He consented, however, to convey a hamper of fruits and other dainties to Mistress Winslow, and promised to do all in his power to promote her comfort.

So Master Lane was obliged to content himself by despatching a consignment of delicacies to relieve the ordinary prison fare, which, however, owing to the oc-cupation of the governor, busy with a thousand prisoners on his hands, and the venality of gaolers, never reached its destination.

It had been with a twinge of remorse that he had ascertained, amongst other details, that Barbara was confined in the very shed which he had himself lent to the government; still he had done his utmost to prove his interest in her cause and having brought Cicely news of his mission with a further promise to do what he could to influence the authorities in Barbara's behalf, he went to his work leaving her to pass the day as best she could.

Long and wearisome were the hours to the tender heart of Cicely as she sat over Mistress Lane's tambour frame, seeking by such occupation to drive from her mind the ever rising fear of what the morrow might bring.

Mistress Lane was busy about her household duties, Deborah helping her, but Prudence brought her work to the window-seat where Cicely had seated herself and soon her busy tongue broke through the thin veneer of shyness which she felt towards this lady, so beautiful, so unhappy, and in her eyes, so eminently interest-ing, and she was presently chattering busily, her work neglected on her lap.

Her eagerness and admiration banished Cicely's reserve, poor Cicely, so anx-ious for sympathy, and Prudence had soon learned the whole story of the betroth-al to Sir Rupert, of their last meeting, and of Barbara's daring escapade.

Prudence was charmed. 'Twas so romantic, so venturesome, so brave. She lis-tened eagerly to Cicely's description of her lover, of his reckless daring and his tenderness. With all the ready passion of an emotional nature she worshipped the heroine of so distressful a love-story and with the eagerness of a romantic child espoused her cause.

Cicely was grateful for this ready sympathy and the mutual confidence thus inspired induced her companion to tell her story too.

"Yes—'tis true, Robert saith he loves me, and though he be but a 'prentice, he is brave and—and splendid, and methinks I care for him also, though 'twould not do to let him know how dearly. He is not as the others. You marked him, per-chance, at supper yester e'en. How he spake his mind! He would be a soldier, an he had his way, he but bides here to please my father, and and——"

"Perchance to see thee at times?" questioned Cicely, smiling.

"It may be so," was the demure answer. "But he will not be a wool-merchant all his days, Lady Cicely. He means to be a great man, perchance to be in the Parliament; think on't, to rule the kingdom, and he could do it well, though I would not tell him so. But, indeed, I care not what he be, so that he love me truly," she added naïvely.

"And what saith Master Lane to this?"

"Oh, dad likes him well, I doubt not. But we have not thought fit to trouble him with the matter yet."

Cicely shook her head, but could not find it in her heart to be severe with such an outspoken admirer of Rupert. She won Prue's heart more completely still by her kindly wishes for the future, and a few commendatory remarks concerning Master Wilcox's appearance, and the younger girl's tongue once loosened on the subject she chattered busily until they were joined by Mistress Lane, who cast a severe glance at her daughter's neglected work.

The morning passed slowly away, but noon brought a visitor for Cicely in the person of Peter Drew, the smith. He had ridden that morning from Durford to offer his services to his ladies, and Cicely could not but rejoice to see his honest, friendly face, though she was conscious of the dangers of so sturdy a supporter of her family wandering unrestrained in the streets of Taunton, and doubtless speaking his mind to whomsoever he met. Indeed, a large bruise on his forehead and a certain dishevelled appearance about his garments, betokened that he had already met with a dissentient acquaintance.

Cicely questioned him closely on the subject and he reluctantly confessed that such had indeed been the case.

"'Twere but a mon at Inn where I left Black Beauty," he explained calmly. "Muzt needs ask my biznez, which I told un, arl vair and pleazant. But a muzt needz zay 'twere waizer to keep fra mixing wi' rebels and zuch laike, zo I told un my lady were no rebel. And a zaying it appeared her were, I gaäve un a tap on head to quiet un. But host and others, zo plaize your ladyship, coom at me thereupon wi' bezoms, whereat I knocked two flat, and others zhowing little ztomach to teäste my cudgel, I oop on Black Beauty and rid awai. 'Twere but a mizunderztanding, zee, and none hurt, but a zhould laive an honest mon to do her biznez in pace."

Though fain to laugh at the smith's bold narrative, Cicely saw clearly that she could not keep him in Taunton without hourly risk of the recurrence of such an episode. She therefore gently told him that, grateful though she was for his visit, he would yet serve her better by remaining quietly at Durford and helping Phoebe to look after the Manor House. And she prayed him return thither as speedily as possible, and remain there till she sent for his assistance.

Peter was terribly disappointed. He shook his head, sighed, moved restlessly in his seat. Then he rose and made a slow tour of the room, peering cautiously behind every curtain and under every article of furniture, and having ascertained to his satisfaction that he and Cicely were alone, he approached her with an air of deep mystery, and exclaimed in a loud whisper:

"An't plaize your ladyship, carn't her ezcaäpe."

"What, Peter!" exclaimed Cicely, astonished.

"Beggin' your ladyzhip's pardon, but 'twere last naight at the Royal Jaämes. A were there, a-talkin' o' Mistress Barbara i' gaol, and 'twere zaid, why couldn't her ezcaäpe? If it be but a matter o' boltz and barz, I be a zmith by traäde, and they be zoon broken. I would na interfere wi' king's justice i' the main, but vor Mistress Barbara, 'tiz but raight her be freed at once. And zo I be coom hither to do it."

"'Twas very kind of you, Peter," answered Cicely, repressing a smile; "but I fear it could not be done. You see there be sentinels guarding the prison. We could not elude them."

Peter's face fell; he scratched his head for some moments in dubious silence. Suddenly he slapped his leg in delight.

"A boggart!" he cried; "a boggart. 'Tis the very thing. I mind wull my vayther tull me that when a were clapped i' gaol over te Cannington vor—vor zome matter of stalin' a pig, brother skeered gaoler wi' a boggart and a coom awai. Now an thee wull be a boggart and skeer t'zentinels, I wull look to barz and boltz and Miztress Barbara will be vree by mud-naight."

Cicely gasped. She pictured herself dressed as a ghost, hopping about the streets of Taunton, a terror to the soldiery, while Peter in the meanwhile broke patiently thro' the bars that shut in Barbara from freedom. She broke into hysterical laughter. Peter was crestfallen at this reception of his plan.

"I zim to think of nought elze," he muttered disconsolately. "There be many weays o' ezcaäpe, Miztress Barbara herzell a told me, could I but bring un to maind. There have been zome as pazzed vor prizoners to let un ezcaäpe, but I could zcarce paz vor Mistress Barbara, and you, 'twere zmall good to vree her if your ladyship were left behaind. Then there be a taäl o' a mon let down i' a bazket, but I zee not raightly how to do that. And there be birds wi' paäpers under wings, and loaves o' bread wi' a rope inzaide. My waife could baäke one, if your ladyship thinks well on't. Tho' fai," he added doubtfully, "'twould need be a maighty big one."

But Cicely could not allow the loyal fellow further to tax his inventive powers, she knew it was indeed kinder at once to crush his hopes.

"No, Peter, it will not do. 'Tis true such plans have succeeded once, but they could little avail us now. We must wait. Wait till to-morrow, I doubt not she will then be freed. If she be not," she added with a sudden shudder, as the fear of the alternative rose in her breast, "why, Peter, if she be not, I will send for thee, and together we will free her somehow, tho' it cost us our lives."

Peter begged to be allowed to stay in Taunton till the morrow, but Cicely dared not risk it. She was firm in her resolution that he must return, and return at once, and at length he reluctantly departed, still mourning over his shattered dream of rescuing his beloved lady from her prison, and bearing her back to Durford in triumph, even as did the heroes of old whose deeds she so admired, and with stories of whom she had so often dazzled his bewildered brain.

The day passed, and as evening drew near, Cicely was seized with an irresistible fit of restlessness. This patient waiting was straining her nerves past endurance; she longed to be doing something, anything so it be definite action towards the release of her cousin. She could tolerate the quiet house no longer, she must out.

Hearing that the lord chief justice and his suite were to enter the town that evening, she expressed her intention of going into the streets to see them pass. She longed to see this man of whom she had heard so much, the man upon whose lips hung the fate of her cousin, the fate of the thousand prisoners who lay that evening in the city awaiting their trial.

Mistress Lane opposed the wish, but Cicely was resolved; she was obstinate, even irritable, in combating the good lady's arguments against such a course. She scarce understood herself this eagerness to see the judge's entry, she only knew that she must go out, must be interested, distracted, or she should go mad with the thoughts she could not banish from her brain.

So Mistress Lane left her to go her way, and allowed Prudence to accompany her, tho' 'twas with many misgivings that she watched them set out.

The two girls went their way and took up their position in the East street.

The streets were very full, many people having come out to see the entry of the judges. Groups stood at the corners, gravely discussing the impending trial, men and women wandered aimlessly up and down waiting—waiting, they knew not for what. Everywhere was a spirit of restlessness, of suspense, and over all hung the great hush of expectation. Men spake for the most part in subdued voices, nowhere sounded the customary cries and cheerful noises of the streets. There were few outward tokens of grief; sorrow and anxiety had so long oppressed the people they had grown accustomed to their burden.

To-night, however, the thought of the dark morrow looming threateningly before their sight had driven them out into the streets to wander restlessly to and fro seeking to escape from that fear which would not be shaken off, but followed ever behind them, whispering in the ear its dread suggestions. The spirit of that terrible tribunal moved on before; already the shadow of its presence darkened their hearts.

As they waited in the East street, acquaintances of Prudence passed the girls, but none stopped to speak. Despite their kindness of heart the Lanes were not popular with their fellow-townsmen, who, perhaps naturally, felt suspicious of this prosperous Tory merchant.

Presently Robert Wilcox approached and encouraged by a smile from Cicely he joined them, and the three strolled up and down the street together.

A sense of loneliness oppressed Cicely as she watched the covert glances and whispers of the lovers. She tried to forget her own sorrows, tried not to listen to the dismal conversations of the passers by, but in vain. She could not escape from her thoughts, could not dismiss from her mind that dreaded verdict, heard on the lips, written on the faces of all around her, "There is no hope."

But at length a roll of kettle-drums announced the approach of the judges; and as the procession turned into East street, everyone paused instinctively to watch it pass.

Dragoons, halberdiers, and carriages all went slowly past, and last of all came the great coach of the Chief Justice, Lord Jeffreys himself reclining carelessly on his cushions within.

Cicely leaned forward eagerly to gaze at the man of whom she had heard so much, and gave an exclamation of astonishment when her eyes rested on his face. Where was the brutal, the ferocious judge of whom so many terrible rumours had reached her ears? Where was that monster of cruelty at whose name even the rough soldiers trembled? Surely not here. This man so wonderfully handsome, this man with the lofty brow, the noble expression, the sad, weary eyes, this could not be the terrible Jeffreys. Yet if it were indeed he, if it were— — Why surely then— — Her heart leaped high with hope. Surely then these stories must be false, base calumnies of the rebels even such as those which were told of Duke Monmouth by the supporters of the King.

And then a confusion at the street corner, a trooper's horse down upon the cobbles, caused the procession to halt, the coach of the chief justice was stationary but two yards from where she stood.

With a sudden wild impulse, born of new hope in her breast, Cicely darted into the roadway, pushing to right and left the astonished men, who would have barred her passage: darted quickly to the side of the coach and laid her hand on the shoulder of Lord Jeffreys as he reclined among his scarlet cushions.

"Mercy, my lord, mercy for my cousin," she cried, scarce knowing what she did.

The occupant of the coach started from his reverie and turned to her, bewildered for the moment at the suddenness of her address. He had, in truth, been almost asleep, worn out with his painful journey over the rough country roads.

"What is it, woman? What did you say?" he snarled sharply.

"Mercy, my lord, I entreat," she gasped nervously. "'Tis for one of the prisoners, my cousin, Mistress Barbara Winslow. She is indeed innocent enough, and, oh! my lord, she is so young."

The judge gave a sudden harsh laugh, a laugh so full of needless cruelty that Cicely shuddered. She looked in his face and shrank back in dread, wondering could this be indeed the same man whose noble expression had so melted her, he was on a sudden so hideously transformed. All the ferocity of his violent nature, all the brutality of a pitiless heart were stamped upon his features. He was, indeed, at that moment, suffering acutely from the effects of his journey, and his mind, at no time tending greatly towards mercy and tenderness, was now warped and disfigured by weakness and pain into a very hell of cruelty.

"Mercy!" he jeered. "Mercy! Nay, there shall be no mercy. They shall all suffer, not one shall escape, not one. I will exterminate them all. Verily, I will make an example of these turbulent townsfolk, I will teach them a lesson they shall not soon forget. Mercy, aye, they shall have mercy, even such mercy as they have deserved. A merciful death."

"Ah, no, my lord! But for this girl," pleaded Cicely; desperately, "surely for her."

"Drive on," shouted Jeffreys fiercely. Then seeing the coachman hesitate and glance doubtfully at Cicely, who clung to the coach door, he rapped out a string of oaths and roared to the man to whip up his horses and proceed.

The coach moved on.

But Cicely, desperate, still clung to the door of the coach, sobbing out her appeal.

"Ah, no, my lord! on this one at least have pity. No no, not death, my lord, not death."

Then the chief justice, livid with fury, rose in his coach, and shouted to his coachman to lash at her with his whip, and drive her away. Terrified, the man obeyed, striking at her blindly. The lash stung across her hands and with a sharp cry she sank on to her knees on the road as the coach rolled onwards, Jeffreys lying back shuddering on his pillows, his face livid with agony, but the bitter smile still upon his lips.

CHAPTER XII

The morning of the 16th broke bright and fresh from the thin September mists. The sunbeams shot across the rosy sky, and sparkled in the clear dewdrops, the late roses raised their glowing heads to meet the light, and the birds in the woods chorused joyously their Autumn serenade. But in the City of Taunton the morning light revealed the grey and careworn faces of many who, hoping little from the morrow, had watched throughout the night in an anguish of doubt and suspense, and a passion of hopeless prayer. Be the morning sunbeams never so bright, they could not dispel the darkness of that day for Taunton.

The sun climbed over the roofs, and peered into the high windows of the prisons, where the captives roused themselves and prepared to stand their trial.

The newly wedded bride lay sleeping in the arms of her husband, who for many hours had watched in silence, till the pale grey dawn had stolen into the wool-shed, to light the face he loved. She had fallen asleep in the happiness of the present, but when she awoke and looked into his face she knew that the dream had passed, and stern reality was before them. She sat up with a start, gazed despairingly around her, then turned again to meet the hopeless glance of the eyes that yesterday had looked but love. With a deep sob of bitterness she flung her arms around him, and buried her face on his shoulder; for now it seemed that the angel of doom stood at the gate of their Eden to drive them forth into the outer darkness, where each must wander alone. And he had no comfort for her pain.

Barbara was ever strangely susceptible to the influence of sunshine. The depression of the previous night had moderated and her spirits danced lightly as the flickering sunbeams. The freshness of the morning was in her glance and she looked as much out of place in those gloomy surroundings as a delicate wild rose dropped in the mire of a city street. Her cheerful spirits were infectious, the men warmed at sight of her bright glances, and for a moment a sense of happiness gleamed faintly in their hearts.

But not for long. The shadow of the king of terrors lay too heavy to be effaced. The gleam of light grew fainter and more distant, until it vanished in the dark mists of grim reality.

The sitting of the court was postponed till noon, owing to the indisposition of the chief justice, but when the trial at length opened, the work went busily forward. These first days of the Assize were devoted to the trial of the more notable prisoners, the bulk of the peasants taken at, or soon after Sedgemoor fight, being reserved for trial in batches of from fifty to a hundred, later in the week.

One of the first to be called was Mistress Mary Dale, the poor young bride. The lovers parted in silence, all eternity in their glance. When she was summoned from the prison he took up his station by the door, to await her return. He waited in vain. In her case—the one instance perhaps in which it was unsolicited—mercy was shown. Her fine was paid and she was free, free to go whither she would, save only back to the prison where she had left her heart. Free, when freedom was banishment, alive when life had nothing to offer save utter loneliness.

Throughout the day the dreary exodus of the prisoners continued. For some there was no return, punishment following close upon conviction, others returned calm and quiet in the certain expectation of death on the morrow, or of that yet more terrible death in life which lay in the sentence of banishment to the Plantations.

The pathos of the scene struck Barbara deeply, and the sense of her helplessness in sight of injustice and wrong awoke in her a state of subdued fury.

But she had her work to do. The morning had brought new terror to the heart of the delicate child, Katherine Keene, and strive as Barbara would, by all means in her power, to soothe and cheer the terrified girl, her panic but increased as the day drew on, and when at last she and her sister were summoned before the court, she clung passionately to her protectress, sobbing in a very frenzy of terror, imploring her not to allow them to take her away.

Even Barbara's firmness gave way under the strain, she wept out of pure pity for a terror which as yet she could not comprehend.

"Brutes!" she muttered between her clenched teeth, when at last the terrified children were marched away. "Brutes! devils! Can they not see the child is half demented. Ah, were I but king for one day, I would teach them a lesson they should not forget."

But later in the day, when a compassionate gaoler brought her news of the children's fate, her indignation rose to fury. For Judge Jeffreys, recognising in the panic-stricken girls a fit object for an exhibition of his fiercest passion, had so bullied and tormented them, so raged, so sworn, so threatened them, that the delicate Katherine could endure no more. Scarcely had she reached the door of the court house, after her trial, when she fell fainting to the ground, and an hour later died from sheer excess of terror. Her younger sister was freed indeed, after payment of a heavy fine, but she never recovered from the shock and fear of that day. Thus suffered these innocents whose sole offence had been in the embroidering of a banner for the Duke of Monmouth, under the direction of their school-mistress.

Barbara having no longer an object on which to lavish her protecting tenderness, there remained nothing for her to do save to sit in idleness, watching that silent procession of prisoners passing ever through the prison door, while the heart within her breast burned and raged with impotent fury.

The day passed slowly on, and at length, towards six o'clock in the evening, the summons came for Mistress Barbara Winslow to attend court. She was the last prisoner for trial that day.

Barbara rose to her feet with alacrity on hearing her name, and throwing on her cloak, made haste to follow her guards. Here at length was something to be done, some change from impotent watching and waiting. Now, at length, she was to meet face to face with these tyrant judges, to whom she might at least speak her thoughts. All concern for her own case, her own danger, had fled, prudence had no place in her thoughts, her mind was filled with a wild hatred of the perpetrators of this barbarous cruelty, with a mad desire to fling defiance at their threats, and to cry aloud to their faces what she, Barbara Winslow, thought of their sentences.

Escorted by a file of soldiers she was marched rapidly across the market-square and into the court house. There was no great concourse of people in the streets. The majority of the townsfolk sympathised with the prisoners, but dared not openly show their sympathy lest they, too, be accounted rebels; they deemed it more prudent, therefore, to remain quietly within doors, while such as sought merely to derive sensational amusement from the trial had found places within the crowded court.

While Barbara waited in the hall outside the chamber where the court was sitting, a prisoner passed her, hurried along between his guards. He was a young man scarcely twenty years of age, slenderly built, with delicate handsome features, but the look on his face made the girl start back with an exclamation of horror.

"In Heaven's name, what hath befallen him? Who is he?" she gasped.

"'Tis young Master Tutchin," answered one of her guards carelessly. "A hard sentence, for sure, 'tis scarce likely he will live to see the end o't."

"What is it?" questioned Barbara in horror.

"To be imprisoned seven years, and once a year to be flogged through every market town of Dorset, which by calculation should be a flogging twice a month. Aye, aye, 'tis a hard sentence," he continued, meeting her glance; "but what would you? He is a proved rebel."

"Oh! that such devils of judges should go unpunished," was Barbara's fierce rejoinder. It was with a heart burning with rage that she entered the court.

And yet, so strange and uncontrollable are the feelings of women that her first thought, when she found herself face to face with the dreaded chief justice, was one of astonishment and pity.

She had expected, like Cicely on the previous evening, to behold a coarse, brutal ruffian, ferocity and hatred stamped on every feature. When, in place of such a creature, she beheld the handsome face and noble bearing of her judge, she gave a gasp of surprise. Pity also filled her heart, for his eyes were half closed, and there were traces of suffering on his face, as he lay back in his chair with an air of extreme exhaustion. The terrible malady to which he was a victim tortured him, and the long day in court had tried him severely; but no amount of physical suffering could overcome the iron will, or prevent him even for a day from pursuing that strange course of relentless cruelty which he had elected to follow.

When Barbara took her place in the dock he roused himself with an effort, and looked at her with a sharp piercing glance.

"What!" he exclaimed. "Yet another of these women rebels. Are we never to have an end of them? Can they not find mischief enow to do in their own homes, but they must needs interfere in affairs of state? What is the prisoner's name?"

"Mistress Barbara Winslow, my lord."

"Winslow! Winslow!"

"Aye, my lord," answered one of the crown lawyers. "Her brother followed the rebel duke, but through her connivance, so it is submitted, he hath escaped the country."

"Ah, ha! so she comes of a fine rebel stock, eh?"

The several counts in the indictment were furnished by Barbara's participation in the escape of Sir Peter Dare, her interference with the whipping of the boy at Durford, and other incidents of a trifling character in themselves, but of which the prosecuting counsel did not fail to take full advantage. The first witness called Corporal Crutch, who took no pains to conceal his malignant satisfaction in prejudicing the chances of the prisoner by every means in his power. Barbara's pride, and her contempt for the man forbade her to question the corporal's evidence, even though she was urged to do so by Sir William Montague, the chief baron of the court; and after corroboration of the corporal's story by other troopers the case for the crown being closed, Barbara was asked whether she had anything to say in her defence before the jury considered their verdict and the court pronounced sentence.

"So please you, my lords," answered Barbara, ignoring Jeffreys pointedly, and addressing herself to the three judges who sat with him, "that I am a traitor I deny utterly. As for the stories these men tell of me, why, they are true enough I must admit. But what then? I did but give food and assistance to those in dire distress and misery, I did no more than we are e'en commanded in the Gospels."

"The Gospels! The Gospels!" interrupted Jeffreys scornfully.

"Aye, my lord," answered Barbara, turning on him sharply. "The Gospels. In which books methinks your lordship hath made but scant study."

Judge Jeffreys started forward, and stared at her in astonishment, then his face grew purple and distorted with fury, and his eyes gleamed horribly as he broke into a fierce tirade.

"What! What! I am to be browbeaten, contradicted in my own court, am I? What! You shall learn that the majesty of the law, the representative of our gracious sovereign is not to be thus lightly answered. Gospels, forsooth! 'Tis ever the same excuse, the same prating of Gospels and conscience and I know not what. Is this yet another of these pestilent dissenters? Do these wretched creatures deem they may rebel with impunity against his gracious Majesty, can plot and scheme against such a loving, such a merciful, king, and then shelter themselves behind such a babble of Gospels and conscience. Faugh! 'Tis monstrous. 'Tis beyond endurance! The prisoner pleads guilty to the charges brought against her but appeals to the Gospels for evidence in her favour, eh? 'Tis but little evidence she will find there in justification of rebellion."

Barbara's anger had risen during the foregoing scene, and was now beyond her control. Twice she had endeavoured to interrupt the judge's comments, and now when at length he paused, she burst forth in almost as great a frenzy as the judge himself.

"And I must needs say this much more—not indeed in mine own cause, for that I care nothing, but rather in the cause of the many poor wretches whom ye have to-day tortured and slain, of the ignorant and helpless peasants whom ye have condemned without fair hearing, of the delicate women whom ye have threatened, of the innocent children whom ye have terrified even to death. Nay, I will *not* be silent, I *must* speak. Ye who are judges, what judgments are these wherein is neither truth nor mercy? Ye prate of the law, what law is this that knows no justice? Ye speak of his Majesty. Oh! an ye be in truth the representatives of his Majesty, the workers of his will, then do I say he is no true king, and 'twould be a good day indeed for England were such a king overthrown."

She ceased speaking. She had said her say, she had poured forth all the pent-up fury of her thoughts, she had defied the judge to his face, and in the dead silence that followed her words, the first grip of terror at what she had said clutched at her heart.

The court gasped in horrified amazement, but the face of Judge Jeffreys was terrible to behold. Always strangely, morbidly sensitive to opposition, or to rebuke from whatever source, the judge lost all control over himself. His eyes seemed starting from his head and glared horribly; his face grew purple and swollen, his lips were drawn back in a fierce snarl. He ground his teeth, and rolled from side to side in his chair, partly in rage and partly in the agony which such rage caused him. His unrestrained fury was horrible to witness. It was as though some fit were upon him, and Barbara shrank involuntarily at the sight of such appalling ferocity. At length he regained some measure of his self-control.

"What! Heaven help us," he exclaimed. "Why, this is the very incarnation of rebellion, a very headspring and source of treason. Oh! that such a woman, so young, should be so far gone in iniquity. Beware, madame, beware! I see death standing beside thee——"

"Then, my lord, I doubt not 'tis an infinitely preferable vision to that which mine eyes behold," she answered, staring full at him, and goaded into recklessness by an awakening sense of her own danger.

For an instant it seemed as if the judge would give way to another paroxysm of rage, but he restrained himself with a supreme effort, and with a calmness that boded even worse for the prisoner than his former fury he turned to the jury and continued:

"What say you, sirs? Methinks you can find but one answer as to the prisoner's guilt."

But Barbara's youth, beauty and courage had not been without effect upon the minds of the jury. Slavish time-servers though they were, they could not without protest see condemnation passed upon a young girl whose only real offence lay in a too-unrestrained tongue. This feeling was readily apparent to the practised eye of the judge and lest it should serve to balk his purpose he added: "The prisoner is young it is true, but what of that? Rebellion must be crushed in the bud, must be slain in the shell or 'twill grow to a most pernicious monster. Come, what is the verdict? Do you find the prisoner guilty or no? Beware, gentlemen, how ye condone guilt; lend no cloak to protect treason."

The jury, thus admonished, held out no longer. They found the prisoner guilty, but salved their consciences by commending her to mercy.

But ere the chief justice pronounced sentence, a protest came from an unexpected quarter on Barbara's behalf. Sir William Montague, leaning forward in his seat, addressed the judge in low earnest tones which could not fail to arrest his attention.

"My lord, I anticipate what sentence you purpose to pronounce upon the prisoner, even such an one as was passed upon the late Lady Lisle. But bethink you, my lord, the cases are very different. For Lady Alice Lisle was the widow of a noted rebel, she was advanced in years; both her age and her experience should have warned her of the full significance of the offence she committed. Moreover, my lord, there are those who consider that even in her case, the sentence erred in severity. But this is but a girl, too young indeed to realise the criminality of her actions. She hath pleaded guilty it is true, but thereby has thrown herself upon the mercy of the court. That she hath incurred the penalty of the law by sheltering rebels, 'twere idle to deny, but she did so from motives of humanity, and in no way from a desire to further the cause of rebellion. For the rest, my lord, you cannot condemn the prisoner because she hath, as indeed what woman hath not, an over-free tongue, and hath on this occasion, it must be confessed, used it most ill-advisedly. Further, I would remind your lordship," he added in a meaning tone, "that there be occasions when to show mercy is not only a divine action, but also an expedient one."

Lord Jeffreys sat for some moments in silence, gazing sullenly at the prisoner. The words of the chief baron had not been without their effect. He knew well what universal indignation his condemnation of Lady Lisle had aroused, and he judged that in face of the interest the affair had excited in high quarters, to pass another such severe sentence upon a woman were not politic. For however much the orders of the King might demand seventy, Jeffreys knew well that his master was not one to screen his servants from the general opprobrium attendant upon the committal of an unpopular act, even were that act the outcome of his express commands.

Meanwhile a deep hush of expectation had fallen upon the court while the judges had conferred together, broken at length by the harsh tones of the chief justice.

"Mistress Barbara Winslow, you have been found guilty of the crime of harbouring rebels, and of interference with the lawful actions of the agents of his Majesty, the King. Yet as the tender heart of his Majesty, our most gracious sovereign, doth ever incline to pity and leniency, you shall, in consideration of your youth, meet with a mercy you have in no wise deserved." Here he paused and scowled vindictively upon Barbara.

"The sentence of the court is that you shall be imprisoned for the space of two years in the common gaol of this city. Furthermore, ye shall to-morrow, and once every month in the two years of your imprisonment, be scourged publicly by the common hangman, in the open market-place. By this discipline it may be that the hardness of your heart shall be melted, and you shall recognise the power of that justice which you have dared to condemn."

A shudder of horror went round the court at the pronouncement of this brutal sentence; but Barbara controlled herself; indeed, she did not yet fully realise what had befallen her.

She raised her head defiantly and returned the judge's glance of triumph with a calm smile.

"Farewell, my Lord Jeffreys," she cried, "and may God prosper you as you deserve."

She walked proudly from the chamber and still scarce realising the horror of her sentence, she passed from the court house, surrounded by her guards, and emerged into the street.

In the centre of the market-place stood a crowd of loafers, rough fellows, and troopers of Kirke's horse, to whom, however, she gave but little heed. But as she was being escorted by the outskirts of the crowd, a sudden sharp cry rent the air, followed by horrible shrieks of pain. The crowd parted for an instant, and she beheld a woman, one of the peasant-women who had shared her sleeping-room the previous night, bound to the whipping-post, her back bare, and streaming with blood, her face distorted with suffering. Then the shrieks were smothered in a shout of coarse laughter from the troopers, the crowd closed round the scene, and her guards hurried her forward.

It was but the glimpse of an instant, but in that instant Barbara realised her own doom; it was as though she had beheld a vision of her own fate, and at length she understood.

She reached the shed, still to be her temporary prison, giddy with horror, the shrieks of the woman still resounding in her ears, and worse than these, that sickening shout of brutal laughter which made her blush and tingle with shame as she pictured the coarse jest that had doubtless given rise to the merriment.

With clenched teeth and drawn face, she hurried into the shed, struggling to master this fear which clutched her heart. She knew that she must not think of it. She must talk, work, do anything, anything; but think of it she dared not. But, alas! what else remained for her. The company in the shed was reduced to a few stolid peasants, who could not have comprehended her fears, and some half-dozen rough soldiers, mercenaries in Monmouth's army, who sought to while away the hours and drown their cares with dice and drink procured, no doubt, by the corruption of an indulgent sentry.

All her friends of the previous day had been removed. The only other female occupant of the shed was the strange old woman, the fanatic, who, when the girl timidly approached her, gazed upon her with unseeing eyes and continued to mutter and gabble her tests.

Nowhere was there comfort for Barbara; she was utterly alone. In vain she strode about the shed, tried to fix her mind upon the past, upon the traditions of her family, upon the boasted courage of the Winslows. In vain she repeated verses, recalled stories, anything to distract her mind, she could not control her thoughts, could not drive the face of the tortured woman from before her eyes, nor banish from her ears the terror of her cries.

It was now dark and her nerves were overstrung, worn out completely with the excitement of what she had passed through. The thing had come upon her so unexpectedly she had no resistance to offer, and now in the silence and loneliness of the night the full horror of the future gradually dawned upon her mind. She pictured with all the vividness of a strong imagination every detail of the life before her; death itself seemed easier to face than this nightmare of shame and torture. She sobbed with terror. Fear took possession of her soul, and she suffered as only those of strong will and high courage can suffer in their moments of weakness.

CHAPTER XIII

Lady Cicely, who was overcome with the effects of her encounter with Jeffreys and the attendant incidents of the previous evening, had not the courage to attend the sitting of the court, although Master Lane had ascertained that her cousin's trial might be expected to take place during the day. She sat hour by hour in the quiet house waiting for her host to bring her news of the verdict.

Prudence was unusually silent and depressed. She had been severely blamed by her mother for her share in the expedition of the previous evening; moreover, the sight of her friend's misery sobered her into a quite unwonted gravity. Deborah, on the contrary, passed the day in a state of hysterical excitement. Like so many otherwise kind-hearted women she possessed in a large degree that morbid love of horrors, which is erroneously considered to be an attribute of the uneducated classes alone.

At intervals during that terrible day, she darted in with some fresh tale of misery, culled from the gossip of the neighbours or the chatter of the maids. She poured forth these stories with an air of eager excitement, nay, more, of intense enjoyment, ill-concealed beneath a grave head-shaking and copious exclamations of pity and horror.

"They have built up a scaffold in the market-place," she announced rapturously. "Oh! 'tis terrible to see it. Martha Hemming saith she could not sleep for the sound of the hammering, and thinking of all the poor creatures to be hanged there. 'Tis said they mostly go straight from their trial to be hanged. Think on't. They may be hanging now, the poor fellows. 'Tis said, down Dorchester way, the judges sent three hundred to be hanged, and my Lord Jeffreys hath said it will not be his fault if he doth not depopulate this place. 'Tis terrible. 'Tis as it was in July. Dost mind it, Prudence, after the fight at Sedgemoor, when Colonel Kirke first came here? They hanged them on the signpost of the Inn. Oh! 'twas too horrible. Joan Marlow saw it. 'Twas said that one wretch was strung up and cut down again four times ere he died. Think on't. And the troopers jesting at him the while. 'Twas a fearsome time! I doubt not 'twill be yet more dreadful now. 'Tis a wonder such things should be. One can but pity them though they be rebels."

So she rattled on, while Cicely sat by shuddering with horror.

Later in the day Deborah became still more profuse and detailed in her narratives.

"They say my Lord Jeffreys is fair raging. Some say he is mad or drunk, for he laughs and jests, and then again bellows with fury. What a man it is! But, oh!

Prudence, I had nigh forgot. Philip Harke is hanged. Straight from court they took him, hanged him till he was well-nigh spent, then cut him down and quartered him. The horror of it! And none dare tell his wife; but she was out ere they knew, and saw his head on a pole in High Street, and has turned silly, they say. And small wonder too; I shall not dare to walk the streets for a month. Praise be to God we have no friends among them, saving, of course, your cousin, Lady Cicely, yet 'tis terrible to see the heads and corpses. And the market-place must be a shambles, they say."

"Peace, peace, Deb. 'Tis too horrible."

"Aye, is't not indeed so? They say there be a thousand prisoners, all told. Yet belike 'twill not be death to all, though his lordship has vowed to show no mercy. And the women; there be many among the victims. 'Tis truly awful. Mistress Brown from over by Lyme, I know not rightly of what she is accused, yet I think 'tis but a matter of some rash words, as that she would pay the excise dues to King Monmouth, or some such folly, but she is condemned to be scourged through every market-place in the country. And they say she as like not to be the only one to meet with such a sentence. But to think on't.—A woman—and but for a rash tongue. Why, who is safe? To be scourged! Oh! 'tis brutal."

"Child! Child! Will you drive me mad?" cried Cicely, unable to endure more. "Be silent."

Deborah stared at her in amazement.

"Indeed, I am sorry I have offended your ladyship," she murmured somewhat sulkily; "though I see not how. 'Tis but natural to feel pity for such misery, though they be but rebels and doubtless deserving of their fate. Yet 'tis horrible for all that. Martha Hemming saith she had seen——"

"Be silent, girl, I will hear no more," cried Cicely, springing to her feet in desperation.

And then she stopped, and her heart leaped in terror, for she heard in the hallway without the voice of Master Lane, calling to his wife, and she divined by his tone that the news he brought was ill.

She went out calmly to meet him.

"Prithee, tell me, sir, tell me all," she asked in a strange, quiet voice.

Master Lane started at sight of her. He hesitated, looking for his wife to come to his aid. Then, meeting the agonised look in her eyes he paused no longer, but stepped forward to take her hand between his own, and told her gently, tenderly, the terrible sentence passed upon her cousin.

"Even now I know not truly how it befell," he continued sadly. "The poor child was overwrought. She bandied words with the chief justice, she defied him. He is not a man to brook defiance, and he revenged himself. But 'tis not likely they will carry out their sentence. Money can do much, influence more. We will talk it over together. Perchance you might go to London, 'tis not to be doubted but his Majesty will have pity upon her youth. You must see the Queen; she will surely show mercy to a woman. I will do what I can to work upon my Lord Jeffreys; I have friends who have some influence over his lordship, and they say money can do much; I doubt not she shall soon be pardoned. Come, my child, we must be brave; we must not despair."

He patted her hand kindly, full of pity for her misery. Cicely listened to all in a strange apathy.

"No," she muttered dully, "no, we must not despair, not despair."

Then she turned from him slowly and mounted the stairs to her room in perfect silence.

Master Lane looked after her anxiously.

"Poor thing! Poor thing!" he muttered, his eyes glistening with tears. "'Tis hard indeed for her. Very hard."

Then he turned to find his wife, feeling his helplessness in the face of this strange, silent misery, and seeking to ease his mind of the burden of a sorrow he could neither grapple with nor relieve.

Cicely paced her room dry-eyed, trembling, striving to realise this horror which had befallen them, striving to picture the execution of such a sentence upon her tender, beautiful young cousin. She could not do so. She repeated the words of the sentence again and again till they jangled through her brain, yet she could not believe it, she remained unmoved.

Then suddenly there flashed across her mind the question: "How shall I face Rupert and tell him this?"

And on the instant her strange apathy vanished, on the instant she understood the full horror of the sentence.

Oh! how could she face Rupert? Rupert whose love for his sister and whose pride in that sister had almost excited her jealousy; Rupert, whose last words to herself had been: "Take care of Barbara, and keep her out of mischief." How could she face him, see the love and trust in his eyes, the bright, brave smile upon his lips, and tell him that Barbara had suffered shame, imprisonment, torture, and she had done nothing, nothing to save her? No! rather let her die than face her lover with that tale upon her lips.

She flung herself upon her bed in a passion of weeping.

But what could she do? The Winslows were not rich, she had little money to offer these brutal judges, if indeed a reprieve were to be bought. She had few relations, their influence at court was but small. It would take much time even to gain access to the King, and in the meanwhile— —she shuddered at the thought.

She had made one appeal to the chief justice, alas! how vain an one; even yet the remembrance of it filled her with terror. She could not, dared not again face that terrible man, again kneel to him for mercy.

Aye, but for Barbara? for Rupert? Truly for their sakes she would do even this. But the hopelessness of the attempt, the impossibility of moving, by an appeal of hers, that pitiless heart! The conviction of it crushed her brain.

And yet, surely, there must be one influence to move him, one road to his favour. Surely, no man living can be absolutely immovable, absolutely indifferent. Ah! could she but discover the key to his mercy how eagerly would she sacrifice all to win it!

She opened her window, and leaned her hot temples against the casement, breathing the cool evening air. Two men passed in the street below, discussing gravely the events of the trial. Their words floated up to her on the breeze. She caught the name of the lord chief justice.

"Ah!" said one, "the only sure road to his favour is by the informing of a rebel. He hath been known to extend a pardon, if he may thereby gain information of a more profitable victim. He is drunk with blood, and crazy for gold."

They passed on, their footsteps echoing down the empty street.

"The only sure road to his favour is by the informing of a rebel."

The words rang in her ears, repeated again and again.

So therein lay the secret to win him.

Well, and surely that were easy. Did she not know of many a rebel, in hiding near her own village of Durford? It needed but a word to unearth them all.

"But it must be a more profitable victim," not a poor peasant who could pay no penalty save death.

Well, and could she not supply that information also? While Captain Protheroe went free, was there not a rebel to be apprehended, a rebel or protector of rebels, surely much the same? For had he not himself confessed to Barbara that he had connived at Rupert's escape, though knowing well his hiding place? That surely was enough to hang a man, and a man indeed deserving to be hanged, seeing 'twas undoubtedly he who had betrayed Barbara!

Ah! what was this horrible temptation seizing upon her? She shuddered at the power of it. To betray a man to his death, a man, moreover, who had protected Rupert! She could not—she could not. There was dishonour in the very thought. A Winslow a traitor! traitor to the hand that helped him!

"Oh, God!" she wailed, "what can I do? And how shall I live if I do it?"

And yet that Captain Protheroe had betrayed Barbara in the end, she firmly believed. And Barbara had risked so much for Rupert's sake, and Barbara was in danger, and must be saved. What mattered it then though she, Cicely, were guilty of this treachery, at the despicable thought of which she shuddered? The shame would lie hidden in her own heart, the loss of self-respect would be hers alone to bear, the matter would lie between herself and her conscience. Barbara would be saved, and what was her own peace of mind compared with the life of Rupert's sister?

Impulsively she donned her hat and cloak. She dared not pause lest her resolution should fail her, lest her terror of the man to whom she was going should sap her resolve, or her horror of the treachery weaken her determination.

She descended the stairs softly, unobserved. The house was very silent.

But at the door she encountered Prudence, who hurried forward eagerly to know whither she was bound.

"Do not stop me, Prue," she answered in a strange, cold voice. "I am going to the White Hart Inn."

"To the White Hart! Not, surely, to see— —"

"Yes, to see my Lord Jeffreys. I have— —I have information to give him."

"But Lady Cicely, you cannot go alone. 'Tis impossible. Wait at least till dad can bear you company. Nay, you must, indeed."

Cicely put her aside firmly.

"No, Prue, I cannot wait. That which I have to do I must do at once, or perchance 'twill never be accomplished. Leave me to go my way."

She passed out into the street. Prudence stared after her in hesitation. Despite her youth, her quick burgher-wit taught her, far more clearly than Cicely, the dangers of such an errand undertaken alone. She knew, far better than did the elder girl, with her sheltered life and breeding, the nature of such men as bore the chief justice company in his nightly carouses at the White Hart Inn.

"No, no," she muttered. "She cannot go alone, alone among those devils."

Quickly she snatched up hood and cloak and followed Cicely into the quiet street.

Cicely scarce noted the presence of her companion. She hurried forward rapidly through the half-deserted streets, looking neither to right nor left, heedless of those terrible signs of butchery which greeted them at every corner, and at sight of which Prudence shrank and shuddered with horror.

At the inn the chief justice sat at supper with the circle of boon-companions whom he had collected from among the followers of his circuit.

At the door of the inn a sentry barred the girl's entrance, and to Cicely's request for audience with the lord chief justice, his reply was that the business must wait, seeing that his lordship was at dinner.

In vain Cicely pleaded for an interview however brief, in vain she protested that her business was urgent, her information of the utmost importance, even in vain she offered him money, the man was obdurate.

From the row of open windows above came the clink of glasses, the murmur of men's voices, at times a loud burst of laughter. Cicely glanced from the unmoved face of the sentry up to the open windows of the room in which was the man she sought. She had carried her resolution so far, she could not endure the thought of failure now.

As she glanced upward an officer lounged into view at one of the windows and stared carelessly down on the group below.

"By Mahomet!" he exclaimed. "A petticoat. Two, i' faith, and main pretty baggages into the bargain."

He turned and said something to his comrades, and the jest was greeted by a burst of coarse laughter.

Other men crowded to the windows and stared down curiously at the two girls, and as the first speaker turned away, the babble of voices in the room grew, louder.

Presently the officer appeared in the doorway of the inn, and with a bow of mock politeness requested the ladies to honour him by placing their difficulties in his hands, and telling him the nature of their business with the lord chief justice.

Shrinking involuntarily before the bold appraising looks with which the man surveyed her face and figure, Cicely nevertheless answered bravely enough that she possessed certain information concerning a rebel, but could confide her knowledge to none save Lord Jeffreys himself.

"'Tis not his lordship's custom to deal with any business at so late an hour," answered the officer. "Yet a request from those fair lips can never go ungranted, so, an you will permit me, I will act as your advocate, and plead with him for an interview. He would scarce refuse, did he know what a pleasure his consent would afford him."

He led the girls into the inn, and with another low bow, and a last critical survey left them in the passage and mounted to the room above with his report.

Evidently the report gave complete satisfaction. It was received with roars of laughter and a burst of eager questioning, and in a very short space of time the officer reappeared below, and requested Cicely, with a great show of politeness, to accompany him to the presence of the lord justice.

"I have so favourably reported to his lordship, madame, that he is as eager to see you as ever you can be to see him; indeed, 'tis yourself should be the most powerful advocate."

"You are very kind, sir," faltered Cicely.

The man's manner made her shudder, but as she turned to accompany him upstairs, followed by the reluctant Prudence, her heart leaped in triumph at having so easily overcome the first obstacle in her path. Surely now she was on the road to success. But when her companion flung wide the door, and bowed her elaborately into the room above, she stopped with a low cry of astonishment and fear, and the glad triumph died within her. For then only did she understand that her interview was not to be, as she had supposed, with the lord chief justice alone, in the privacy of his chamber, but that it was in the presence of these half-drunken roysterers, whose coarse laughter heard in the street below had stung her cheeks to crimson; it was before these drinking, jesting, pitiless men that she must tell her tale, and urge her plea.

It was too late then to retreat, but as she stood in the doorway, and surveyed with anxious eyes the room and the company assembled there, a vague, inexplicable fear took possession of her heart, and involuntarily she groped for Prue's hand, and drew the girl closer to her side.

Down the centre of the room ran a long table, plentifully furnished with meats and wines, at which were seated some of the officers of the troops quartered in the town, the judges, and a sprinkling of the officials of the circuit, and several pliable Tory gentlemen of the neighbourhood. Candles were lighted on the table, and as their rays illumined the faces of those who sat at meat they revealed no face that did not bear the clear stamp of debauchery and wickedness. For even in that callous and licentious age it would have been hard to find in all the length and breadth of the realm a viler and more despicable coterie than this company of noted officers, honoured judges, and highborn satellites who sat at the board of the lord chief justice of England.

At the head of the table sat my Lord Jeffreys, the very picture now, despite his ailment, of jovial good-humour. He had laid aside alike the severity of the judge and the ferocity of the man, and as he lounged at ease while the wine circulated freely, he warmed in the flattery of his comrades, and cracking jests and capping stories, was himself the leader and head-spring of their boisterous mirth.

On his right hand sat the commanding officer of the district, Colonel Kirke. And it was at sight of the latter's face that Cicely first realised to the full what manner of men were these before whom she stood. For nature is not to be gainsaid, and now, even as in the days of Cain, she imprints upon a man's features the sure tokens of his sins. But no longer, as in that age of the world's innocence, do men flee forth into the wilderness to hide their shame, rather they walk abroad, regardless of the mark upon their foreheads, knowing well that none will dare to call them to account.

And surely, in all the annals of our history, never was there a man more hardened in cruelty, more steeped in licentiousness than this same Percy Kirke. Yet the man was a great soldier, an able commander, fearless as death itself. But withal one whom no man could hold in honour, whom no woman could trust, for he would accept a bribe or betray a woman with the same ease and satisfaction as he would toss off a cup of wine.

As Cicely and her companion were ushered into the room the colonel was leaning across the table whispering a story into the ear of the lord chief justice. The rest of the company turned silent as the two girls remained timidly in the doorway shrinking from the cold gaze of so many pairs of eyes.

At length, the story ended, Lord Jeffreys burst into a roar of laughter, turned slowly in his chair, and after eyeing the two trembling women for a moment in silence, snarled:

"Come, girl! 'Tis damned wearisome to be troubled with affairs of state at this hour of the night, but since ye are here, say your say. What do you want with me, eh?"

"I entreat your lordship's pardon for this intrusion," began Cicely timidly. "An I might see your lordship alone— —"

"What? An assignation! Oh! fie, madame," cried the chief justice, glancing round at his companions with a mocking smile. Then he continued sharply, "Nonsense, girl. Say what you want here and now, or leave it unsaid and begone."

Seeing no escape Cicely called up all her courage and proceeded to urge her plea.

"I have come hither on behalf of my cousin, Mistress Barbara Winslow, who was to-day sentenced to— —to a most cruel punishment. I am here to beg your lordship to think mercifully of the matter and to grant me her pardon."

Lord Jeffreys glanced at the speaker with a quick scowl.

"How's this?" he cried sharply. "What means this? Am I never to hear the end of this pestilent woman? Is all the world mad concerning her? But we will have no pleading here. You have come, I am told, to lay information against a rebel. Beware, madame! If you have no such errand, if you have tricked us, the worse for you."

"Nay, my lord," answered Cicely, trembling. "I have not deceived you. I have information, not indeed of a rebel, but of one who hath connived at an escape. But I will give it only in return for my cousin's free pardon. On no other consideration."

"Say you so, indeed. And who may you be, madame, who dares to dictate terms to his Majesty's representatives? Have a care, madame, have a care."

"It matters little who I am, my lord," answered Cicely with some spirit, "save only this. I am no spy, no common tale-bearer. I would not willingly lay information against any man, and I vow that, do what ye may, I will not speak a word further on the subject till I have your assurance of my cousin's pardon."

Lord Jeffreys scowled savagely, but she met his glance unflinchingly, and he turned away with an oath and swallowed a glass of wine.

"Well! Well!" he exclaimed testily. "Out with thy story, girl. Who is this rebel?"

"You swear to me my cousin shall be pardoned?"

"Aye, aye. You shall have her pardon, an the affair prove serious enow to merit it—a hanging matter. Now, the name of your rebel, and be speedy, madame."

"'Tis—'tis Captain Miles Protheroe."

"Miles Protheroe!"

A shout of astonishment from the officers present greeted the name, all eyes were turned on the informer. Only Colonel Kirke remained silent, but he turned in his chair, and leaned forward with an eager glint in his eyes, and his teeth gleamed white behind his black beard.

Then Cicely told her story. The silence, the universal attention frightened her. She stammered, broke down, struggled on again. Only the thought of Barbara nerved her to a finish. Jeffreys helped her by an occasional sharp question, the rest of her audience sat in silence.

When she had finished her tale she turned to the lord chief justice eagerly.

"Is—is that a hanging matter, my lord?" she asked, shuddering involuntarily at the question.

"Oh, aye, 'twill serve, I doubt not."

"Then the pardon, my lord," she urged timidly.

"Pardon? Eh, what? What pardon?"

"For my cousin, Mistress Winslow. You swore she should be pardoned, if I spoke."

Jeffreys looked round the table with a low laugh of amusement. Then he slowly drained his glass.

"To be sure," he said. "To be sure. She shall be pardoned, freely pardoned— when her sentence has been executed."

Cicely's heart grew suddenly cold.

"My lord! What mean you?" she gasped. "Surely—you cannot——No! No! You swore to me she should have a free pardon."

"So she shall, so she shall," assented the judge. "A full and free pardon, two years from to-day. I'll answer for it."

Cicely held out her hands in helpless entreaty.

"Ah! no, my lord. Surely you are jesting with me," she cried.

"Tut, you fool," he answered impatiently. "Do you deem a pardon is so easily won? Jesting, forsooth; aye, 'tis a jest, i' faith," he laughed brutally, "but I doubt if Mistress Winslow will find it so. They shall tell her on't after her first taste of the whip, and see if her wits can mark the humour on't."

He laughed heartily at this suggestion, some of his comrades and satellites joining in his mirth.

But Cicely gave way utterly. She fell at his feet; she sobbed out desperate entreaties to pitiless deaf ears.

"Ah! no, no, my lord, it cannot be, you cannot mean it. Say you do but jest. Surely it is enough, this thing that I have done. For I have told you, told you all I know. Ah! tell me what more I can do, what more to win her pardon. Indeed I will do anything—anything, an you will but pardon. Ah! my lord, my lord!"

Jeffreys looked down at her and laughed. Then he poured himself another glass of wine, and pushed the bottle on to his neighbour.

"Take her away! Take her away," he said testily, pushing her with his foot.

Cicely would have renewed her plea, but Prudence Lane, realising that any such effort would be useless, and apprehending that to remain longer in such dissolute and abandoned company might be to court insult even of a more degrading character, leaned down to her companion, and with a whispered entreaty, drew her to her feet. The door was flung open for their departure and the two girls, Cicely clinging to her friend's arm for support, were ushered from the room, and thence into the High street.

In heavy silence they retraced their steps homeward, but had not proceeded far, when upon turning a corner they ran almost into the arms of Captain Protheroe. He had been absent from Taunton since the previous day upon a mission in the west, and was now on his way to the White Hart Inn in search of Colonel Kirke to make his report.

Cicely recoiled from him with a cry of remorseful horror, but he stepped eagerly towards her. Though they had never spoken together, he knew her well by sight.

"Lady Cicely Winslow!" he exclaimed in glad astonishment. "What brings you to Taunton at such a time? 'Tis no ill news, I trust. And Mistress Barbara? Is she here likewise?"

Cicely stared at him, her eyes wide with a momentary terror.

"You know, you must know," she exclaimed in a low, hard voice. "No! I will not believe but 'twas you who betrayed her. I dare not. I should go mad else at what I have done. No! 'tis true, you are but mocking me."

Her words had almost a ring of entreaty in them. She could not, would not believe his innocence; would not be deprived of this last plea in justification.

He stared down at her in amazement.

"On my soul, Lady Cicely, I do not understand one word of what you are saying," he exclaimed.

Cicely remained sullenly silent. He turned to Prue for an explanation.

"What means all this? Where is Mistress Barbara Winslow?"

"In prison, sir, for harbouring rebels, sentenced for two years, and to be scourged every month in the open market-place. If, as her ladyship says, this is your doing, you may be proud of your work." She tossed her head defiantly.

"In prison! Here in Taunton! Impossible, girl. You must be mad to say it," he urged in desperate eagerness.

Prudence would have responded with an outburst of scorn, but Cicely seized her by the arm and dragged her down the street. Indeed the poor lady was half demented. The sudden appearance of Captain Protheroe had brought vividly before her mind the full significance of what she had done, and with that strange stubbornness which possesses those worn out in mind and body, she sought to shelter herself from the stings of conscience behind the plea of justification in view of the criminal and despicable nature of the man she had betrayed. As she herself said, she dared not believe in his innocence. Her only comfort lay in convincing herself that he was even as those to whom she had betrayed him.

Captain Protheroe stared after their retreating figures in the deepest astonishment, but his astonishment quickly gave place to horror as he realised the meaning of their words.

To be imprisoned, scourged by the brutal soldiery, this girl, so young, so tender, so beautiful! He ground his teeth with rage as he hurried forward.

"This is one of Jeffreys' deviltries, I doubt not," he muttered.

He had heard of many such, had heard of them with a shudder of loathing, and passed on in disgust. But that she—that they should dare to lay hands on her! Instinctively his hand went to his breast, where lay concealed the knot of scarlet ribbon. He trembled at the sudden, awful horror of the thought.

But he was a soldier, a man of action, not one to waste time in futile imaginings while there was work that might, that must be done. With an effort he pulled his thoughts together and reviewed the situation, while he strode rapidly towards the White Hart Inn.

"There is but one thing to be done," he muttered. "An appeal from me to Jeffreys or to Kirke were worse than useless. I must to London. General Churchill will refuse me nothing, and he is high in favour with the King. He can procure a pardon—he shall do so. I will get leave at once, and start to-night. When she is free and safe, *then* to find the man who has informed against her. But before all she must be released."

So he determined, as he went rapidly on his way.

Meanwhile in the upper chamber of the White Hart Inn the carouse continued. The babble of tongues and roars of laughter once more disturbed the peaceful silence of the evening.

After Cicely's departure Lord Jeffreys exercised his wits sharply upon the subject of his late applicant's visit, and his companions joined in his humour.

But despite the boisterous merriment an air of depression hung over many members of the company. This sudden accusation levelled at one of their comrades, for an affair so trivial in their eyes, and yet adjudged by the chief justice as worthy of death, roused an anxious terror in their hearts that would not be stilled. For if this man indeed be brought to punishment, upon whom might not the next thunderbolt fall; who could be accounted safe? Were they not all equally guilty, and equally open to betrayal? They eyed the judge nervously, and trembled while they laughed.

Only Colonel Kirke made no attempt to hide his preoccupation, though it sprang from another cause. He sat grave, silent, biting his lips in thought, while that strange gleam of ferocity deepened in his eyes.

At length Lord Jeffreys turned to his neighbour, and rallied him good-humouredly.

"Come, Percy," he cried, "you don't drink. Why, what ails you, man? Have you lost your heart to yon fair fool, eh?"

"No, my lord. I' faith, I have clean forgot her."

"But not her story, eh?" asked the judge, glancing at him with a sinister smile, for he was quick to read men's thoughts, and guessed at the anxiety in his companion's thoughts. "Come, about this rebel officer of yours. What of him? Shall we wink at the matter?"

His lordship was no hypocrite; that which he did, justly or unjustly, he made little attempt to hide, and certainly among his boon-companions, the taking of a bribe, or the winking at a fault were subjects for free discussion.

Kirke pushed aside his glass, and leaned across the table, speaking in a low voice:

"This is my affair, my lord. This is a matter for court-martial. Let me try the man."

Jeffreys laughed good-humouredly.

"What! you dog. You want to handle the crowns, eh! Is it a rich prize?"

"There'll be no crowns in this case," said Kirke with a grim smile. "This is a matter for punishment."

"What, colonel! Turned honest, eh! Why, man, if all reports are true you've done the same yourself, a thousand times, tho' certes you've more frequently pocketed the reward than spared the life."

"Maybe. But they have grown restive on the subject at Whitehall of late, damn them! My Lord Sunderland has been pleased to complain. Well, we'll make an example of this one."

"Tut! man. Have your way, court-martial an you will, but never hang the fellow. His friends won't pay for his carcase. There are enough and to spare for hanging; this fellow should yield a goodly profit."

"Years ago, my lord," answered the colonel grimly. "this man and I were in France together. We quarrelled concerning a slip of a girl; he professed to mislike my methods of dealing with her and laid his cane across my cheek in public. When I cried for satisfaction he refused, saying he did not measure swords with a bully. He is a swordsman, curse him; it was useless to brand him as a coward; I had no redress. That was twelve years ago. I feel the stroke of his cane on my cheek again to-night and here at last is a salve to the bruise. I've watched and waited, knowing that my chance would come, and now at last he is in my power. No, my lord, crowns will be of no avail; he shall be tried at sunrise to-morrow, and shot like a dog at noon."

Throughout this speech the colonel's tone had grown ever louder, and as he uttered the last words with a savage ferocity, the door opened, and Captain Protheroe walked into the room.

"Hullo! colonel, another victim?" he exclaimed. "Who is the wretched devil who is to be shovelled out of the world so speedily?"

There was deep silence. Captain Protheroe gazed round in astonishment at the circle of grave faces, all turned eagerly towards him. Only Lord Jeffreys gave a sudden short laugh, as he lay back in his chair and watched the scene. For he loved to watch human comedies, if tragedy lurked behind them.

Then Colonel Kirke spoke:

"Captain Protheroe, you are under arrest. You will give your sword to Captain

Harrington, and accompany him at once to the guard-house. I refuse your parole."

The Captain faced the speaker in astonishment.

"I! Arrested! What devil's foolishness is this?" he cried. "On what charge?"

"Set a watch on your words," answered Kirke shortly. "You are charged with connivance at the escape of a noted rebel, Sir Rupert Winslow."

Captain Protheroe started. So there was ground after all for the accusation; it was no imaginary charge, easy to refute; it was a serious affair, an affair he saw well that might cost him dear. He hesitated a moment, then:

"I claim at least to have the matter referred to the General," he said resolutely. Neither Churchill nor Feversham, he knew well, would be severe upon him.

"You are at present under my command, Captain Protheroe," answered Kirke shortly. "You will be tried by me. Captain Harrington, remove your prisoner."

The Colonel had risen to his feet, and for a full minute the two men faced each other in silence. Then Captain Protheroe smiled. He knew his enemy's inveterate hatred, he read the full significance of that glance. And yet he smiled. It was too simple, too obvious. Not a man in that room, he knew well, but had been guilty a dozen times of the same breach of duty as that of which he stood accused, yet they went free, unpunished, while for himself he saw well there would be no mercy. The malice was too palpable, he laughed in his enemy's face.

Not, though it were for his life, would he urge one plea before this man; his pride forbade him to stoop to entreat the favour of one whose vengeance he so utterly despised. Without a word he handed his sword to Captain Harrington, and turned to accompany him from the room.

"Where is he to be lodged, Colonel?" inquired Captain Harrington doubtfully. "In the guard-house?"

Colonel Kirke hesitated.

"No," he muttered to himself. "'Tis not secure enough. The fellow is too devilish popular with the men. I scarce think my lambs would dare to revolt, but yet there might be an escape. I'll not risk it. I must ask you to keep the prisoner for me till to-morrow," he added aloud, turning to the governor of the prison, who was seated among the officers at the lower end of the table.

The governor shrugged his shoulders.

"I' faith, we are full enough," he muttered. "Tho' his lordship has cleared us out a little to-day," he added with a laugh.

"Any hole or corner will serve till morning," persisted the Colonel, "so it be secure."

"Secure enough; I'll answer for that," answered the governor as he scribbled an order for imprisonment.

He tossed the paper to Captain Harrington, an escort was called, and in a few minutes Captain Protheroe was marching through the silent streets to his prison.

He was no coward, yet no man in his inmost heart can jest when he finds himself face to face with a prospect of meeting death. And as he passed by the swinging corpses and trunkless faces hoisted on poles in the market-place, and reflected that in twelve hours he might be even such as they, he was seized with a wild impotent fury against the fate which had brought him to such a helpless pass. Only his soldier's pride held him from throwing himself desperately upon his guards, and making one last, vain, hopeless struggle for freedom.

The distance from the inn to the gaol was not great, and having arrived at their destination, Captain Protheroe was duly handed over to the charge of the head-gaoler, who in the governor's absence consigned him to one of the large sheds situated near the castle.

Then Captain Harrington, having fulfilled his commission, paused to bid his prisoner good-night.

"I am grieved about this, Miles," he said anxiously, for the two had been comrades. "But keep up your heart; the Colonel cannot really mean to treat seriously such an affair. Why, zounds, man, none of us have an over-clean record in that respect. He is bound to take some notice of the accusation, of course, and he bears a grudge against you, we know, but it can't mean more than a night or so in prison."

"Do you think so, Will?" answered the prisoner, pressing his outstretched hand. "No, Kirke and I have met before, we know each other. He's not the man to forgive an injury, and I'll be hanged if I ask him to; tho'," he added with a smile—"there's not a doubt on't I'll be shot if I don't."

"Tut, man, it's never so bad as that. Keep up your spirits. And anything I can do——"

"There are one or two commissions—— But there will be time enough in the morning to speak of them. You'd best return now and report to the colonel, or you will get a lick of the rough side of his tongue yourself, as my Lord Jeffreys hath it. Good-night.—And Will, here's a word of advice from a dying man, beware of women, and it may be you'll live to be drowned after all. Now, my man, I am ready," he added, turning to the gaoler, and with a final nod to his friend, he passed into the shed.

Captain Harrington stood for some minutes in thought. But despite the colonel's threats, he could not believe that he would carry out sentence of death for so trivial a matter, on one of his own officers. So with a shrug and a whistle he turned away, and strode back to the White Hart Inn.

CHAPTER XIV

Captain Protheroe leant against the wall, and gazed round his prison with an expression of deep disgust.

In a corner sat a noisy group of men, seeking as he judged by the dismal light of a flickering oil lamp, to drown their fears in drink. For the rest, the place was silent, and as it seemed to him, deserted, the prevailing darkness being broken only in places where the moonlight filtered through the high windows, and fell in splashes of brilliance upon the floor.

It was in truth a dreary place and one not calculated to raise the spirits of the new occupant, who stared moodily before him, cursing his luck. For he saw no hopeful prospect in the situation and he was by no means resigned to death now, when he was but beginning to realise the full joy of living. Two months ago, he told himself, it had been different; the world had not so much to offer then, indeed he had not known that it held so much. And now, with the new sense of this knowledge of the world's gifts teeming in his brain, to go forth and be shot down like vermin with never a fight for life! A man should not be called upon to endure so much.

And then, with a rush, his thoughts turned to Barbara. He could do nothing for her now. He could not even save himself, far less afford protection to another. He groaned aloud as he pictured her suffering, and again he bitterly cursed his utter helplessness.

Then, as he reviewed the events of the preceding hours, the question flashed across his brain: "Who had betrayed him? Who?" And quick as an answering flash came the reply, though he strove vainly to deny it entrance to his thoughts, "Who, but this girl herself, this girl who led him to the deed, for whose sake he was to die?" For to none but to her had he confessed his interview with Sir Rupert, none but she and himself knew of her appeal to his mercy or of her disclosure to him of her brother's hiding-place. Clear as day the facts lay before him, they would not be denied; she alone in all the world had the knowledge to betray him. And had she not already twice tricked him? Had she not plainly refused his friendship, denied him her trust?

This was but the consummation of her scheme. But that she should have wheedled him to spare this man, and, when danger threatened have betrayed him coolly, hoping thereby to save herself! He raged at the thought, at the black ingratitude of the action. And a woman with eyes as true as heaven, whom he would have trusted even to death! Where then could a man repose his faith, if she were worthless? Better indeed to die, and be out of a world where women could be guilty of such baseness.

Then a softer mood asserted itself. He recalled her face, the strong, proud face with the deep eyes, earnest and sincere behind the mask of mischief. He thought of her look when she had stood against him, sword in hand, to fight for her good name, fearless, resolute, even when driven to a stand with death seemingly staring her in the face. Here was no cowardice, no treachery. And she had risked her safety to give her brother an hour's happiness.

No, it was past belief that such a woman could be guilty of such devil's work. She must be innocent. There might be others—a woman always chattered—-he knew well she had a glib and hasty tongue. Or perchance they forced the story from her, tricked her to the telling of it. No, come what might, he would not believe that she had of set purpose brought him to this pass. And even if she had, if she had in a moment of weakness betrayed her benefactor, bartering his life for hers, even then— —

Passionately he drew out the knot of ribbon and pressed it to his lips.

"God bless her!" he murmured tenderly. "Strong or weak, true or faithless, God bless her."

And still with that strange density which at times overclouds the instinct, a thought of the real culprit never crossed his mind.

Again he strove to turn his thoughts back to his own position, to weigh the prospects of release; but with scant ardour. Life had little to offer if he must stand by and see her suffer, and in face of his present disgrace, he realised his helplessness to assist her.

He continued to gaze moodily before him, idly watching a ray of moonlight steal across the floor of the shed. To his surprise he saw it reveal the foot of a woman, and as it climbed to her knee he marked the desperate tension of the clasped white hands that lay thereon:

"Poor soul," he muttered. "There is trouble there."

Higher still crept the beam of light till the whole figure was illumined, and then, as at the drawing aside of a curtain of darkness, the face of Barbara Winslow emerged slowly from the black shadow, and appeared before him bathed in a glory of light.

Barbara! Yes, though at first sight he barely knew her, barely recognised those pallid cheeks, the dropped jaw, the fixed, staring eyes wide with fear, all the agony of her terrified spirit written on her face.

He sprang forward with a cry and crossed the room to her side. She turned to him quickly and seized his outstretched hand, all other feelings submerged in the great terror that held her.

"Oh! I am frightened, I am frightened," she sobbed in utter abandonment. "Indeed I cannot bear it. Sure they cannot truly carry out the sentence? I could not endure it, it would kill me, and I cannot die yet. Help me, help me. Do not let them scourge me. I am so frightened, help me."

What could he do? He held both her hands tightly in his own, and passed his arm round her as though to shield her from all hurt. And she, forgetting all else in the face of this fear which she felt for the first time in her life, crouched against him in a paroxysm of trembling and sobbing.

"Oh! I know I am a base coward, but what can I do? For I was so happy, and life was so good, and now I—I, Barbara Winslow, must be scourged openly in the market-place by the common hangman, month after month, till assuredly I must die of the shame. Think! The troopers will watch and laugh, and I shall be— — Oh! no, no, indeed I cannot bear it; what shall I do!"

He ground his teeth in helpless, desperate rage. Wild vague assertions of help and protection rose to his lips and died away unuttered, for he knew himself powerless. His heart surged with impotent fury, while she sobbed in his arms in the very abandonment of fear and misery, the natural reaction after the proud restraint of the past few days.

But it was only for a little space; the firm clasp of his hands, the pressure of his arm, gave her the sense of human support and strength that she lacked. In a few minutes the cold terror left her, she was herself again save for backward shudderings at the remembrance of the emotions through which she had passed.

Drawing her hands gently from his grasp, she lifted her white, tear-stained face to his with a smile.

"Thank you," she said simply. "I know not what ailed me. 'Twas mighty foolish and yet 'twas terrible enow," she added with a shudder.

He laid his hand on hers again firmly, and she did not withdraw it. For a few minutes they sat in silence.

Presently Barbara's glance wandered to the far end of the shed, where the group of drinkers sat.

"They are to die to-morrow. I would I were a man, and knew no fear," she murmured enviously.

He smiled.

"Think you they know no fear? That is the very height of fear that dare not face the morrow, but seeks forgetfulness thus."

"Could I forget thus?" she asked.

"I would not have thee try, Mistress Barbara: 'tis but a coward's way."

"Yet 'tis but for one night," she cried hurriedly. "And I cannot bear this torture of waiting and thinking. Let me not be a coward again. Let me not think. Ah! when I think I see it all; the troopers and the prison and the post, month after month till— — Ah, no, I will not think. Talk to me—tell me—tell me why you are here," she continued, for the first time filled with curiosity as to the reason of his presence.

His heart leaped gladly at her question.

"Do you not know, madame?"

"Indeed no; it cannot assuredly be that you too are a prisoner?"

"Yes. A prisoner even as yourself, condemned for treason."

"You—a traitor. Impossible!" she exclaimed naïvely.

"I thank you for the compliment, Mistress Barbara," he answered with a smile.

"And the sentence?"

"Imprisonment—until to-morrow," he answered lightly.

"And to-morrow you will be free?" she questioned doubtfully.

"Aye, free from every fetter."

Something in his tone startled her.

"It is not so," she cried quickly. "You are deceiving me."

"Nay, madame. Is not freedom the supreme gift of death?"

"Then you are to die to-morrow?" she asked in a tone full of awe.

"Court-martial at sunrise, shot like a dog at noon. That is my sentence. Come, will you not wish me a pleasant voyage? I confess myself no good sailor, and do heartily trust they have no storms on the Styx."

He spoke lightly, but she turned from him suddenly with a choking sob.

"Oh!" she cried bitterly. "How you must despise me for a true coward."

He laughed tenderly.

"Nay, Mistress Barbara, we be all cowards at heart, I warrant, only some have learned the trick of hiding it. And indeed to one who has faced him many times, death loses somewhat of his grim aspect. Besides—" he continued cheerily, "when a man bethinks him how many of his fellows in past ages have faced death un-flinching, it seemeth but a small matter for him to follow in their footsteps. I doubt not we shall meet with gallant company across the bourne."

"And have you no regrets?" she asked wonderingly.

He looked down at her and his face clouded.

"Aye, madame, one." He hesitated, then continued in the strange hurried tones of one who has at last resolved to speak his thoughts, and risk the consequence.

"Men on their death-beds make strange confessions, madame; here is mine. For fifteen years I have asked and expected little of life save to win a name in my profession, and for the rest, to enjoy to the full all the pleasures that the world had to offer. I deemed that I had succeeded fairly in both these, my ambitions, and I was content. But—two months since, on a certain sweet night in July, I met a wom-an. Not such an one as the courtesans of Whitehall, not such as are they whom a soldier most often meets in his way thro' the world, but such a woman as a man might dream his mother was, such as he would wish to be the mother of his sons. And when I looked into that woman's eyes I understood for the first time that all I have sought and won from life was worthless, and tho' I have drunk deep of the cup of pleasure, yet all my days I have been but as a child playing contentedly in the desert, while the door of an enchanted garden lay unnoticed at my side."

"Were the woman's eyes indeed so beautiful?" asked Barbara softly.

"Madame, they are as the clear depths of the heavens, wherein a man may read all the perfection of life. I have seen her but thrice since first we met, yet one look into her eyes has taught me more of the reality of life, of happiness, of love than I ever dreamed of even in the age of a man's most golden hopes. And so, madame, I cannot die without one regret, the regret that I may not live to deserve the pressure of that woman's hand, nor hope to make myself worthy to feel the touch of her pure lips."

He paused, looking down upon her doubtfully; she did not meet his glance, but he heard her sigh softly, as she gazed before her into the darkness. At length she spoke.

"Then you had been happier had you never seen the woman? Is it not so?"

"Happier! No, Mistress Barbara, is it not better for a man to die, having gazed once upon the glories of the heavens, than to live a thousand thousand years, nor lift his eyes from earth?"

There was silence between them.

Then Barbara rose from her seat.

"I am weary," she said softly. "I think I could sleep now, and I would fain be rested for to-morrow. I must be strong then; they shall not think I fear them. I must rest. But not in there," she added, gazing shudderingly at the dark corner behind the screen. "Not in there, lest I wake."

Near them lay a pile of straw and loose wisps of wool. These he gathered together, and spread his cloak upon them.

"It is not much," he muttered discontentedly; "yet it is better than the bare boards."

"It is perfect," answered Barbara, snuggling down into the warmth of the cloak.

He knelt to draw it more closely round her.

"Good-bye, Mistress Barbara," he said, raising her hand to his lips.

But she, suddenly raising herself upon her elbow, drew his head down towards her and kissed him on the lips.

"Good-night—good-bye—and thank you," she whispered simply.

Then she lay down peacefully, and drew the cloak once more around her.

The moon dipped behind a bank of clouds and the prison was in darkness.

Captain Protheroe rose to his feet, and stood for some time gazing before him, as one half-dazed. Then he recovered himself with a start, his eyes flashed, he looked round quickly, his whole body alert for action.

Die! No surely not now, he could not die now. It was impossible; there must be some way of escape for them both. If he could but think of it!

But the more he thought thereon, recalling all the tales of prison breaking and rescue that he had read or heard of, picturing the security of the shed, the disposition of the sentries, the surer did the knowledge of his utter helplessness overwhelm him, and yet the more persistently did he fight against this knowledge, assuring himself continually that death must be impossible now.

CHAPTER XV

Prudence sat on a stone seat at the bottom of the high-walled garden behind her father's house. Around her fell the soft moonlight, clothing the daisied grass and the shimmering trees in a veil of glory. The air was full of rich scents, remembrances of the dying sweetness of the roses, the noises of the street were hushed, and there rested over all a soft whispering silence, broken occasionally by the rapturous notes of the nightingale, as he poured forth his soul in an ecstasy of love. The scene was redolent of the sweet witchery of love, and Prue with her soft eyes, her glittering hair, and the mischievous dimples deepening in her cheeks, seemed in the moonlight like some fair enchantress weaving the spell of her sweet beauty over all around.

There were no traces on her fair face of the horrible scenes of which but half an hour since she had been a witness, no indication on her smooth brow of the strain of the last two days. She had not forgotten Cicely's misery and how she lay so still, so silent in the room above; but the weight of a sorrow which did not touch her personally lay but lightly upon her young heart, and she had been conscious of a feeling of relief when she left her friend to the tender care of Mistress Lane and crept out into the silent, peaceful garden.

A thorough child of nature, she sat calm and happy, her spirits in harmony with the scene immediately around her, though in the streets without the drying corpses of innocent men waved their limbs weirdly in the breeze, and women, their hearts breaking with despair, sat silent in a grief too deep for tears.

Prudence sat deep in thought. She had an enterprise in view for the furtherance of which she foresaw the necessity of laying resolute siege to the will of Master Robert Wilcox. She would require his co-operation, and as she traced out the lines of her campaign, her eyes glistened brightly, and her lips curved into a roguish smile. For Prue was one to scorn an easy dominion, else had she never given her heart to so resolute a lover as Robert.

So intent was she upon her thoughts that she did not notice the approach of Master Wilcox himself, walking with rapid step down the trim garden path; in fact he had been watching her for some minutes in a lover's rapture, before she raised her eyes and noted his presence. Then he sprang eagerly to her side.

"Ah! Prue; sweetheart," he cried, with outstretched arms. "I hoped I might chance on you here, and yet indeed I scarce dared to hope it."

Prue slipped quickly aside from the proffered embrace. "Good-evening, Master Robert," she answered with a demure assumption of indifference. "And pray what may be your errand to me?"

Robert's hands fell to his side; he stared at her in amazement.

"Why, Prue, my darling," he exclaimed.

Prudence eyed him coldly.

"'Tis a fine evening, Master Robert, and I was enjoying the silence and solitude of the garden. Prithee then—your errand?"

Robert hesitated a moment, then he seated himself upon the bench beside her, and laid his hand on hers.

"Come sweetheart, what is wrong?" he demanded resolutely.

"Nought that I know of," she answered calmly, withdrawing her hand, "saving only that methinks you are somewhat free with your 'sweetheart' and 'darling,' Master Wilcox."

"What! Must I not call thee sweetheart then, my dearest?"

"In truth I had as lief you did not," she answered curtly.

Robert eyed her a minute doubtfully: then he plunged boldly into the subject.

"See here, Prue, what is the matter; for what art thou so angry with me? An it be concerning Janie Medlar, 'tis mere foolishness. I met her down by the river, 'tis true, yet 'twas but by chance, and then I could not, in courtesy, refuse to walk home with her. Now could I? And the rose—she asked for it herself—I swear she did. But no more passed between us, save the merest—er—nothing whatever. 'Tis utter foolishness, Prue."

Prudence smiled to herself; she was learning secrets. But she answered coldly enough:

"I' faith, Master Robert, and what is it to me what passes betwixt you and Mistress Medlar? 'Tis much, indeed, if I am to call her rival—pale-faced chit."

"'Tis not that? Then in Heaven's name, Prue, what is it? What have I done?"

Prue turned and faced him:

"Ah, well said. What hast thou done, Master Robert? What hast thou done all thy life save sort wool and enter ledgers? And yet you would be one to call a maid 'sweetheart' and kiss her on the lips. I tell you, you must seek elsewhere then, Master Robert, I am not for such as you. I will have nought to do with any, save brave men, men proved by action, not swollen with boasts."

Robert groaned aloud.

"Lord, Prue," he muttered; "not that all over again."

"And wherefore not, Master Robert? Has a man nought to do save sit till the apples fall into his lap? Thinkest thou a girl can be wooed by words alone? I tell thee thou art mightily mistaken. If a maid be worthy of love she is worthy of winning, and winning by deeds, not by empty vows and foolish boastings."

"Perchance thou wouldst have me join Kirke's band then, and win thee by such deeds as those in the market-place yonder," muttered Robert angrily.

"Indeed that were better than nothing," answered the girl with a mocking toss of her head. "Better be one of Kirke's Lambs, brutes tho' they be, than a white-livered wadcomber, caring for neither king nor country so he have a full belly and a whole skin."

"Now by Heaven, Prue, this is too bad. 'Tis unfair to taunt me thus when thou knowest I had ridden gladly with the Duke if I had but been given the chance, and that I do but bide here at the work to please thy father, and so clear my way to winning thee."

"Is't verily so?" laughed the girl scornfully. "Truly I marvel what men would do, if they had not women's petticoats to hide behind."

But this was too much for Robert to endure with patience. Though he more than half suspected she was playing with him, for he had watched her smile as she sat on the bench alone, yet he felt that no man should be called upon to endure such mockery; for the sake of future peace he resolved to teach her a lesson.

Roughly dropping the hand which he had taken again to strengthen his plea, he moved to the far end of the bench, and turned an angry shoulder to his tormentor.

"So be it, Mistress Prue," he answered. "An those be your opinions, 'tis useless to talk further on the matter. I am sorry that my actions fail to please thee, but on my honour, I do not see that I am in any wise bound to alter them to suit every whim and fancy of thine. The evening is chill; would you not be wiser to go indoors?"

Prue gasped, and gazed at the sulky shoulder with eyes wide open in astonishment. The affair had taken a sadly different turn from that which she had contemplated. It looked greatly as though this attack upon the fortress would prove a failure, nay more, as though it would turn to a defeat and rout of the attacking party itself, did she not with all speed change her tactics.

Accordingly, with a celerity worthy of a great general, she changed, upon the instant, her whole plan of campaign, abandoned this frontal attack, and devised a more subtle method of overcoming such unexpected resistance.

She tried first the effect of silence; but experience had taught her that Robert was better skilled in the use of that weapon than she herself, and indeed it was a struggle to her to keep silence for five minutes at any time. She abandoned this course after a very short trial.

Then she sighed. Twice, thrice, with the suspicion of a sob in the last sigh, which she felt must sound infinitely pathetic. She looked eagerly for signs of relenting in that stubborn shoulder; Robert was resolute.

The affair was beginning to assume a most serious aspect. If it continued thus much longer, she would be forced to haul down her colours and abandon the siege entirely. And then what would become of her schemes?

No. She must bring all her forces to the attack, and—and—Robert could not see her where she sat.

She rose and stepped quietly into the deep glow of the moonlight, standing full before the gaze of her offended lover.

She stood first with her back towards him, plucking nervously at the petals of a withered rose. Robert looked at the trim, white figure outlined against the darker trees, at the soft curve of the averted cheek. He looked and wavered.

Suddenly she turned and faced him, standing before him in all the charm of her saucy beauty. She shook out her curls till the gold glistened in the moonlight, she turned her eyes full upon him, and she smiled, a smile full of mischievous invitation that lurked in her eyes and curved round her rosy dimpling lips.

It was enough. Robert stared at her for a moment in silence, then he sprang towards her and seized her in his arms.

"Ah, Prue, you witch! You witch!" he cried. "How could I resist thee? Say what you want, sweetheart. I will do it, aye, that I will."

"Wilt thou really promise that, Rob?" she asked, nestling into his arms.

"Aye, sweetheart."

"Anything, Rob?"

"Anything you ask," he answered, gazing into her eyes.

"Then, oh, Rob; help Mistress Winslow to escape."

He stared in astonishment.

"What sayest thou? Prue! Prue! 'Tis impossible, 'Tis madness to dream on't," he cried.

"You promised to do anything I asked," she complained reproachfully, straining against his embrace.

"Aye, sweetheart, so I will, so I will." He pledged himself rashly to keep her in his arms. "But this— — How is't possible? Would you have me break into the castle and bear her out by force?"

"She is not in the castle; she is lodged in one of the temporary sheds," corrected Prue reproachfully.

"Well, 'tis the same thing, sweet. Gaol or shed, 'tis prison enow, and i' faith, I see not how it be possible to fetch her out."

"Pooh! What is the use of thy wits, Rob, if thou canst not get the better of father's old wool-shed."

"Master Lane's shed, sayest thou?"

"Aye, truly, she is there. Dad told me so this morning. The door bolted and barred, sentries in the street without, and many more in the guardhouse opposite. I saw them there last Sunday when I passed. But what of them. You can surely outwit such fudge-heads as they."

"Master Lane's shed," cried Robert again, a strange note of excitement in his voice. "Art certain she is there?"

"Aye, certain, Rob. What then?"

"Prue, who guards the little door in Blind Man's alley?"

Prue looked at him eagerly.

"What door, Rob? I mind it not."

"Yes, thou knowest it. The master's private door at the near end of the shed. They say 'twas put there years ago for old Master Lane, thy grandfather, to enter secretly and count his bales; maybe for the entrance of other sorts of goods,—folks say. For 'tis known he hid arms and ammunition for the king's troops in the last war. It has not been used for years, and on the inside 'tis still hid behind a pile of sacks, I doubt not. But 'tis there."

"Oh, Rob! I had forgot it entirely. And oh, I doubt not they have forgot it too, for I passed thro' Blind Man's alley last Sunday even, and there was no sentry stationed there."

"No, sentry, Prue? And the key hangs on thy father's chain."

His voice was hoarse with excitement, he stared before him in dawning thought.

Prue clasped her hands eagerly.

"Oh, Rob," she whispered. "What shall we do? What shall we do?"

He turned his head slowly and looked down at her.

"Ah! sweetheart, it's madness, madness!"

"Yes, Rob, dear, but—let us be mad. Ah! do, do."

He hesitated, but his inborn love of adventure tempted him as much as her eyes. He yielded to her pleading, and sealed the bargain with a kiss.

Then they sat down on the bench, hand in hand, and proceeded to mature their plan.

"Now, sweetheart, we must think with all our wits."

"It must be to-night, Rob," Prue urged. "They might carry out the sentence to-morrow. It must be to-night."

"To-night be it."

"And what shall we do?"

"There is but the one way that I can think of. Enter the shed by the hidden door, and fetch her out thence."

"Oh, Rob, that sounds so easy," cried Prue, a note of disappointment in her voice.

"Does it indeed, madame?" he laughed. "And what if the door be barred within, or I meet with a sentry, or the other prisoners should betray me, or I cannot find the lady, or she will not come?"

Prue gasped in dismay at this terrible list of possibilities.

"Oh! it is too dangerous, Rob," she urged with a sudden shrinking terror.

"Nay, but we'll e'en try it. For indeed I do not think any such misadventure likely to befall us."

"Then let us set about it at once, Robert."

"Nay, there is much to think on yet. Where shall I hide her when she is free of the prison?"

"Bring her here, Rob, by the garden door. I can hide her in the old attic for a night or so, and they will never dream of seeking in father's house for an escaped rebel, and in a few days Lady Cicely may win her pardon. But I am coming with you, Rob."

"Certes, no. Why, I had as lief have my Lord Jeffreys. No, Prue, I mean it. If I cannot go alone, I go not at all."

"Oh, but Rob. I must do something."

"Ay, i' faith, thou must. 'Tis for thee to get the key."

"The key!"

"Aye, the key of the shed. It hangs, as I said, on Master Lane's chain, tho' he hath doubtless forgot the fact, it has been so seldom used. But I know it well. Now, how wilt thou get it for me?"

"Oh! Rob, I know not, i' faith. How is't possible?"

"Pooh! Where are thy wits, Prue?" he asked teasingly.

"You shall not mock me," she panted. "But in good earnest, Rob, 'tis impossible."

"Come, Prue, no despair. Why, I have seen him hand thee his keys a hundred times."

"Aye, but that was for the cellar, when he fancied a certain wine at supper, or maybe for his bureau in the counting-house, to fetch papers or moneys. Not—not—Rob!"

"Well!"

"Thinkest thou not, perchance that a glass of hot port wine might help my Lady Cicely to sleep."

"Prue! Thou has hit on the very plan. And once the chain is in my hands, the key of the shed is ours. But go to thy father quickly, sweet, or 'twill be too late, and Lady Cicely will fall asleep before her drink be prepared."

"Oh! Rob, I shall laugh when I ask him; I know I shall."

"Not you, Prue. I've too good cause to know your powers of acting a part."

Prue laughed and blushed at this reference to the evening's quarrel. Then she sprang quickly to her feet.

"Well, I must do my best. Do you wait here, Rob, and in ten minutes I'll be with you."

She darted across the grass and disappeared into the shadow of the trees.

Robert awaited her return in a frenzy of impatience. So much depended upon the success of the girl's errand, so many obstacles presented themselves before his mind. For Master Lane might hand her the cellar key alone instead of the chain, though that were never his way. Or Mistress Lane might be with her husband and disapprove of her daughter's request. Or Deb might accompany her sister to the cellar, or Prue herself, in her excitement, might betray the plot. Of the danger, the madness of the undertaking he thought not at all. Once embarked upon the enterprise he was carried along by the excitement of the adventure it promised. Like Prue, he lost sight of other considerations in view of the daring of the attempt.

Presently he saw her coming towards him, her white dress gleaming through the trees, and as he darted to meet her, he heard the jingle of the keys. She had succeeded in her quest.

"Here they are," she whispered, her eyes dancing with triumph. "Take it quickly, I must not keep Dad waiting. He was alone. He gave them without a question. 'The whole cellar full if 'twill aid Lady Cicely,' he said. Is that the one, art sure? Then give me the chain, and go. Here is the key of the garden gate. I will watch. Keep out of danger and be careful. But oh! Rob, is it not fine? You and I to outwit them all, my Lord Jeffreys and the governor, and—and the very law itself."

He laughed aloud, sharing to the full her excitement. Then without further parley he set out on his errand, leaving Prue to her eager watch for his return.

So these two laid their wild plans in the solitude of the peaceful garden, while in the castle near, the prisoners rested quietly, resigned to their fate, and in the brightly lighted room of the White Heart Inn Judge Jeffreys and his comrades feasted and drank till the night air rang with their boisterous revelry.

CHAPTER XVI

Robert Wilcox hastened on his way to the prison with joy in his heart and excitement in his eyes, at thought of the adventure that promised, while in the darkness of the prison Captain Protheroe sat with his head buried in his hands, sunk in the misery of an impotent despair.

No man who has not himself endured it can understand the agony to a man of Captain Protheroe's disposition, of acknowledged helplessness. For he was essentially a man of action, strong, capable, alert for every danger, with a ready wit to cope with every obstacle that rose in his path. He had never yet learned the meaning of failure. And now, when life at last offered him the full cup of his desire; when but four bare walls stood between him and a freedom so rich that beside it his past life seemed but an empty waste; now when his whole being clamoured for action, he could do nothing but sit helpless and inactive, while the hours slipped slowly away and the day drew near when the woman he loved must suffer shame and torture with none to support or comfort her. He knew it was useless to struggle against his fate, but his whole soul cried out against submission. Yet he could do nothing, nothing, but sit rigid, silent, his hands locked together in the fierce misery of impotent revolt.

Suddenly he stirred, every sense on the alert and listening intently. At the farther end of the shed his fellow prisoners lay silent, their sleeping forms dimly visible in the faint light. Close beside him, where a pile of bales and sacks was heaped against the wall of the shed, he seemed to detect the noise of a key turned gently in a rusty lock, followed by the creak of an unused hinge. He waited with bated breath for what should follow. After a pause the hinge creaked again.

Half incredulous, he crept forward to investigate the cause of the unmistakable sounds, and began noiselessly to remove the sacks from that portion of the wall which they concealed. Two he moved easily, but the third resisted his efforts. In vain he pulled, exerting his strength in an obstinate determination to have his way. As he became dimly conscious that the resistance was rather active than passive, it suddenly ceased, and he stumbled backwards, with the sack in his arms.

Like the full moon on an Autumn evening the fiery head and rosy countenance of Master Robert Wilcox rose slowly into view above the top of the piled bales, and peered cautiously into the shed.

For a moment the two stood staring at one another doubtfully. But as Master Robert slowly perceived the captain's uniform, his jaw dropped, and a look of horror and consternation crept into his face.

"Good Lord!" he gasped, and with a sudden swift movement, his head disappeared from view.

But Captain Protheroe was no whit behind him in rapidity of thought or action. Quick as lightning his arm darted over the sacks, and he grasped firmly the tousled hair of the intruder.

"Hist, you fool!" he whispered. "All's well. I'm one of the prisoners myself. Is it a rescue?"

Slowly the face reappeared and stared doubtfully at the speaker, then having subjected him to a critical survey, and being at length assured by the captain's tone and bearing of his good faith, Master Wilcox heaved a sigh of relief, and rubbed the sweat from his forehead.

"Phew! What an escape," he muttered. "I made sure you were one of those damned sentries. Yes, 'tis a rescue, but not for you," he continued curtly.

"Nevertheless, my friend, I purpose to be one of your party," answered Captain Protheroe coolly, "I and a lady who is here with me."

"A lady; what lady is she?"

"What is that to thee?"

"Nought, only 'tis a lady I am here to aid; Mistress Barbara Winslow."

"What! Even so? Why, well met, friend. 'Tis even she of whom I spake. She is sleeping yonder. I will go bring her and we can slip out quietly without rousing the others."

Robert eyed him half-doubtfully.

"Be speedy then. Every minute is danger, for I know not when the sentries will be round."

"True, there's no time to lose."

The two had carried on their conversation in whispers; the other inmates of the shed were undisturbed.

Captain Protheroe now went swiftly to Barbara's side. She was sleeping quietly, her cheek pillowed on her hands. He aroused her gently.

"What is it?" she gasped, in sleepy bewilderment.

"Freedom," he whispered, smiling down at her.

Silently they stole back across the shed, and soon the three stood side by side in the narrow alley outside.

"Come!" cried Rob, seizing Barbara's arm eagerly. "There's not a moment to lose. Come!"

But Barbara was now thoroughly awake. She drew back quickly.

"But the others!" she exclaimed. "Surely you will not leave them behind. They are to die to-morrow."

Captain Protheroe shook his head.

"Mistress Barbara, the risk is too great."

"Oh, but that is rank cowardice," she exclaimed angrily. "You may do as you choose, sir, I shall— —"

He laid a restraining hand upon her arm.

"Captain Protheroe," she exclaimed indignantly, eyeing him haughtily.

He smiled at her serenely.

"Yield to reason, Mistress Barbara. You cannot go back."

Barbara turned away angrily, and addressed herself to Rob.

"Cannot you go back?" she asked.

"Not I, madame," was the ready answer. "You are not safe yet."

Barbara sighed, looked at the pair of them contemptuously, and yielded to necessity.

"But you can leave the door open," she urged.

Rob hesitated.

"'Twill be a clue," he muttered, but yielded to her plea. "Now, come, madame, we must wait no longer."

"Where are you going?" she demanded quickly.

"To Master Lane's house," he answered impatiently. "Lady Cicely is there, and— —"

But Barbara shook her head obstinately.

"No," she said, "I will not bring trouble upon them. They are loyal folk, and were I discovered there, 'twould bring misfortune to all. Did Master Lane send you to me?"

"No, madame, he knows nought of the venture as yet, but— —"

"Then, indeed, I will not go. I will not endanger them, and Cicely. 'Twould be most cruel."

Rob groaned in desperation.

"Lord! These women!" he muttered. "Nay, madame, trust in me and come at once. We may be discovered any moment."

Barbara turned to Captain Protheroe.

"Whither are you going, sir?" she asked abruptly.

"I' faith, I cannot say," he answered doubtfully. "But for you, madame, it were certainly wiser to follow this gentleman, if he can bestow you safely."

"I will not," she answered resolutely.

"We'll all swing for it, an we bide here parleying much longer," began Rob desperately.

He broke off abruptly, for even as he spoke, a window in the wall opposite was flung open, and a man's face peered out into the alley.

Instinctively the three drew back into the shadow. But it was too late. The disturbed burgess had seen the three figures, and in an instant he suspected the truth of the situation.

With an exclamation his head disappeared from view, and a moment later they heard the bolts of a door round the corner of the building shot back and the man rushed into the street shouting:

"The prisoners are escaping! Look to your prisoners."

Captain Protheroe seized Barbara's hand, and they began to run rapidly down the alley. They heard the sentinels running up the street and shouting. They darted round the corner as their pursuers turned into the alley.

Rob had disappeared.

The alley led into a wider street, parallel to that in which the sentries had been posted, at the main entrance to the shed. Down this the fugitives turned, but were met by a knot of men running towards the shouts. Captain Protheroe tightened his grip on Barbara's hand, desperately, and ran straight towards them, waving his free arm in the direction of the prison.

"The prisoners!" he shouted. "They are escaping, look to them."

The ruse succeeded. The men hesitated a moment, staring doubtfully at his uniform, and then proceeded at a run towards the prison, shouting confusedly. On they ran right into the arms of the sentries, who at that moment turned out of the alley.

A few moments of confusion ensued ere the identity of each party was made clear to the other—moments precious to the fugitives, who ran on blindly from street to street, little heeding which way they went.

Barbara stumbled as she ran, and her breath came in sobs. Captain Protheroe's grip upon her wrist was like a vice. Again they turned a corner, and for an instant they stopped dead; for halfway down the street, full in their path, the bright light from an open doorway flared across the road, and in the light stood a group of soldiers eager and alert. They had run into a trap.

Their pursuers behind shouted a warning, the troopers in front wheeled round quickly to face them.

To go back was impossible, to stand still, madness, to run forward into the arms of these expectant troopers, a desperate chance. This time no ruse could avail them.

And then, a few yards on the near side of the lighted doorway, Captain Protheroe espied a dark opening in the line of buildings. He darted towards it and slipped between the black shadows of the houses.

Barbara was spent, but even as they ran into the narrow alley, and as he felt further effort was hopeless, Captain Protheroe noted an open doorway, dimly lighted. It was a desperate chance, his only one. With an effort he dragged Barbara into the house, and shut the door behind him, listening intently, while the girl sank exhausted at his feet. He heard their pursuers turn the corner, pass the door unheeded, and running eagerly on, turn again into the street beyond. Their shouts and footsteps died away in the distance, and all was still.

Captain Protheroe turned and surveyed his surroundings. They were in a narrow, dimly-lighted passage, flanked by a doorway on either side, and leading to a third door at the end. The door on the left was open, and the room to which it gave access, a small parlour, was deserted.

He glanced at Barbara. She raised her head and smiled at him bravely, though her breath still came in shuddering gasps, and her face was white and drawn.

He stooped down, and helped her to her feet, then leading her into the little parlour, laid her, unresisting, on the settle, and closed the door.

"Where are we?" she whispered, looking wonderingly around her.

He shook his head.

Just then a door was heard to open in some distant part of the house. There was a babble of sounds, a shrill voice singing through the verse of a song, followed by a loud burst of boisterous laughter.

Captain Protheroe, with a quick exclamation, crossed to the window of the room, drew aside the heavy curtain, and peered out.

Then he turned with a strange expression in his eyes.

"We have walked into the lion's den, Mistress Barbara," he said. "This is the White Hart Inn."

Barbara started to her feet.

"Oh! let us go, let us go instantly," she cried.

Captain Protheroe stood irresolute.

"I don't know," he said slowly; "it may be we are in the safest place. At least 'tis the last place where they would dream of searching for us."

As he spoke, the door at the end of the passage opened, and they heard a dragging footstep slowly approaching.

Barbara clasped her hands in desperation.

"Lie down!" he whispered sharply. "Lie down, and turn away your face."

The footsteps drew nearer, the door was pushed open, and a girl carrying a dim rushlight entered the room. Her dress was untidy, her hair tousled, her eyes heavy with sleep.

She gave a quick cry at sight of the occupants of the room, and almost dropped her candlestick in her surprise.

"Why, Sue, what ails you?" Captain Protheroe asked cheerily.

The girl stared at him in bewilderment.

"La, Captain Protheroe, sir, eh! but ye frighted me. I took thee for a ghost.

What ever be thee here for? Why," she continued with dawning recollection, "I heard tell as how thee wert took prisoner, and in gaol along wi' rebels."

"Arrested, I! What nonsense," he answered coolly; "'twas but a jest of Colonel Kirke's. They don't arrest the king's officers, Sue, my girl. But look you, this lady hath but just recovered from a swoon. There was a disturbance in the streets, and she was thrown down and frightened. I brought her in here to recover, before I take her home."

"Eh, poor thing!" exclaimed Sue, eyeing Barbara pitifully. "The street is no place for the like o' her this time o' night. But you're kindly welcome, sir, and the lady too. We could not give her a bed, sir, I'm afraid; but an she wish to rest on mine——"

"Oh, there's no need to put yourself about, she will be well enow shortly."

"Would you be wishing for supper, sir?" asked in girl sleepily.

"Supper! Good heavens, no. Why it must be near midnight. I'm for my bed presently, and methinks 'tis the place for you now. You look tired to death, my girl."

"Aye. I've been about since five o'clock this morning," she answered, yawning. "Their lordships make a deal of work. But I'm going to my bed now, if you want no more, sir."

"Nothing, thank you, Sue."

"I'm sleeping in yonder," nodding her head across the passage. "Perhaps you'd call, sir, if you want anything." Then she added, hesitating, "We be so full o' guests now, father sleeps on the settle here. But he'll hardly be down yet, he must see their lordships safe to bed first. Good-night to you, sir."

She crossed the passage and disappeared through the doorway opposite.

Captain Protheroe broke the silence which followed:

"If you are rested," he said briskly, "I think we had best be gone."

"Must we go?" she asked lazily.

"The sooner we are free from the houses, the better. The landlord may come here any moment. They are quieter above stairs already."

Then he glanced across the room.

Through the half-closed doors of a cupboard in the corner he espied some dishes of meat—cold bacon, a half eaten pasty, several loaves of bread.

"Fugitives cannot be over and above honest," he muttered with a laugh, as he swept the contents of the cupboard into a cloth, and tucked the bundle under his arm. "We can make the loss good to mine host, some day, perchance, and food we must have. Now, Mistress Barbara, if you are ready."

He stopped with a look of consternation, for even as he spoke, the passage door again opened, and they heard a man's voice calling aloud:

"This way, Master Peters, we can transact our business somewhat more privately here."

The only possible hiding place the room afforded was the space between the high-backed settle and the wall. In an instant the two had stepped back into its shadow, and crouched there, scarce daring to breathe, hoping only that the dim uncertain light might conceal their presence from the two men who a moment later entered the room.

The first was a big, burly farmer, with round, red, solemn face and somewhat wooden cast of countenance. He took up his stand by the table, facing the settle, but with the light between him and the fugitives.

His companion afforded a marked contrast; a small, thin, wiry, sharp-featured man. His pale face was alight with intellect, but his narrow-set blue eyes were hard as steel, and while seeming to pierce a man's inner-most thoughts, yet gave in return no vestige of answering confidence. He was soberly suited in black, and carried in his hand an open letter, and a small bag of gold.

This was no other than Master Stephen Jewars, my Lord Jeffrey's clerk and secretary, one in whom it was commonly averred his lordship trusted more nearly and confided more honestly than in any other living man.

The secretary, laying the letter open upon the table, turned and faced the farmer.

"You are after your time, Master Peters," he began, "I had expected you yestere'en."

"Aye, aye," answered the farmer slowly. "I were in Taunton then, sure enow, but the mare were took bad and I could not leave her."

"Hum," answered the other somewhat sharply. "You should recollect, Master Peters, time is precious."

"Aye, your honour," answered the farmer imperturbably. "But so is hosses."

The secretary started angrily, and eyed the solemn face of his companion doubtfully. Then satisfied by his scrutiny, his lip curled slightly, and he proceeded:

"Well, well, now you are here, I need not detain you. I see by this letter that you successfully carried out your undertaking."

"Aye, aye, sure enough. I took Master Ferguson to— —"

"Master Peters," interrupted the other sharply, "you will do well to remember this is a matter requiring much circumspection. We will, therefore, have no names, if you please."

"Why, there be none here to hearken," answered the farmer, in aggrieved surprise.

"There is a saying that walls have ears. You cannot be too careful."

"As your honour pleases," answered the man with a shrug. "I took the man, you know who, safe to Lime right under the noses of the troopers, he lying hid in my cart. He bided three nights in my house, and then I shipped him to France wi' my wife's cousin."

"'Twas well done, Master Peters, and here is the price for your task."

The secretary handed the man the bag of money, and watched him secrete it in his belt. Then he laid his hand on the farmer's arm, and eyeing him steadily with those piercing blue eyes, addressed him in a slow impressive tone.

"And now, Master Peters, there remains but one thing to say to you; a warning. You will remember that this matter is an affair of state, and he who has had aught to do with such affairs does well to keep his eyes blinded, his ears deaf, and above all, his tongue dumb. If by word of yours, spoken be it in anger, in boasting, or in drink—if ever, I say, word of this matter escape you, you will——"

"I'm paid to be quiet; I'm not a man to babble i' other folk's affairs," interrupted the farmer in an aggrieved tone.

"I knew it, otherwise you had not been chosen for the work. Nevertheless, bear my words in mind. The man I serve is all-powerful. He can reward generously, but he never forgets an injury, and he never forgives a foe. Good-night, Master Peters, and remember to bear yourself discreetly."

The secretary let the man out through the door leading into the alley. He returned to the room muttering to himself.

"I doubt the fellow must be disposed of, he knows too much," he said slowly. Then he picked up the letter from the table, and stood for some minutes gazing at it abstractedly, lost in thought.

"Fool! Fool!" he muttered at last. "Madman, to put himself in the power of such a man. Of a surety it must work his ruin in the end. And all to no purpose, since the papers are still lost. And yet, what is't to me? For an he rise, I shall rise with him, and if he fall—his carcase must serve as a stepping-stone, whereby I may rise alone."

Thoughtfully he folded the letter, and placed it in his pouch, then turned again from the room. They heard him go slowly down the passage, a door closed, and all was still once more.

The fugitives emerged cautiously from their hiding-place.

"Ferguson! Ferguson!" muttered Captain Protheroe to himself, as he wrapped his cloak round his companion's shoulders. "Ferguson and Jeffreys! for assuredly 'twas Jeffreys of whom he spoke. Now, what the devil—— But come, Mistress Barbara, we'll away from here, and leave them to brew what plots they will."

Barbara pulled the cloak closely round her, and followed him silently out of the house. He walked quickly down the alley, and turned into the silent street behind the inn. The moon was down, and save for the occasional glimmer of a lamp, the streets were in darkness.

"Where are we going?" asked Barbara, wonderingly.

He shrugged his shoulders.

"We must get clear of the town, first. You will not go to your cousin?" he asked doubtfully.

"No, indeed! I would not risk danger to Cicely. And besides I know not where lies the house."

"Then we throw in our lots together?" he asked, smiling down on her.

"Indeed, sir, I see not what else remains for me," she answered simply, committing herself to his protection with an implicit faith.

Under his breath he prayed Heaven he might be the means of saving her.

The streets were very silent, they passed on unheeded, avoiding the watch by careful detours. Of their former pursuers they heard nothing; and, indeed, these latter had given up the chase in despair.

As for Robert, with the quick wit of one well versed in such adventures, experience culled from many encounters with the watch, when his two companions set off down the alley he had scrambled without more ado through the very window whence the alarm was first given, and biding there quietly till the pursuit had passed, he escaped thence as silently as he had entered, and made the best speed he could back home.

So none hindered the fugitives in their progress, and they hurried on, with hope ever dawning more brightly before them.

Suddenly a man reeled out of a cross-street, and ran straight into Barbara's arms. He started back with a drunken curse, stared stupidly down at her, and then passed on.

But when he had gone a few paces he paused irresolutely, looked back over his shoulder, and then turning, ran unsteadily after them and seized the girl's arm.

"Mistress," he said in a hoarse whisper, "I saw thee in court to-day."

Barbara gave a cry of horror and shrank back, Captain Protheroe clenched his fists, and glanced cautiously up and down the quiet street.

But the man laughed drunkenly.

"Bah!" he cried, "I'll not betray you, my beauty. 'Tis too pretty a face to lie hid in prison, and kissing, not scourging, were meeter for thee. Aye, and so I'd tell my Lord Jeffreys himself. I'll not betray thee. But get you from the town. Taunton streets are not for you. That bonny face is not soon forgotten, my angel."

Captain Protheroe scowled. His fingers itched to be at the man's throat, for though the warning was kindly, the tone was insolent, and the fellow leered at the girl with his bleared eyes. But a disturbance was not to be risked. With a curt nod, and a gently murmured word of thanks from Barbara, they hurried on, leaving the belated traveller leaning up against a wall chuckling over their hasty retreat.

But their progress was doomed, nevertheless, to meet with yet another check that night.

They had turned into a quiet street, on the outskirts of the town, when they were aware of three men coming towards them, carrying amongst them a ladder.

Captain Protheroe drew Barbara into the shade of a doorway, and they waited for the party to pass. They stopped, however, before a small house, and laid their burden on the ground; then lighting a small lantern they stooped over the bundle on the ladder, and busied themselves over it for some minutes with muttered curses and ejaculations. There was a silence and a mystery about their proceedings that excited the captain's curiosity, and he craned forward eagerly to watch them.

Presently they rose and rearing the ladder against the house, held it there, while the leader of the three, an old man, small and hunchbacked, clambered up and entered the half-opened casement of a chamber in the upper story. He disappeared for a moment into the room, then returning to the window, proceeded to haul up the bundle by a rope to which it had been fastened.

With a sudden quick movement Captain Protheroe put his hand across Barbara's eyes, that she might not watch them, for he recognised in a moment the thing they were hauling up so eagerly, he understood too well the meaning of that dangling shadow on the wall. A hanged man was a common enough sight in those days, but what meant these silent men, with that helpless body here?

The man in the chamber hauled up the corpse, until the helpless, drooping head was on a level with the window ledge. He secured it there, descended the ladder, and stepped into the middle of the road chuckling and rubbing his hands, to see the effect of his handiwork.

His accomplices stared at him curiously.

"Well, master," growled one, "there he hangs for sure, and we're well paid for the job. But what a murrain a man wants wi' a hanged corpse dangling outside his chamber, is more than my wits can tell."

The hunchback turned slowly and faced the speaker, and his face was as the face of a madman.

"Harkee, my man," he said grimly. "The wench sleeping in yonder chamber is my niece, was my niece, for she's none o' mine now. She was a devil with her whims and tantrums, but for all that, she should have wedded my son, for she hath a pretty fortune of her own. But she would none of him, calling him 'fool' and 'dotard' because, forsooth, he is not so quick in his wits as some. And he my son. But I kept her close, and she should have gone my way in time, when Monmouth's army came to town, and with him this cursed fellow. They met, I scarce knew how, and she drew him on with her devil's eyes. But I kept her close, so I deemed, till at length I learned the fellow had been in secret night after night to visit the girl, thus, by her chamber window. Then we waited for him, I and my son, and fell on him in her room. But he worsted us, two to one though we were, and my son a giant in strength; and he slew my son. He slew my son, and she laughed when she saw him lying dead before her. And he my son. Her lover fled by the window, and I saw him no more. After the battle I sought him high and low until I found him. I brought him to his trial, and saw him hanged for a rogue. But she has heard nought of him as yet. Presently will we rouse her, and see how now she greets this lover of hers."

The man told his story in a cold, even tone, and at the end broke into a sudden savage chuckle; the light from the lantern illumined his face, and his companions shuddered at the sheer brutality of its expression.

But the two eavesdroppers who had heard the story, horror-struck, could endure no more, indeed, Barbara was trembling from head to foot. With one accord they crept from the doorway, fortunately unobserved by the three men, who stood so intently contemplating the horrible spectacle before them, and passed rapidly from the spot, horrified by the experience, and ever pursued by a wild unreasoning terror lest the sleeping girl should wake and come to the window, lest they should hear the greeting she gave her lover's corpse.

And so at length they left the town behind them, and reached the quiet country beyond.

The night lay dark and silent around them. The pure fresh wind blew on their faces, bearing the sweet scent of the woods upon its wings; the trees and hedges shadowed darkly above them, whispering soft answers to the wooing breeze. The air was full of the sweet mysterious noises of the night, when nature murmurs, in those voices which know neither sound nor language, yet speak so clearly to the listening heart.

The wide arch of the clear heavens stretched above them, spreading before their gaze the infinite glories of their star-lit space, teaching alike the infinite littleness and the infinite greatness of man; since though he comprehend so little of what lies around him, yet hath he in his being the breath of that spirit who "or ever the earth and the world was made, is God from everlasting, and shalt be, world without end."

The joy of freedom coursed through their veins, a great peace enfolded their hearts, and the Spirit of God rested upon them as they walked on in silence, side by side, into the darkness of the night.

At length, when they had walked three miles or more, Captain Protheroe stopped and stooping down carefully scanned his companion's face.

"We will go no further now," was the result of his scrutiny. "I fear me we must dispense with a roof for to-night at least. Can you endure a night in the open, think you?" he queried doubtfully.

Barbara smiled, stretching her arms out towards the sky.

"Indeed I can. Three nights in prison have wrought such effect upon me, I could wish never to behold a roof again."

"Good! then follow me. I know of a hiding-place that should shelter us safely for many a day."

He turned abruptly from the road, and helping her through the bordering hedge, struck across several rough fields, until a dark shadow of a wood loomed before them, and in a few minutes more they were enveloped in the blackness of its depths.

"Give me your hand," he said, drawing her nearer to him. "The paths are difficult to follow."

Indeed she could distinguish nothing in the intense darkness, but he walked on unerringly, leading her along a maze of narrow paths, bordered by thick brushwood, and a tangle of undergrowth.

"I played here as a lad," he said in explanation of his ready pilotage. "There is no better way to learn the lie of a country than to roam it as a boy. I verily believe I could go every step of the way with my eyes shut."

Presently he stopped, and turning, looked at her doubtfully.

"We should leave the path here, madame, but I fear 'tis a difficult passage, and scarce fit for you to traverse. Think you — —"

Barbara laughed.

"Fear nothing for me. Be sure, sir, a woman can go through most things if she ardently desire to come out at the further end."

So they turned from the path, and plunged into the tangle of brushwood. Despite her boast, Barbara found the difficulties of the way far greater than she had expected, for the darkness was so deep she could distinguish little of what lay around her, and the briars and thorns caught her skirts at every step. Captain Protheroe went before to part the branches for her, where it was possible, or to help her to scramble over the tangle of bushes that barred their way. In spite of her fatigue the girl's spirits had quite recovered their customary buoyancy, and as they struggled forward, she climbing and scrambling, he pulling her on, she shook with laughter.

At length, after ten minutes' tedious struggle, their way was barred by a network of branches and creepers so tightly enlaced that the barricade was clearly not due to nature alone. Captain Protheroe after a few paces to the left, paused, and pushing aside a branch which yielded to his efforts with but slight resistance, he stepped through the opening, and their journey was at an end.

Barbara found herself in a small clearing, a sloping hollow in the ground, enclosed by a ring of trees and a network of branches. The ground was thickly carpeted with moss, she felt the spring of it beneath her feet; the faint sound of running water announced the near neighbourhood of a spring; far overhead, through the thick interlacing leaves she could see the stars.

"This is our camp," said Captain Protheroe, glancing round with a proprietary air of old acquaintanceship. "'Twill be nigh twenty years since my cousins and I first made it. We were Oxenham's men then, an I remember rightly," he continued with a smile, "fighting against the Spaniards in the Neck of Panama. My father had read us the history, and we built our camp according to the fashion therein described. By the look of it, one would say that none had been here since. The forest stretches far, and 'tis an unfrequented place. 'Twill shelter us well for to-night at least, and then we can lay our plans. And now, madame, you must rest."

He turned to one corner of the clearing, where the moss grew thick and soft, and pulling down some branches, together with long fronds of bracken, he built a rough bower to shelter her from the cool breeze, and give her at least a thought of privacy. Then he spread his cloak upon the ground, and rolled the wide cape over a pile of leaves and grass to form a rough pillow.

He eyed his handiwork with an air of dissatisfaction.

"'Tis a poor place," he muttered; "but I can do no more to-night."

Barbara crossed to his side; she looked up at him with a sudden smile, but her eyes were soft and dark with unshed tears.

"For this, for a thousand kindnesses, Captain Protheroe, I must remain forever in your debt."

She held out her hand; he stooped low before her, and pressed it to his lips.

"Madame, I am amply rewarded."

So he answered her, and had she met the look in his eyes she had known that his words were true.

Long after Barbara's tired eyes had closed in sleep, Captain Protheroe lay silent, motionless, lost in thought.

Twelve hours ago he had held rank in the royal army, rich in wealth, in power, in all the prosperity and happiness of a favoured officer. Now he was an outcast from his profession, an exile from his home, a rebel over whose head hung the penalty of death.

Yet he did not blame his fate. For there, beside him, an outlaw as he, helpless save for his protection, was the one woman in the world who throughout his life had awakened the worship of his nature, and though the star of his fortunes hung low and dim on the horizon, yet before him, in the darkness gleamed the rising star of love.

Yes, he was amply repaid.

So these two rested peacefully in the shade of the sheltering leaves, while behind them in Taunton, Prudence and Robert tossed sleepless, in a consternation of wonder and doubt, and Cicely, to whom Prue had confided the whole story, prayed desperately the night through in an agony of newly awakened hope.

CHAPTER XVII

Barbara opened her eyes wonderingly and gazed upwards into a maze of soft shimmering green. She had slept long and soundly on her improvised couch, and some moments passed ere she could collect her thoughts, and solve the mystery of her surroundings. But gradually the events of the previous night took shape from the mist of dreams that clouded her brain, and she awoke to the new day. With a prayer of thankfulness for her safety she sprang from her couch, and stepped out of her bower into the wider enclosure beyond.

But there she paused, with a quick gasp of wonder and delight at the scene which met her eyes.

She was alone in a strange, green world. The ground was carpeted with thick, springy moss. The walls were of green leafy bushes, and intertwining branches festooned with trails of creepers hanging from tree to tree. Far overhead the giants of the forest greeted each other in a close embrace, each tree trunk arching high to meet its neighbour, and all veiled in the delicate shimmer of the ever-moving leaves. Here and there a shaft of green light pierced through the branches and lit up to a brilliant sparkle the emerald dewdrops which lay thickly encrusted on the moss.

"Sure it must be even thus under the sea," murmured Barbara, "except that there, men say, is ever silence, and here is ever sound."

She paused again to hearken with wondering delight to the thousand voices of the forest, the never ceasing whisper of the leaves, the ripple of water, the songs of the birds, clear among them the trill of the robin, even then beginning his winter serenade, all the mysterious sounds heard only in the heart of woodland life.

Close at hand a spring bubbled up and trickled away in a tiny silver stream. Barbara plunged face and hands into the clear, cold water, and the blood went tingling through her veins. She hesitated a moment, glancing round to make sure she was alone. Then with a half defiant toss of her head, she drew off shoes and stockings, and sitting on the soft moss, dabbled her feet in the stream.

The fresh air of the morning blew upon her face. She was gay with freedom, with health, joy, sheer animal happiness. She laughed aloud, and flinging back her head burst into a wild song of life and love which she had heard Rupert sing a score of times, but which she had never until now fully understood.

But as she sang she stopped abruptly and sprang to her feet, crimsoning with blushes, for the bushes where she sat were parted, and Captain Protheroe stepped out and stood before her, on the other side of the tiny stream.

"Good-morning, Mistress Barbara," he cried gaily. "Is it you indeed, or has some nymph of the forest sought haven in our glade?"

Barbara looked down at her bare feet guiltily, and then as her glance travelled slowly up her figure, she gave a sudden gasp of helpless dismay.

The bottom of her skirt hung limply about her, in veritable shreds and tatters; it was covered with green and brown stains and was torn in a score of places. Her bodice was equally dishevelled, one sleeve had been pulled right out of the gathers, and her dainty lawn fichu hung round her neck in a long draggled string.

For a moment she was filled with consternation, then gradually the ridiculous in the situation tickled her humour, and after one minute's pause her face dimpled into mischief and she broke into a merry laugh.

As for Captain Protheroe, he vowed to himself that never before had she looked so lovely. Her cheeks glowed with health and freshness, and her eyes danced, her pretty feet and slender ankles peeped from beneath her skirt, and her face and figure seemed infinitely attractive, a harmonious part of the beauty around her. She was adorable, and he longed to tell her so; aye, more, he longed to tell her of his new-born love, to plead for her mercy, to lay his life, his worship in homage at her feet.

But he dared not speak his thoughts, he dared not let himself be carried away by her beauty, lest losing for a moment his self-restraint, he lose it forever, and destroy at once his honour and the hope of her love.

So with an effort he turned his gaze aside and assumed once more his customary manner of careless raillery.

"Ah! Mistress Barbara," he cried gaily, again glancing at her garments disarranged and travel-stained, "I vow 'tis too bad of me. I knew it was no path of roses we followed last night, but I little dreamed the journey was so severe an one as this betokens. It was indeed careless of me, and yet I knew no other way. I pray your forgiveness."

"Indeed, there is nought to forgive. Is it not ever a path of thorns that leads to Paradise, and methinks e'en Paradise can scarce be more lovely than this."

He flushed with pleasure.

"You like our camp, madame!"

"'Tis perfection. I have never seen aught so lovely. The forest is a new world to me."

"A new world, and you the queen on't."

"A pretty queen i' faith, in rags and tatters. More like a beggar-maid methinks."

"An all beggar-maids were so, madame, one would judge King Cophetua a man of infinite discernment, and wisest choice."

Her eyes danced in recognition of the compliment, but meeting his glance she deemed it wiser to bring him back to earth.

"An I be queen, prithee, fair subject, give me my breakfast, for I am hungry as a trooper."

"'Twill be a somewhat cheerless meal, I fear," he muttered discontentedly; "I have been abroad in search of something better to offer than the cold bacon and pasty we purloined from the inn, but I met with little success. Here are all my spoils."

He unfolded two large leaves filled with wild plums and berries, and together they sat down to the meal. Barbara laughed lightly at the extraordinary collection of viands her companion produced from his bundle, but Captain Protheroe regarded the food scattered about on the ground with a rueful countenance.

"'Tis poor fare indeed, Mistress Barbara. But that foul witch, Misfortune, has driven us forth into the wilderness, and we must needs endure the distresses she showers on us with as bold a heart as we may."

"Fie, fie! sir," answered Barbara gaily, devouring her bread and blackberries with infinite gusto. "Where are your eyes? This is no wilderness, but a sweet enchanted isle. Some gentle enchantress hath led us hither, and now encloses us with a hundred magic spells safely guarded from the malice of our foes."

"And here we shall dwell happily ever after. Runs not the story so? For my part I should be well content," he added softly.

Again Barbara ignored the tenderness in his voice.

"This is no pasty, neither is it mere greasy bacon that you eat," she continued her parable calmly, "though to your eyes so it may appear. 'Tis magic food that our enchantress hath supplied. While this water," she added, stooping with cupped hand to drink from the spring, "sure no ordinary water could have so sweet a taste. 'Tis the nectar of the gods, and whosoever drinks it shall remain forever young."

"I' faith, madame, you are a lesson in contentment. For myself, hard fare is nothing, but I feared for you. I went fishing also this morning, but with ill success, my hand has lost its cunning since boyhood. But you shall have trout for supper, or I will drown in the attempt."

Barbara laughed brightly.

"Tell me of your camp here when you were a boy," she commanded.

So he told her of his boyhood, becoming boy again as he talked. Told of his games, adventures, beliefs, of life in those golden days when the forest had been to him a place of magic, each rock a fortress, each rotting tree-trunk a fearsome beast of prey, each flower-clad glade a dwelling for the fairies. And she listened to all with a sweet eagerness, a ready comprehension, a quick sympathy which led him to another and yet another tale, till his whole boyhood lay open before her like a book, and through the boy she learned to know the man, the man as he really was beneath his veneer of careless gallantry, brave, honest, simple, and chivalrous. For the man who looks back with love to the days of his childhood preserves one treasure in his heart which the world may never sully.

Thus they talked, these two, cut off from all their world. Naturally, openly they talked, disclosing to one another their deepest, purest thoughts, for the spell of the forest was upon them, and for the nonce the man and the woman met face to face, simple and unashamed The sunlight played about them, the leaves danced and whispered, and the air thrilled with the song of the birds.

"THUS THEY TALKED, THESE TWO, CUT OFF FROM ALL THEIR WORLD"

"And were there no women in your camp?" asked Barbara at last, smiling.

"Yes, one. We would have appointed her our cook, our slave, as is the manner of lads towards most maids of their age. But not she! How that chit of a maiden ruled us, and how presently we worshipped her! She would sit here, our queen, enthroned and crowned, while we must scour the forest for fruit and flowers, rare gifts for her Majesty. We must wait upon her pleasure, fight for her favours, be in all things her slaves. Young as she was, she knew her power well, she tyrannised over us even then, and we—we loved her for it with all our hearts."

His voice was soft and tender, and a shadow fell on Barbara's heart.

"Where is she now?" she asked, with eager, too eager, Interest.

Again he hesitated, and answered in a cold, slightly restrained voice:

"She hath been, for some years, at the court of his Majesty, King Louis."

Then there fell a silence between them, but no longer the silence of sympathy, for he was lost in recollection, and she in wondering doubt.

Presently he rose abruptly to his feet.

"I think, Mistress Barbara, 'twere well I should go and reconnoitre. I will soon return; but I would fain see, if possible, what our enemies are about. Are you afraid to stay here alone?"

"Afraid?" she asked in astonishment, "why, what should harm me?"

"Yes, 'twas a foolish question to ask you, Mistress Barbara, I might have known the answer," he replied admiringly.

He paused a moment, smiling down at her, turned with a nod, and vanished into the wood.

For some time after his departure Barbara lay still, nestling in the luxurious couch of moss, wrapt in dreams. But the fresh joy of the morning had passed, and her dreams grew less bright.

She remembered now for the first time the helplessness of her position; an outcast, with no shelter save such as Captain Protheroe might provide, no escape save through his contrivance, no protection save his arm; she was utterly dependent upon him.

And then she remembered, with a sudden hot rush of blood to her cheeks, that it was she herself who had brought this about.

For he had not offered to take her with him, rather had he advised her to seek out the Lanes and take shelter with them; but she in her heedlessness had refused his advice, had forced her company upon him. And he could not in courtesy refuse, but was bound by his honour to undertake the task, to provide for her, and protect her, even at the risk of his life.

No, she had thrust herself, unwelcome, upon him, and had now no hope save in him.

So she mused, growing each moment more ashamed, more angry, her pride stinging her afresh at each recollection of his kindness and her dependence on it.

For this dependence, which might once perchance have been a sweet thought to her, was now turned to gall and bitterness by the shadow of another, the aforetime queen of the forest, whose presence seemed to her to haunt the little glade, the girl who had claimed his homage, whom he had loved with all his heart.

For if he loved the girl of whom he spoke so tenderly, then she, Barbara, could be nothing to him, save that perchance her beauty gratified his eyes; her presence was but an aggravation of his distresses, her helplessness a burden, unwelcome as unsought.

Her first impulse, nay, her firm intention was to flee from him at once, relieve him from his forced task, and win or lose her safety for herself. Thus her pride urged her to act.

But more gentle thoughts held sway. For Barbara was practical, and above all things, just. She saw clearly that to leave him now, in secret, would but add to his troubles, since he would without doubt seek her again, nor rest until he found her, fearing for her safety. Further, to urge him to leave her were useless; such a man as he did not lightly relinquish a task he had once taken in hand.

No, clearly she could not escape from the position in which she had thrust herself, her punishment must be to remain with him, dependent on his care. Nor must she accept his kindness grudgingly, but with a free heart, simply, confidently, else her conduct were indeed unjust. For since she had imposed the task upon him, she must not make it bitter by any act of hers.

So she resolved, though it hurt her pride sorely to accept his favours, deeming that she had nought to give in turn. For the Winslows were ever proud folk, giving gift for gift, blow for blow, in fair exchange, and Barbara had by no means consented to give nought and receive all at the hands of any man, save that her wonderful sense of fairness (no such common attribute of her sex), forced her to give his feelings the consideration she felt was but his due.

But for that other woman! The woman who had once sat there, enthroned, accepting his homage, perchance in the very spot where new she lay. She rose abruptly and walked to the far side of the hollow, where she seated herself stiffly on a fallen tree, and glanced distastefully at the soft bank of moss that had lately formed her couch.

Presently she grew restless, and so to escape from the folly of her thoughts, she resolved to make a short voyage of exploration on her own account.

She had no difficulty in discovering the opening in the bushes which enclosed the hollow, and passing through she found herself on a narrow green path leading through the forest. The brambles crept close to her side, and at times even stretched their long arms across her path, but in the clear light of day she had no great difficulty in making her way along a road which in the darkness of the previous night had appeared fraught with almost insuperable difficulty.

She tripped along at a fair pace beneath the towering branches, pausing ever and anon to gaze with wondering delight at some newly opening scene of woodland beauty.

Now she would pass a stretch of bracken, higher than her head, through which the sunlight streamed in a blaze of emerald fire. Anon she came to pause in a grove of beeches, gazing up in awe at the giant branches above her, curving in graceful arches far above her head; or she stooped in delight over some gnarled old tree-stump, alive with feathery ferns and delicately coloured lichens; and once she came to a wide, green bank o'ercovered quite with delicate cobwebs, dew-flecked, shimmering like silken gauze, beneath which swayed the tender lily-plants, like the slender forms of eastern beauties, dancing in their jewelled veils.

It was a world of magic delight, and as she wandered on, she fell again beneath the forest spell, and forgot her cares in the sheer joy of beauty. For the forest has a magic charm for all who will yield to its influence. The song of the sea is restlessness; the teaching of the hills is aspiration, but the spell of the forest is peace.

But suddenly she stopped, with a quick indrawing of the breath, for close beside her, separated only by a leafy screen, she heard a deep, shuddering sigh.

Her first impulse was to flee at once along the road she had come, back to the safe shelter of the hollow. But her curiosity stayed her, and she waited, hand on heart, for what should follow.

Again came the groan, and this time she could distinguish some muttered words.

"My God! I will endure no more. It must end now."

Barbara had been no true woman had she turned back now. But it was perhaps as much pity as curiosity that prompted her to push gently aside the branches, and peer through them at the speaker of these despairing words.

Before her, on a fallen tree sat the dismallest figure of a man she had ever seen. Pale, emaciated, with haggard face half concealed by a tangle of matted hair, and clad in that most melancholy of apparels—soiled and tattered finery. His right arm hung limply at his side, a pistol in the hand. His head was bowed upon his breast, but even as Barbara looked, he raised it, and she marked his desperate glance, his eyes hardened in despair.

As she looked upon his face the beauty of the forest vanished, it showed but as a drear wilderness of thorn and bramble, a fit setting to the desperate figure of the man before her; even so does the sight of a drowned corpse rob the sea of all its glory.

The man raised his face for a minute to the heavens, as though he would fling a look of defiance at the pitiless gods; then slowly lifted the pistol in his hand and turned the muzzle towards his temple, curling his finger round the trigger.

Without thought of aught save that the deed must be prevented, Barbara did not pause to consider her best course of action; she sprang through the bushes and confronted the sufferer, holding out her hands entreatingly towards him, and, with a sudden flash of instinct, crying in half-pleading, half-commanding tones:

"Hold, sir, hold. I require your protection."

The man sprang to his feet, and stood for a moment staring in amazement at this unexpected apparition. Then he fell on his knees before her, his eyes fixed adoringly upon her eager face.

"Barbara," he whispered, "Barbara! You! You!"

It was the girl's turn to be astonished. She drew back a step, and regarded the speaker with a frown of bewilderment.

"Do you not know me, Barbara?" he whispered again. "You can't have forgotten me, Ralph Trevellyan."

"Ralph!" she cried in amazement. "Is it possible?" It was indeed difficult to recognise in this haggard figure the gay debonair youth she had known in former days, her brother's boon companion, and a favourite playmate of her childhood.

"Ralph Trevellyan!" she repeated again doubtfully.

Then glancing down quickly at the pistol still in his hand, she cried reproachfully, "Oh, Ralph!"

He understood her meaning, and flushed hotly.

"And why not, Barbara?" he questioned defiantly. "What else remained to do? I am sick of this life, and here in this cursed forest is neither food nor shelter. It had to be death one way or another, better thus than on the scaffold."

"But not now, Ralph," she pleaded; "surely not now."

He took her hand and kissed it.

"Not now, Barbara, if you have need of me."

"Oh! indeed I have great need," she answered quickly. "For I am a fugitive even as thou, a rebel tried and condemned, and but yesterday escaped from Taunton gaol."

His face gleamed with anger.

"What! Did they dare! The fiends! But tell me how it befell, Barbara."

"No, I will have your story first. Tell me — — But stay, I had forgot. You are worn and hungry. Come. I know where there is food in plenty. Come!"

So she led him back to the hollow, and on the way he told her his story. How he had been left for dead on the field of Sedgemoor, but was saved by some pitiful peasants, who hid him in their cottage and nursed him back to life. But a few days since, while his strength was still but half-restored, a raid was made upon his hiding-place, he having been betrayed, and he had but just escaped to the wood in safety. There he had lurked for three days, feeding upon berries and such wild fruits as he could find, until at last, his strength well-nigh spent, and his spirit hopeless, he had resolved to give up the struggle and end his life.

As he finished his story, to which the girl listened with eager sympathy, they reached the enclosure, and parting the bushes, Barbara led him proudly into the hollow.

"Here is our camp, Ralph, is it not a Paradise? And now sit, and I will fetch you food."

"But tell me, Barbara," he asked suddenly. "You are not alone here. Surely you cannot have wandered all night alone in this wilderness."

Now Barbara hesitated, wondering how best to explain the apparent inconsistency of her conduct in having declared herself in urgent need of his protection, when she was provided with a most capable protector already. And while she paused, choosing her words, Captain Protheroe himself suddenly appeared at the entrance and stopped in wonder, gazing questioningly at the intruder.

Then a strange thing happened. Before Barbara could explain matters to either of her companions, Ralph turned, and saw the cause of her sudden silence. He stared wildly at the captain for one moment, then springing to his feet, he drew his sword, and rushed full pace to throw himself upon the intruder.

Captain Protheroe was unarmed, and the attack was utterly unexpected, but he was a man of ever ready wit, quick to meet all turns and shifts of fortune, and was accordingly in no wise overthrown by the onslaught. He stepped back a pace, into the shelter of the bushes, and pulling down a large leafy branch, he entrenched himself behind it, as behind a shield, and peered cautiously through the twigs at his opponent.

As for Ralph, he stopped dead for a moment in absolute amazement at this manoeuvre, then with a new rush of anger at what he deemed the cowardice of the fellow, he flew fiercely to the attack, slashing aside the leaves, and thrusting through the branches in a fury of rage. But Captain Protheroe's spirits rose to the fight, and he on his part did good work with his branch, swinging it from side to side, warding off the blows of his opponent, and occasionally getting in a thrust on his own account with the leafy mass, at his enemy's face.

The twigs snapped, the branches cracked, the leaves flew round them in a wild shower at the sweeping strokes of Ralph's sword. Sure never before was such a mad confusion.

Barbara stood for some minutes transfixed with astonishment at the strange turn of events, then with a quick cry she rushed to Ralph's side, and seized his arm firmly with both hands.

"Patience, patience," she cried. "Ralph, this is my good friend, Captain Protheroe, through whose help I have escaped from prison."

The two men eyed one another angrily for a moment, then Captain Protheroe cautiously lowered his branches, and Ralph sheathed his sword.

"Your pardon, Barbara," muttered the latter; "I did not recognise the gentleman as one of your friends. I had thought from his dress— —"

"Captain Protheroe was indeed an officer of the royal army. But he hath been imprisoned— — You have never told me wherefore you were imprisoned," she interrupted suddenly, turning to the captain.

He turned to her in amazement.

"Why, madame, do you not know?"

"I!" she cried. "What mean you? Is it possible you were condemned for the affair at Durford! Indeed I knew nought of it! I am sorry—I——"

He turned the subject quickly.

"Then this gentleman, madame— —?" he queried doubtfully.

"This is Sir Ralph Trevellyan; an old, a very dear friend of Rupert's—and of mine. He was wounded at Sedgemoor, and is now a fugitive as we are. He hath agreed to join our company, and we will all three travel together."

Captain Protheroe bowed stiffly, and glanced jealously at the newcomer.

"I am sorry, madame," he muttered sulkily. "You do not consider my protection sufficient."

"Hoots!" exclaimed Barbara crossly. "Two are ever better than one."

"Possibly. I doubt not this gentleman is also of that opinion," he answered with a slight sneer.

But here Ralph broke in hotly.

"If this gentleman like not my company, Barbara, I will right willingly rid myself of his."

"Certainly not!" cried Barbara, thoroughly exasperated, fearful also lest, removed from her influence, Ralph might again attempt his life. "If Captain Protheroe like not my friends, he may e'en journey alone."

Captain Protheroe looked up in astonishment.

"Do you desire me to leave you, madame?" he demanded coldly.

"As you please. An you care to do so, of a certainty I would not prevent you," she answered angrily, but her voice faltered. Here was the opportunity she had told herself she desired, the opportunity to free him from her dependence. But now her pride wavered, and despite her angry words, she prayed he might not go.

But he also had pride, pride now stung by jealousy. Without a word he turned on his heel, and strode from the glade.

Barbara stared after his retreating figure in dismay, but she could not call him back. She turned fiercely upon Sir Ralph.

"And pray what right had you, Ralph, to quarrel with Captain Protheroe?" she cried in a fury.

"Tut! Barbara," he answered coaxingly. "We shall do better without him. I doubt not the fellow is but a spy."

"He is no spy," she answered, stamping her foot in her rage. "He is a most brave, a most chivalrous gentleman. And—and I would to Heaven he had not left me."

She turned angrily away from her astonished companion—and found herself face to face with the captain himself.

The gloom had vanished from his face, and he looked down at her with a smile in his eyes.

"I pray you pardon me, Mistress Barbara," he began; "I did not willingly play the eavesdropper. I returned to fetch my cloak. But now——" he paused, and looked down at her whimsically. "Now, may I stay?"

In vain Barbara endeavoured to preserve her anger, gazing back haughtily into his laughing eyes; she was too delighted to see him again, and presently her lips twitched, and the dimple appeared.

"You—you are very troublesome," she answered, turning away.

Being a wise man and well versed in the ways of women Captain Protheroe sought for no more definite expression of relenting, but seated himself cheerfully on a fallen tree, and awaited her pleasure.

Presently Barbara continued, as though nothing had occurred.

"Come, you two must be friends. Give Captain Protheroe your hand, Ralph, and crave pardon for your rough welcome."

She accompanied the words with a glance in the direction of the discomfited Ralph, and he dared not refuse, but he complied with the request in a somewhat sulky fashion.

"Believe me, sir," he said, with the slightest curl of his lips, "I deeply regret that in my eagerness to protect this lady, I did not observe that you have been—er—deprived of your sword."

Captain Protheroe flushed at the implied insult, but accepted the extended hand.

Barbara hastily continued:

"That is well," she said cheerfully, affecting to ignore the rising quarrel. "Now will we be all friends together. And now, Captain Protheroe, the result of your expedition?"

"I fear I have but little to tell. One patrol indeed passed on the road to the south, but for the rest the country looks quiet enough. Yet we can scarce hope to pass another day here in safety; if you are ready we should move on to-night."

"Whither, then?"

"Aye, that is the question. We—" then interrupting himself with a bitter laugh—"I had forgot, 'tis we no longer,—they, the King's troops, are guarding the coast from Watchet to Parret mouth, since so many have escaped thence; there is small hope to the north. We might turn south, and lie hid among the Blackdown Hills, yet there is little to be gained by that; 'twill be some months ere the country be quiet, and you cannot lie all that time in the open. My plan, an it meet your pleasure, is to strike eastward to-night, skirt Bridgewater, and so make for Wells. There lives in that city an old woman who was my foster-nurse. She's a faithful soul, and would do aught for me, I verily believe. I could bestow you safely enow with her, indeed 'tis like enough the three of us could lie hid there a day or so, until we hear of some means of escape to Holland. There you can rejoin your brother, and we can take service with Brunswick."

"But how to reach Wells?" queried Barbara.

"We must journey by dark, and lie hid in the day-time in whatsoever corner it pleases fate to lead us to. We must press on rapidly, and should be there in three marches at most. I confess to the risk, but know no better plan. What say you?"

"I know nought of the matter," answered Barbara somewhat helplessly. "Do what you think wisest."

"To Wells be it then. I know the disposition of our—the troops, and the search is like to be less stringent there than elsewhere."

"We will leave the matter in your hands," continued Barbara. "But I must go to Durford before we start for Holland, if you please."

"To Durford, madame! Impossible! 'Tis the one place where you would be in greatest danger. What in Heaven's name would you at Durford?"

"Why, marry, collect my gowns of course. Do you dream I would leave them behind for any trollop to flaunt her person in them? My French silk, and the blue taffeta, and—oh! my new gold brocade. I cannot go away and leave my new gold brocade. I must have it; 'tis a matter of absolute necessity."

"But it is impossible," he cried desperately.

"Yet I can't go to Holland in these tatters," she persisted in exasperation.

"Indeed, madame, I see not how the effect could be improved," he answered, smiling at her admiringly. "But an it be indeed a matter of absolute necessity, tho' it seemeth at present an utter impossibility, I will bear the matter in mind when I lay my plans."

"That is kind," answered Barbara, with an approving smile.

Then she turned to Ralph with a sudden exclamation of distress.

"Oh! you poor boy," she exclaimed, "I had forgotten you entirely; you must be famished. See, here is our store. Eat what you will, and then rest; you must be wearied out with fatigue."

There was a tenderness in her voice and actions as she hovered over her old playmate seeing to his wants, a tenderness that sounded bitterly in the ears of Captain Protheroe. It was after all only the 'mother' feeling, natural in all women towards one whom they instinctively know to be weaker than themselves, but it was capable of a very different interpretation, and small blame to her companions did they thus interpret it, the one with a quick gladness, the other with a sudden pang.

When Ralph's wants had been supplied, and he had at last stretched himself out to sleep, Barbara came slowly and seated herself by Captain Protheroe's side.

"Captain Protheroe," she began hesitatingly, "were you indeed imprisoned solely on account of what you did for Rupert?"

"Nay, madame," he assured her quickly; "that was but the pretext I was imprisoned on account of an old grudge."

"Yet had there not been that pretext," she began.

"They had invented another, madame."

"But none save I knew of it. How could they hear it?" she questioned wonderingly.

"That, Mistress Barbara, is what I have been wondering ever since my arrest."

She looked at him curiously.

"And did you ever, in the midst of your wondering, suspect me, Captain Protheroe?"

He dropped his eyes before her clear glance.

"I am ashamed to confess that I did."

"That was unjust," she exclaimed quickly. "Despite all testimony, I never believed that you had betrayed me."

"I betray you!" he cried indignantly. "Why, how could you dream it, madame?"

"And how should you then deem it possible in me?"

"Oh; that was different."

"I do not see it," she answered with a smile. "But you know now that I am no traitor?"

"My faith upon it, Mistress Barbara," he cried earnestly. "I knew it the instant I looked again upon your face."

"And yet——" she mused, "'tis passing strange. It would seem we have a mutual enemy. I would I knew who had betrayed us."

"And I," he answered grimly.

"You would be revenged?" she questioned curiously.

"There should be a reckoning, Mistress Barbara."

"You believed me a traitor when we were together in prison?"

"I deemed it possible. Consider, Mistress Barbara, I knew no other who could have——"

"And yet, believing that, you saved me?"

"And yet, I saved you," he answered, smiling.

"Was that then your revenge?"

"Revenge! On you! Ah! Mistress Barbara, that were indeed different. Is not my life yours to do with as you wish?"

"The forest is no place for compliment, sir," she rebuked. "This pure air puts such empty words to shame."

"I know it, madame," he answered quietly. "'Twas indeed for that reason I dared to speak the words, trusting that you would know them to be true."

She had no answer to his words. Her heart trembled with gladness, but she despised herself for the weakness. "His life was hers." Aye, but might not a man speak so, look so, a hundred times, and mean no more than empty courtesy? And in her heart she cursed this cruel art of compliment, the meaningless gallantry to-wards her sex which permits a man to stale his homage at every maiden's feet, and forbids a woman to place credence in aught a man may say, lest she shame herself by seeming to take that which was never offered.

For Barbara had met too many such light gallants, men who, in all innocence doubtless, yet with deep cruelty, juggle with maiden's hearts as lightly as they throw a main; and she had already learned to don her armour, and enchain her free heart in the heavy fetters of her pride.

So she answered him nothing, wotting not what to say. And he, fearing to displease her, spoke no further.

Silence hung about them, the heavy stillness of the noonday hour accentuated by the drowsy hum of insects.

Presently Captain Protheroe glanced up at the sun shining high above their heads, and looked across at Barbara with a smile.

"Noon, Mistress Barbara," he said in a meaning tone.

She understood instantly the drift of the allusion, and shuddered fearfully.

"Ah! we are not yet far enough from Taunton," she cried anxiously.

"On the contrary, we should rejoice that we are already so far. Tho' I sup-pose," he added with a sudden smile, "had we waited, in a few minutes from this hour I for one should have journeyed much further."

"Indeed we should be greatly thankful," continued Barbara seriously. "For here we are, free and"—glancing at the loveliness around her—"one would almost say in Paradise. Why only last night I bade you farewell, and——"

She stopped abruptly, their eyes met, and her face crimsoned with blushes; for as she spoke the words, she remembered, on a sudden, the manner of that farewell.

He understood the cause of her confusion and pitied it. With a sudden impul-sive movement he leaned forward and laid his hand upon her knee.

"Nay, Mistress Barbara," he began hurriedly. "I beg of you not to be so dis-tressed about so small an act of charity. The events of yesterday are as a bad dream; we will look upon all we said and did as the acts of delirium."

To his surprise Barbara sprang to her feet, her face crimson, her breast heaving with anger.

"Indeed, Captain Protheroe," she answered in the coldest tones, "you need have no fear I should otherwise have understood your words. The whole affair was but a jest."

She strode haughtily past him and disappeared into her bower.

Captain Protheroe looked after her with a long, low whistle of astonishment and dismay. Then he shook his head solemnly and drew out his pipe.

"The longer a man lives," he remarked to that trusty confidant, "the more surely he learns that the only safe method of dealing with women is to preserve an absolute silence. Thus only may he chance to escape offence, for they can interpret it as they will."

CHAPTER XVIII

Not until evening did Barbara emerge from her retirement. She found Sir Ralph seated by the spring, mightily refreshed with his sleep, but gazing somewhat gloomily at his surroundings.

He greeted her appearance, however, enthusiastically.

"Ah! Barbara, that is well," he cried joyously. "Methought you had vanished entirely. Come, sit here and talk. I have a thousand things to say to thee, now we are alone. This is like old times again, is it not?"

Barbara assented absently. She was wondering whither Captain Protheroe had vanished. She paid small heed to the look of admiration in her companion's eyes.

"You haven't forgotten the old days, have you, Barbara?" he questioned, with a suspicion of tenderness in his voice.

"Of course not," she answered gaily. "My memory is scarce so short. Why 'tis but five years since you were with us."

"And I have thought on you every day since we parted, Barbara," he continued softly.

Barbara started, there was no doubt as to the tenderness of the tone. She was on her guard.

"Indeed, a most profitless proceeding," she answered sharply.

There was a pause during which Ralph feasted his eyes upon his companion's face. Then he continued in a meditative voice.

"Do you remember, Barbara, how Rupert and I were wont to play we were knights tilting for our lady's favour? You were ever my mistress then."

"You had no choice," she answered laughing. "Rupert took all others unto himself."

"Yet had you still been mine, Barbara, were there a thousand others, you alone. I wore your favour, and vowed to serve thee all my days. You have not forgotten that, Barbara? The day I took my vow?"

"Alack-a-day," murmured Barbara to herself. "Here now is Ralph gone crazy. Ah, me! what shall I do? And 'tis five years since we met. Can a man indeed remain so faithful?"

She looked at him doubtfully, but the look in his eyes left no room for doubt. Then she grew angry at the folly and the wilfulness of man, who seeks ever for love where it may not be found. Yet her anger was slight, seeing no woman is ever angry at love, however unsought, and she pitied him and liked him the more for his love.

So she answered lightly, striving to drive him from his course.

"We played many games in those days, Ralph, I cannot mind them all."

But he leaned across and laid his hand upon hers. "'Twas not merely a game to me, Barbara, surely you know that? You knew that when we parted, Barbara."

Then springing to his feet, he burst out eagerly: "Oh! Barbara, I swear I have thought on you each day these five long years. And now to find you again! You were lovely as a child, and I loved you. You are ten times more lovely now; why may I not love you still? And loving you, why may I not tell you so, as in the old days."

"Because—because—Oh! 'tis folly. We were but children then, and——"

"Then let us be children again, Bab," he answered softly. "See, the forest has brought us together again, and——"

But Barbara sprang to her feet, too angry with herself and shamed for having conjured up, in former days, this love which she could not still, and womanlike, angry with him for persisting in a love which pained her. For even the best of women look upon the heart of man as an unbreakable toy. They tread upon it unthinkingly.

"Indeed the forest has done nothing of the sort," she retorted angrily. "Do not be so foolish, Ralph, or I will talk with you no more. 'Tis unfair to tease me with matters that are past and done with."

He looked at her gravely.

"I am not foolish, Bab, and 'tis not past and done with yet," he answered stubbornly.

"Then, 'tis high time it was. Look you, Ralph, I am glad you are here, 'tis good to see you again, but an you pester me with such talk, I shall—I shall—— I won't have it, Ralph; 'tis unfair."

He looked at her doubtfully, not knowing what to make of her anger. Then he submitted with a quietness that surprised her. Yet he deemed his cause not hopeless, only unripe.

"I am sorry I angered you, Barbara," he answered quietly. "We will talk no more on the matter. Yet, perchance I seemed somewhat sudden. But I have always longed for you, Barbara, and when you came to me suddenly, in the wood, 'twas as tho' Paradise had opened to me again."

Barbara answered nothing. She had seated herself again by the stream and was now plucking the grass and dropping it bit by bit into the rippling water, pondering the while why love may not beget love, and blaming herself for her ungracious acceptance of a constancy of homage a woman should be proud to win.

Presently Ralph sat down again by her side, and eyeing her for a minute doubtfully, he began with some hesitation:

"Barbara!"

"Well?"

"Who is this fellow?"

"What fellow, pray?"

"Why, this Protheroe. Where did you meet with him, eh!"

"I—I knew him first at Durford. He was quartered there with some troops, and rendered us some courtesy."

"Hum! I like him not."

"'Tis a pity," she answered drily.

"No," he continued gravely; "and I like not that you should be wandering thus in his company. Why not send him away now, Barbara?"

"Certainly not."

"But wherefore not?" he urged.

"Because I do not choose," she answered tartly. "Besides 'twould be foul ingratitude. He saved me from prison."

"That is no reason why you should burden him with your protection now I am here. Indeed, Barbara, 'twere wiser to—to thank him, and leave him now."

"I will not. 'Twere most ungracious. And, prithee, how should we fare without him?"

"Well enow, I warrant. See here, Barbara, he may be honourable enow——"

"He is."

"Yes, but he is not one of us. He is but a soldier of fortune, and I like not that you should have to do with such an one. 'Twas vastly unseemly that you and he should be trapesing the country alone together, and I only hope no harm comes o't."

"And 'tis vastly impertinent of you, Ralph Trevellyan, to suppose that I cannot guard my honour and my own good name," she broke out hotly; for the suggestion in his words startled her, and stung her to the quick. "How dare you speak thus? Upon my word, Ralph, you may be an old friend, but, certes, you presume on the fact."

"Good Heavens! Barbara. What is the matter? I only suggested——"

"Then do not do so again. Captain Protheroe is a most honourable gentleman. 'Tis base of you to distrust him."

"Well! Don't be angry, Barbara," he pleaded quickly. "You know in Rupert's absence——"

"You put yourself in Rupert's place, eh? It suits you ill. Rupert hath both greater knowledge of me, and greater trust in me than thou hast, it would appear."

"Now, Barbara, dear — — *Damnation!*"

He dropped her hand and turned aside angrily, for a rustling of leaves and crackling of twigs announced the return of the third member of the party.

Barbara greeted him brightly; she was relieved at his return.

"Whither have you wandered, sir? You have been absent for hours."

"I have been fishing, madame; behold my success."

He crossed to her side, and with an air of deep pride laid before her three tiny trout.

"Is that all?" she asked doubtfully, fearing lest a smile might hurt his feelings.

"All!" he cried indignantly. "Why, what would you more? There is one apiece."

"Assuredly, but — —" then she noted the twinkle in his eyes and burst into a merry laugh.

"Indeed, sir; you have kept your promise nobly. Yet I think we must thank the fates that we are not entirely dependent for our supper upon your skill."

"Ingratitude, thy name is woman! Here have I lain, arm deep in water, for three mortal hours, to catch these — er — tempting morsels, and all I meet with is contempt. Never again, Mistress Barbara."

"And have you not even the story of some monster who hath escaped you, to comfort your heart?" she queried solemnly. "I believe Rupert ever derived much solace from such illusions when he could produce no more substantial triumph."

"Alas, madame, I fear illusions are but little to my taste. But since you scorn my offerings, we had best make as good a meal as we can of the somewhat stale viands which remain to us, and then if you are rested, we ought to make a move."

So they supped, and bidding farewell to the hollow, presently set out on their tramp.

Their way led for some time through the wood, and when they finally emerged in the open country the night had already fallen.

But Captain Protheroe knew the country well, he led them unerringly through meadows and along lonely and deserted bye-lanes, never pausing to doubt his path.

They were, in truth, an ill-assorted party, these three, so strangely thrown together by Fortune, to tramp the night through. For the two men were divided by every difference of life, rank, opinion, and character; they were followers of different leaders, supporters of widely opposed causes, and but two months before they had been adversaries in one of the bloodiest battles of their time. And to this was yet added that fatal gulf twixt man and man, which even a lifelong friendship can scarce hope to bridge across — love for the same woman.

By all tokens they should have hated each other, and assuredly they did.

And Barbara? She had in hand a task which called for all the gentleness and tact of her nature. For with her lay the task of keeping these two at least in outward friendship, seeing from the one she could not, from the other she would not part. And yet, with neither, was her heart at ease. She could not rebuff Ralph, lest he in despair be again driven to desperate ends; moreover, the affection of a lifelong friendship, the gratitude for a constant love, above all, the loneliness of her position, forbade her be ungracious to one who loved so well. Yet even while she showed him kindness, her heart reproached her, knowing she was but leading him to hope for more. For 'tis ever so with women, their tenderness towards all misery leading them to be kind when they should be cruel, far more often than cruel when they should be kind.

'Twixt Captain Protheroe and herself, checking the free flow of her spirit, lay the ever-widening barrier of her pride. For when she discerned the tenderness in his voice, or worship in his eyes, while her heart leaped towards him in the sweet simplicity of her love, her pride cried to her to beware, telling her that it was nought but pity for her weakness. The words of Ralph had done their part, bringing, like the words of the serpent, evil to the breast of Eve. For an it were in truth so unseemly, this wandering with him alone which before had seemed to her so sweet, so natural, what then would men say of that embrace in the prison, given, indeed, in all simplicity, yet given unsought? Nay, but what mattered it what men said? what would he think? Would he think her light o' love? Her heart burned at the thought. So she mused ever, growing morbid in her weariness, with the strain of those last fearful days. So she mused, scorning him in a fierce defiance lest perchance he deem her simple, shrinking from him in a fierce shame, lest he deem her unashamed.

Thus her troubled thoughts strove within her brain, but to all outward seeming she was as before, gay, gracious, natural as a child.

Only in her terror lest she seem to ask for love, she devoted herself more and more to Sir Ralph, whose love was assured, chatting with him of days gone by, laughing over the remembrance of childish mischiefs.

And for a time Captain Protheroe submitted to be set aside, striding on ahead in gloomy silence, thinking on the journey of the previous night, and cursing the Fates for sending them this interloper to part their company.

But after a while his heart accused him of cowardice, thus to stand aside and leave to a mere foolish boy, so he deemed their guest, the winning of a treasure that he yearned to make his own.

Truly he had not over-many pleasant recollections to recall to her mind, yet one he had sweet to him, since the knowledge of it lay between their two hearts alone. So suddenly, as they walked, he fell back a pace or two, and in a pause turned to her with the question:

"Where learned you the art of fence, Mistress Barbara?"

She started and blushed. Then answered with a spice of mischief:

"My master is beside me. Ralph initiated me in the art, and hath even greater skill than I, but we cannot all be experts," with a saucy glance. "Of late years I have practised mostly with Rupert."

He saw the mischief in her face, but forgave it freely.

"Methought I recognised a trick or two of Jules Berin when we crossed blades. Has your brother studied with him?"

"No, but of his pupil. What know you of Jules Berin?" she asked quickly, a note of suspicion in her voice.

He laughed, and answered unheeding:

"Faith, I have been often to Paris, and we always have a bout together. For a soldier picks up many tricks in his wanderings, and, indeed, I have studied the art both in France, Italy, and the Low Countries. 'Tis one of the finest pleasures in the world"—he continued with enthusiasm—"to be pitted against a skilled adversary, straining every effort of wrist, eye and nerve."

There was a moment's silence. Then Barbara demanded quietly:

"Then where learned you the trick of disarming yourself, sir?"

He started.

"Madame?"

"Was it a trick or no? I had not deemed it so before, yet now I fear—— Confess, sir."

He laughed softly. "Alas, madame, you have entrapped me. I must confess to the trick. I learned it then, madame, when I learned many other matters 'twould scarce interest you to hear of."

Barbara sighed and smiled.

"See how we poor women may be deceived by our own vanity. For ever since our meeting I have deemed myself a most excellent swordswoman, and gloried in my skill."

"But so indeed you are," he protested eagerly. "And when we have the opportunity, I will teach you passes that perchance none save I and half a dozen others understand."

But here Barbara must turn again to Ralph, who was listening jealously to the conversation which he could in no wise comprehend. Skilfully she drew him on to talk, and presently the two men were engaged in a deep discussion of their favourite pastime, waxing for the nonce almost friendly over their eager comparison of rival styles of fence.

So they talked, merrily enough, well-nigh forgetting they were fugitives in fear of their lives. For brave hearts do not brood on distresses, but rather despise them, defying the oppressions of crabbed Fortune, and reaping gladness even from the sorrows she has sown.

They walked the night through, halting at times to rest, jet for the most part pushing on as rapidly as possible, that their wanderings might be the sooner ended. Many a time, when the night had grown old, and the silence of weariness had fallen upon them, did Captain Protheroe glance anxiously at the girl at his side, for he knew nothing of the powers of a woman, and doubted whether he were not pushing her strength too far. But she answered him ever with a bright smile and quickened pace, though her limbs ached and her body was heavy with fatigue. For she would in no wise endure to be a drag upon his purpose, and he, marvelling at her endurance, let her be. Yet he was very tender towards her, wrapping her in his cloak whenever they halted for a rest, fetching her fresh water to drink, doing all in his power to ease her journey; and all without question or explanation, but with a gentle, quiet courtesy that softened even her pride, and led her to submit to his ministrations with a sweet gladness.

Onward they journeyed, until with the first grey tinge of morning light they found themselves upon a wide moor, intersected by deep ditches, stretching wild and drear before them in the cold light of the dawning. Here and there on the wide expanse loomed dark and shadowy the outline of some village, the clustering houses pressing round the sheltering tower of the church. Here and there the light gleamed coldly on the dead waters of some still dank morass; it was a scene well suited to the corpse-like grey of dawn, a scene of utter desolation.

The two men glanced quickly at one another as the growing light revealed each minute more distinctly their surroundings.

Then with one accord they turned to Barbara.

She was gazing about her in astonishment.

"What place is this?" she questioned. "'Tis like a field of the dead."

"And so it is, Barbara," answered Ralph quietly. "This is Sedgemoor."

She shuddered fearfully.

"Truly a scene well fitted to the death of such a cause," she muttered. "One would call it the haunt of devils. Why did you bring me here?"

Captain Protheroe shrugged his shoulders. "It lay upon our way, madame, and I fear I thought no more on the matter. The world has many battlefields——"

"But none as this one—to us." Then she continued more brightly, "Whither go we, then?"

Captain Protheroe pointed across the plain to one oil the villages just emerging from the mist.

"Yonder is our destination, Mistress Barbara. 'Tis the village of Chedzey. In that village is an inn, an inn so atrocious that neither officer nor man of the royal troops would ever willingly put head inside the door. I lay there once, in ignorance, and had hoped never again to be so led astray. But times have changed, and it must be our refuge."

"But how? Surely the folk will suspect. Our dress——"

"I purpose to go there as an officer of the royal army, who hath made an important capture of two desperate rebels, yourself and Sir Ralph, to wit. The capture was made this morning before daybreak. I have sent my men on to Wells to fetch an escort; we remain all day at the inn, and at night, our escort not arriving, we set out to meet them on foot. What think you of the scheme?"

"'Tis a mighty lame story," muttered Sir Ralph scornfully.

"Zounds, man, then devise a better," was the angry retort. "What matter the story an we carry it off with a high hand? These rustics are simple enow, and they know better than to carp or question the words of an officer of the king. Besides, we cannot lie out here all day, and Mistress Barbara requires rest and food before she set off on another tramp."

"As you will then," answered Ralph somewhat sulkily, "But the danger is great."

"Of course the danger is great. What then? In a great game a man must play high if he stands in to win. What say you, madame?"

"That I fear you are a gambler, sir," she answered quickly, eager to dispel the quarrel. "But since there seems no alternative, why talk further? Let us to Chedzey and trust to fortune."

"We must needs wait a little space. 'Tis somewhat early hours for calling."

So they sat to rest, and watched the golden light sweep up the sky and shade softly into the pale rose of the sunrise.

Presently Barbara turned to Captain Protheroe.

"Tell me a little how the battle was ordered," she commanded.

"Faith, madame, that is no easy task," he laughed. "A man hath little time to note much of a fight save his own men and those immediately opposing him. And the greater part was fought in darkness, to boot. But—yonder at Chedzey lay our camp, the militia was at Middlezey and the cavalry with the general over there at Western Zeyland. 'Twas a night attack, you must know, and should have been a surprise, but the Duke's army, being stopped by the Bussex Rhine—yonder it lies."

"What! That little ditch to stop an army?"

"Aye! But 'twas flooded then, full twenty feet across. And they made such a to-do being held up by a strange river that our outposts discovered them and we soon turned out. We couldn't get across at them, but drew up our men on the far side of the ditch and fired across. We were twenty feet apart, mind you, but their fellows fired too high and there was small slaughter on our side the ditch. Later we bridged the Rhine and got fairly at them, and then our cavalry came round from Western Zeyland and then 'twas soon over. There was no doubt of victory from the beginning, and but for the darkness and some confusion at first the fight had not lasted so long. The peasants fought bravely enow, I confess,—I would I had the training of some of them,—but the attack was bungled. Nothing was provided for, their guides led them astray, their ammunition was lost, they had no competent leaders, and not knowing whether to advance or retire, they stood still and were cut down like grass. The leadership was a disgrace. Lord Grey and the cavalry ran away, at the first shot, and the Duke and most of his officers directly after."

"By Heavens, sir! I will endure no more."

Sir Ralph stood beside them, his hand clapped to his sword-hilt, his face crimson, his eyes blazing with fury.

"I will endure no more o' this!" he cried. "Is it not enough, sir, that you force yourself upon this lady's company, but you must needs poison her ears with lies concerning your damned victory, with dastardly slanders against myself and my friends? By Heaven, sir, but you shall answer for those words ere the world be a day older."

Captain Protheroe stared for a moment in amazement. Then he gave a quick exclamation of annoyance and embarrassment.

"Peste!" he muttered. "I had entirely forgotten you were o' the other party."

"Maybe, sir, but that is no excuse for your words."

The officer rose to his feet, looking annoyed and troubled.

"My words! I am sorry they offend you. Had I but remembered your presence I had not spoken so rashly, perchance. But—the words are spoken, and"—with a shrug, "i' faith, I cannot alter facts."

"Facts! The whole story is a dastardly lie."

"Sir!"

"And you shall give me satisfaction."

"With the greatest pleasure, sir, as soon as I can come by a sword. I shall enjoy nothing more."

Barbara gazed desperately from one angry man to the other, hesitating what best to do. Then she stepped between them with quiet dignity.

"Ralph! Captain Protheroe! Gentlemen! You forget yourselves, I think."

Captain Protheroe flushed and bowed stiffly. "Your pardon, madame," he said coldly.

Sir Ralph looked moodily at the girl.

The danger was not yet past.

"Captain Protheroe," she continued, with the same quiet air of command, "I have dropped my—my kerchief in yonder ditch, I think. Will you have the goodness to go in search of it."

He stared at the audacity of the request, for as Barbara had never approached the place she indicated, his search promised to be a somewhat fruitless one. But meeting her resolute glance he turned without a word, and strode down into the deep tangle of gorse and bracken that covered the bottom of that dried-up ditch.

Then Barbara turned to Ralph, and used all her arts to bring him to a more peaceable frame of mind.

"Indeed, Ralph," she urged, "'tis sheer folly to be so enraged; you could scarce be more so had you run away in good truth. He meant not to offend thee, I am sure on't. He spoke but what he knew. Doubtless all the royal side think thus of the fight."

"But 'tis a sheer lie to say we ran away at the first shot, or for that matter, ran away at all. A foul, dastardly lie."

"Oh, hush, Ralph. He speaks but as he has heard, and doubtless he believes it to be true. Anyhow, 'tis nought to fight about."

"You don't understand, Barbara," persisted the enraged man impatiently. "What should you know of a man's honour, and when it behooves him to fight for it? I tell you he must answer for his words."

"And I tell you you must not fight. Think, Ralph, suppose you killed each other, I should be alone."

There were tears of desperation in her eyes; he was moved to pity.

"There, there! Barbara, don't you be troubled," he said, patting her hand with an air of humouring kindness. "I promise you we will not fight yet, not at least till you are in safety. I doubt not 'twill need both our wits to get out of this pother. A quarrel does not stale with delay, we'll postpone it till more favourable date."

And with that Barbara was for the present content. She had staved off the fight; who could tell what the future might bring?

So they turned to seek Captain Protheroe, but he was not in sight, neither did he answer to their call. But hurrying to the edge of the fosse they peered down and saw him, on his knees, in a tangle of bracken, all his attention riveted upon a small packet which he held in his hands.

Barbara called to him eagerly.

"I have found my kerchief, 'tis needless to seek further. What have you there?"

Then he rose to his feet, and climbed up to her side. The two on the bank stared at him in amazement; his eyes blazed with a strange light, and his voice trembled with excitement.

"Mistress Barbara! Sir Ralph! What think you I have found? Nay, you would never dream it. 'Tis a miracle of wonder. 'Tis well-nigh inconceivable."

"But what is it? What mean you?" they cried in amaze.

His hand shook with eagerness as he held out his prize. 'Twas a small letter-case in green silk, richly embroidered in gold; a maze of scrolls, in the centre of which were the letters J. M. entwined beneath a coronet sewn with pearls. Barbara looked at it in doubt; what might be there to cause such desperate eagerness.

"J. M.," she questioned. "That is— —"

"James, Duke of Monmouth, madame, who else? And were there a doubt, the contents dispel it."

"The contents?"

"Aye. I have already searched it. It contains five letters, so precious, madame, that it would seem he bore them ever about his person. How they came here is a mystery; he must have lost them in the hurry of his flight. 'Twas indeed irony of fate that he should lose them just in the time of need."

"But what are these letters?" interrupted Ralph impatiently.

"Three are from Lady—from a woman."

"You did not read them!" interposed Barbara quickly.

"Nay, madame, they are sacred. We will leave them to the grave Nature herself has prepared."

He tore them in pieces and scattered them slowly into the ditch. Then as the last scrap of paper settled into the shadow of the gorse, he muttered softly:

"There lies, I doubt not, the story of a hopeless love."

"But the others!" interposed Ralph sharply.

"The others!" Here Captain Protheroe laughed quickly, all the excitement returning to his face. "Ah! the old fox, how he duped us! These other letters are from no less a person than George Jeffreys, Lord Chief Justice of England."

"From Jeffreys, and to the Duke?"

"Even so. Faith! I knew the scare at the Duke's invasion was great, but I never dreamed 'twas so serious as to lead so cautious a toad as Jeffreys thus far to commit himself."

"Read!" commanded Barbara, in a maze of thought.

So Captain Protheroe again unfolded the letters and read their contents aloud, while his companions listened with breathless eagerness.

To his Grace the Duke of Monmouth by the hand of my Secretary Stephen Jewars:

> YOUR GRACE.—Concerning the matters upon which Mr. Ferguson hath already spoken with me, I do assure your Grace that I am your Grace's most devoted servant in this affair, and I do earnestly pray that your Grace's present undertaking may meet with success. The time is well nigh ripe for the attempt. The nation hath been much discontented with the manner of the late elections, and the speech of Master Edward Seymour (of which doubtless your Grace hath heard), is the subject of conversation throughout the town, having awakened much thought in the minds of the people. His present Majesty sits but unsteadily upon the throne, and his power will be yet more greatly shaken when he hath carried out that which is in his mind. For 'tis his fixed intention to forward by all means the cause of the Papish religion so abhorrent to the people of England, and to this end he purposeth as soon as may be to seek to bring about the repeal of the Habeas Corpus and the abolition of the Test Act. It needeth but the introduction of such measures to awaken in all power the indignation of this people, and to turn their eyes at once to him who alone is

at hand to save them from tyranny and oppression, your Grace's self. Therefore, your Grace, I do most humbly beseech you to delay yet a little while, this undertaking, till His Majesty shall have so deeply committed himself in defence of his religion that his person shall have become abhorred of all the people, and your Grace shall indeed be welcomed as the saviour of an unhappy nation. And to this end, I will with all diligence seek to abuse the mind of His Majesty with regard to the will of his subjects, and so urge him more speedily on his course.

I rely upon your Grace's sacred promise, to preserve this letter a secret even from your Grace's most intimate followers, for rumour is many tongued, and as you will readily conceive should a breath of suspicion light upon me, my power to assist your Grace with information of the Council Chamber will be forever destroyed.

Ever your Grace's most devoted servant,
GEORGE JEFFREYS.

"This second is dated June, written after the Duke's landing, when all London was in a ferment as to what should befall."

YOUR GRACE.—I do greatly rejoice to hear what manner of welcome hath been accorded your Grace. Only a consciousness that I may better serve your Grace in my present post holds me back from hastening to your side. But I must warn your Grace that many preparations are about to be made to withstand your progress. General Feversham will start for the West in three days, and with him all the forces collected in this neighbourhood; General Churchill hath already departed thither with the Blues. His Majesty hath further summoned home such regiments as are at present abroad in the Dutch service, but their loyalty is greatly questioned, and 'tis also feared that the militia of Devon and Somerset will at the first encounter go over to the side of your Grace.

It were wise, an it meet with your Grace's approval to strike rapidly for London, avoiding encounter with General Feversham (of whose route I will keep your Grace informed). For here be few troops and those of doubtful loyalty, and the late arrests in the City have won for your Grace many waverers.

Again relying upon your Grace's promise to keep this matter secret I remain deeply grateful to your Grace for your most generous offers, and I pray Heaven to send your Grace all success in this undertaking.

Ever your Grace's most devoted servant,
GEORGE JEFFREYS.

"So they run. Treason clear enow, is't not?"

"Pah! the traitor!" cried Ralph furiously. "And now, having himself conspired against the King, yet he goes free and sits high, judging his fellow conspirators."

"And such judgments," cried Barbara. "Such wicked, brutal judgments. Oh! 'tis unbearable."

"And yet, Mistress Barbara, methinks his lordship is himself in no very enviable position. I doubt not he would give much to know the whereabouts of these letters. And when he sits in court, and rolls out his bloody sentences, I dare swear his own head feels somewhat unsteady on his shoulders."

"That which we overheard in the inn at Taunton, was not that also part of his treachery?"

"By Heavens, yes. This explains his dealings with Ferguson. Doubtless Ferguson acted as go-between; he knew the secret and he is no man to spare his friend an he can use him. It was indeed highly important Ferguson should leave the country in safety."

"But why did not Duke Monmouth betray him?" asked Barbara.

"Because the Duke was no traitor," answered Ralph sharply.

"Possibly," answered the captain drily. "And otherwise, he had lost the proofs. Men say the Duke wrote to his Majesty, claiming to have some secret to confide in him after his arrest; is't possible he referred to this treachery of Jeffreys? But 'twould have been useless to bring such accusation without proof."

"Well, here are the proofs. Now what were best to do?" began Ralph eagerly.

"Nothing."

"Nothing! What! when you hold in your hands such perfect revenge, wouldest leave the scoundrel free to guard his neck in safety?"

"The safety of Jeffreys' neck is a matter of small importance to me compared with the safety of my own. Jeffreys is a man in power. There are, certainly, other men in power, who would give substantial consideration for the possession of this knowledge and who would joyfully work his ruin. Sunderland or my Lord Halifax, for example. There are such men, I say, but unfortunately, it is—er—far from convenient for me to appear before them at present. No, we are outlaws flying from the justice of the country, and the faster we fly, the wiser we shall be. Let us get safely to Holland, there will be time enough for revenge when our own necks are in safety."

Ralph submitted reluctantly. 'Twas natural that to him, whose own friends and followers had suffered so horribly at the hands of the lord chief justice, revenge should appear more sweet than life itself, but he recognised the truth of his companion's words, and for Barbara's sake, if for no other, consented to leave the matter in Captain Protheroe's hands.

The sun was now risen, and the clear light revealed the pallor of Barbara's face, the dark rings of weariness round her eyes. Reproaching himself for having so long forgotten her, Captain Protheroe proposed they should at once repair to the village.

Their preparations were soon completed. The captain buckled on Ralph's sword, tied the latter's hands behind him, and drawing Barbara's arm through his they marched forward.

CHAPTER XIX

The village of Chedzey was little more than a collection of mean cottages, the largest of which was the inn. The inhabitants were already stirring, and the wife of the innkeeper was standing at her door when the party approached.

She stared in amazement and pity at Barbara's tattered garments and weary face, and cast a scowl in the direction of the officer whom she recognized as one of the hated Tangiers regiment, lately the scourge of the countryside. To his demand for beds and breakfast she answered sulkily that he must seek further, the house could provide him nothing, and even when he sharply urged his commands, she advanced grumbling objections and refused to move from the doorway.

But upon this her husband appeared, in fear at sight of the officer, and sharply bade her hold her peace, and let the strangers enter.

"Art mad, wife?" he whispered. "Wouldest have the house burned about our ears, that thou darest to thwart one o' Kirke's officers? Stand by, and let him have his way."

"Thou wast ever a chicken-hearted fool, John," retorted the woman scornfully. "This is an honest house, and not for such wastrels as they o' the royal army. But have your way and don't blame me an you like not your customers."

"Pardon, your honour," cried the man, bowing low before the captain. "The woman's tongue runs out of all holding. Peace, jade, and get you in, or 'twill be the worse for you."

With an angry glance at her husband the woman withdrew, and the host led the way upstairs into a poorly-furnished parlour, where after some little delay breakfast was served, no very tempting meal, but welcome indeed to the famished travellers.

Judging that where most is told, least is surmised, Captain Protheroe gave mine host a detailed account of the capture of his prisoners, adding such realistic details as most appealed to his sense of fitness. His horse, he said had been shot by the rebel, hence his journeying to the village on foot, his only trooper having been despatched to Wells for fresh horses and escort.

Barbara and Ralph listened with great interest to the dramatic account of the latter's desperate struggle, with difficulty refraining from applause at the close of his picturesque statement.

But the woman's eyes filled with tears, when she learned the nature of her guests, and when later she conducted Barbara to her chamber, she hung over her with a thousand tender offices, bathing her tired feet, brushing out her tossed hair, doing all in her power to increase the comfort of the weary girl.

"Eh! my dearie, my dearie," she cried pityingly. "What will they do to thee? And so young, too, as thou art. But 'tis a black-hearted crew they are, and no denying it. My heart bleeds for thee, my beauty. Curse them! Curse them to hell, say I. Nay, my tongue runs wildly, I know, but who could help it. Look you, my pretty, I have a son, even such as thy brother yonder, but younger by some years. To the fight he would go, I could not hold him back. And I sat here all that bloody night, hearkening to the firing, dreaming that each shot bore his death. He came not back. Then I went out to search; I sought night and day among the slain, but he was not there. So I blessed Heaven, and waited his return. But he comes not, nor sends, and I know not where he lies; at times 'twould seem I can bear no more, but must e'en go seek him through the world, till I find him. Ah, my lamb! my son, my bonny son, where art thou?"

Thus she wailed, and Barbara, despite her weariness, comforted her as best she might, praying to Heaven for pity on this sorrow no earthly hand could soothe.

Presently the woman recovered, and with many apologies, rose to leave the room, yet she turned once again before she reached the door.

"My dearie, it seems not possible to aid thee, yet be sure, an I can do aught for thee, I will do it. And who can say? A chance may offer. I will watch. Now sleep, I will weary thee no more."

In order to give more realism to the story of his capture, and also to prevent their disturbance, Captain Protheroe chose to rest in the parlour, out of which both the sleeping chambers led. As luck would have it, they were the sole visitors to the inn, a little-frequented place, and were consequently left to sleep in peace throughout the day. They were full wearied, and it was not until five in the evening that Captain Protheroe roused his companions, and summoning mine host, gave orders that dinner be presently served.

The three adventurers were thoroughly refreshed by their long rest, their spirits were high, and when they assembled at the meal they were all prepared to play to the utmost advantage their several parts in the game of chance upon which they had embarked.

Therefore, while mine host prepared the table, Captain Protheroe, remembering his story, enquired most particularly whether his escort had not yet arrived, expressing great indignation when he learned that it was yet to be expected.

Barbara laughed mockingly behind mine host's fat back while this conversation was toward. Her amusement increased as the game proceeded. She longed to add dramatic touches of her own, but prudently refrained. Nevertheless, she challenged the officer mischievously with her eyes, and he, accepting the challenge, cursed the lazy trooper roundly, rated mine host, and bade him keep sharp lookout lest the escort, missing the house, ride past unheeding.

So they sat down to dinner, mocking at Fortune, jesting over the gulf which yawned at their feet.

And Fortune, in revenge for their confidence, turned her wheel.

For, as danger oft shows least when nearest to hand, scarcely had they commenced their meal when the sound of approaching horses broke upon their ears, and two minutes later after a confusion of shouts, the door was burst open, and mine host hurried into the room.

"Your honour!" he cried joyously. "All is well. Your honour's escort has arrived."

Ralph dropped his knife with a rude clatter, and half started from his seat, while a quick gasp of fear escaped from Barbara's white lips.

Captain Protheroe paused for a moment, his glass to his lips; cool soldier though he was, his hand trembled and the red wine splashed over the brim and stained his sleeve.

Then he turned on mine host with a sudden oath:

"What mean you by this intrusion, blockhead?" he thundered. "Shut the door and say your say. What is't?"

"The escort, your honour," stammered mine host. "'Twas even as your honour supposed. They had mistaken the place, and would have ridden past, had I not hailed them, saying your honour was even here. They wait in the street below."

"Let them wait, we cannot set out yet, before we have dined," retorted the captain sharply. "See the men have drink, and leave us. Shut the door behind you," he shouted as mine host left the room, "'tis most infernally cold here."

Directly the door was closed, all three sprang to the window. 'Twas even as the man had said. In the street below six mounted troopers were drawn up; but their leader was not in sight, he stood talking to mine host at the door.

"Heaven help us!" cried Ralph desperately. "What to do now, I wonder. What in heaven and earth can we do?"

Barbara was silent, her eyes fixed on Captain Protheroe's face.

He strode the room fiercely as his custom was, in thought. Then he gave a short laugh.

"So much for vainglorious boastings," he muttered. "Out of our own mouths we are betrayed. Certes, the game is against us now. We could hold the room—but that were folly. And escape is not to be thought on. Yet—Pah! what a fool! No. I see nought to be done, save wear a bold countenance, and play out the game to the end. 'Tis a wise maxim when the luck turns. And it may be the men have not yet heard— —"

Again the door was opened and mine host entered once more; the joyous importance had died from his face; he looked depressed and dubious.

"Your honour!" he began nervously, "I seem, in my zeal to obey your commands, to have mistaken the matter. These men are not your honour's escort, but a party of dragoons riding from Bridgewater to Wells. Nevertheless, seeing the escort does not yet arrive, and learning your honour's difficulty, they put themselves at your honour's service. And their honourable commander craves the honour of waiting upon your honour in your honour's room."

A moment's perceptible silence, then with a curt "'Tis well, bring him here," mine host was dismissed.

The three fugitives waited in silence for the man's return. Only when the soldier's footstep sounded on the stairs, Captain Protheroe leaned forward and laid his hand on Barbara's arm.

"Do not be afraid, Mistress Barbara." he said quickly. "We will win safe through this somehow. Trust us."

And Barbara, with trembling lips, smiled bravely back at him.

"I am not afraid," she said simply.

Then mine host, with many obsequious bows, ushered in the visitor.

The officer was a big, blustering fellow, coarse of face, and rough in manner. He strode noisily into the room, and on seeing the captain burst into a boisterous laugh.

"Ha, Protheroe, my boy! Well met. The fellow below couldn't tell me your name or I warrant you I'd have been up here long before. What's all this about your escort, eh? Lost your horse, two captures, and the fool of a trooper not yet returned. Ha, ha! Protheroe, you go well to work. 'Tis good I came this way, you'd scarce fancy passing the night here, eh? We are riding to Wells and can take you on with us."

"Good!" answered the captain quickly. "But we've no hurry to start yet awhile. Sit down and drink, man, the night's young enough yet, and my men may still come. Look you, fellow," —to mine host,—"set out more wine, and then begone and see to the men below. And harkee, don't come crashing in like a wild bull again; if we want you I will call. And if my men arrive, let them wait below. Now begone."

Then he turned to his guest.

"Come, Jonas, sit down, and drink; there's no need to start for another hour."

Captain Jonas was standing in the centre of the room, hat in hand, bowing elaborately to Barbara, and ogling her the while with his great protruding eyes.

"By Jove, Protheroe!" he drawled, "is this your capture. Zounds! What a prize. You're a hard man to keep such a beauty in limbo. Best put yourself under my protection, mistress; I'll keep you safe. I'll not swear to set you free, but at least I'll wager that pretty face shall never waste in prison."

Checking swiftly an angry movement from Ralph, Barbara curtsied with quiet dignity, and moved again to her seat at the table.

"Oh, ho! a lady, eh? Who is she, Protheroe?" asked Captain Jonas in an audible whisper.

Captain Protheroe shrugged his shoulders.

"Pah! Only a rebel. Come, drink, man, and tell us news. Where do you hail from?"

"Bridgewater! As dead and drear a hole as ever man was quartered in. Praise be to the devil we're moving on to Wells, and in a month we'll be quit o' this cursed west country, where there is neither a pretty woman—saving your presence, madame—nor a decent bottle of wine for a man to solace himself withal. I thought you were at Taunton, Protheroe!"

"I was—till yesterday. Is there no news from your way?"

"By-the-way, Protheroe!" he exclaimed with a sudden burst of laughter, setting down his glass and slapping his knee. "How could I have forgot it! I' faith there is news, news o' the queerest, and you are the very man it concerns."

"Ah! What then?"

"A fellow came over from Taunton yesterday morning with the wildest tale. Some cock-and-bull story of your arrest, and then later of a prison-breaking, and your disappearance with some woman. But 'twas but a half-drunk trooper, and as I was over in Taunton on Monday and heard nought o' the matter, I beat the fellow as a slanderer of the King's service. 'Twas all a lie, I suppose."

Captain Protheroe glanced quickly at the speaker. Then he leaned across the table and poured out a fresh glass of wine.

"Well, no, not entirely a lie," he answered coolly. "I was arrested, a jest of the colonel's, some wager with my Lord Jeffreys. I was released in the morning, of course. The prison-breaking is true, too, 'twas the same night. But a tale grows like a mushroom in the telling. Heard any news from town?"

"What should I hear in a hole like Bridgewater?" answered Captain Jonas indignantly.

Then he turned to Barbara, at whom he had been staring with insulting openness ever since his entrance.

"I could swear I have seen your face before, madame, but I can't for the life of me recollect where. 'Tisn't a face one forgets soon, neither," he continued, ogling her afresh.

"My poor face is honoured by your recollection, sir," answered the girl coolly. "It must be some time ago that we met. Since my escape I have necessarily had little converse with the King's officers."

The man laughed loudly.

"I don't doubt it, madame. Your escape, eh? So you broke prison, did you? Was that long since?"

Barbara bit her lip in irritation at her slip.

"Some while since, sir. But few words make least mischief, so, an't please you, I'll keep my story for the crown lawyers to devise. You can hear it then, an you care to attend my trial."

"By Jove, madame, you have courage," laughed the man admiringly. "Come, what is your name?"

"That also, sir, 'tis the lawyer's business to discover," she answered calmly.

The soldier laughed once more, and turning to Captain Protheroe, he entered forthwith into a keen discussion as to the merits of the new regiments the King was then raising and the possibility of the formation of a large standing army in the country.

The three conspirators drew sighs of relief at the change of subject, and for some little time there was peace, while the new arrival chattered, drank, and ogled Barbara, and they waited with anxious hearts for the next move in the game.

Suddenly Captain Jonas broke off abruptly in the middle of a dissertation concerning the absolute demand for more careful training of cavalry, and after staring for a moment fixedly at the girl, he burst into a quick laugh.

"By Jove! I have it," he shouted. "'Twas in court at Taunton, I saw you, madame, and not later than Monday last. I saw your trial. What a fool I am! And the name, the name? What was it now? Ha, ha! madame, I'll have it in a minute, we'll not leave it to the lawyers to devise."

"Well! Lydia Philbeg, an you must have it," answered Barbara calmly.

But Captain Jonas shook his head.

"Softly, madame, it ran not so. Philbeg! No, I swear that was not the name."

"What a pother about a name," interrupted Captain Protheroe impatiently. "Leave the girl in peace, an she wishes to be unknown. Fill your glass, man, and pass the bottle. 'Tis poor stuff, but what can one expect in such a hole? Where are you quartered in Wells, eh?"

"We put up at the Green Buck. 'Tis not much of a place, but the wine is fair, and old Dame Barbara has—By Heavens! the very name. That's queer now. Barbara——Barba—Barbara Winslow or I'm a Dutchman! Your health, Mistress Barbara Winslow. Ha, ha! I knew I'd remember it soon. We toasted you after the trial, before I rode back to quarters. Lydia Philbeg, forsooth! Ha, ha! madame, I've got you now!"

"'Well, I hope to goodness you're satisfied now, Jonas," answered the Captain impatiently. "What a man you are for hunting a hare to death!"

But a sudden gravity had come over Captain Jonas.

"Barbara Winslow!" he muttered. "Zounds! Protheroe, that's queer. 'Tis the very name of the woman they said you had run off with from Taunton gaol."

Captain Protheroe set down his glass suddenly. He saw suspicion dawning in his companion's eyes. "Hang it all, Jonas! The fellow must have been a d——an infernal fool. Mistress Winslow escaped indeed, and I was posted after her in pursuit, and caught her this morning. That's the length of the story. Why, devil take you, man, if I had run off with her, should I be here now? Not unless I was a greater fool than—than you are."

But suspicion still hardened in the soldier's eyes.

"Then did the lady escape alone?" he questioned cunningly.

"I bore Mistress Winslow company," interrupted Ralph quietly.

Captain Jonas turned to him sharply.

"You?" he asked contemptuously. "And who may you be?"

The youth drew himself up haughtily.

"I am Sir Ralph Trevellyan," he answered, eyeing the captain defiantly.

"Ralph Trevellyan. Why that's the name o' the fellow who escaped us at Burrows' Farm, four days syne. Burrows' son told me so himself, under the whip. You never saw the inside of Taunton gaol, my friend."

"Tut! man," interposed Captain Protheroe lightly. "Let them have their little romance. We can prove their identity well enow, so a lie more or less is no matter, and seems to cheer their spirits mightily. Fill your glass, and tell us the latest about the fair Arabella."

Captain Jonas darted a sharp glance at the speaker. Captain Protheroe leaned back in his chair, and met the suspicious glance with a lazy smile. But behind his nonchalant demeanour his wits worked shrewdly, and he never for an instant took his eyes from his companion's face.

There was a slight pause. Then in an altered voice Captain Jonas asked:

"Where did you take them, Protheroe?"

"Peste! What a man you are for detail. If you must have the story, I ran them to earth between four and five this morning, in hiding in Mart Mill three miles south of Bridgewater."

A strange light crept into Captain Jonas' eyes. There was dead silence for a moment before he answered in a strange voice:

"That is strange, Protheroe. I drew that cover myself this morning at four o'clock, and I'll be sworn it was empty."

Then suddenly dashing down his glass, he sprang to his feet.

"By Heavens, Protheroe!" he shouted fiercely, "I believe you've been lying to me from beginning to end."

But he got no further. Ere Captain Protheroe could snatch his sword from its sheath, Ralph was at the man's throat, burying his fingers deep in the soft flesh.

Captain Jonas was a strong man, and despite the suddenness of the attack, he fought with desperate fury. They swayed together, tottered, fell; rolling over in a wild indistinguishable mass of struggling limbs. There was no sound, save only Ralph's quick breathing and now and again a choking, inarticulate cry from Captain Jonas. Over again they rolled, and now the man's struggles were weaker. Ralph's grip had told.

"Oh! are you killing him?" whispered Barbara, watching the struggle in horror.

"No, he's not dead yet," gasped Ralph. "Out of the way, Barbara, while we finish him."

"Ah, no! You will not kill him now!" she gasped.

"There will be no need if he is quiet," answered the captain quickly. "But we must get him out of the way as soon as we can. Give me a cloth to gag him."

Quickly Barbara tore off her kerchief, and together the men gagged his mouth, and strapped his arms with his own sword-belt. They rifled his pockets of money, and took sword and pistol, for necessity knows no law.

Meanwhile Captain Protheroe devised his plan.

"We must get out of here as soon as possible," he urged, "or these cursed troopers will be down on us. And 'twere useless to slip away secretly, 'twould but arouse suspicion, and bring mine host to the search. We must play high again and carry it off by a bold show. What then? The gallant captain is drunk, he would have been so in another hour, had he been left in peace. We will put him to bed, and bid the men leave him undisturbed. Then we take three of the troopers' horses and ride off, leaving them to follow. when their officer is returned to his senses. What say you?"

"But is there no risk— —" began Barbara.

"Good Heavens! madame, of course there are, a thousand risks, but we have no time to stop and count them. Once let the men discover us, and it's all over. Now to bed with this gentleman. We must wait a little to give him a reasonable time to get drunk, and then—away."

They carried Captain Jonas into one of the bed chambers, tied him securely to the bed with one of the sheets, and covering him over well, they left him, locking the door behind them.

Then they sat down to wait, their hearts leaping at every footstep, watching the light fade in the west, and listening to the distant sounds of the troopers carousing at the back of the house.

But after half an hour they could endure no more. Ralph's nerves were shaken by the struggle, for his strength was not yet returned after his wound, and Barbara was trembling from head to foot. So Captain Protheroe resolved to wait no longer, but to make their escape while they could.

Accordingly they descended the stairs, and summoning mine host, they paid their reckoning generously, telling him at the same time that the captain had gone to sleep and must in no wise be disturbed.

Mine host showed no surprise. He knew his wines, and doubtless was accustomed to the speedy overthrow of his guests. Moreover, it was not often that his house met with such patrons, and he blessed Heaven secretly for his good fortune in sending him a second officer in need of a night's shelter.

Then, with some misgivings Captain Protheroe summoned one of the troopers, and bade him bring up three of the horses. But the man was half-fuddled with drink, and only stared stupidly at the officer. So they thrust him aside and un-hitched the horses themselves, and the cool, leisurely manner in which they went about the business disarmed suspicion, and none made a motion to gainsay them.

Captain Protheroe lifted Barbara into the saddle. She was perforce obliged to ride astride. He felt her tremble in his arms, but her face was calm and firm.

The woman came out of the house with a cloak and wrapped it round her.

Barbara stooped down quickly.

"The troopers!" she whispered; "keep them here. I may escape from him, but from the troopers never."

The woman patted her hand tenderly.

"Trust me, my dearie," she answered softly. "An wine can make them drunk they shan't move till morning. God keep thee safe, my dearie."

"And bring your son to you again."

"I ride to Wells," said Captain Protheroe as he mounted. "If my men arrive send them after me. Tell Captain Jonas I hope to meet him there anon. Good-even."

They clattered off into the darkness.

"Was that wise?" whispered Barbara when they had left the village behind them. "Will they not seek us in Wells?"

The captain smiled sagely.

"Truth is often expedient, Mistress Barbara, because no one believes it. Captain Jonas is one if those crafty fools who if they would ride secretly to Wells say loudly: 'I ride to Taunton,' and follow the road a mile or so before they double back, chuckling at their wisdom. I trust him to judge me by himself."

"Is not horse-stealing a capital offence?" queried Ralph cheerfully.

Captain Protheroe laughed.

"I' faith, I have committed so many capital offences during the last three days, that one more or less is of small moment. Prison-breaking, petty larceny, assault and robbery, and horse-stealing; 'tis a lively record."

"We are well out of the last danger," sighed Barbara.

"By Heavens! Yes. I thought not to get off so easily. My only plan was to make the fellow drunk, or to lead Mistress Barbara to feign illness when 'twas time to set out, and so we remain behind. But the stars are on our side, we have not only routed the enemy, but got off with their supplies and transport, into the bargain. We should be at Wells by nine o'clock."

"And what then? How shall we enter? Will not the gates be shut?"

"I think not. An they be 'tis no great matter to have them opened. They make small difficulty of letting any enter, 'tis in getting out the trouble lies."

"Aye! 'tis ever easier to go into a trap than to get out again," muttered Ralph doubtfully.

"Oh, Ralph! what words of ill omen!" cried Barbara with a shudder.

"In truth, I see not why we should go to Wells at all. Why not ride straight to the coast?" he queried, discontentedly.

"Simply because Mistress Barbara cannot lie out in any hole and corner, until we have the luck to find a vessel bound for Holland. She is not as we are," answered Captain Protheroe sharply. "In Wells she will be at least comfortably housed."

"But indeed I am strong. I can endure hardship," cried Barbara eagerly. "Think not of that. Let us to the coast an it be indeed the safer plan."

"On my honour, Mistress Barbara, I believe the boldest plan is ever the safest. I know that the coast is strictly guarded, escape in these garments would be impossible; we have 'fugitive' writ large upon us. But who would dream of seeking us in Wells? Where should we be safer than under the protecting care of my Lord Jeffreys himself?"

So they acquiesced, and galloped on rapidly through the gathering darkness. But half-a-mile from the town they halted, and dismounting, drove their horses into the fields, deeming it wiser to enter the town on foot. Half-an-hour later they were safely sheltered in an old rambling house, situated in the lower part of the towns where Mistress Fytch dwelt.

CHAPTER XX

Mistress Fitch was a quiet old dame who, unlike the majority of her kind, concerned herself but little with her neighbours. Her connection with the Protheroe family had imbued her with a certain show of pride, and the gossips in their turn—finding that she displayed a disposition to resent their advances, and finding, moreover, that the old lady's uneventful existence furnished no scope for their curiosity—had ceased to interest themselves in her and her affairs.

She lived in a house larger, indeed, than her needs, where one room was ever kept prepared for the occupation of her beloved Master Miles, should he chance to be in the neighbourhood. The main feature of her life indeed was a devotion to her foster-son; nothing he could do ever came amiss to her, and she had the most absolute confidence in his judgments.

Accordingly, when he and his companions arrived late one night, and abruptly informed the old lady that they must take up their abode with her for a while, it required only a word or two of explanation of the circumstances of their position to satisfy the old lady, and to cause her to set about her preparations for their accommodation.

They found but little difficulty in concealing their presence in the house. Lest an arrival had been noted, Mistress Fytch was instructed, if questioned, to speak of a visit from her nephew and niece from Taunton; but their entry into the house had been at a late hour, when the neighbours had already retired to rest, and as a matter of fact none had marked them.

They dared not venture forth save after nightfall and then with extreme caution, but, although at times the hours hung somewhat heavily on their hands, the rest and the peaceful atmosphere of the house were very welcome after the turmoil of the past week.

Barbara soon found full occupation for her time. With intent to relieve Mistress Fytch, she took into her own hands the greater part of the housework, and busied herself about parlour and kitchen with all the delight of a child engaged in a new amusement. She had certainly slight knowledge of the art of cookery, but it was never her nature to anticipate difficulties, and she applied herself to her new tasks with the same grave resolution, the same hopeful self-confidence that she was ever wont to bring to bear upon all her undertakings.

Some of her experiments certainly horrified poor Mistress Fytch, but the old lady speedily grew to love the girl, despite her whimsies, and despairing of controlling so determined an assistant, she let her have her way.

But Barbara had also another task to her hand. For Ralph, his strength exhausted by exposure and starvation, was laid low with a fever, and for two days lay delirious, dependent on her care. She nursed him with unwearying tenderness, though the duty was no light one, and she shrank in dread at his raving, which wrung her heart sorely. For ever his talk was of Barbara, Barbara his perfect woman, Barbara whom he worshipped with his heart and soul. And as she listened to his words, and learned the story of his years-long devotion, her heart grew heavy with pity and she redoubled her tenderness towards him, crying to herself that she was cruel, cruel, to have nought to give him in return.

Even when the delirium passed, and he was on the speedy road to recovery, her self-reproach, her gratitude, led her in cruel kindness still to continue her tender ministrations, and as he watched her waiting upon him, hovering over him, ever watchful to supply his wants, it seemed to him that Mistress Fytch's simple rooms were changed to a veritable paradise, and those few short days passed like a glimpse of heaven.

But for Miles Protheroe life during those days was alternate heaven and hell.

For howsoever rapturously a man may love a woman, regarding constantly her courage, her beauty or even her disdain, yet is his love made more devout when he may watch her, moving simple, gracious, sweet, about her household work. Then first is revealed to him the full influence of her nature. No haughty queen, no unapproachable goddess she, but the bright light of a man's life, the very homemaker, glorifying by the beauty of her gracious presence the humblest tasks.

Captain Protheroe thus day by day grew to love Barbara more, but with the growth of his love his despair increased at sight of her devotion to Sir Ralph.

As she listened perforce to the sick man's ravings, he would steal from the room with despairing heart and maddened thought, that another could pour out to her so freely the words which he might not speak.

So the days passed, until preparation for their escape from the country could be perfected. Captain Protheroe had not been idle in searching for news of a vessel bound for Holland. There was a certain old shipmaster, John Quelch, whom he had known since boyhood, and to him he resolved to turn for help, for Master Quelch, he knew well, was a frequent visitor to Wells, where his sister kept an inn. Accordingly at the inn he ventured secretly to seek news of him, and there, luck being with him, he discovered the man himself, and confided to him his difficulties. Master Quelch owed something to the captain's kindness in former days, and having readily promised his help, two days later brought the welcome news that his brother's vessel, the *Roaring George*, was shortly to sail from Listoke and the skipper would take them on board. He further suggested that they journey to the coast as his companions, and thus there would be less danger of interruption on their way, since such journeys of seamen and their relatives were frequent betwixt Wells and the sea, and he was a man well known upon the road.

The fugitives accepted the offer right willingly, and this matter being arranged, time again hung heavily on Captain Protheroe's hands until the day arrived for departure. It was easy for Barbara to wait, busy with her many duties; it was easy for Ralph, still weak from his fever; but he had nought to do save sit hour-long watching Barbara at her work, and wondering wherein exactly lay the magic of her charm. All her ways fascinated him, and he could not keep his eyes from following her every movement.

This persistent watch upon her doings for a time annoyed and embarrassed Barbara. She felt sadly conscious of a want of habitude in her work, and feared lest a critical brain lurked behind his observant glance. She endeavoured to appear perfectly confident even with the results of her cookery, but 'twas at times a trying effort. Yet, finding no comments were offered, and her failures passed unnoticed, she grew emboldened to meet him glance for glance, and what she read in his eyes was so unmistakable that it brought the blush to her cheek, and the mischievous smile to her lips, and, for women are at best but mortal, sent her about her work with added daintiness and allurement.

But at length he could no longer satisfy himself with watching in silence; the force of his love, hopeless though he feared it to be, overpowered his prudence; he could not restrain his tongue.

Barbara was in the kitchen, concerned with the making of a pasty. She was alone, nor aware of his presence in the next room, and as she worked she sang a plaintive little song concerning the mystery of love. Thus it ran:

> "Oh! what is love? Some say it is but sorrow,
> Passion unholden, joy a three-part pain.
> Here for to-day but gone for aye to-morrow,
> Leaving behind a memory and a stain,
> If this be so, my heart it shall not move.
> Let me not love. Let me not love.
>
> "Oh! what is love? Some say 'tis but a dreaming
> Born in the Spring-time of a single sigh.
> Blazing in glory, earth an Eden seeming,
> Dying of passion as the roses die.
> If this be so, if love a vision prove,
> Let me not love. Let me not love.
>
> "Oh! what is love? A worship all undying.
> Faith looks to faith, and heart to heart has fled.
> Faith is fulfilled, no more the soul goes sighing.
> Love is for aye, and time itself is dead.
> If this be so, if earth a heaven may prove.
> Ah! give me love. Ah! give me love."

Scarcely was the song ended when Captain Protheroe strode abruptly into the room, and crossing to her side seized her almost roughly by the arm.

"Mistress Barbara," he asked hoarsely, "know you aught of what you sing?"

She paused, silent, wondering at his tone.

"Ah! Mistress Barbara," he continued more gently; "would it were mine to teach you the meaning of your words."

But, though she dearly loved to read that look upon his face, yet at his words a spirit of mischief possessed her; and, maiden-like, loving him she loved to show him cruelty that she might hereafter prove the kinder in atonement. So drawing from him she turned to place her pasty in the oven, at the same time asking mischievously:

"What! Wouldest teach me that love is sorrow, sir?"

He smiled at her and shook his head.

"Nay, that was not all your song, Mistress Barbara."

"A worship all undying," she repeated softly. Then she turned to him demurely.

"Captain Protheroe, how long is't since you saw the lady of whom you spake to me in the forest, she who was once your queen?"

He started back angrily.

"Mistress Barbara! Who hath been spreading scandalous stories concerning me?" he cried in a fury of indignation.

She stared at him in amazement.

"Nay, sir, none that I know on," she faltered.

"Then what— —"

"I did but wonder how long a man's 'worship undying' lives," she answered mischievously.

He eyed her keenly for a moment, then he laughed.

"Sure a man can scarce be writ down inconstant because he remain not true to his childhood's love."

"Yet some men have proved themselves so constant," she murmured softly.

"That should be easy, madame, to one who hath known you all his life," he answered quickly, disarming her by his gallantry. Then he continued: "'Twould indeed go hard with me, must I forfeit all other loves for that one, seeing the lady hath been wed for more than ten years."

"She is wed! Ah!" Then she looked at him curiously. "You loved her once?" she asked gently.

"Love!" he cried quickly. "What should a boy of eighteen know of love? Oh! he may dream he loves, but he knows nought of life; to him all women are angels. But when a man loves, a man who knows his world, who hath seen both what is good and evil in woman, who hath outgrown his illusions; when he loves— — Ah! madame, what must a man feel, who, having learned to detect the flaw in every gem, yet finds one perfect pearl; who, having come to fear that purity in woman is but a dream of youth, yet meets one to restore to him his hope. Ah! truly, a boy may love a perfect woman, but a man must worship her with all his soul."

There was silence between them. Presently he continued more lightly.

"That, Mistress Barbara, is a man's love; what do you know of a woman's?"

"A woman's love!" she began dreamily. Then on a sudden she sprang to her feet with a sudden cry.

"Oh! my pasty, my pasty! I had altogether forgot it."

She flew to open the oven-door, but alas! it was too late, the pasty was a cindered crust. She drew it out and laid it on the table, then turned to Captain Protheroe with a look of deep reproach. To her indignation he was laughing heartily at the disaster.

"Oh! 'tis too bad!" she cried indignantly. "'Twas you who made me forget it."

"'Pon my honour, Mistress Barbara, I am very sorry," he answered penitently; "is't indeed ruined. Could we not scrape it or—or in some other means——"

"No," she answered in melancholy tone; "'tis useless. I must e'en set to work upon another."

"But I may stay and talk to you?" he pleaded.

"Certes, no," she cried sharply; "'twould but cause me to forget again. Prithee, leave me alone, I do better so. Indeed I will not have you here. Go!"

She frowned angrily, and he fled from her in despair, nor marked the blank look of disappointment on her face when he obeyed her, nor the sigh with which she turned again to work. For man will never understand that he was not born to obey woman, and that woman, true to nature, does not require obedience at his hands.

'Twas that same evening. Ralph was rapidly recovering health and spirits, and the three were seated together in his room, chatting merrily.

Presently Mistress Fytch climbed the stair, and entered the room, her face beaming with pleasure.

"Mistress Barbara, my dearie," she began. "There is a pedlar below."

"A pedlar!" cried Barbara, springing up with an alacrity that drew a laugh from both her companions; "a pedlar!"

"Aye, dearie. 'Twas Master Miles here bid me find one, saying you had need of matters for your journey. This fellow hath but just come to town, and they tell me he hath some rare stuffs to show, so I e'en bade him bring them here to-night."

"Oh! Nannie, how good, how—how heavenly of you," cried Barbara with shining eyes. "I will go to him on the instant, I will buy of his best, I will. Oh! how I have grown to hate the very sight of this gown! To think that I need no longer wear it!"

She clapped her hands in sheer delight.

"Don't buy the whole pack, Barbara," cried Ralph cheerily as she hurried away; "or we must charter a special vessel to carry your wardrobe to Holland!"

"You grow well too fast, Ralph," was the laughing reply. "I must needs put you on bread and water an you wax too impertinent."

She shut the door behind her, and tripped down the stairs humming a merry tune, all a woman's inexplicable joy of purchase dancing in her eyes. The visitor was in the parlour, into which opened alike the door of the staircase and the door of the street. He was standing with his back towards her, busily unstrapping his pack, but turned upon her entrance.

On a sudden her cheeks grew white as her kerchief, and her eyes filled with fear. It was none other than Simon!—For a moment she hoped wildly that he might not recognise her or, even recognising her, might not be aware of her arrest and trial, but the hope was destined soon to fade. For an instant the man stared at her in amazement, then a quick gleam of satisfaction flashed across his face, and he broke into a low chuckle.

"Mistress Barbara Winslow!" he cried with an ugly grin at the trembling girl. "I come from Taunton, Mistress Winslow, from Taunton, where there be those who mightily desire your presence. There's an empty cell in Taunton gaol for your ladyship, there's an idle whipping-post awaiting you there, Mistress Barbara Winslow!"

Again he chuckled and rubbed his hands with malicious glee.

Barbara's first impulse was to cry for help, and so bring down the two men from above stairs to her aid. But with an effort she controlled herself, for she perceived on the instant what must be the result. The pedlar was but a step from the street door; at her first alarm he would make his escape, and returning speedily with the guard, would secure not herself alone, but her friends. Her wit seemed to desert her now, in her greatest need; she could devise no plan of escape to insure the safety of the three. As yet the others might be safe, the man knew nothing of their presence in the house. Was it not better, braver, to go with him at once, surrender herself, since clearly Heaven willed not her escape, and so shield her companions from the danger that threatened them? For had Captain Protheroe rescued her from prison (she gave poor Rob little credit for his share) only that she should, by cowardice, betray him now? And Ralph! Had she saved him from death in the forest, only to insure for him a death a thousand times more horrible? Ralph, so weak, so lightly despairing, who loved her so truly. Yes, she might still save these two who had done so much for her. She would not shrink from the sacrifice.

Her mind was made up.

"God wills it," she said. "You have found me. I will go with you."

"That is wisdom, mistress," grinned the man. "'Tis not here as at Durford." Quickly he put up again his pack, and shouldering it, laid his hand upon her arm.

Firm and unflinching Barbara followed him to the door. Simon laid his hand upon the latch, another moment and they would have been in the street. Suddenly he paused. He turned his head to listen, and a smile of low cunning crept slowly into his eyes. For they heard the opening of a door, and a man's cheery whistle sounded in the room above. Barbara gave a quick gasp of terror, she felt the pedlar's eyes were fixed upon her face.

"Quick, quick," she cried losing her wits in her excitement; "let us be off. Someone is coming."

"Aye," said the man slowly; "someone is coming. And there are two rewards to be won in Taunton."

He released her arm, and still with his hand upon the latch, turned to confront the newcomer.

Barbara could do no more. With a sigh of desperation she sank into a chair and covered her face with her hands.

The door opened and Captain Protheroe appeared.

For a moment the two men stood staring at each other, then the truth flashed to the brain of the soldier and he made a spring forward to secure the pedlar. But the man was too quick for him; he darted through the already opened door, into the street, slamming the door behind him.

Captain Protheroe was about to follow, but recognising the hopeless folly of such action, he stopped, and having fastened the door turned to where Barbara sat, white and trembling.

"The fellow knew you?" he asked sharply.

"Yes, he was about to take me to the guardhouse," she answered, trembling.

"Good Heavens! why didn't you cry for help? We might have seized him perchance."

"I—I feared, an I did so, he would discover that you and Ralph were here," she stammered. "'Twould have undone all three. And Ralph——"

"You would have gone without a word?"

Barbara hesitated.

"I—I could not bear that Ralph should be taken," she muttered, shy even then, of confessing her fear for his capture too.

He looked down at her for a moment with deep pain in his eyes:

"I see," he said gently; "I—I understand."

She knew that he did not understand but she could not tell him so, and indeed he gave her no time. In an instant he was alert, ready for action.

"No time to lose, Mistress Barbara," he said cheerily. "We must be out of this directly. I'll give your friend a quarter of an hour to tell his tale and return with the guard."

"But how! Where?" she cried desperately. "Ralph can't travel yet."

"He must. You don't know, Mistress Barbara, what can be done when it's a case of do it or hang. Come."

They hurried upstairs, summoned Mistress Fytch, and quickly told their story.

Ralph was up in an instant.

"I'm ready," he cried abruptly. "What are the orders?"

He had learned much during the past ten days. Despite his jealousy of Captain Protheroe he knew him as one to be relied on, and his love for Barbara forbade him do aught that would increase the difficulties of the one man who could save her.

"We've little time to consider ways and means now," muttered Captain Protheroe, striding about the room as was his wont when in deep thought. "You'll take Mistress Barbara at once out by the north gate ('twill not yet be closed) and go by the fields to Mallet, 'tis but a mile hence. Nannie must go too—'tis safe here for her no longer; and she knows the road."

The old dame was called and matters quickly explained to her.

"Very good, Master Miles," she answered, as calmly as though he had bidden her serve his supper. She had implicit faith in her foster-son in all matters save those appertaining to the care of his health.

"To Mallet then, and wait there. Is Johnny Dean still living, Nannie?"

"Why, for sure he is, Master Miles, why not? Shall I take the young mistress thither?"

"Yes, go to Johnny Dean's and wait me there."

"But you? What will you do?" cried Barbara suspiciously.

"Why, Mistress Barbara," he answered, smiling and drawing from his breast the green silk letter-case found in the Sedgemoor ditch. "I purpose to see an these letters will fetch their price."

"But how? Of whom?"

"Of whom but the man most likely to pay it, my Lord Jeffreys."

"What? you would go there, to him, alone! Oh, no, no, you must not, indeed you must not. 'Tis too rash, 'tis madness. Better risk all than that you—you should—— Oh! Captain Protheroe, we can't leave you behind."

Her voice trembled, her eyes were full of tears. For a moment he hesitated, gazing at her with surprise, with a faint, wondering hope; but he shook his head.

"Do not be afraid, Mistress Barbara," he said lightly; "I have faith in the power of these bits of paper. Trust me, I'll join you ere two hours are passed."

Somewhat comforted by his words, Barbara said no more. She had learned to know by his face when he had made up his mind, and recognised that further argument would but waste time.

When the two women had left the room in search of cloaks, Captain Protheroe turned abruptly to his companion.

"Look you, Sir Ralph, this is a desperate strait. You can await me at Mallet till nine o'clock. If by that time I have not come, then go north, make for Listoke, try to get aboard the *Roaring George*. And, look you, take these letters (I have made copies of them). If you are ta'en, get them to Churchill, or, better still, Rochester.

They may save you yet, even if I fail."

"But, Heavens, man! if you fail it's death for you. Why not come with us, and try to win to Holland? Why go to Jeffreys at all?"

"Because, tho' a desperate chance, 'tis worth risking. Zounds! man, you don't think. What hope have two women and a man weak with fever of escaping the royal troops? Practically none, unless I can buy free pardons for all and a safe conduct into Holland from Jeffreys."

The women being now ready to set out, Captain Protheroe went with them to the door at the back of the house, from whence a short labyrinth of streets led to one of the gates of the town.

There he turned to the girl who stood beside him, her dark eyes gleaming in the shadow of her hood. It was a crimson hood and reminded him of the night he first met her in the country lane at Durford.

"Good-bye, Mistress Barbara," he said wistfully.

A sudden fear awoke in her eyes.

"But you will come after us, you will see me again?" she cried quickly.

"Assuredly, Mistress Barbara," he answered softly; "if there be pity in Heaven I shall see you again."

She looked at him doubtfully, but urged him no more.

"God keep you," she said gently.

Captain Protheroe watched them disappear in the darkness. But he failed to note a dark figure flit from the shadow of a neighbouring house, and follow them on their way.

CHAPTER XXI

Chief Justice Jeffreys sat alone in his lodging at Wells.

The long sitting in court was over. All day he had stormed and bullied, reducing prisoners and advocates alike, and even his brothers on the bench, to a state of terrified submission. He had poured forth abuse on the heads of timorous witnesses, cracked his jests and thundered his threats at the miserable victims of the law's severity. He had sworn, wrangled, and blustered, and now he was alone.

The wearying journey, the tedious days of work, the long nights of carouse, above all the unrestrained passions in which he daily indulged had conduced to the inevitable result; on his arrival in Wells his malady had become greatly aggravated, and his physicians had urged on him the absolute necessity of quiet and abstinence. Accordingly to-night he followed their advice; the officers and other jovial gentlemen who formed his escort feasted apart, and, sick in body, weary in mind, he sat alone.

And as he sat there in all the luxury of his surroundings, despite his high position, despite his success, despite his wealth, power, and influence, 'twould have been hard to find in all the length and breadth of the kingdom a more wretched man than George Jeffreys, lord chief justice of England, lord chancellor elect.

For the man was cursed with a double curse, and the burden of his life seemed at times too heavy to be borne. Cursed with an ambition which would not let him rest, which ever urged him to new struggles, new extravagances, new ventures, and contrariwise cursed with a sensitiveness, a cowardice that made each step in the path of his career an added terror to his brain, each rough encounter a fresh misery, each rebuff a stinging agony.

The mainspring of his character was an overweening vanity. He must be first of his company, he must, by whatever means offered, rise to the highest; but on the other hand he could brook no opposition, a taunt or a rebuke was torture to him, a threat a terror that moved him at times to tears. The rebuffs and sneers which to a braver nature appear but the natural pricks of life, were to him a veritable torment from which he shrank with all the horror of a keenly sensitive soul. While his ambitious vanity drove him to assume airs of overweening insolence, to bully and overawe all who came before him, to delight to see men shrink and tremble at his words; yet if he met with opposition, his haughty mien vanished in a burst of childish passion, and if he found his aims thwarted he became reduced to a state of helpless misery.

Thus his ambition drove him into a struggle with the world, but the very enmity and hatred naturally evoked were to him the source of misery unspeakable.

Such was the man who had elected to climb the highest rung of the ladder. Verily he paid his price.

As he sat alone, forced no longer to wear his mask, to preserve an air of proud assurance and command, the reflection of his thoughts played across his face, and 'twas a bitter tale to read. His brows frowned in pain and perplexity, his lips twitched nervously, and in his eyes lurked a look as of one cowering beneath an ever-present dread. He leaned weariedly back in his chair, his hands idly resting on its arms, his face drawn with suffering.

On the table before him lay many letters from friends of the prisoners he had recently condemned, heart-rending pleas for mercy, despairing appeals for a mitigation, however slight, of the agonising sentences he had pronounced; and among them was a letter from his father, the old man whom still in spite of all he respected and in his own way loved, a letter entreating him to show pity in his judgments, threatening to disown him should he still persist in his bloody methods. And Jeffreys himself, save in his outbursts of rage, was not a cruel man, and took little enough delight in his brutal task. Still he had no choice. For the King's commands had been absolute; no mercy must be shown and the King's commands he dared not disobey.

And in addition to these commands, apart from his hope to win by his zealous service the office of lord chancellor, there was jet another reason, more poignant than all, why he dared show no mercy to those associated with the late rebellion; why, if he could have had his own way, every man who had so much as looked at Duke Monmouth should be put to death.

For he himself, in one of those sudden fits of alarm which formed the cause in him of so much double-dealing, had intrigued secretly with Monmouth, and the haunting fear of discovery had sent him down into the west like a savage beast of prey, panting to sweep from sight all traces of rebellion, striving to prove, by the very ferocity of his judgments, his loyalty to the King and his repugnance of the course of his enemies. So he was driven, by the very desperation of his ambition, to win for himself a hatred and contempt that almost broke his heart.

And to-night, as he sat alone, he wondered wearily whether the struggle was worth the torture it created, and his heart cried to him to give up the contest, resign his office, and in retirement find rest for his suffering body, and peace for his weary soul. So spake his heart, and he longed for determination to follow its dictates. Yet he knew too well the while that peace was not for him, for the curse of Lucifer was upon him, and so long as there remained power to strive for, or enemies to overthrow, so long must he struggle on in misery, until death should bring to him the only rest such as he may ever know.

He was interrupted in his musings by the entrance of his secretary, Master Stephen Jewars. Perturbed and anxious the man hurried into the room, and after a moment's pause advanced to his master's side.

"My lord," he began nervously, "there is an officer without, asking to see your lordship."

Jeffreys moved impatiently.

"Not to-night, Jewars," he said sharply; "I will see no one to-night. His business will wait."

"Pardon, my lord, even so I answered him, but he declares his business will not wait. Moreover, 'tis a matter of the most absolute importance, so he states, that he see you."

"Devil take you!" cried Jeffreys angrily. "Why, fellow, have you not heard the same tale ten thousand times of late? 'Tis another o' these petitioners, I'll warrant. I will not see him."

A moment the secretary hesitated. Then he stooped over his master and said in a low, cautious tone:

"My lord, it may be I am mistaken, but—methinks the man knows something."

Jeffreys started.

"What mean you, fellow?" he asked quickly. "What does he say?"

"Nay, my lord, 'tis mostly by his manner I judge it, for he demands to see your lordship as tho' 'tis nought to him yet for your sake 'twere wise. And then also his words—for he claims to have information concerning an intrigue with the late Duke, an intrigue which may not astonish your lordship as much as most folk, yet 'twill be of greater moment to your lordship to be the first to hear on't."

"Tut!" cried Jeffreys nervously. "Any man might say that."

"Aye, my lord, any man might say it, but an I be any judge of men, this man hath meaning in his words."

Jeffreys was silent.

"Well, well, Jewars," he said after a pause; "I will see the man. But not alone. You will remain in the room, and look you, have an escort ready at hand, lest the man must be—lest he prove an impostor."

"Very good, my lord," answered Jewars with a sigh of relief. "I will bring him in at once."

Two minutes later he ushered Captain Protheroe into the judge's presence.

At sight of his visitor Jeffreys started, and eyeing him sharply for a moment, rapped out a fierce oath.

"What's this!" he cried. "What do you here? How dare you come here? I know you, fellow, I know your face well."

"'Tis possible," answered the other coolly. "I have been frequently before your lordship—er—unofficially. I was one of Colonel Kirke's officers."

"Truly, you do well to say *was*," shouted Jeffreys angrily. "I mind you well, sir. You are he who was committed at Taunton and who afterwards escaped. I have not forgot you, sir."

"Indeed! I congratulate your lordship upon an excellent memory," was the cool reply.

"Zounds! Jewars. What is the fellow here for?" blustered the judge. "A condemned rebel! A traitor! Call in the guard."

"Nay, my lord," interrupted Captain Protheroe quietly. "I have that to say to your lordship of the deepest import. You will do well to hear me out. The guard afterwards—an you will."

Jeffreys eyed him, frowning.

"You are a cool fellow," he muttered. "Have a care, sir, have a care. Do not trifle with me. Your life is not worth one——"

"I am aware of that fact, my lord," he interrupted coolly. "Judge then whether the business which led me to place myself in your power be likely to be of import or no. Indeed, my lord, you will do well to hear me."

For a moment the judge hesitated, trying to outfrown the officer's cool glance, but finding here was a different man from those whom he was accustomed to bully in the law courts, he submitted with a bad grace to the demand.

"Well! Well! say what you desire, sir; but look you, waste no time."

"I have no desire to do so, my lord. In fact waste of time were more fatal to me than ever it could be inconvenient to your lordship. Briefly then, I am here to give your lordship an opportunity of exercising mercy."

Judge Jeffreys stared for a moment in amazement, then dropped his fist upon the table with a fierce oath.

"Mercy! Mercy!" he shouted. "And have you dared, fellow, to force your way into my presence, to interrupt my rest, solely to beg for mercy on your miserable life. Have you indeed so dared, fellow?"

"My name is Protheroe, since it seems to have escaped your lordship's otherwise excellent memory," was the cool reply. "But indeed I certainly have not intruded on your seclusion merely to beg so slight a thing as my pardon. 'Tis a most wide-reaching exercise of mercy I offer your lordship, the release of four rebels at least."

Jeffreys sprang to his feet, trembling with fury, and roared out a torrent of oaths that startled even the accustomed ears of his hearer. But Captain Protheroe did not change a tittle of his cool, resolute mien. He knew his man, and knew well that the only way to master such as he was to meet insolence with insolence, and rage with cool contempt.

"To the guardhouse with the insolent fellow," shouted Jeffreys, glaring with passion. "Away with him!"

"You forget, my lord," shouted the officer, endeavouring vainly to win a hearing; "I do not come empty-handed, I bring my price."

But the Judge was beside himself with fury, and Captain Protheroe had hardly escaped immediate arrest, had not the secretary stepped quickly forward and whispered a few words in his master's ear. At first he could gain no attention, but gradually the storm subsided, the judge's fury wavered before the calm indifference of the soldier, and after a moment's silence he submitted sulkily to his secretary's persuasion.

"Well! Well! Jewars. I will hear him," he muttered. "Look you, sir, say clearly what has brought you here. You claim to have information to give. What is it? What have you to offer?"

"Two letters, my lord."

"Letters!" The judge started forward, grasping the table with his hands, his eyes glaring at the officer. "Letters, say you?"

"Aye, my lord," answered the officer nonchalantly. "Certain letters of your lordship's own hand, which have come into my possession. They are, I venture to believe, a most sufficient guarantee for my trust in your clemency."

Jeffreys dropped his hands and fell back into his chair, his eyes fixed on the speaker with horrible intensity. His fingers moved nervously and his lips twitched. Jewars touched him on the shoulder, and with a start he recovered himself.

"Show me the letters!" he snarled abruptly.

Captain Protheroe drew the papers from his breast, and handed them across the table. He was purposely deliberate in his movements, revelling in the anxiety of the judge's face.

There was a dead silence in the room while Judge Jeffreys perused the letters. He bent his head low over the paper, therefore his face was hidden from the officer, who waited breathless for the pronouncement upon the contents.

At length after a long pause, the judge raised his head.

His face was calm, his voice as usual loud and raucous.

He eyed the officer firmly.

"These" —he said slowly, tapping the papers—"these are forgeries."

A sudden cold chill crept round Captain Protheroe's heart. He stared at the judge in amazement, in slowly rising despair.

"Forgeries, sir," said Jeffreys again coldly. "Have you no more to say?"

But even while he spake, Captain Protheroe noted, though the face and voice were calm, yet the hand which held the letter trembled till the paper shook like an aspen leaf. He noted this, and took fresh courage from the sight.

"Pardon me, my lord," he drawled politely; "not forgeries, but—er—copies."

The judge glared at him.

"Copies," he cried sharply. "Then where are the originals! Show them to me?"

"Indeed, my lord, you underrate my very high opinion of your lordship's—er—ingenuity, if you deem I have brought the originals with me," answered the captain with the same slow politeness. "They are in safe-keeping elsewhere."

Jeffreys swore under his breath. Then he turned to the officer with a scornful laugh.

"And you dream, by these letters, you can prove me traitor, eh?" he asked mockingly.

"Certainly not, my lord, if your lordship can prove your innocence," was the cool answer.

There was silence. The two men eyed one another defiantly. Then Jeffreys laid down the letters, and leaned across the table.

"You are a fool, sir," he said sharply, "an you think to reap any advantage from these letters. I tell you the plain truth. I have intrigued with Monmouth, but solely that by gaining his confidence, I might prove of greater assistance to his Majesty."

"Indeed, my lord, I never held so low an opinion of you as to suppose you would confine your treachery to one party only," answered Captain Protheroe insolently. But his heart beat quickly, for he liked not the suggestion in the judge's words.

"Have a care, sir," shouted Jeffreys angrily. "Recollect you are in my power."

"With reservations, my lord. For, if I join not my friends within two hours, the originals of these letters will, before to-morrow night, be in the hands of one likely to take a deeper interest in the matter than your lordship seems to do."

"Devil damn you, fellow! Have I not told you wherefore these letters were writ?"

"You have. For your lordship's sake I trust others may place more credence in your story than I do myself."

"What! Do you dream his Majesty will believe there is one word of truth in your story if I deny it? Your letters are powerless to destroy me. Heavens, man, do you suppose his Majesty would disgrace me on such evidence? I tell you, sir, I am as necessary to him as his crown."

"My lord, you yourself undoubtedly are the best judge as to what extent his Majesty finds your services a necessity. But 'tis said he is easily suspicious, and 'twill not be the first time such accusations have been brought."

Jeffreys winced at the suggestion.

Captain Protheroe continued quietly:

"But 'tis not to his Majesty the papers would be delivered. He is the head of the kingdom, but by no means the only power therein. It might be, my lord, that the accusation once brought, he would be powerless to save you."

"What do you mean?" snarled the judge.

"I think, my lord, 'twas his late Majesty who remarked that your lordship was not 'parliament-proof.'"

Jeffreys started back and glanced uneasily at the speaker.

"Parliament," continued the officer slowly, "is indeed almost entirely Tory, but yet, as your lordship has good reason to know, it hath no great love for your person. There may not be many honest men among the members, but 'tis certain there are many cowards, and cowards will not brook traitors. If this accusation be brought forward it will not be lightly set aside, And it should not be necessary for me to remind your lordship that you have many enemies in the House."

Jeffreys sat silent, gnawing his nails, and gazing moodily on the ground.

After a pause Captain Protheroe continued with rising courage.

"Now, my lord, should these letters fall into the hands of the Duke of Rochester for example."

Jeffreys started to his feet with a sudden wild cry.

"Your price, man, your price?" he shouted fiercely. Then he sank down again and leaned his head wearily upon his hand.

Captain Protheroe's eyes flashed with triumph.

"My price!" he cried eagerly. "My lord, I might ask much, but I refrain. All I demand is a free pardon for four rebels, Mistress Barbara Winslow, Sir Rupert Winslow, Sir Ralph Trevellyan, and myself. That is my price, and no dear one for such evidence as this."

"Pardons! Pardons!" cried Jeffreys testily; "what have I to do with pardons? 'Tis his Majesty alone who can grant such."

"Truly, my lord," answered the officer politely; "yet knowing the great confidence his Majesty places in your lordship, I venture to believe you will find no great difficulty in procuring what I demand. In the meantime I will content myself with a safe pass to Holland for myself and my companions."

A sudden light gleamed in the judge's eyes. Drawing towards him ink and paper he wrote the necessary orders, signed and sealed them and laid them on the table beside him.

"That will serve your purpose, sir," he said quietly. "My secretary will now accompany you to fetch the originals of the letters; on your return with them this passport shall be delivered to you."

Captain Protheroe laughed quickly.

Then he turned to Jeffreys with an air of deep reproach.

"Alas! my lord," he cried, "you do indeed underrate my opinion of your ability; moreover, I fear, you take me for a fool. No, no, my lord; that plan likes me not."

Judge Jeffreys started up with an oath, and made a movement to tear the paper in pieces. Captain Protheroe stopped him sharply.

"Hearken, my lord," he said sternly, "you will hand that pass to me now, you will take no steps to interfere with our departure, and you will at once apply yourself to obtain the pardons I demand. If money be required to win them I doubt not your lordship has sufficient to meet all expenses. In the meantime I and my friends will ride in safety to the coast, stopping a night or so at Durford Manor house——"

"Durford," cried Jeffreys sharply, "what would you at Durford?"

"Er—a small matter of an old gold brocade, I believe," answered Captain Protheroe, with a little smile of reminiscence. "From there we will take ship and sail for Holland. On the day your lordship procures our pardons, the letters you require shall be delivered into your hands."

"And if I refuse?"

"Refuse! why, then, as I have already explained, the letters have another destination. His Majesty, I believe, has now left Winchester, but the Duke——"

"I should at least soon see you hanged," interrupted Jeffreys furiously.

"I believe you, my lord," answered the captain drily; "but I do not anticipate I should have long to wait before your lordship followed me."

There was a pause. Then Jeffreys continued testily.

"What assurance have I these letters will be delivered to me?"

"My word."

"Pah! What faith put you in my word that you should have your pass?"

"None whatever! but the parallel is hardly just. I am a man of honour. That is one of the few titles to which your lordship has never aspired." Then he continued sharply, "Come, my lord, there is no time to lose; I beg you to come to a decision. I will not insult your intellect by repeating the facts of the case. Briefly, the matter runs thus: Whose head do you count of greatest value, mine or your lordship's?"

There was a full minute's silence. Then without a word Jeffreys picked up the passport and handed it to the officer.

"Ah, my lord! I thought I should not be mistaken in your answer," said the captain coolly. "I need not impress upon you the advisability of doing all in your power to facilitate our safe journey. Our interests will doubtless be dear to you as—as your own neck. My lord, I bid you good-evening."

The judge made no answer. He leaned wearily back in his chair, staring moodily before him. Behind him stood the secretary, silent, immovable, but with an expression of deepest relief upon his face. Captain Protheroe turned on his heel, and strode across the room, but scarcely had he reached the door when it was opened suddenly from without, and he found himself face to face with Colonel Kirke.

Both men gave a sharp exclamation of astonishment and sprang back. Then the colonel with a sudden quick movement stepped into the room, shut the door, and set his back against it.

For a moment all was still, the two stared at each other in dead silence, measuring glances of hatred and contempt. Then Jeffreys rose from his chair and stepped quickly forward.

"What do you want, colonel?" he asked hoarsely.

Kirke turned abruptly to the judge.

"What is this man doing here, my lord?" he demanded sharply.

Jeffreys moved nervously.

"Captain Protheroe is about to start upon a mission to Holland, at my direction," he answered nervously.

"But, my lord, have you forgot? this fellow is an escaped rebel, committed for treason."

"I know, colonel. But he is pardoned."

"Pardoned! By whom? For what reason?"

"In return for information received," answered Jeffreys quickly.

"Hell-fire! That he is not!" shouted the colonel fiercely. "I know you, Jeffreys, you've made your money out of him, and now you would let him go. But, by Heaven! an you do, I'll noise it abroad till all London hear on't. And you know, none better, his Majesty's commands concerning these rebels, not one is to escape. Pardoned! Now, by the light of the Prophet's beard, the man is a traitor and shall hang e'en if I had to do it with my own hands. Pardoned! Pah! The man shall hang as sure as my name is Percy Kirke."

He ceased, and there was another silence. Captain Protheroe loosened in its sheath the sword he earned and glanced rapidly round the room. He turned to the chief justice, but no further help showed there. Jeffreys had sunk back in his chair, and looked the picture of helpless dismay. The man was a mass of nerves, sensitive as a girl; he trembled under Colonel Kirke's fierce attack, and had no words with which to defend himself.

"Do you understand me, Jeffreys?" the colonel again shouted. "By Heaven, I'll publish the facts."

"My lord," interposed Captain Protheroe quietly, "'tis but a night's ride to Winchester."

Jeffreys looked from one to the other hopelessly calculating his chances with a desperate cunning.

"Tut, colonel," he began nervously; "what is the man to you? Let him ——"

He was interrupted by a sudden knock at the door, and the entrance of an orderly.

"A messenger from London, my lord," he said.

He marched across to the chief justice, and handed him a packet, then saluting, turned and left the room.

Partly with the idea of gaining time, partly with a faint hope of there finding a way out of his difficulty, Jeffreys broke open the packet and began to read. Colonel Kirke stood silent, watching him angrily, but Captain Protheroe glanced hurriedly up and down the room, puzzling his wits to devise some method of escape.

Suddenly the chief justice started to his feet and turned to the colonel. There was a look of excitement on his face, and triumph in his eyes.

"Colonel Kirke," he exclaimed harshly, "you are recalled to London!"

With clenched hands and blazing eyes Kirke turned on Jeffreys.

"Recalled! I! What in the devil's name do you mean?"

"Here are your orders. The regiment will proceed there in the course of a week. You are to set out immediately."

Kirke stared at the paper in amazement; then he threw it to the ground and stamped on it in a sudden fury. "Recalled! Disgraced! Bah! Have you had a hand in this, Jeffreys? Recalled! Now, by — —" He roared out a torrent of oaths.

Presently he grew calmer, picked up the paper, read it once more, and locked moodily at the chief justice.

"I must set out at once," he muttered. "But look you, Jeffreys, a word of warning; this is but a passing affair, the work o' that meddlesome Sunderland, I'll be bound. I shall soon return, so be careful what you do. I've set my heart on this matter" — pointing to the captain. "When I return, an that fellow be not handed over to me for court-martial, then, by all the devils in heaven and hell, I'll be revenged. You know me, Jeffreys, and you know what I can do. Take warning."

He swung to the door, then pausing, turned to Captain Protheroe, and eyed him with a scornful glance.

"A narrow shave for you," he said; "but I'll hope to see you hanged yet, my fine fellow."

Captain Protheroe smiled scornfully.

"I'm afraid, colonel," he answered drily, "unless our executions take place simultaneously on the same spot, we can't both realise our mutual hope."

With an oath Colonel Kirke swung out of the room, and the door was shut. Then Captain Protheroe turned to Jeffreys. The judge's face was a study of indecision. He stared moodily at the letters before him, he glanced nervously at the door through which the colonel had retired. He was a man standing betwixt two abysses, doubting over which to risk a jump. At last he raised his head, and faced the captain defiantly.

"Captain Protheroe," he said, "I must withdraw your passport and place you under arrest."

Captain Protheroe stared at the judge in dismay. The secretary took a rapid step forward, and stooped over his master's chair.

"My lord," he whispered, "think what you do. These letters — —"

"I know! I know!" cried Jeffreys testily; "but I also know Kirke. 'Tis one or the other, and Kirke is not a man to deny."

Again the secretary stooped to argue, but Jeffreys thrust him aside.

"No, no, Jewars, I tell you 'tis the safer way. This is the only evidence" — tapping the letters — "and it may be disproved."

Then, with a sudden inspiration Captain Protheroe stepped forward, and leaning over the table, fixed his eyes on Jeffreys.

"The only evidence, my lord?" he asked quietly. "Tell me, has your lordship ever heard of a certain Master Hugh Peters, of Lime?"

"Peters!" gasped the secretary, with a sudden start of horror.

"Aye," answered the officer slowly. "A worthy man who can give much valuable information concerning the manner of Ferguson's escape, about which there has been so great a pother in London. And, my lord, he is not the only man who knows the secret."

With a sudden cry the secretary caught the chief justice's arm; his face was livid, he trembled from head to foot.

"My lord," he cried, "there is no help for it, this man must go. There is no safety else. He knows—Heavens! what does he not know? My lord, Colonel Kirke may be dangerous, but he is disgraced, and he hath but little evidence, and 'tis but a matter of bribery after all. But this man—oh, my lord! let him go, out of the country with him, and Heaven grant we may never see him more."

Jeffreys turned and stared at the terrified man, and slowly the fear passed into his own heart. Fiercely he clutched the arms of his chair, his eyes rolled, he moved his head from side to side, as one hounded to death, and seeing no escape. Then with a loud cry of rage and despair, he sprang to his feet, and pointed wildly to the door.

"Go!" he cried. "Go! You are free! But have a care. For an you come within my power again, by God! you shall pay for this. You shall die a thousand times; at the cart-tail, at the post, at the gallows, at the stake. You shall feel a thousand torments, till hell itself shall show more merciful. I will— —"

"Silence!" shouted the captain sternly. "Peace, fool, I will hear no more o' such vapourings. I go now, but first, mark you this, my Lord Jeffreys, see to it you carry out our contract to the smallest detail, for should harm befall me and mine thro' your doing, I vow to heaven, my lord, I will not hang alone. So, an you value your own neck, leave us in peace."

For one moment Jeffreys stood gasping open-mouthed, gazing at the speaker in a fury of impotent rage, then he suddenly collapsed and sinking into his chair, he fell forward across the table and burst into bitter tears.

But Captain Protheroe waited no longer, but tucking the passport into his breast, proceeded calmly to the street. Nor did he pause until he had passed out of the north gate and left the town behind him.

"Phew!" he muttered, wiping his forehead, "I've played high in my time, but never for such stakes as these. Heaven help me! what a hand I held, and God forgive me, but how I played it!"

CHAPTER XXII

Captain Protheroe walked on rapidly across the dark field-path which led to the little hamlet of Mallet. It was already late, and he did not wish to keep his friends in suspense longer than was needful.

Suddenly he paused, as he became aware of a confused clamour of sounds proceeding from the direction in which, he was going, but only for a moment, then with a sudden misgiving he commenced to run rapidly forward through the darkness.

The cottage where the fugitives were to await him lay on the outskirts of the hamlet, separated from the cluster of other cottages by some fields, and the sounds, now becoming more distinct, came from that direction.

A confused murmur of voices met his ears, punctuated by a succession of heavy blows of musket-butts (so he rightly guessed) upon the cottage door; then followed the crash of a door falling, more shouting, above which he could distinguish a voice raised loud in authority, and then the clash of two encountering swords.

A moment later he reached the gateway of the croft within which the cottage stood.

There he found a group of peasants, held in check, in spite of much shouting and menacing gestures, by a small body of mounted troopers. Nearer the cottage were some unmounted men, those evidently who had been responsible for the attack upon the door, one or two of whom carried lanterns, and by the combined light this afforded, and that which streamed from the dismantled doorway, there was revealed to Captain Protheroe the incident which formed the central feature of the picture.

At the doorway of the cottage two men were fighting. The swordsman with his back to the doorway was Sir Ralph. With white set face, and his breath coming in quick gasps, 'twas clear he was sore pressed, and wellnigh spent.

His opponent, who was slowly but surely driving him to retreat into the passage-way, was a small, dapper little man, in the uniform of an officer of the King's troops. He fought with a cool precision, and ever and anon as the fight proceeded, he exclaimed admiringly:

"Well thrust, sir, well indeed. Keep back, men, let be. 'Tis a fair fight."

For a few moments Captain Protheroe stood in amazement, watching this extraordinary scene, then suddenly realising that unless he quickly intervened

Ralph must be overcome, he thrust his way past the startled troopers, and ere they could prevent him, seized the little officer round the middle and lifted him aside.

The latter, with an exclamation of anger, wrenched himself free, and turned upon the intruder.

"And by what right, sir — —" he began furiously; but ere he could get further in his speech his hand was seized in a hearty grasp, and Captain Protheroe broke out eagerly:

"Harrington! Will! You! By all the powers, but luck is with us wherever we go. This is splendid."

"Miles Protheroe!" cried the little man in delight, but restraining himself suddenly, he stared hard at the captain. "What are you doing here, Protheroe?" he asked sharply. "D— — me, I had forgot, you are a rebel, too."

But the other's light laugh quickly reassured him.

"No more a rebel than are these, my friends, here," he cried cheerily. "Look" — and he handed his passport to Harrington—"that is all right, isn't it? By Jove! what a mercy I arrived in time; you were about to make a pretty mess of things, Will."

"Plague take that meddlesome pedlar, who brought us out with such a cock-and-bull story as this," cried the little officer indignantly. "Here have I been forced to put your friends—and a lady, too—to most distressing inconvenience and—er—danger, and all to no purpose. Alas! I doubt she will never forgive me. Plague on the fellow! where is he?"

But the pedlar, who had followed them to the cottage, and having given information had then served as guide to the patrol, was not to be found. He was quick to appreciate that the game again had gone against and had vanished into the night.

"But what were you after when I arrived, Will?" asked Captain Protheroe with a laugh.

"This gentleman thought fit to hold the doorway, against me. I—I was—-er—about to remove him."

Then he turned politely to Ralph, who had sunk wearily into a seat within the doorway, whence he smiled faintly up at Barbara as she came anxiously from an adjoining room to his side, to ascertain whether he had received any hurt.

"I must apologise, sir," he said with grave politeness, "for so rudely forcing myself upon your company. 'Twas a misconception, which I trust you will pardon. But I fear I can never hope the lady will be equally forgiving."

Barbara looked up with a bright smile.

"Indeed, sir," she said softly, "we should rather be grateful to you, for the generous manner in which you conducted the attack. We owe you thanks for your courtesy in staying your men from firing upon the house when you discovered I was here, and for your chivalry in insisting upon fighting Sir Ralph single-handed."

The little man flushed with pleasure.

"Faith! madame," he cried gallantly; "'twas nothing. However hard pressed a man may be, nothing would excuse discourtesy to a lady. And for the rest, 'twas a most enjoyable fight whose interruption is condoned only by the acquaintance thus created."

Captain Protheroe laughed lightly.

"Zounds! Will, what would the colonel say to your new methods of rebel hunting, eh? He is ever the same, Mistress Barbara; he rides the country with a cumbersome escort, yet doth all the work himself."

Captain Harrington again turned to his recent adversary, who still leaned back, with half-closed eyes.

"I trust, sir," he said anxiously, "I have not been so excessively clumsy as to wound you in our affray. 'Tis a thing I never do, unless mortally."

Ralph smiled faintly.

"Rest assured, sir, your hand is still sure."

"Sir Ralph Trevellyan is but recovering from a fever," interposed Barbara gently; "the encounter hath exhausted him."

"I am well enough, Barbara," exclaimed Ralph, struggling to his feet.

"Indeed, you are not," she answered firmly. "Sit still while I fetch some water."

But now Captain Harrington was all contrition. He flew for water, he sent his men for wine. He hovered over Barbara with most assiduous attentions, while she ministered to her exhausted companion.

"What may I do now?" implored the little officer, when Barbara had finished her task; "what may I do to further atone for my mistake? Where are you bound for now, eh?"

"We are on our road to Durford; it lies north of Taunton, you know; but we can hardly set out to-night. Is there any place hereabouts fit to spend the night in?" asked Captain Protheroe doubtfully.

"My quarters are but five minutes' distance from here," cried Captain Harrington eagerly; "if I dared hope to be so greatly honoured."

"Oh, no," cried Barbara quickly; "indeed, we cannot take your rooms."

"Alack! madame, I feared 'twas too great an honour to hope for," sighed the little man mournfully. "After my error, too. And yet, if it might have been— —"

"Nay, sir," interposed Barbara, somewhat puzzled how to meet such unexpected humility. "If you will indeed be so generous— —"

"It will be the best thing we can do," interposed Captain Protheroe. "And to-morrow, perchance, you can lend us mounts as far as Durford."

"Willingly, willingly," was the eager reply.

"Then let us be off. Where is Nannie?"

"I'm here, Master Miles," answered the old lady, calmly entering from the adjoining room where she had been soothing the terror of the bed-ridden owner of the cottage.

"Ah! that's well. We must be moving. Set the old fellow's mind at ease and come along. You shall come back to him to-morrow, an you choose."

All was quiet when they came out of the cottage.

"Straight along that path, Miles!" cried Captain Harrington eagerly, pointing out the direction; "you can't miss the way. I will escort the lady."

"Not so," answered Captain Protheroe resolutely, putting Barbara's cloak about her; "I will escort Mistress Barbara. You can best lead the way."

Captain Harrington glanced for a moment at the speaker, then with a deep sigh, and a mournful shake of the head, he shrugged his shoulders, and taking Ralph's arm, turned along the path towards the village.

"Alack!" he muttered to himself, "Alack! The early bird!"

"Mistress Barbara," pleaded Captain Protheroe, as they followed the others along the narrow way, "Mistress Barbara, you have not said one word to me since I arrived."

"I had nothing to say," she answered, smiling. Then she added softly, "I knew you would come."

And with that he strove to be content.

CHAPTER XXIII

Next day they rode merrily to Durford. At early morning they set out, when the white mist curled in the valley, and the russet trees, sun-kissed on the hills, gleamed like fiery tongues of flame above a silver sea; through the bright noonday they rode, when the mists like evil witches of the night had vanished before the sunbeams, the broad earth lay smiling up into the deep blue heavens, and the myriad creatures of earth and sky raised their tiny voices in harmonious *Te Deum* for the glory of life. Through a world of joy and sunshine they rode, until early in the afternoon they climbed the last hill and saw in the valley below the red-roofed cottages of the village and the tall grey chimneys of the Manor House hiding among the burnished leaves.

And from that point their ride was a royal progress.

Like lightning the news spread about the village that Mistress Barbara was come home. Cottage doors were flung open, women and children rushed headlong into the street to meet her. They crowded round her to kiss her hands, to shower greetings upon her; the women wept, like the foolish creatures they are; all the village was agog with joy. And Barbara, with shining eyes, laughed and waved her hand, and rode through them like a queen. At length they reached the park gates, and there was Cicely, her ribbons streaming in the wind, her hands outstretched in eager welcome, running full-pace to meet them.

Barbara leapt from her saddle, and with a sudden queer little sob rushed into her cousin's arms.

There they stood crying and kissing, while the villagers flung up their caps and laughed with delight, and the bells broke out into a wild peal of music because Barbara Winslow was come home.

Presently Cicely released Barbara and ran towards Ralph with a world of delighted greeting in her face, and as she took his hands her eyes fell on Captain Protheroe. For a moment she stared at him as one amazed, and then slowly the first bright joy died in her face, her cheeks flushed crimson, and her eyes filled with misery and shame. Yet he, guessing nought, wondered at her glance, and felt himself unwelcome.

But Barbara saw nothing, her joy to be home again filled all her thoughts. She seized her cousin's arm, and broke into an eager chatter of explanations, rejoicings and questionings, till Cicely was fain to laugh in sheer bewilderment.

"Softly, softly, Bab," she cried; "I must have it all from the beginning. Come in, and tell me all. You are safe, and you are here, and that is all I care."

And so, Barbara, waving farewell to her followers, came at last to the house, and the tale was told.

Some hours later Captain Protheroe was alone in the large hall of the Manor House. Explanations had been given, questions answered; the excitement in the village had died away, and all was still and peaceful, with the sweet peace of a September evening.

He had been for some time alone.

Ralph, yielding to Barbara's insistence, had retired for a rest after his long ride, and the two cousins had early slipped away together to revel in a long talk.

He sat in one of the deep window-seats, gazing idly at the fading glows of the sunset, dreaming of the night when he had last stood there and struggled against the influence of the girl, who now was all the world to him. And as he looked back and thought on all she had been to him since that night, he wished with all his heart that Time would turn his hour-glass, and let him live those days again. Nay, give him back but three sweet hours again, and he would be content to endure even banishment from her side, with such a memory to soothe his pain. So he mused, concerned not that to many the shadow indeed proves dearer than the substance, nor that he whose memories are tender Is ofttimes happier than he who in the attainment loses the remembrance forever.

He was disturbed in his dreaming by the sound of his own name cried softly, and, turning, he found Lady Cicely standing close beside him, her hands tightly clasped, her head half turned away.

"Captain Protheroe," she said in a strained voice; "I—I have somewhat to say to you."

"To me?" he asked wonderingly. Then catching sudden sight of her face, he started back. "In heaven's name, Lady Cicely, what is it?" he cried. "Is Mistress Barbara——"

"Oh! Barbara is well," interrupted the lady quickly, with the faintest attempt at a smile. "'Tis of yourself I must speak, yourself and me."

He placed a chair for her, then took up his position opposite, leaning against the window frame, and looking down on her in wonderment.

Then, seeing she hesitated to speak, he asked gravely:

"In what have I been so unfortunate as to offend your ladyship?"

She glanced up in distress.

"Oh! 'tis not that. 'Tis I who have offended you. I have done you grievous wrong.'

"Done me wrong, madame?" he asked, smiling down at her, marvelling at the small troubles with which women love to torment their minds. "Nay, an it be so, madame, 'tis forgiven. Prithee, think no more on't."

"Oh! but I must," she cried wildly; "I have thought on it day and night since 'twas committed; thought on it every moment till I felt I must go mad an I could not see you to confess to't."

"Nay, madame, indeed it was not worth your thought, whatever it be," he answered gallantly. "That you have given me place in your gentle thoughts should be sufficient atonement."

But she, covering her face, burst on a sudden into bitter weeping.

"Oh, do not talk so!" she cried. "You do not know. You do not know."

His face grew grave. He took a step forward and leaned over her in deep distress.

"Nay, madame, I entreat you." he said gently; "indeed, you must not weep for such a thing. Come"—he coaxed lightly—"what is this grievous wrong? Why, you could scarce be more distressed had you betrayed me."

Then she dropped her hands and faced him.

"You have said it," she cried in a dry voice; "'twas indeed I who betrayed you."

He started from her and stood upright, looking down on her in amazement, in slowly gathering wrath.

"'Tis true," she sobbed; "I betrayed you to my Lord Jeffreys."

"You did?"

"Yes. I—came even from so doing when I met you—that night in Taunton."

"That night! And yet, madame, having done so, you allowed me to go on, without word of warning, into the trap which you yourself had set?"

His face was in the shadow, but she trembled at the suppressed anger in his tone.

"Is this true, madame?" he continued sharply.

She had no answer save a sob.

"And may I ask," he continued presently in the same stern tone, "may I ask your reason for—er—taking such an active interest in my affairs?"

"I—I deemed you had betrayed Barbara," she answered timidly.

"Your suspicion was as unjust as your revenge," he cried angrily. Then he checked himself, and presently continued coldly, "Your pardon, madame, I forgot myself. I believe,"—he drawled with a slight sneer—"in affairs of honour, 'tis not—customary to judge women by the standard usually applied to men."

Cicely winced at his words, but sobbed on helplessly, making no attempt to defend herself. Captain Protheroe walked slowly to the far end of the room and having partially mastered his anger, slowly returned to her side.

"Come, madame," he said sharply, "there is no need to weep more about the matter. The thing is done; there is an end on't."

"I—I did it for Barbara," she sobbed, stung by his tone to seek for some self-justification.

"Ah!" His tone was startled, questioning.

"Your life was to be the price of her freedom."

"Her freedom!"

"Yes. But, fool that I was, as well as traitor, they took my information and cheated me of the reward."

She burst into a fresh passion of sobs.

But now all trace of anger had left his face, he was eager, glad.

"But, Lady Cicely," he cried, "this is, indeed, a different matter; I had misunderstood. You were justified, perfectly. What a villain I was to doubt you. Madame, can you ever forgive me?"

Cicely stared at him in amazement.

"Nay, sir, I see no difference. Your words were just."

"Just! madame, they were shameful, infamous! I cannot hope to win your pardon for them. Why, Lady Cicely," he continued with boyish eagerness, "I am grateful to you for your action, most grateful. I count it the highest honour to have been privileged to serve Mistress Barbara, for," he added softly, "I would gladly die a thousand deaths to shield her from pain. I beseech you, madame, be comforted. 'Twas no betrayal, I was a most willing victim at the sacrifice."

But though she smiled faintly Cicely still wept.

"Ah! 'tis kind to say so," she cried, shaking her head, "But for me—for me who betrayed you! What respect, what honour have I left me?"

"Ah! madame, would my tongue had been cut out ere ever I spake those words," he cried miserably.

"Nay, the words were nought. But the deed! The deed remains the same. What must you think of me? Nay, what must I think of myself?"

Bitterly she wept, and he looked down on her in helpless despair.

Then he bent over her tenderly, and gently took her hand.

"Lady Cicely," he said softly, "what would you think of me, had I betrayed you to save Sir Rupert?"

"Ah!" Her sobs were arrested. She looked at him a moment, then gave a long sigh of slow-dawning comprehension.

"Yes, madame! Would you look upon me as worthy your contempt? Would you not rather be glad?"

"Yes! Yes!" she whispered eagerly.

"And for the rest," he continued gently, "'tis well enow, for Colonel Lovelace to write that love be little if honour be not more, yet there may be a love so self-forgetting that a man counts himself as nothing in comparison with it, and would gladly give his dearest part, even his honour, to serve his beloved. 'Twas with such a love, Lady Cicely, you loved your cousin, and by Heaven! she is worthy of it."

Cicely smiled and shook her head.

"These be somewhat indiscreet doctrines, sir," she said.

"Nay, madame, when was love noted for discretion?" he answered, smiling at her. "And, moreover, if your act were a betrayal, 'twas a right courageous one. I warrant me, 'twas no easy task for you, madame, to play the traitor."

She looked at him gratefully.

"How is it you understand so well?" she asked.

"I' faith, Lady Cicely," he answered with a sudden smile, "I fear me my record is not overclean. Not a month since, in this very room, I entered into a bargain, hardly consistent with my honour."

"And that, too, was for Barbara," she murmured softly.

"Even so. She has required much of us, has she not?" he continued, smiling. "Yet whoso is greatly loved, to her must much be given."

"And you do not regret it?"

"Regret, madame?"

"It hath cost you much."

"Maybe, but it has won me more." Then he added, half to himself, "For whatsoever befall me now, in this world or the next, I have at least had my hour of heaven."

There was a silence, broken only by Barbara's voice, singing in the room above.

Cicely rose to her feet.

"She is coming, we must go to supper."

Then she turned and laid her hand upon his arm—"You have been so good to me, Captain Protheroe," she said gently. "And what I may do in return, I gladly will. You love Barbara! Ah! I could tell you so much, so much, for who knows so well as a woman how women may be wooed. Could a man but have that knowledge, he might win every maid in Christendom. Therefore"—she smiled—"perchance 'tis better withheld. And for this present matter—certes! methinks you are doing very fairly well for yourself. Only remember 'Woman loveth a bold wooer.' Let there be no despair. More love is lost by want of hope than ever was won by diffidence."

"Alas! Lady Cicely! How can a man such as I hope greatly to succeed?"

"Tut, sir, we women are for the most part easy of credence. An a man tell us oft enough and resolutely enough that we need him, we needs must be convinced at last."

"Indeed, Lady Cicely, you give me hope. If 'twas e'en thus Sir Rupert won you——"

"Rupert!" she laughed; "nay, sir, 'twas of ordinary mortals I spoke. There was small need for Rupert to assure me that I loved him. But come, we must to supper."

She led him to the adjoining room where Ralph already awaited them.

And presently Barbara came down and joined them there. She was attired in an amber brocade, and wore her jewels; her hair towered high in a mass of wavy curls. After ten days of vagabondage she revelled in the luxury of an exquisite toilet, and every detail of her appearance was perfect.

Captain Protheroe had seen her in many garbs, in many phases, but never before had she seemed so queenly, so alluring, so worthy of a man's absolute homage, and as they looked upon her, each man gave a gasp of hopeless adoration.

She was in the highest spirits, glowing with happiness, yet wearing withal a certain air of gracious dignity, which suited well the mistress of the Manor.

The two men feasted their eyes upon her face, hung upon her words. And to each she talked with equal friendliness and vivacity. But Cicely, who watched her closely, noted that in her manner toward Ralph there lurked a certain tenderness, of pity or remorse, while towards Captain Protheroe she seemed more distant, more reserved. And though she met Ralph's looks of admiration with a merry open smile, yet when she raised her eyes to Captain Protheroe, and read the worship in his glance, she blushed faintly and the lashes quickly fell. So noted Cicely, and learned her cousin's secret from her face.

Yet from the men these signs were hidden, alternately they hoped, and then they despaired. Only as they felt the power of her presence, his passion cried to each to win her spite of all, and they trembled at the fascination of her beauty.

There was much to talk of during the meal, for Cicely would hear each detail of their adventures, and on her side related all she knew of Robert Wilcox's part in the affair.

"I would I could see him to thank him," said Barbara; "'tis a courageous youth. And I fear I was—er—somewhat curt when last we parted."

"More than curt, Mistress Barbara," answered the Captain, smiling; "some might even say exceedingly obstinate. We were well-nigh reduced to desperate measures, Lady Cicely, to bend her to our will."

Barbara laughed.

"I am glad you did not so far forget yourselves," she cried saucily; "but I trust no harm hath befallen good Master Lane on my account, Cis."

"No, he is safe, and in ignorance of the share he had in the matter, for so I advised. He is so stout a royalist, so well-known and honoured by the governor, and all the Tory gentlemen of the district, that upon his denial of any complicity in the matter, he was honourably acquitted, and the inquiry dropped. 'Tis true, some do say that money changed hands ere the incident was closed, but an it be so we will make it up to him anon. He is safe, and the escape remains a mystery."

"I warrant me the fiery-headed youth passed one or two anxious days while the inquiry was pending," remarked Captain Protheroe, smiling.

"Nay, neither he nor Prue are wont to expect trouble before it comes; they were so triumphant over their success they thought but little of possible consequences. And I doubt not Robert found ample reward at his mistress's hands."

"'Tis pity so brave and adroit a lad is not a soldier," said Barbara.

"Aye, so says Prue. And indeed 'tis his own desire."

"Would we could help him to his wish."

"He shall be helped," answered the captain quickly; "an you take interest in his fate, Mistress Barbara. When I get the command I expect, in Holland, I will send for him, and see to his advancement with all my heart."

Barbara repaid, with a grateful glance, this ready offer to fulfil her wish, and so the matter was decided.

They sat long over their meal, talking over what had befallen them in their wanderings, discussing plans for their future, wondering on the life that awaited them abroad.

At length, when the evening was far advanced, Barbara pushed back her chair and cried to her cousin that 'twas time for rest. But ere she rose she filled her glass and looked up with a merry smile.

"Come!" she cried, "here we sit together safe after all our troubles, and it seems 'tis occasion for a toast, and yet I know not exactly what it should be."

"May I not give the toast, madame?" asked the captain gravely.

"Certes, an you will. I feel I must drink to something."

"Nay, you must not join in this," he answered with a smile. Then springing to his feet and raising his glass, he turned and faced her boldly:

"What think you of this toast, Sir Ralph?" he cried: "I drink to the bravest comrade in misfortune, the sweetest companion in peace, and at all times the most courageous of women— —"

"Barbara Winslow!"

Ralph sprang to his feet, and for a moment the two men stood together, their glasses raised aloft, looking down with adoration where she sat blushing and laughing in all the pride of her beauty. Then crying her name again, they drank the toast, and with a simultaneous impulse turned and dashed their glasses against the wainscot, so that the shining fragments fell like showers upon the floor.

The moment of enthusiasm passed, the two men turned sharply and glared at one another, with a silent challenge in their eyes.

Cicely saw the look and trembled, and deeming it wisdom at once to remove this apple of discord from the feast, she rose quickly, and smiling good-night to her companions, carried her cousin off to bed.

When they were left together the two men seated themselves at the table, but there was a silence between them, and a shadow brooded over the room.

At length Ralph pushed aside his glass, and leant across the table towards his companion with the air of one who has determined on his course.

"Whither are you bound now, Protheroe?" he began. "What are your plans?"

Captain Protheroe hesitated a moment.

"There is no chance for me in England yet," he said slowly, "though General Churchill would give me his help. But there is no room in the army for Kirke and myself—at present. No, I shall to Holland, I have a cousin there already, and take service with the Prince of Orange, he is a man to be served."

There was a moment's pause. Then Ralph continued with a would-be careless air.

"Doubtless you will set off to-morrow. I will escort Mistress Barbara to her brother, and we need—er—burden you with our company no longer."

Captain Protheroe stared for a moment at his companion.

"For the present," he answered coldly, "my way lies with yours."

Ralph eyed him angrily.

"Pardon me, sir, but in Mistress Barbara's interests, it were wiser you should leave her, now your company is no longer necessary to her safety."

"Heavens! man, what would you imply?" asked the officer sharply.

"Your escape and wanderings with this lady, the whole story of your intercourse together, is enough to set many scandalous tongues wagging about her name. The sooner this intercourse ceases, the better."

"If that be your fear, then, on the contrary, the longer I remain at her side, the better," answered the captain drily. "Seeing that tongues do not long speak scandalously of a lady whom I have the honour to protect."

"Captain Protheroe," cried Ralph sharply, "I were loth to quarrel with you, but if you will take no hint, I must e'en speak plainly. This lady is nothing, can be nothing to you. After what hath passed betwixt you, part I know and part I guess, your attentions but trouble and embarrass her; nay, more, they are an insult. I insist that you at once cease to burden her with your company."

"You insist?" repeated Captain Protheroe slowly.

"I do. An it be necessary I will prove my right to do so." He touched the hilt of his sword menacingly.

Captain Protheroe rose to his feet.

"You are mad," he cried angrily; "'tis impossible for me to fight you."

"Indeed!" scoffed Ralph, "would you have me brand you coward then?"

Captain Protheroe laughed scornfully.

"Bah! Perchance that would prove no easy matter. Seeing that those who know me would know it for a falsehood, and those who do not know me could be taught. No, Sir Ralph, I will not fight you. And for the other matter——" he paused. "You say that my attentions are a burden to Mistress Barbara?"

"I do. And that both for the sake of her fair name, and her own peace of mind, you must leave her."

"And I think, sir, you are mistaken. I will only leave Mistress Barbara at her express command."

"Since you know well she is too courteous ever to urge her way," sneered Ralph sharply.

Again there was silence. The captain was thinking now on all that had passed betwixt Barbara and himself; remembering her sweet trustful ways, her gentle words; treasuring that one golden hour together in the forest, ere discord had sent this man to part their souls.

Then he rose to his feet and faced Ralph, eyeing him keenly, hanging on his answer.

"Tell me, Sir Ralph," he asked abruptly, "has Mistress Barbara given you the right to protect her?"

See now how strange a thing is a man's love for woman, since it may inspire him alike to deeds of highest purity or words of deepest shame.

After one moment's pause, Ralph set honour behind him, and answered quietly:

"I have that right."

But even as Ralph spoke the words, a wild passion leapt into Captain Protheroe's eyes, a passion of hatred, of jealousy, of unbelief.

"Now, by Heavens! Sir Ralph," he shouted fiercely; "I believe you lie."

"Have a care, sir," cried Ralph sharply; "for one who will not fight, you are strangely free with your words. 'Tis easy to speak that for which you may not be called in question."

"Man, you will drive me mad. 'Tis impossible that I should fight you."

"Even with this to warm your blood?" Sir Ralph flung the contents of his glass into his companion's face.

Then the last shred of resolution to avoid a quarrel vanished. That had passed between them which could not be overlooked. Captain Protheroe drew his sword and bowed stiffly to his opponent, the gleam of the death-harbinger in his eyes.

"It is enough, sir," he said furiously; "I am at your service."

But Ralph was now the calmer of the two.

"'Tis impossible here," he cried; "we should be interrupted. If it will suit your convenience I will meet you at sunrise to-morrow in the meadow behind the stables. There we shall be undisturbed."

"As you will. I am at your service whensoever you choose to appoint."

So they bowed and parted for the night, with murder in their hearts. While above in the sweet calm of her chamber, the cause of their quarrel lay dreaming peacefully, innocent of all wrong, save only of a heart too tender to give pain, and of a face too fair to leave a man his peace.

Alas! for a woman, since though many seek, she loves but one. Alas! for a woman, since if she too quickly perceive and ward off love, false tongues cry shame upon her vanity, but, if not perceiving, she foster it, then belike must a man's life be laid to her charge, aye, or a man's soul.

CHAPTER XXIV

As the first rays of the sunrise flushed the sky with glory, Barbara awoke on the morning following her home-coming. She sprang from her bed and crept softly to the casement, intending but to greet the morning, and then slip back to sleep. But the birds, the flowers, the sunshine all called to her to join them, and casting away all thoughts of further rest, she hastened to the adjoining room, and rousing her reluctant cousin, begged her to rise and join her in an early ramble.

But Cicely declined firmly to leave her cosy bed, so Barbara was forced to dress alone.

Presently, however, she reappeared at her cousin's bedside, and kissed her into wakefulness.

"Cis, you must rise," she cried; "'tis disgraceful. All the world is stirring. Even Ralph and Captain Protheroe are abroad, I have just seen them go down the garden together."

"Plague take you all for a set of fools," cried Cicely sleepily; "what should they want out at this hour o' the morning?"

"Why, Cis, 'tis heavenly."

With a deep sigh Cicely relented.

"Well, Bab, I will come. But not one step do I take without some breakfast, so bid Phoebe prepare it."

And with that Barbara must perforce be content. Yet she herself would wait for no breakfast, but snatching up her hat, ran into the garden to drink in the joys of the bright September morning.

Full speed she ran down the garden, and there came to a sudden halt, remembering with a pang of remorse that she had not yet greeted Butcher since her return. So, with intent to free him to join in her ramble, she turned into the copse, a short cut to the stables. But there she again came to a pause, puzzled at the sounds which reached her ears.

"Now, what in Heaven's name— —"

Then she ran through the copse at fullest speed, for of a sudden she divined what was passing beyond, and with a loud cry darted into the open meadow, and ran towards the two men who were thus engaged in the settlement of their quarrel.

At sudden sight of her, Captain Protheroe leapt quickly back out of his opponent's reach and lowered his swordpoint, at the same moment Barbara seized Sir

Ralph's arm.

She seized his arm, but her eyes were fixed on Captain Protheroe in wide-eyed indignation and reproach.

"Oh! This is too much," she gasped; "you might have killed him."

The possibility of Ralph killing the captain had not entered her head, but the insult and the compliment went unheeded by each. They thought only of the anxiety implied in her words.

"This must end now, forever," she continued firmly; "Captain Protheroe, 'tis for you to apologise."

"Madame!"

"Certainly, sir, you are in the wrong."

He stared at her in wonder.

"Do you know the cause of our quarrel, Mistress Barbara?" he asked doubtfully.

"Assuredly," she answered in surprise, for she deemed it but the consummation of the quarrel she had interrupted on Sedgemoor. "Assuredly. I am of one mind with Ralph in this matter; he is in the right, and you have been mistaken."

Slowly the light of hope died in the captain's eyes, and left there only a great yearning. He drooped his head for one long minute in silence, then drew himself up and slowly sheathed his sword.

"Yes," he said quietly; "I have been mistaken." Then he turned to Barbara, and his voice was full of tenderness.

"Mistress Barbara," he said, "a man should not be blamed, if having once looked on heaven he become blind to things of earth. Forgive me the mistake. In this, in all things, I remain ever your devoted servant. Your happiness is mine, I—I am content."

He turned and walking slowly out of the meadow, disappeared amongst the trees.

"What does he mean?" asked Barbara wonderingly, staring after his retreating figure.

But she had no time for further conjecture.

Directly Captain Protheroe disappeared, Ralph snatched her in his arms, and covered her face with kisses.

"Oh! my darling, my darling," he cried; "is it indeed so? In truth I dared to hope it, overbold that I am. But now—to be convinced! Ah! Barbara, mine! mine!"

So he cried in the intervals of his kisses. But he stopped abruptly in the midst of his ecstasy, becoming suddenly conscious that the lady was struggling in his embrace, struggling violently, passionately, to be free.

He freed her, gazing at her in surprise, as she stood confronting him, her face crimson with anger.

"Ralph!" she gasped furiously, "are you mad? What mean you? How dare you—touch me?"

He stepped back a pace in astonishment.

"Why, Barbara! Barbara!" he cried.

"How dare you touch me?"

"Nay, sweetheart," he pleaded, "I have not really angered you?"

"Angered me!" cried Barbara in desperation; "angered—! Good Heavens! am I gone crazy? What right can you think, can you dream you have, to treat me so?"

"But, Barbara!" cried the amazed man; "did you not say, e'en now, you were one with me in this matter."

"Assuredly. But if I dislike his slander of Monmouth's officers, must it follow that you may treat me thus? For shame, Ralph."

"If you dislike—Barbara! Is't possible you deem we fought for the affair at Sedgemoor?"

"For what else, pray?" she asked indignantly.

But he turned aside with a groan and leaning his elbow against a tree, buried his head in his arm.

Barbara eyed him doubtfully.

"Ralph! Ralph! What is't?" she asked sharply. "Why did you fight?"

"Because—and on my faith, Barbara, I believed it to be the truth—I told that fellow, Protheroe, that his presence, his attentions pestered you, and I insisted he should leave you."

Barbara drew herself up royally.

"You did, Ralph?" she asked coldly. "And pray what reason had you for so insulting a guest in my house, a man to whom we owe everything? Your reason, Ralph?" she urged with an imperious stamp of her foot.

"Ah! Barbara," he moaned; "look in your glass and there seek my reason. Your face is reason enough to send a man to hell."

Barbara's indignation gave way at this unexpected retort. She was subdued, silent.

Then Ralph raised his head and turned to face her.

"Barbara! I must know the truth. Do you not love me?"

She looked at him with eyes full of pity.

"No, Ralph, I cannot. Indeed, I wish I could. But love comes at no man's bidding, comes unsought, and"—she added with a break in her voice—"so oft, alas! comes when it is not wanted."

His face was white and strained, his eyes hard as he looked at her.

"If this be so, Barbara," he cried harshly, "you have deceived me, cruelly. Why did you save me in the forest? Why did you nurse me back to life at Wells? Better to have left me to die then, deeming you worthy my love, than let me live to learn such love in vain. No, by Heaven!" he cried passionately, "I care not what becomes of me; I will not live if I must lose you."

Barbara laid her hands softly upon his arm, and in her eyes as she raised them to his face, a strange light gleamed.

"Ralph," she whispered, "am I so unworthy of your love?"

"What mean you?" he cried, staring down at her.

"Nay, perchance I am wrong," she answered, "only it seemeth to me sad that love must turn to bitterness an it be not crowned by possession. And methinks a man's love for a woman, an the woman be worthy, should be so high a thing, that whether he win her or no, yet is his life dedicated to her forever, and for her sake should be lived in all honour and purity. For think not, tho' a woman may not love a man, her heart is hardened at his suit. Rather does she strive her life thro' to be more pure, more true, more noble, even for his love's sake, to grow more worthy of that highest gift which he has offered to her. Thus in their separate paths thro' the world, two lives shine brighter in honour of each other, and love that seemeth but to lead to bitterness and despair, proves rather a mighty power strengthening and glorifying her to whom 'twas offered, and him who bore it. Nay, Ralph, I cannot rightly say my meaning, but sure true love should make a man strong, not weak; strong to love even without reward."

She paused, and as he looked into her eyes, the enthusiasm of her soul passed into his, and his heart went out to her in worship, wholly unselfish, wholly pure. For he perceived how fair a part it is for a man, rather than seek ever wages for service in just exchange, to give life in service unrewarded if his soul be wakened to the sacrifice.

Low stooping he kissed her hands.

"You are right, Barbara," he said softly; "who was I to speak to you of love? Yet now, God helping me, my life, my love, shall prove as worthy of you as you are worthy of the best a man may give."

But still her eyes looked on him pityingly.

"And, Ralph," she pleaded, "surely love is not all to a man. There are other prizes worth the winning: fame, power, knowledge, may not these fill your heart?"

He smiled at her, shaking his head.

"Nay, Barbara, when I ask for bread, wilt throw me a stone? Leave me my love, dear, it sufficeth me. All I ask of life now is grace to prove me worthy to live in your memory."

So he spake, nor dreamed that in a few short years, his love would have faded to a tender memory, and life, fame, honour, again be all in all.

So they turned and went back through the copse into the sunlit garden, and

Ralph, his heart still heavy beneath his sorrow, passed on into the shadow of the house.

But Barbara lingered in the full blaze of the sunshine, on the glittering, dew-encrusted lawn. And since love is ever selfish, the memory of Ralph's trouble faded quickly in the glory and the triumph of her own sweet dream of love. For in reading Ralph's heart she had learned at last to read her own. She knew now that God's great gift was hers, that her heart had learned the world's secret, and she loved with a love that crowned her life with glory. So her heart leapt out to the sunshine, and it seemed to her, as she stood thus, in the beauty of the garden, that all nature knew her joy; the wind whispered it to the trees, the birds sang it to the sunbeams, and the great deep-hearted roses, pouring forth their souls in a passionate sigh of fragrance, bowed their heads at her passing as to their queen, to whom was given all the kingdoms of the world and the glory of them, to whom was revealed all the beauty and the treasures and the wonders of the earth.

For so is ever the first coming of love to a woman; loving, purified, one with all the world, she walks innocent as Eve in the garden of Eden, dreaming that God hath blessed her above all women, and that from thenceforth the purpose of her being is fulfilled. So Barbara dreamed away the time, in the glory of the sunshine, and the sweetness of her joy-crowned youth.

Soon Cicely stepped from the deep shadow of the wide doorway, and came slowly down the garden, stopping ever and anon to gather one of the delicate roses, late-blossoming on the trees. And as she approached she eyed Barbara questioningly and smiled at her own thoughts.

Presently she reached her cousin's side, and then, as she stopped to free her skirt from an entangling branch, she began in careless, cheerful tone:

"Oh, Barbara! Captain Protheroe prayed me to bid you adieu; he has gone."

"Gone!"

The sun had vanished from her sky; the glory of the world had faded.

"Gone!" she cried again. "Left us? Whither should he go?"

"To Watchet, to take ship to Holland, so he said; there to seek service with the Prince of Orange," answered Cicely casually, still gathering her flowers, still smiling to herself.

"But, wherefore?" cried Barbara, in desperation. "Wherefore should he leave me thus, leave me without a word?"

"Nay, the riddle is more than I can read. Yet from what he said, methought you yourself had bid him go."

"I! Cis, what madness! What were his words?"

"Why, marry, that Sir Ralph had told him his presence wearies you, and that you have declared that you are of one mind with Ralph in the matter."

"Cicely!" she cried, a world of desperation in her tone; "sure, 'tis impossible."

Yet even as she spoke she knew it to be true, for if Ralph had so misunderstood her words that morning, why might not others also?

"Oh! Cis, what shall I do?" she questioned hopelessly. "'Tis all a mistake. I meant not—no, indeed, I meant not that he should leave us. What can I do?"

"Nay, child," answered Cicely calmly, "I see not what can be done now. The man has gone. 'Tis pity you have sent him so discourteously away, but he has gone."

As she spoke she glanced once more quickly, questioningly at her cousin, then gathering together her flowers, she turned back towards the house.

But as she went she smiled mischievously and hummed a light ditty she herself had learned from Sir Rupert, and thus ran the words:

> "When maiden fair, to rouse despair,
> Doth ponder long 'twixt yea and no,
> The man who sighs, an he be wise,
> Will lightly turn his back and go.
> For tho' he fear, while he be near,
> Of love for him the maid hath none;
> Yet when, alack! he turns his back,
> He'll find her heart is quickly won."

Cicely passed into the house, leaving Barbara standing alone by the sun-dial heedless alike of song or smile; for her, song and laughter seemed to have died forever. As she watched the shadow creep along the dial, it seemed to her like the shadow creeping over her soul, darkening each succeeding moment of her life as her sun passed further on his way. And as the shadow crept, so must her life creep on henceforth; slowly, in silence and in shadow to the end.

And all her heart surged up in the despairing cry:

"I love him, I love him; he has gone!"

Gone! Aye! but not past recall.

She started, the crimson flushing to her brows at the thought.

Could she—could she not follow him and beg him to return, seeing he had gone in misunderstanding, deeming her ungrateful, unkind? Nay, did she not owe it to her love to do so, seeing he had left her apprehending that she loved another?

But could she, indeed, do this? Could she, Barbara Winslow, follow any man and beg him to return to her, as it would seem, kneeling before him to entreat his favour; she who hitherto had walked ever as proudest among women? The thought angered her.

And yet, she loved him, and perchance, nay, surely, he loved her. Must two lives be darkened because she feared to lower her pride? Men might look askance upon her deed, but—she loved him. Was her love so poor a thing that it could be dishonoured by so small a thought? If love was worthy of aught, surely it was worthy of courage.

She loved him, was he not her king, a man to whom a queen might be proud to stoop!

Thus was she tortured, now daring, now shrinking, till her pride faded in the glory of her love, and she raised her head proudly to the free heavens, resolved upon her course.

She hastened to the stables, and with her own hands saddled her horse. There Cicely joined her, wondering.

"What would you, Barbara?" she asked.

"I will follow him," she answered calmly, "to beg him not to leave me."

"Barbara! You cannot!" cried Cicely quickly; "think what will be said! Think of the shame!"

But Barbara looked at her with a strange smile.

"I love him, Cis," she said softly; "what has love to do with shame?"

And so saying, she mounted her pony, and rode off.

Her heart sang in wild triumph, for pride lay dead within her and love was all in all.

"He loves me," she sang, "he loves me. I go to tell him of my love."

"And if he loves me not!"

Her heart trembled at the thought; yet since her love was strong, she did not pause.

"For," she thought, "I think, indeed, that he loves me. But an he do not, what then? I can but return alone. For what harm to him to know he has my love? 'Twill be no burden to him, rather an added triumph to his life. Surely he shall know I love him. Men do not shame to speak their love to women, is women's love then so poor a thing that they must shame to speak of it to men?"

So mused Barbara, deeming herself more or less than woman.

Then on a sudden, turning the corner of a quiet lane, she saw him. Slowly he rode, his reins hanging loosely on his horse's neck, his head bowed upon his breast in thought.

And at the sight she drew rein and paused, her eyes wide with doubt and consternation.

For, so strange is woman's heart, at sight of him, there, close before her, all her resolution fled, and she could but stand at gaze, trembling at the thought of his near presence, shrinking in a horror of doubt, fear, shyness from what had, but a moment since seemed so simple, so natural an action. No. 'Twas beyond question impossible, she could not speak the words.

So, at a sudden pride-awakening thought, she resolved, and had even then, turned her pony's head and softly ridden away, but for the intervention of an un-expected occurrence.

For while she paused in hesitation, a rabbit darted out of the hedge beside her, and the pony, restive at the check to their progress, on a sudden swerved aside, and ere she could fully recover her seat and regain tight control of the reins, had bolted along the road, in a senseless panic, past the astonished object of her thoughts.

Then, since perforce it must be, slowly, reluctantly, with cheeks a flaming crimson, she turned to meet him.

As for Captain Protheroe, suddenly interrupted in his reverie by the sight of the lady of his dreams flying past him in a whirl of hoof-thundering, hair-flying disorder, his astonishment knew no bounds. He reined up his horse and stood regarding her in amazement, half doubting the reality of the vision.

"Mistress Barbara!" he exclaimed, "you here! What do you here?"

But she trembled and flushed yet more at sight of his surprise.

"I—I do but ride abroad, sir," she faltered; "may I not ride these roads as well as another?"

"Assuredly," he answered gravely. But there was an eager gleam in his eyes, for he thought on the words of Lady Cicely, spoken ere he rode away:

"I know nought of this affair," she said. "But I am a woman, Captain Protheroe, and 'tis we women who see the truth. And trust me, Barbara loves you, whether she yet know it herself or no."

And he had ridden away, deeming the words but gentle folly, spoken to ease his pain. But now, as he looked upon her flushed cheek, and downcast eyes, he thought on them again, and his heart beat quickly.

Then he looked at the pony, sweating with the fury of the ride, and he smiled, thinking:

"Assuredly, 'twas even me she came to seek."

He dismounted and standing beside her, after a pause asked quietly:

"Madame, why did you ride after me?"

"I—I——"

"Have you nought to say to me?"

Then she gathered her courage, and turned on him to escape his questionings.

"Why did you leave us so discourteously?" she asked.

"Alas! madame," he murmured, "I lacked courage to bid you farewell."

"But, now——"

"Now, Mistress Barbara! Think you it were easier now to bid farewell, now, while I look upon your face? Ah, no! in truth, I cannot leave you now. For, ah! Mistress Barbara——" he broke out passionately, laying his hands on hers—"I love you—I love you, and to leave you is to go from the joys of heaven out into the darkness of death. Ah! Barbara, if you know mercy, bid me not leave you now."

"'AH! BARBARA, IF YOU KNOW MERCY, BID ME NOT LEAVE YOU NOW'"

He paused, then as she sat dumbstricken by the force of his passion, he continued with a sudden bitterness:

"And yet how should I stay, seeing my love is nought to you. Better to leave you now. For in truth, a man must not ask too much of Heaven. But to leave you—to see your face no more! Ah! madame, madame, what is this you have done to me, seeing I cannot leave you now, and yet I dare not stay?"

There was silence. Then Barbara, turning away her face, said slowly:

"Captain Protheroe! I supposed you and Ralph fought concerning the affair on Sedgemoor. I—I knew of no other cause of quarrel betwixt you."

Captain Protheroe raised his head with a quick hope. "Ah?" he questioned breathlessly.

"Yes. And"—she continued hurriedly—"in this quarrel Ralph was in the wrong. I—I do not wish you to leave me."

A moment he paused. Then he answered in a low restrained voice:

"While I can serve you I will remain. But, an you need me no more, I pray you then, in pity, turn away your face and let me go."

But Barbara turned her head and looked at him, and she whispered softly, so softly that he but caught the words ere they died away:

"Nay, sir, but what an I need thee all my days?" And having so spoken again she turned away her head.

The birds' chorus rose loud and triumphant in the human silence that followed, while he took her hands in his and pressed them to his lips.

Then he tried to see her face, but 'twas still turned from him, he could but see one crimson cheek and the curling lashes resting upon it. He sighed softly, but smiled withal.

"Mistress Barbara," he pleaded, "have I not told you your eyes are like unto the clear depths of the heavens? Alas! why are the heavens so oft veiled from the gaze of man?"

She answered not, but turned her head slightly, and he saw a smile was playing round her lips.

"Is it lest by too long contemplation of their beauty, a man should lose himself in longing?" he asked again.

Then Barbara turned her head and faced him, but still her lashes drooped, and she whispered very softly:

"Nay, but rather lest by too long contemplation a man should learn their secret."

"Ah, Barbara," he pleaded; "be merciful. Show me the secret of the heavens."

So she raised her eyes to his, and far in their depths he read her secret.

And she, stooping, gave her face to his kisses, and her life to him for all its span.

Lector House believes that a society develops through a two-fold approach of continuous learning and adaptation, which is derived from the study of classic literary works spread across the historic timeline of literature records. Therefore, we aim at reviving, repairing and redeveloping all those inaccessible or damaged but historically as well as culturally important literature across subjects so that the future generations may have an opportunity to study and learn from past works to embark upon a journey of creating a better future.

This book is a result of an effort made by Lector House towards making a contribution to the preservation and repair of original ancient works which might hold historical significance to the approach of continuous learning across subjects.

HAPPY READING & LEARNING!

LECTOR HOUSE LLP
E-MAIL: lectorpublishing@gmail.com